"I Want yo
his eyes glowing silver.

Jo suspected that was a tell with him: Molten silver meant hot and horny. Which was fine with her, as she was feeling rather hot and bothered herself.

"But I can't claim you," he added.

"Claim me?" she echoed, then gave a laugh. "You make me sound like lost luggage. No one can *claim* me. I have free will." She moved around the table and dropped into his lap. She slid her arms around his shoulders. "Fortunately for you, I'm free and willing."

"Jo," he said, but she didn't want to hear it and covered his mouth with her own.

She smiled, slid her lips to his ears, and nibbled briefly before whispering, "I ache for you."

He sucked in a harsh breath, then something snapped. Suddenly his head jerked around so his lips could claim hers.

By Lynsay Sands

THE RENEGADE HUNTER
THE IMMORTAL HUNTER
DEVIL OF THE HIGHLANDS
THE ROGUE HUNTER
VAMPIRE, INTERRUPTED
VAMPIRES ARE FOREVER
THE ACCIDENTAL VAMPIRE
BITE ME IF YOU CAN
A BITE TO REMEMBER
A QUICK BITE

Coming Soon

TAMING THE HIGHLAND BRIDE

LYNSAY SANDS

THE RENEGADE HUNTER

A Rogue Hunter Novel

AVON
An Imprint of HarperCollins*Publishers*

This is a work of fiction. Names, characters, places, and incidents are products of the author's imagination or are used fictitiously and are not to be construed as real. Any resemblance to actual events, locales, organizations, or persons, living or dead, is entirely coincidental.

AVON BOOKS
An Imprint of HarperCollins*Publishers*
10 East 53rd Street
New York, New York 10022-5299

ISBN 978-0-06-147431-6
www.avonbooks.com

First Avon Books paperback printing: October 2009

Printed in the U.S.A.

10 9 8 7 6 5 4 3 2 1

For
Margaret Isabel Willan

Chapter One

Nicholas came to the edge of the small copse of woods and quietly cursed. Somehow he must have missed the rogue, must have walked right past him. The thought made him turn and glance back the way he'd come, but Nicholas was sure there was no way he could have missed him. The woods lining the road were only ten feet deep and he'd moved through them slowly, eyes searching the trees as he'd gone. He couldn't have missed him, but it was the only thing that made sense.

Nicholas retrieved the signal receiver from his pocket and glanced at the screen. The small blip that was the rogue's car was still exactly where it had been earlier. The fellow hadn't doubled back and driven away. He slipped the device back in his pocket and turned to peer at the driveway before him.

There was no way the rogue had gotten in there on foot, he was sure. It was the entry to the new enforcer house. The equivalent of a police station for vampire hunters, it had better security than a mortal prison from what he could see. The gate blocking the driveway was ten feet high and made of thick wrought iron. There was an equally high brick wall that disappeared into the trees on either side of it. Every foot or so along the wall, metal spikes shot up and three lengths of barbed wire were threaded through them, running along the top as a deterrent to anyone trying to climb it. A sign on the fence warned that it was electrified. If that wasn't enough security, there appeared to be a second gate some fifteen feet inside the first with a chain-link fence, also topped with barbed wire and no doubt electrified.

He shook his head slightly. This was something Nicholas never thought he'd see. The enforcers had always been rather loosely based, run out of Lucian Argeneau's home. However, it seemed his uncle had decided to make it all more official and organized. It was about time, Nicholas supposed. This should have been done centuries ago.

His gaze slid away from the gate and to the woods on the other side of the drive from where he stood. It was hard to believe the rogue he was following had slipped across that wide open expanse under the nose of the guard inside. Aside from that, there was a pillar before the gate with a camera and intercom system built into it. The rogue wouldn't have risked trying to cross the open area and getting caught on that camera. However, either the rogue had risked it and snuck across, or Nicholas had somehow managed to move right past the man as he'd made his way here.

Nicholas glanced over his shoulder at the woods at

his back. While his mind was telling him he couldn't have walked right past the rogue without noticing, he was starting to worry that perhaps his instincts weren't as good as they used to be.

The sound of an engine caught his attention and Nicholas turned back to the driveway just in time to see a catering van pull in. He watched silently as it stopped between the pillars.

"Yes?" a metallic voice asked over the intercom.

"Cally's Catering," the van driver announced. "We're here to pick up our people and dishes."

"Come on in." The first gate slid open.

Nicholas expected the vehicle to be stopped between the two gates and inspected, but instead the guard in the small guardhouse inside the second gate came out and manually opened the inner gate for the van to enter. He did wave it to a stop, however, the moment it was inside.

The guard spoke briefly to the driver, and then moved around and opened the back door of the van to check inside. With his attention on the guard, Nicholas almost missed the man who suddenly slid out from under the side of the van, shifted to a crouch, and sprinted for the woods behind the guardhouse.

The sight almost made him shout out a warning, but Nicholas caught himself and instead reached for his phone. It was the damned rogue, of course. The tricky bastard must have waited at the side of the road for a likely vehicle to approach, taken control of the driver to make him stop, and then slid under the van and clung to something on the undercarriage to hitch a ride in.

Clever little prick, Nicholas thought, frowning as he continued to search for his cell phone. He had to warn them inside and tell them to put a guard on the sisters and then start searching the property for the rogue that had gotten in. He'd tell them to start having the guard check under the vehicles as well. At least he would if he could find his damned phone, Nicholas thought with frustration as his search came up empty. What the hell had he done with it? It had been beeping a warning that the battery was low earlier in the evening and he'd plugged it into the car lighter with its special adapter to charge it up, and—

"Hell," Nicholas muttered, glancing back the way he'd come. He'd left the damned thing in the car. He briefly considered running back to get it, but while the rogue he was following had merely pulled over and parked at the edge of this property, Nicholas himself had parked in the woods nearer the next property to avoid being spotted. The man, Ernie Brubaker, was one of Leonius's spawn, and Nicholas hoped if he followed him long enough, Ernie would lead him to Leo's hideout. Leonius Livius was one nasty rogue who needed to be dealt with, and Nicholas had set himself the task of doing just that. However, his caution meant that his van was a good distance away . . . and by the time he ran back and grabbed his phone to make the call, Ernie could have grabbed one of the girls and gotten out again.

That was the only reason he could think that the fellow was here. At least that's what Nicholas had come up with when he'd realized he'd followed the man to the new enforcer house.

Nicholas sighed and swiveled back to peer at the gate and the driveway beyond again. The guard had already returned to his little shack and the van had disappeared from view. No doubt at that very minute the rogue was racing through the trees toward the house. He had to warn them, but the only way to do that without his phone was to walk up to the gate and flat-out tell the guard . . . and that would pretty much toast his cojones, Nicholas acknowledged. Unfortunately, he didn't have much choice. If he didn't—

Nicholas was distracted from his thoughts by the arrival of another vehicle. He turned his head to watch a van approach the gate, and felt a grim smile curve his lips as he noted the cleaning service name on the side of the vehicle stopped beside the pillar. It was blocking the camera and intercom from his view . . . and him from the camera's view, he realized.

Without pausing to think about how risky it was for him personally, Nicholas slid from the cover of the trees and raced across the short open expanse to the back of the van. Once there, he took hold of the handle on the back door and stepped onto the back bumper, careful not to cause unnecessary motion in the vehicle with his weight. He then held on for dear life and waited as the driver explained into the intercom that they were there to clean up after the party.

The guard repeated his invitation to "come on in," and after a short pause as the outer gate swung open, the van started forward with Nicholas clinging to the back like some bad imitation of Spider-Man. He was passing the camera on the pillar before he recalled its presence, but by then it was too late. Telling himself the guard wouldn't be inside the guardhouse to see him riding by, but had no doubt headed out to open the inner gate, Nicholas stayed on his perch until the back end of the van was even with the second open gate. He then leaped off and made a charge for the bushes by the guardhouse as he'd seen the rogue do. Nicholas prayed the whole way that the guard stuck to the routine he'd used the first time. If so, the van would block the guard's view of his mad dash for the trees. If not, he was likely to get a bullet in the back.

Nicholas didn't release the breath he was holding until he reached the safety of the woods behind the guard shack without anyone shouting out or shooting at him. He then allowed himself to breathe out and suck in a fresh gust of air, but barely slowed his step as he followed the trail he suspected the rogue had taken, heading straight toward the house on the hill.

"Oh brother," Jo muttered.

"What?" Alex asked, lowering her glass and raising an eyebrow.

"More arrivals." Jo nodded toward the doorway where their sister, Sam, and her fiancé, Mortimer, were greeting a newcomer. It was yet another tall, well-built hunk in leather. Every male here appeared to be wearing leather of some description or other, either leather pants, a leather jacket, a leather vest, or some combination of the items. One or two were even wearing the whole deal. It was like a biker convention without the tats. That was the one thing Jo had noticed; while all the men looked mean and gruff, and several even had long hair, not a single one had a tattoo or piercing of any kind. They were the most clean-cut bikers she'd ever seen.

If they were bikers, she thought. Maybe they were all in rock bands like Mortimer and his friends Bricker and Decker. If that was the case, then it made them the most clean-cut rockers she'd ever seen.

"Come on, it isn't that bad," Alex said with amusement.

"Isn't it?" Jo asked dryly.

"No," Alex assured her. "I mean look around. We are presently in a room full of really good-looking men. I haven't seen this much eye candy in one place in a long, long time."

"Eye candy?" Jo asked.

"Yes, eye candy. Look around you, Jo, every single guy here is built. They all have muscly chests and narrow waists." She shook her head, her marveling eyes sliding over the men gathered in small groups that were dotted throughout the room. "There isn't a paunch, a set of crooked teeth, or a knobby knee to be seen."

"Yeah, and if they weren't treating us like lepers it might be nice," Jo said.

"They aren't treating us like lepers," Alex said with a laugh.

"Are you kidding me? Are we at the same party or are you just not paying attention?" Jo asked with amazement. "Alex, they come in, Sam and Mortimer greet and have a little huddle with them, and then they bring them over to us, and the men all—every last one—stare at us with this weird intense look for a minute, saying absolutely nothing. They then glance to Mortimer, shake their head, and move off. Some even just turn around and leave right away. The rest just stand around talking to each other and ignoring us," she pointed out, and then asked, "And you don't think this is strange?"

"Well, when you put it that way," Alex said wryly and shrugged. "It *is* kind of weird."

"Yes, it is," Jo said firmly. "And it isn't the only weird thing here. What about the security on this place? That's a bit over the top, don't you think?"

"Yeah, but Sam explained that Mortimer and the boys are having trouble with a stalker fan," Alex reminded her.

"Right," Jo snorted. "A stalker fan for a band who hasn't even agreed on a name yet."

"I thought they were going with Morty and the Muppets," Alex said with a frown.

"Alex," Jo said. "Even if they have a name now and a stalker from some Podunk little town they've played, where the heck did they get the money for this place and all its security? For God's sake, they're tricked out here like a third world dictator or big-wheel drug dealer. I doubt even the president of the U.S. or the prime minster here in Canada have twenty feet of barbed wire between them and the world."

Alex grinned and said, "I have a theory about that."

"Oh?" Jo asked. "And what is that?"

"That Mortimer isn't really in a band. That the story was all just some cover to hide the fact that he's really some big-deal rich guy. Like Gates maybe."

Jo raised her eyebrows. "Gates is a skinny old dude

with glasses and graying hair. Mortimer is not Bill Gates."

"Well, his son or some other rich guy then," Alex said with exasperation. "The point is, he just pretended to be some poor schmuck in a band so that Sam wouldn't fall for his money rather than him."

"Right," Jo said doubtfully, although, really, it made more sense than that Mortimer, Decker, and Bricker were in some little band and having trouble with a stalker fan. She supposed Sam probably knew the truth of the situation by now, and would eventually clue them in. In the meantime, Sam and Mortimer had finished their little huddle and were now leading over the latest arrival at the party—*late* being the key word since it *was* late and the caterers and cleaners were moving through cleaning up around the guests. Turning, she handed Alex her drink. "Here. Hold this. I have to go to the bathroom."

Alex accepted the drink, but narrowed her eyes. "You'd best really have to go. You are *not* leaving me here to handle all these men by myself."

Jo gave a wry laugh. "As far as I can tell, there's nothing to handle, they're all more interested in each other than us. They're probably all gay."

"You think?" Alex asked with wide-eyed alarm.

Jo merely rolled her eyes and slid quickly away before Sam, Mortimer, and Mr. Late-to-the-Party could reach them. She had to wonder about the question, though, as she moved through the milling men. They all looked kind of perfect. Not perfect as in model gorgeous. Despite Alex's words, there were some men there who were not picture-perfect pretty. Some were tall, others a little shorter, some white, some darker-skinned, one had a nose that was a little large, another had narrow eyes, and so on, but they were all perfect versions of themselves, with perfect complexions, healthy hair, and *very* healthy bodies. There wasn't a blemish to be seen, not a single split end on a single head, and not an ounce of fat. It was enough to make a gal feel a bit inferior. Most men she was acquainted with didn't know from a split end or good blemish creams and moisturizers . . . unless they were gay.

Maybe she hadn't been far off the mark, Jo thought as she reached the door. A glance back as she stepped into the hall showed that Sam and Mortimer had reached Alex with the latest man, and he was doing that weird staring thing, peering intensely at Alex's forehead as if she had a huge zit growing in the center of it.

Shaking her head, Jo hurried up the hall. She bypassed the bathroom, however, heading for the kitchen instead. Much to her relief, the room was empty. Jo moved quickly through it to the dark and equally empty dining room and the sliding glass doors that waited there.

A small sigh of relief slipped from her lips when she managed to step outside without being discovered or stopped. Jo eased the door closed behind her and then paused to glance around. She and Alex had arrived earlier in the evening when it had still been light out. The yard had been large and peaceful then; a beautifully manicured lawn surrounded by trees softly swaying in a light breeze. But spooky seemed more fitting now, Jo thought with a grimace. The bucolic scene from day became a mass of unrecognizable shapes in the darkness, and all of it was rustling in the gentle night breeze. It was enough to make her glance warily around and consider heading back inside, but she didn't. Instead, Jo took a breath and started out. She wanted a little walk and fresh air before returning inside to suffer more of the weird encounters that made up this party. She'd really like to cut out and head to her apartment to relax and put her feet up, but she'd ridden here with Alex, and they were supposed to spend the night. Now Jo wished she'd driven herself. If she tried to retire early, Sam would no doubt be all over her, asking what was wrong and why she wasn't still at the party. Jo didn't want to hurt her older sister's feelings by telling her this was the lamest party she'd ever attended.

Heck, working at the bar most nights was more entertaining than this party, Jo thought wryly. The only people here who had really talked to her and Alex were Sam and Mortimer, and his supposed bandmates Bricker and Decker, as well as Decker's girlfriend, Dani, and her little sister, Stephanie. They were all nice enough, but Decker, Dani, and Stephanie had disappeared directly after greeting them, which had left Jo, Alex, and Sam as the only attendees who were female. That fact, added to the fact that every single one of the males in attendance had avoided them after their brief weird behavior on being introduced . . . Well, it had all put her on edge. Some fresh air and quiet was what she needed, and if she was going to be walking at night, this was the place to do it. Spooky or not, with all the security, she was definitely safer here than anywhere else, Jo thought as she started out across the lawn.

She'd taken only a few steps when it occurred to her that Bricker was working the gate tonight. He'd said he'd volunteered for the job since he already knew her and Alex. Jo had found that comment a bit bewildering. Sam had said the party was to introduce them to Mortimer's friends, and it was true they'd already met Bricker, but still . . .

Maybe she'd walk down to the guard station at the front gate and see if Bricker was bored or wanted anything, she thought, turning her feet toward the end of the house. Jo liked Bricker. Not in a kiss-me-you-fool type way. He was cute, but it was obvious there was no real spark between them. He was more like the jokester younger brother of a friend—easygoing, fun to be around, but not boyfriend material. That was all right, though. Jo wasn't looking for a boyfriend. Heck, she didn't have time for one. Between working full-time at the bar and the full load of marine biology courses she was taking at the university, there was little time for friends, let alone a love life.

Maybe Bricker could tell her what the deal was with the guys inside, Jo thought as she turned the corner of the house. He'd know if they were gay or not.

Jo had barely started along the side of the house toward the front yard when movement out of the corner of her eye caught her attention. She turned, a gasp of surprise slipping from her lips as she saw the fair-haired man charging out of the darkness, but it became a cry of pain when he crashed into her, body slamming her back against the side of the house. Her head hit the brick wall hard enough that stars exploded behind her eyes, and the agony shooting through her left her gasping for breath.

The man was saying something. Jo could hear the rumble of his voice, and smell his vile breath, but his words weren't making it to her stunned brain, and then he was suddenly gone.

Without his body pinning her to the wall, Jo immediately crumpled to the ground, groaning as her knee landed on something terribly hard that sent more pain shooting through her. It took Jo a moment to even care about where her attacker had gone, but then the pain slowly began to recede and she became aware of the sounds of grunts and curses nearby. Forcing her eyes open, she lifted her head and spotted the two men grappling several feet away.

Jo didn't recognize either of them from the party and was pretty sure she would have had she met them. The blond who had attacked her had a feral look about his face, and his hair was long and lank. As for his clothes, they were dark but sloppy, with various stains on them that could have been dried blood. The other man had dark hair that was not long like the fair-haired man's, but not exactly short either. He also wore faded, but clean jeans and a dark T-shirt.

The two men were grappling and spinning, each fighting to subdue the other. They also appeared to be playing for keeps, Jo realized as she saw that the blond had his hands at her savior's throat and was trying to choke him. In the next moment, the men crashed to the ground and were rolling.

Jo decided she had to get help for her would-be savior and started to get to her feet, but her knee banged against the rock she'd landed on earlier, drawing another hissing breath from her mouth and drawing her eyes down. Spotting the small, palm-sized boulder, Jo instinctively picked it up. Holding the rock tightly, she reached for the wall with her other hand, dug her fingers into the uneven brick surface, and began to force herself upward.

Once on her feet, Jo found she was more than a little shaky and the dark yard had an alarming tendency to spin. Going back around the house and inside to get help no longer seemed a very feasible idea. By the time she got there, this battle would be over, and Jo wasn't at all sure who the winner would be. She had to help. Taking a deep breath, she released the wall and stumbled toward the men as they rolled themselves across the paved driveway. She was only steps away when the dark-haired man managed to throw the blond off him. In the next moment he was on his feet, had grabbed the blond by the collar and dragged him to his feet as well, and the two were struggling again.

Jo stood, blinking her eyes and shaking her head, a bit bemused. The speed the man had moved at was just too quick. It was like watching a movie with several bits cut out; one minute he was on the ground, and then he was up, and then he'd crossed the several feet he'd tossed her attacker and caught him up. Obviously, she'd slammed her head into the wall harder than she'd realized, Jo thought, but continued forward, raising her boulder when she saw the dark-haired man had turned the blond so that his back was to her. She grasped the boulder in both hands, lifted it over her head, and brought it down on the blond with all her might. Too much might maybe, Jo thought worriedly as she heard the cracking sound it produced. There was one bad moment where she feared she might have done some serious damage, maybe even a killing blow, but then realized that wasn't the case at all. All she'd done was get the blond's attention . . . and piss him off, she realized as he suddenly turned his head to growl at her like a dog, baring fangs not unlike a dog's as well.

Jo's eyes widened incredulously at the sight and then shifted to his golden eyes glowing with fury. She took a nervous step back, but before he made a move, the dark-haired man punched him. At least she thought he punched him. She saw her savior's arm and shoulder shift and heard the thud. Whatever he'd done was enough to distract the blond from her. He turned back to the man who'd hit him and started to strike out at the dark-haired man in retaliation, but before he could finish the action, the dark-haired man struck again. This time, a small gurgle of sound slid from the blond's lips, and he began to crumple to the ground.

Chapter Two

"Are you all right?" Nicholas stepped over the rogue lying on the ground, moving toward the female standing just a few feet away. Her expression was shocked, her face pale, and he could smell blood in the air. Frowning with concern, he caught the woman by the shoulders and turned her away to examine the back of her head, silently cursing himself for not moving quickly enough to prevent her getting injured. He'd just arrived at the edge of the woods closest to the house when he'd spotted Ernie charging across the clearing toward the building. He hadn't spotted the woman the rogue was headed for until the man was nearly on her.

He should have shot him then, Nicholas supposed. It would have saved the woman one hell of a head banging, but he'd been worried the noise would bring Mortimer and the others down on him. He'd rather take care of the rogue and slip away than straight-out sacrifice himself, but Nicholas would if it became necessary. It wasn't like he had much to look forward to now anyway, but flat-out suicide wasn't in his nature, so he'd kept his gun in its holster and gone for brute strength instead, dragging the man off her and battling him hand to hand.

Unfortunately, Ernie was a wiry little bastard and he fought dirty. On top of that, Nicholas had been a tad distracted trying to see if the woman was all right. When she'd taken it upon herself to help him out by slamming a boulder over Ernie's head, Nicholas had decided it was time to stop playing. It had been obvious the woman wasn't smart enough to go for help, but would instead stick around and make herself a target should Ernie have gotten in a lucky shot and incapacitated Nicholas. So he'd resorted to his blade, stabbing the man in the chest but missing his heart the first time. He'd then stabbed him again, piercing the heart with the second blow. At least he hoped he had. Otherwise the guy would heal in a few minutes and be up causing problems again.

The thought made him release the woman to turn back to Ernie, but a gasp made Nicholas glance back in time to see that he'd released the woman so abruptly, she'd lost her balance and was even now tumbling to the ground. Nicholas reached out quickly, grabbing her up before she hit the dirt. He set her back on her feet, a frown plucking at his lips.

"Are you okay?" he asked, holding her to be sure she was steady on her feet.

"Yes," she breathed. "Thank you."

Nicholas released her more carefully this time, and then glanced to Ernie.

"Is he dead?"

The question from the woman brought his gaze back around to find her leaning to peer around his bulk at the man on the ground.

"No, he's just incapacitated for now," Nicholas said grimly.

"You must have hit him pretty hard to knock him out," she muttered, starting around him toward the body. "I've never seen anyone knocked out from a punch to the chest and I've seen a lot of bar fights."

Nicholas caught her arm to keep her from going near Ernie and raised an eyebrow in question when she glanced his way. "Have you now?"

"Hazard of the job," she explained, and then added, "I manage a bar by the university. Fights are a regular occurrence. Not in the bar itself," she added quickly. "We have bouncers to prevent that, but they start up outside sometimes."

Nicholas merely nodded and shifted to block Ernie from her view. It was obvious she hadn't yet noticed the knife sticking out of the rogue's chest, but then it was dark and she was mortal, without the night vision he enjoyed. He suspected she'd be upset if she did see it, though, so shifted to the side again when she tried to peer around him.

"You should go to the house. It's safer," he said quietly.

"Yes, but what about him?" she asked, trying to look around him once more.

Nicholas merely shifted his bulk to block her again. "I'll take care of him."

"Oh, well . . ."

She frowned, her gaze moving back toward the house uncertainly, and Nicholas turned her in that direction and gave her a little push both physically and mentally. "Go on."

As far as he was concerned that should have been enough to send her on her way, so forgetting about the woman, Nicholas moved back to kneel beside Ernie. He needed to be sure the knife rested in the rogue's heart and that the man wasn't likely to get up and make a nuisance of himself. Then he could slip off the property, get back to his vehicle, and call to let Mortimer know he'd left him a little gift.

"What's your name?"

Nicholas stiffened and glanced over his shoulder with surprise. The woman should be halfway to the house by now; he'd pushed the thought at her to go back inside. Instead, she was standing right behind him, peering over his shoulder at Ernie. He saw her frown and squint to see better and then she asked, "What's that in his chest?"

Cursing, Nicholas stood and caught her arm to urge her toward the house. This time he actually tried to slip into her thoughts rather than simply send out a general thought. However, his footsteps came to an abrupt halt when he came up against a blank wall in her mind.

"What is it?" she asked, peering up at him curiously.

"I can't read you," Nicholas admitted with bemusement.

"Read me?" she asked with confusion.

Nicholas merely shook his head and tried again to penetrate her thoughts, but again he came up against a blank wall . . . which could mean only one thing: She was his life mate. It was a shocking revelation. Some immortals only ever met one life mate in a lifetime. Some found and lost one and then waited centuries, even millennia to meet another. Nicholas had found his first life mate fifty years ago and lost her a few short months later. Truthfully, he'd never thought he'd encounter another. He hadn't thought he'd live that long.

"Oh jeez, not you too."

Nicholas blinked his thoughts away and quirked one eyebrow in question. "Not me too what?"

"The penis-eye thing," she muttered.

"Penis-eye thing?" he asked with complete confusion. It was a term he had never heard before.

She shifted impatiently, but explained, "Sam is holding a party tonight to introduce my sister Alex and me to some of Mortimer's friends. They're all male, and every single time one of them has been introduced to us, they stop and stare at our foreheads like we've got penises growing out of them."

"Ah," Nicholas murmured, and had to hide the smile that wanted to creep across his face. The desire to smile died as he realized he was actually having it. Nicholas hadn't had anything to smile about in a very long time. Clearing his throat, he asked, "And what happens after they stare at your foreheads?"

She shrugged, managing to look even more irritated. "They wander off without a word and talk to each other. Right now there are probably twelve decent-looking guys in the house all talking to each other while Alex is either standing by herself or is talking to Sam and Mortimer." She pursed her lips briefly and then admitted, "I think they're gay."

Nicholas raised his other eyebrow. "Sam and Mortimer?"

"What?" she asked with amazement and then clucked her tongue impatiently. "No. Sam is my sister, Samantha. She and Mortimer are a couple."

"I see," Nicholas murmured, and then offered, "My apologies for giving you the penis-eye look."

"Hmm," she murmured, and started to turn back toward Ernie.

"What's your name?" Nicholas asked, drawing her attention back to him.

She turned back, but merely arched an eyebrow and pointed out, "I asked you that very thing several minutes ago and you still haven't answered me."

"Nicholas Argeneau," he said quietly, and waited for a gasp of horror, or for disgust to enter her eyes. Instead, she held out her hand.

"Nice to meet you Nicholas Argeneau. I'm Jo Willan."

"Jo," he murmured, and thought it suited her. "Short for Josephine?"

She wrinkled her nose, but nodded. "I hate that name."

"I like it fine," he said, and then added, "But Jo suits you better."

She laughed at that. "You hardly know me. How could you know whether it suits me or not?"

"I know," he said solemnly.

She peered at him in silence for a moment, then shook her head and glanced away muttering, "Must have hit my head harder than I thought."

"Why do you say that?" Nicholas asked, eyes narrowing. "Are you having pain? Double vision?"

"No," Jo said quickly, and then grimaced and admitted, "Well, my vision is acting up. I could have sworn that guy had glowing gold eyes and fangs a minute ago, and just now your eyes kind of looked like they were glowing silver."

Nicholas relaxed. There was nothing wrong with her vision, but while her lack of reaction told him she had no idea who he was, this comment made it obvious she knew nothing about the people in the house she was visiting. She was an uninitiated mortal, completely ignorant of the fact that immortals walked among them.

Recalling that she'd mentioned a party here tonight, he asked, "Why are you at this party?"

Jo shrugged and smiled wryly as she admitted, "Because my sister Sam would have skinned me alive if I'd tried to duck out on it."

"Your sister Sam?" he asked. "You said she was Mortimer's friend?"

"His girlfriend," she corrected, and then added, "They're pretty tight. I'm thinking they'll be announcing a wedding date any day now."

"Ah." Nicholas nodded. Mortimer had found a life mate. Good for him. He'd always liked the man. No doubt this Sam was now trying to find life mates for her sisters to prevent having to leave them behind in the future. It wasn't an unusual reaction from a new life mate, and sometimes it even worked, but that was a rare event.

It just figured that fate would play its normal nasty tricks and make her his own. Jo's sister Sam certainly wouldn't be pleased about it if she knew who he was, and Jo's being his life mate would bring neither of them joy since Nicholas couldn't claim her. Well, he could, but he wouldn't. It would mean subjecting her to life on the run as he was; always hunted and always hunting.

"I guess I should thank you for saving me."

Nicholas peered down into her solemn face. Her eyes were wide and a beautiful brown that would probably turn golden were she turned. Her nose was tipped up and adorable and her lips were over full, swollen as if bee stung. They were kissable-type lips, sweet and soft-looking, and without giving himself time to think better of it, he reached out to catch her by the arms and lifted her up slightly even as he bent his head to claim her lips. He'd intended it to be a quick kiss, all he would allow himself. However, the moment their lips met, an explosion went off inside his body. It was as if little fireflies were doing a frenzied dance through his bloodstream . . . and she wasn't fighting him or pulling away.

Nicholas couldn't resist deepening the kiss. Slipping his tongue out, he urged her lips apart to taste her fully . . . and was lost. She was as sweet as he could have wished, her mouth opening for him fully, her breath carrying a hint of lime and tequila. She was a margarita drinker, he thought. Nicholas had tried the drink fifty years ago when he was eating and drinking and never forgot the flavor. He'd enjoyed the sweet tartness of the beverage. He enjoyed it now as well as he kissed Jo.

It was her moan that brought Nicholas back to his senses. He was in the middle of enemy territory with a temporarily disabled rogue just feet away and a party full of enforcers just inside the building behind him . . . and he was stopping to kiss a life mate he could never claim. Nicholas had never realized he was such a masochist. This was like tasting the frosting of a cake he could never eat, he thought unhappily, and slowly eased and then broke the kiss. When he lifted his head, Jo's eyes were still closed and her lips still slightly parted and damp from his kiss. He was hard-pressed not to kiss her again, but resisted, and when she opened her eyes, he growled, "Consider me thanked."

A small smile curved her lips, and then Jo reached up to caress his cheek, saying, "Surely saving my life is worth more than one little kiss?"

Nicholas's eyes widened at the invitation, and he didn't resist when she drew his head down and pressed her lips to his once more. This time Jo was more than quiescent in his arms, this time she was the aggressor, pressing her body against his even as she urged his lips apart with her tongue. Nicholas managed not to respond for half a second, but then gave in to what he wanted rather than what was smart and unleashed the passion exploding inside him. His hands slid around her, one at her back pressing her closer, the other sliding to her bottom, cupping her there and lifting her slightly.

This time when Jo groaned, he didn't end the kiss, but deepened it further still, trying to devour her with his mouth. She responded in kind, her arms sliding around his shoulders, fingers digging into his skin as she kissed him back.

Jo had a lot of passion in her, a hunger to match his own, and Nicholas was actually considering carrying her off with him after all and fully tasting that passion when a blinding light suddenly hit his eyes. It had the same effect as a bucket of cold water would, and Nicholas and Jo broke apart at once. He turned sharply toward the first beam of light, but before he could even consider making a run for it, a second beam flashed on to his left and then another to his right. The one that suddenly came on at his back was completely superfluous.

"Nicholas."

"Mortimer?" Jo said uncertainly.

Feeling her bump up against his arm, Nicholas glanced down to see that she'd raised a hand to shelter her eyes from the light and instinctively moved closer to him. Frowning, he growled, "You've made your point. I'm surrounded. Now turn off the damned flashlights. You don't need them to see and you're just blinding Jo."

The lights weren't shut off as requested, but all four of them were lowered to point at the ground.

"Are you all right, Jo?" Mortimer asked, moving close enough to catch her arm and draw her away from Nicholas.

"Yes, of course. My head hurts a little, but Nicholas saved me before anything too bad happened."

"Nicholas *saved* you?" Bricker asked, and Nicholas grimaced at the surprise in the man's voice.

"Yes, from that blond guy." Jo gestured behind Nicholas, and all flashlights and eyes turned to where Ernie Brubaker should have been, but all they found was a bloody knife lying on empty ground.

"Christ," Nicholas muttered with disgust. He'd known he should have checked to be sure he'd hit the heart. Instead he'd— Nicholas caught himself, shook the self-recriminations away, and shifted his thoughts to what was important now. His eyes slid over the four men surrounding him: Mortimer, Bricker, Anders, and Decker. His gaze halted on Decker. "His name is Ernie, he came for your woman and her sister. He's probably fled, but you'd best get inside and stick close to them until you're sure."

Decker nodded and turned away at once, but Mortimer stopped him by saying, "Take Jo with you."

"But I don't want to leave Nic—" The sudden halt to her words and equally abrupt blankness to her expression told Nicholas that one of the men, probably Decker, had taken control of her. He understood the need, but it still bothered him that he did. Nicholas didn't comment, however, but merely watched silently as Decker led Jo Willan away, knowing it was probably the last time he'd ever see her. It was a sad reality to acknowledge, and he felt heartsore and weary when she disappeared around the corner with Decker.

Feeling every one of his five hundred and sixty years, Nicholas turned his gaze to Mortimer. "You need to cut back the trees at least twenty feet from the driveway outside the gate and inside. You need to stop the vehicles between the closed fences for inspection rather than inside both gates, and you need to check under and all around the vehicle instead of just inside before you let them past the second gate. The rogue came in on the undercarriage of the catering truck, slid out, and ran into the trees while Bricker was talking to the driver."

Mortimer didn't look pleased at his lecture, but merely asked, "And you?"

"I had to improvise when I saw that Ernie had got in. Ernie Brubaker," he added. "He's one of Leo's immortal sons. I've been tracking him in the hopes of finding Leo's hideout and followed him here."

"And how did you get in?" Mortimer asked again.

Nicholas shrugged. "Fortunately, the cleaning truck pulled up right after he got in. I rode in on the back bumper of the van and slipped off into the woods inside while Bricker was checking the driver."

Bricker glanced to Mortimer and then back to Nicholas and asked, "Why?"

"Why what?" Nicholas asked quietly.

"Why would you risk coming in here?" he explained.

"Ernie," Nicholas said simply. "I knew you weren't aware he was in here and I thought I'd best run him to ground before he got to one or both of the girls."

"You expect us to believe that you risked coming in here to—"

"Believe what you want," Nicholas interrupted grimly.

"Why not just call?" Mortimer asked.

"I didn't have my phone," he admitted and then

glanced toward the house as a small army of enforcers came hurrying around the corner. Eyebrows rising, he asked dryly, "Jesus, is there anybody on the streets tonight?"

Mortimer ignored him and moved to meet the men. He started giving orders. Within moments the enforcers had spread out in all directions, some returning to the house to stand guard there, the rest heading off to begin searching the grounds. Mortimer then turned and made his way back to where Nicholas waited with Anders and Bricker.

"You'll be our guest tonight, of course," Mortimer announced quietly, and then smiled slightly as he added, "We won't take no for an answer."

"Ha ha," Nicholas muttered bitterly.

Mortimer gave up any attempt at humor, his expression becoming solemn as he added, "I'll call Lucian once we have you locked up."

"You have somewhere to lock up rogues here?" Nicholas asked with interest.

Mortimer gestured toward the building at the back of the property. It was a large structure sided with corrugated metal, Nicholas noted as Mortimer said, "It used to be an airplane hangar. It holds our SUVs now, and we built an office and three cells as well. You should be comfortable enough."

"Great," Nicholas muttered, moving forward when Mortimer gestured with his gun for him to do so.

"We put up the brick wall and fencing too," Bricker announced as they urged him along the side of the house. "And furnished the place. It's been a busy summer."

Nicholas merely grunted. He knew this wasn't the first house the enforcers had inhabited. They'd been in the other one only a couple of weeks when trouble with Ernie's father, Leonius, had made them pack up and move to a new location. It made him wonder if they'd decide to move again now that one of Leonius's sons knew the new location. He doubted it though. They couldn't keep the location a secret for long, and couldn't move every time their whereabouts were discovered. He supposed that was why they'd gone so hard on security . . . and if they listened to the advice he'd given them moments ago, they should be safe enough here. Not that it should matter to him, he supposed. Once Lucian was called in, he was a dead man.

Jo closed the door behind her and crossed the room, headed for the bed. She was very tired and eager to climb under the covers and sleep. That was the thought circling through her mind as she passed the window and spotted the men on the lawn.

Pausing, she moved closer to the window and peered out, recognizing Mortimer and Bricker, but not the third man with them. They were quite a distance away, but the stranger appeared to be a good-looking man. She didn't recall meeting him at the party, however. Curious, she moved to the balcony door and slid it open to step outside.

The low rumble of the men's voices drifted to her on the night breeze, and Jo frowned at the cadence and rhythm of the stranger's voice. It sounded vaguely familiar, but she was sure they hadn't met. She watched them walk to the building at the back of the property, listening to them talk and trying to place where she'd heard the voice before. Even after they disappeared inside the building, the question of where she knew the man from continued to nag at her rather irritably. Jo had the feeling it was important, but couldn't seem to figure it out.

She was still fretting over the matter when the sound of a door closing drew her attention. Mortimer and Bricker had come back out of the building where her sister Sam said he housed his car collection, and were walking toward the house. Jo watched them for a moment, but then turned and slid back into the house before they could spot her. She really was very tired and eager to climb under the covers and sleep. Unfortunately, she now had a rather nasty headache. Frowning, she raised a hand to the back of her skull as she headed for the bed once more, but her footsteps slowed and then stopped as she felt the bump there.

What the heck? Wincing as her fingers slid over the swelling, Jo changed direction, heading for the bathroom instead. She stepped into the small room, flipped on the bright overhead light, and then moved to the mirror, turning her head to the side in an effort to see the goose egg she had. Of course, that didn't work. Grimacing, she started opening drawers and cupboard doors in search of a hand mirror or something she could use to see the back of her head, but there was very little in the cupboards and drawers, just towels, washcloths, and various soaps.

Jo closed the last door and straightened with a sigh. Not only had she not found a mirror, but there was no aspirin or pain relievers of any kind in this guest bathroom either. It seemed, tired and eager to climb into bed and sleep as she was, she would have to go downstairs and find some sort of pain reliever first. There was no way she was going to sleep with her head pounding as it was.

Maybe she could find out what had happened to her head while she was at it, she thought. Jo had no recollection of bumping it or anything and certainly should, considering the whack she must have taken to cause the swelling there now. In fact, she couldn't understand how she didn't recall what had happened to cause it, and began to worry that something might have been dropped into her drink tonight, one of those date rape drugs or something.

The thought raised enough worry in her that Jo suddenly wasn't so tired and eager to climb into bed and sleep anymore. In fact, she was wide awake and alarmed as she slid into the hall. Jo was halfway to the stairs when she heard the front door open below. Heavy footsteps entered the house, and then there was the tap of high heels rushing up the hall.

"Oh, Mortimer," she heard Sam say anxiously. "What's going on? Decker brought Jo inside all blank-faced and wouldn't tell me what had happened. He took Jo upstairs and sent her to her room and then went to check on Dani and Stephanie and hasn't come back. He was controlling Jo, wasn't he?"

"Yes, honey, he had to."

Jo froze in the upper hall at Mortimer's words. Decker had been controlling her? He had to? What the . . .

"Why?" Sam asked. "What's happened?"

"A rogue got onto the property," Mortimer explained. "One of Leo's sons. He attacked Jo. It's all right," he added quickly as Sam gasped in dismay. "She's fine. Nicholas was following the rogue and saved her before he did more than bang her up a bit."

"Nicholas?" Sam asked even as Jo repeated the name in her head. She suddenly had a flash of the man she'd seen on the lawn with Mortimer and Bricker. They were standing in the dark and he was peering down into her face, telling her his name was—

"Nicholas Argeneau?" Sam spoke the name running through Jo's mind, and then added, "The *rogue* Nicholas Argeneau. He was here too?"

"Yes. He was apparently tailing Leo's son and followed him onto the property to keep him from causing trouble. He saw him attack Jo and stopped him."

A moment of silence fell below and Jo eased forward, moving close enough to the railing that she could see the tops of Sam and Mortimer's heads, but no more. She had no desire to be caught. Jo suspected they would stop talking if they knew she was there.

"So this Nicholas Argeneau," Sam said grimly, "the *rogue* Nicholas Argeneau . . . helped save Dani and Stephanie at the beginning of summer and has now, again, risked getting himself caught to save my sister?" Sam asked slowly in what Jo fondly thought of as her sister's lawyer voice. "Does that make any sense to you?"

"No." Mortimer sounded weary, and his hand came into view as he ran his fingers through his hair. "But that's what's happened."

"Why would he do that?" Sam asked, and then, voice serious, said, "Are you sure he's a rogue, Mortimer? A man who'd risk himself to save complete strangers just doesn't sound like a—"

"He's a rogue, Sam," Mortimer interrupted firmly. "And I don't know why he did what he did tonight. Maybe he's trying to make up for the past. Just be glad he did and Jo is safe."

Sam released a little sigh, and her head moved as she nodded. "I should go check on Jo."

"Leave her be, honey," Mortimer said, and Jo eased a little closer to the rail to see him catching Sam's arm as she made for the stairs. "Decker wiped her memory and put it in her head that she's tired and wants to sleep. Leave her be until morning. You might stir some of her memories if you talk to her tonight. They'll be more likely to stay wiped if you leave her until morning."

"Are you sure?" Sam asked, sounding worried.

"So long as she doesn't see Nicholas or Leo's son again, those memories should stay buried," Mortimer assured her. "Now come on. I need to call Lucian and I'd rather not be too far away from you until we're sure Leo's son isn't still prowling the property."

"Is there a possibility he is?" Sam asked with dismay.

"We think he's fled. The gate was open when the men went to search. We think he slipped back through the woods while Nicholas and Jo were kissing and slipped out through the gate when Bricker left his post to investigate the noises he heard."

"Nicholas and Jo were *kissing*?" Sam asked as if Mortimer had said they'd been having sex on a coffee table in the living room in front of the whole party. Jo understood, however; she was a little shocked at this news herself. She'd been kissing some guy she didn't know but who'd saved her from some guy who'd attacked her?

"I'll explain in a minute," Mortimer promised. "I really have to call Lucian. Come on."

"But why were they kissing?" Jo heard Sam ask as Mortimer led her away from the entry and into the library.

Much to Jo's regret, the door closed before Mortimer could answer. She would have liked to have heard that answer herself.

Jo stayed where she was for another moment, her mind spinning a little. Most of what had been said made no sense to her. Decker had wiped her memory and put it in her head that she was tired? She'd been attacked by a rogue, whatever that was, and some fellow named Nicholas, also a rogue, had saved her . . . apparently risking himself in some way to do so? And she'd been kissing him?

It was the bit about wiping her memory that bothered her most. What did that mean? And how could it have been done? Oddly enough, however, while she wondered about that, Jo was also having strange flashes of memory in her head, just bits of memory that were very disjointed and didn't make a lot of sense. Mostly she just kept seeing the dark-haired man's face.

Raising one hand to her head, Jo closed her eyes as the headache she'd been suffering suddenly increased tenfold. Forcing herself to breathe deeply and not think at all, she waited for the intense pain to ease a bit. It had just reduced to being bearable when she heard the front door of the house open again.

Jo stiffened where she stood as what sounded like a small army stomped into the house. She heard the library door open then and Mortimer asked, "Well?"

"All clear. He definitely got away," someone answered.

"Right. I want two men on the gate in future. We stop all vehicles between the gates and do a thorough search, inside, outside, under, and on top before the vehicles are allowed past the second gate from now on. I don't want this happening again. Understood?"

There were several murmured agreements and then Mortimer sighed. "Nicholas is locked up, but I couldn't reach Lucian. I left a message, but he and Leigh have been traveling a lot since she lost the baby and it could be a couple hours before he gets back to us. So, in the meantime, I want you . . ."

Jo couldn't hear the rest of what he said. His voice had grown fainter, as if he'd turned back into the library, and the sound of shuffling feet as several people moved out of the entry completely muffled the rest of his words. The men had followed him into the library, she supposed, and peered cautiously down over the railing when the sound of a door closing was followed by complete silence.

Sure enough, the entry was now empty.

Jo stared at the closed library door for several moments, and then began tiptoeing down the stairs. She didn't know what the hell was happening, but suspected the only way she was going to find out was to talk to the man who was locked up. Any other time she would have gone straight down and confronted Mortimer and Sam, but that bit about Decker wiping her memories as well as the strange flashes of memory that had come to her moments ago had combined to make her wary of doing so. And Mortimer had said that as long as she didn't see this man, the memories would stay wiped.

If they really had messed with her mind, Jo wasn't giving them the chance to do so again. She would rather go down and talk to this Nicholas fellow who had risked himself to save her, get those memories back, and keep them. They were hers, dammit, and no one was taking them from her.

Chapter Three

Jo managed to make it out of the house without being spotted. She paused just outside the sliding glass doors to the dining room to peer over the dark yard. She was pretty sure everyone was in the house right now, but considering the events of the evening, it certainly couldn't hurt to be cautious.

Aware that the longer she took, the better the chances were of getting caught, Jo gave up her position by the door and broke into a run, sprinting straight for the back building. She was actually pretty impressed with her speed as she flew across the grass. She'd never been much for athletic pursuits, preferring things like rock climbing and diving for physical activity, but her feet were pedaling so fast they seemed to barely touch the ground.

A little sigh of relief slipped from Jo's lips when she reached the door to the building and found it unlocked. She eased it silently open and then slid inside with one nervous glance back at the empty yard. Once she had the door safely closed behind her, Jo paused to get her bearings. She was standing in a small lit hall with glass windows running along either side of her. The windows on her right revealed a large, well-lit garage with several vehicles inside. Every single one of them was an SUV.

It didn't look like much of a car collection to her. The SUVs all appeared to be brand-spanking-new. She was getting the distinct impression that Sam hadn't been completely honest with her about things.

Deciding that was something she was definitely going to have to take up with her sister later, Jo slid her gaze to the windows on her left and found herself looking into a dark office. There was a desk, filing cabinets, chairs . . . Her eyes paused on a large, boxy-looking shape and she squinted a little, trying to make out what it was. When that didn't help, Jo moved slowly to the open office door. She reached inside and felt along the wall on the left and then the one on the right, relieved when she found the light switch. The moment she flipped it, light exploded overhead. It left her blinking briefly, but then she was able to see that the large boxy shape was a medical refrigerator with a glass front revealing row after row of bagged blood.

Jo gawked at the sight, bewilderment rolling through her as she tried to sort out what that could be about. Was Mortimer a closet hemophiliac or something? The question slid through her mind as she took a quick glance over the rest of the office and then flipped the light off again. There was a small window in the room, and she didn't want to alert anyone at the house to her presence by having lights shining in windows where there shouldn't be lights.

At least not until she knew what was going on, Jo thought as she eased away from the office door and peered around. A hallway ran off the left side of the small hall she now stood in. It was well-lit and had three doors leading off it—two along the opposite wall, and one on the same side as the office. Not really doors so much as cell doors, Jo realized as she passed the first one and saw it was made of bars one would expect to find in a prison. This first cell held a small cot, a sink, a toilet, and nothing else. It was empty, and Jo continued on her way, quite sure she would find the man named Nicholas in one of the other two.

She was right. While the lone cell on the left also had no one in it, the second one on the right held a man. He lay flat on his back on the narrow cot in the room, hands under his head, and legs crossed at the ankles in a completely relaxed pose. He also had his eyes closed when she first saw him, but either she made a sound without realizing it, or he simple sensed her presence, because his eyes suddenly opened and his head lifted, turning in her direction.

"Jo." He spoke her name softly, but it was enough. The sight of his face and the sound of his voice triggered a whole landslide of memories in her mind. Images and sensations flickered through Jo's brain one after another. They were all out of order and disjointed, a kaleidoscope of confused scenes flashing one after the other, and they were accompanied by a searing pain as what felt like a hatchet slammed into the top of her skull.

Screaming, Jo grabbed for the top of her head as her legs buckled. For what could have been seconds, minutes, or hours, she was aware of nothing but the pain. Then it began to ease and she slowly became aware of her surroundings again.

The first thing Jo realized was that she was lying on the cold concrete floor. She lay curled on her side in a fetal position with her hands over her head. Fortunately, her head wasn't bleeding. The pain had been inside, not from a hatchet that had split her skull open, she realized, and then slowly became aware that someone was speaking to her, voice urgent as he said her name over and over again.

"Jo. Are you all right? Jo, talk to me. Jo?"

Nicholas, she recalled. The man who had risked himself to save her and got locked up because of it. Jo closed her eyes briefly, taking another moment to let the pain ease further, but he continued to call her name with what sounded like growing agitation. She wanted to say something to reassure him she was all right, but the pain had left her panting and breathless, and all she could do was remove one hand from her head and wave it weakly to let him know she was okay. The moment she did, she felt something brush the tips of her fingers. It startled her eyes open, and she tilted her head enough to see that Nicholas was now lying on the floor of his cell, his arm extended as far through the bars as he could reach, which was just far enough to touch the tips of her fingers with his own.

Releasing a little sigh, Jo stretched her arm out a bit

until he could actually hold her hand with his own. Nicholas fell silent then, but his expression was still concerned. Jo was still too spent to reassure him, however, so simply lay still and allowed her eyes to close briefly as she tried to sort out the collection of memories that had just bombarded her. They were all there now; the party, the walk, the attack . . . Nicholas. He'd kissed her and she'd kissed him back and it had been . . .

Jo closed her eyes again. Those two kisses had been pretty wonderful, like nothing she'd ever experienced, and the man had saved her from that other fellow. If what she'd overheard Sam say was true, he'd also apparently helped save two other women earlier in the summer . . . So why was he locked up in this cell?

"Jo?"

She tilted her head again and peered at Nicholas.

"Are you all right?" he asked.

Jo nodded slowly, and when the action didn't bring on any more pain, let her other hand slip away from her head.

"I'm guessing they wiped your memories and you just got them back?" he asked quietly.

That made her eyes widen in question. "How—?"

"I've seen it before," he said dryly.

Jo simply stared at him for a moment and then pulled her hand free of his to sit up.

Nicholas did the same, shifting to his hands and knees, and then maneuvering himself to sit cross-legged on the other side of the bars.

They stared at each other for a moment and then Jo asked, "What the hell is going on?"

Nicholas smiled wryly. "Feeling better, I guess?"

A small, weary laugh slipped from her lips, and she brushed a strand of hair that had escaped her ponytail back behind her ear. "My head hurts."

"It will for a while," he said solemnly. "Aside from the blow you took earlier, your brain cells are all a bit scrambled at the moment."

Jo nodded. She could believe that. "I overheard Mortimer tell Sam that Decker wiped my memory."

"Yes. I suspected he would when he took control of you to lead you to the house," Nicholas admitted, and then tilted his head curiously. "Is overhearing Mortimer what started the memories coming back?"

Jo considered the question, but then shook her head carefully. "No. It was when I saw you crossing the lawn with Bricker and Mortimer from my bedroom window. You seemed familiar but I couldn't remember where from and my head started to hurt."

Nicholas nodded as if that made sense and then explained, "Seeing the subject of the memories that were wiped can bring them back."

She frowned. "What do you mean wiped?"

"It's kind of a misnomer. The memories aren't really wiped so much as veiled or . . ." He frowned, obviously unsure how to explain what had been done to her. "The memories are still there, obviously, or you wouldn't have just got them back, but they're buried deep in the subconscious, and if nothing triggers them they stay there."

"How did he do it?" Jo asked at once, horrified at the thought that anyone had the ability to bury her memories. "Is there some machine or something?"

She waited as a struggle took place on Nicholas's face. She recalled his saying he'd suspected that Decker had wiped her memories when he'd *taken control of her* to lead her to the house. Now that she thought about it, Jo didn't recall walking back to the house and up to her room earlier. The memories that had returned to her carried her right up until the men had surrounded them in the yard while they were kissing and then started again with her in the guest bedroom afterward. She wasn't even sure how long afterward that had been, the memories between were all missing.

Frowning at that realization, she asked, "And how could Decker take control of me? What is going on here?"

"I can't explain it to you, Jo," Nicholas said finally. "If I could claim you, that would be one thing, but I can't . . . and they'd just wipe your memories again afterward."

The bit about claiming her made no sense, so she concentrated on the last part of what he'd said, and pointed out dryly, "Well, if they'll just erase the memory anyway, then there shouldn't be any problem telling me."

"I can't explain," he repeated firmly, shaking his head. "And you shouldn't be here. Mortimer will probably come back out to question me after he calls Lucian, and if he finds you here he will take control of you again and he *will* wipe your memories."

Jo stared at him silently for a minute, and then stood up. When Nicholas did as well, she moved to the bars and peered up at him. "Sam said you were only caught because you risked yourself to save me. She said you risked yourself earlier in the summer to save Decker's girlfriend Dani and her little sister too. Is that true?"

Nicholas nodded solemnly.

She considered that briefly and then asked, "Do I need to worry about Sam? She loves Mortimer. Is he—"

"He's a good man," Nicholas said firmly. "Your sister is perfectly safe with Mortimer. He will never stray, never harm her, give his life for her, and always keep her safe. You needn't worry about her future. Please trust me on that."

Jo considered him silently, debating whether she should trust him and finding that in her heart of hearts she did. If he said Mortimer was not a threat to Sam, she believed him.

"And what about me?" she asked. "Is he a threat to me?"

"He would never hurt you either," Nicholas said solemnly.

"Fine." Jo turned away and started up the hall, saying, "I'm not sure what's going on here and I can't make you tell me, but these guys aren't cops and you only got caught because you saved me from that blond guy. I'm not leaving you locked up here. I'm going to go check the office and see if there are keys in there to your cell."

"Wait, Jo. I—"

"I'll be quick," Jo promised, turning the corner into the entry hall before he could protest again. Not that she would have listened anyway. She was determined to set him loose. It made perfect sense to Jo. Nicholas never would have been in this mess, whatever it was, had he not troubled himself to save her from blondie with the bad breath. Besides, what she'd said was true, Nicholas might be locked up in a cell, but this wasn't a police station, and Mortimer and Bricker were not cops. While she distinctly recalled Mortimer telling Sam that Nicholas was a rogue, as far as Jo knew, that was just a devilish, womanizing male. Considering how good a kisser he was, she wasn't shocked at the revelation. Her lips had been tingling ever since she'd regained her memories of the two toe-curling kisses he'd planted on her. The man showed some serious skill there, but it wasn't a good enough reason to be locking him up like a criminal. She was cutting him loose.

Jo peered out the window of the office before she did anything else, checking to make sure no one was heading toward the building. Finding the yard empty, she then turned to the shadowed room and began to move cautiously around, feeling the desk surface and then opening and groping the contents of drawers in the hope of finding a key to the cell Nicholas was locked in.

When that didn't turn up anything, Jo checked the window again, intending to risk the lights for a few moments if no one was around. However, the sight of two men crossing the lawn toward the building made her heart lurch up into her throat.

Panic suddenly pumping through her, Jo glanced wildly around the shadowed room, and then her eyes landed on the dark hole that was the knee cubby under the desk. Without pausing to consider the merits of the hiding spot, she quickly dropped and crawled into it. Jo had just gotten into the spot and squeezed her eyes closed—as if that might help make her invisible—when she heard the outer door open and the murmur of male voices.

"I don't know, Mortimer," Bricker was saying. "Nicholas just keeps risking himself to save women. Maybe he isn't the rogue we thought he was."

"Sam said the same thing," Mortimer admitted, and Jo's eyes opened with alarm as his voice suddenly became clear and loud and the office light came on overhead. Oh Christ, they were coming in here. She was so dead, she thought with horror as Mortimer continued, "But you know what he did as well as I do, and—"

"Where are you going?" Bricker interrupted.

"To get the keys to the cells," Mortimer answered, and Jo's heart stopped as his legs came into view between the desk chair and the kneehole where she crouched.

Please don't sit, please don't sit, she began to pray, sure he would bump her with his legs if he sat at the desk, and then she'd be discovered. Jo could have howled with frustration when his knees began to bend as he started to sit.

"I have the keys still," Bricker said, and Mortimer paused and straightened again. As the legs moved out of sight, Bricker asked, "Why do you think he keeps risking getting caught then?"

"I don't know," Mortimer muttered as the lights

in the office went out again. "Maybe he has a death wish."

"You think so?" Bricker asked with surprise, his voice growing fainter as the men moved out of the office. "I never would have figured him for the suicidal sort."

"I didn't say suicidal, I said death wish. There's a difference."

Jo remained where she was as the voices moved farther away, not daring to breathe, let alone move until the deep rumble of Nicholas's voice joined them. She couldn't hear what they were saying now, but it told her that Mortimer and Bricker had reached the end cell and it was relatively safe to move. Certainly it was safer to move and get the hell out of the office than it was to wait there for them to return. Jo didn't think she'd be fortunate enough to avoid getting caught a second time if she stayed where she was. She had to get out of the office before they finished talking to Nicholas and returned.

Crawling out from the knee cubby, Jo crouched behind the desk and peered nervously over it toward the door just to be sure, but when she didn't see anyone at the door or through the windows, she quickly stood and tiptoed out of the room, only to stop when she heard the voices up the hall.

"Nothing to say?" Mortimer was asking.

"He was talking earlier," Bricker commented, and she could hear the frown in his voice.

"Well then, I guess we just wait for Lucian. He'll find out anything we need to know," Mortimer decided and Jo realized she'd best get her butt moving. She glanced around briefly, her gaze moving back toward the exit, and then shifting to the garage where the SUVs all sat lined up silent and waiting. She headed for the garage. It seemed the smartest option to her. Jo didn't trust that Mortimer and Bricker wouldn't lock the door of the building when they left this time, and she might not be able to get back in. Besides, there was obviously no sense looking for the keys in the office since Bricker had them. But perhaps she could find something in the garage to hack through the bars or jimmy the lock or something.

"Lucian might come tonight and put you out of your misery, but it could be morning before he gets here," Mortimer was saying as Jo reached the garage door. "You might as well make yourself comfortable. Do you want anything?"

Nicholas's response was just a rumble of sound as Jo carefully opened the door to the garage and slid through it. As she eased the door carefully closed, she heard Mortimer say, "Then we'll leave you to your thoughts."

Jo hurried to the first SUV in the garage to duck on the other side of it. She waited there for one heartbeat, but then couldn't resist easing up to peer through the windows of the SUV. She was just in time to see Bricker and Mortimer enter the small entry hall and move into the office.

As she'd feared, Mortimer did drop to sit in the desk chair and scoot his knees under the desk as he leaned back in the seat. Had she remained, she definitely would have been caught, Jo thought as she watched Bricker settle himself on the corner of the desk. The two men looked like they were settling in for a long chat, and she sighed to herself, wishing they'd get their butts out of there even as she wished she could hear what they were saying. Jo even briefly considered trying to sneak to the door and cracking it open to listen, but the risk of being caught was enough to put that idea in the "not very smart" category so she remained where she was.

They talked for only a moment before Bricker stood and moved to the medical refrigerator she'd earlier noted held a stock of blood. As she watched, he opened the glass-fronted door to retrieve a couple of bags.

Jo frowned, wondering what on earth he was going to do with them. Her confusion only increased when he tossed one of the bags to Mortimer, and she eased up a little higher to see better, only to drop quickly out of view again when Bricker suddenly glanced in her direction.

Biting her lip, Jo waited, sure she'd been spotted and that Bricker would come bursting into the garage any moment. But a moment passed and then several more without the sudden sound of the garage door opening. Still, she gave it another moment and then eased up just high enough to see through the windows again. What she saw was Bricker throwing out what appeared to be a now-empty blood bag as he followed Mortimer out of the office.

Jo ducked back down and waited until she heard the slam of the outer door. She then eased back up to peer through the windows of the SUV again. The office was empty, Mortimer and Bricker were gone. Jo hesitated and then got to her feet and moved to the large garage door in front of the SUV she'd been hiding behind. Rising up on her tiptoes, she managed to peer out the high window and saw Mortimer and Bricker moving off across the lawn toward the house. She watched, waiting until they entered through the sliding glass door, and then turned to peer around the garage.

Unlike the office, the garage lights had been on when she'd entered the building and still were. Jo had no idea why, unless some of the partygoers had arrived in some of the SUVs in here. Which meant they'd be coming in to collect their vehicles when they wanted to leave. She had to get moving.

Jo moved to the long worktable along the back wall of the garage, her eyes quickly scanning the tools hanging from hooks in the pegboard above it. There was everything from screwdrivers to chain saws on that board. Jo briefly considered the easy route, taking the chain saw and just cutting through the bars, or failing that—because she wasn't entirely sure even a chain saw could cut through metal bars—simply cutting through the plasterboard walls. However, chain saws were bloody noisy, and the sound might reach the house or the front gate and bring someone running, which meant she had to do it the hard way. She'd have to pick the lock. It wasn't an impossible task, but she was rusty and it might take a bit of time. She hoped the men didn't return for a while as she grabbed up several likely-looking tools.

Moving quickly, Jo hurried out of the garage, but instead of heading right back to Nicholas's cell, she made a quick detour into the office for a brief look out the window. Reassured to find the lawn empty and still, she hurried out of the office with determined strides.

Chapter Four

Fate was a fickle bitch with a very bad sense of humor, Nicholas decided, lying on the cot in his cell and staring up at the ceiling. Here he was, caught and about to meet his Maker, and Madam Fate throws a life mate at him just to muddy the waters. How sick and twisted was that?

He grimaced at the ceiling, his ears straining to hear any sounds of movement in the building. Mortimer and Bricker had arrived not long after Jo had slipped away in search of keys. Since there had been no uproar or stir after they'd left him, it seemed obvious her presence hadn't been discovered. She must have hidden, he supposed, and wondered why he hadn't warned the men of her presence.

That would have been the responsible thing to do, Nicholas knew. Her being here and the fact that she'd regained the memories that Decker had wiped could cause problems. However, Nicholas hadn't been willing to give up the opportunity to talk with her again, maybe even steal another kiss, and possibly even escape. He'd like to take her with him, but he had nothing to offer her except life on the run, and that was no life for a woman like Jo. He could already tell she was the free-spirited type, and they couldn't be free-spirited when they were on the run. They had to be cautious and careful about every little thing they did.

Mind you, he hadn't been much of either lately, Nicholas acknowledged. He'd been taking too many chances and too many risks. It was what had gotten him caught this time and nearly got him caught at the beginning of summer. But he couldn't regret what he'd done in either instance. Even if he died tomorrow, Nicholas wouldn't regret saving Jo from Ernie. The rogue would have either killed her, or hurt her badly and gone after Dani and her sister, or have simply taken Jo back to his father. None of those conclusions was acceptable to him. He might not be able to claim Jo as his life mate, but Nicholas would do what he could to keep her safe while he could.

Unfortunately, that meant he couldn't explain the situation to her. Not that Nicholas had it in him to tell her the truth anyway. He had no desire to see the horror and disgust enter her eyes when she learned what he'd done fifty years ago. If she even believed him and didn't simply decide he was spaced out on drugs or just plain crazy. After all, he didn't look like he could have been around for fifty years, and explaining the whole I'm-a-vampire bit wasn't likely to be that believable to her.

Nicholas smiled faintly at the thought of her expression if he tried to explain that. *Really, I am a vampire, but a good vampire . . . except for that one time I murdered an innocent.*

He grimaced. Yeah, except for that one inexplicable evil deed he'd performed while in the throes of grief, he was a swell guy.

The slam of the outer door caught his ear, and Nicholas opened his eyes, straining to listen for other sounds in the building, but the steady hum of Mortimer and Bricker's voices from the office was gone. Absolute silence seemed to resound from the hall. He waited another moment, but there wasn't any noise at all now except for his own breathing.

Nicholas was starting to worry that his life mate had decided to leave him to his fate and had slipped back to the safety of the house when he heard the soft "shush" of air being moved as a door opened. It was followed by the scuff of someone walking quickly, and Nicholas smiled to himself. He was sure it was Jo and that she was still here. It might be selfish of him, but he was glad. He could talk with her a little bit and maybe learn something about this woman who could have been his salvation had he not made one stupid, irreconcilable mistake all those years ago.

Standing, he moved to the bars to peer out. She appeared just moments after he reached them, expression fretful and eyes nervous as she hurried down the hall toward him.

"I couldn't get the keys, Bricker has them," Jo babbled as she approached. "But I found these and think I can pick the lock."

"Pick it?" Nicholas asked doubtfully.

"Yes. I worked as a locksmith's assistant the summer

between high school and university. He taught me a few tricks. I can do this," she assured him, dropping to her knees in front of his cell door. She examined the lock briefly and then grimaced. "It might take me a little time, but I can do it . . . and if not, I'll go back and get the axe and just chop through the wall."

Nicholas found himself smiling for no reason. Really, the woman was adorable, he thought, and asked, "So you've worked with a locksmith and now manage a bar. What else have you done in your short life?"

Jo paused and raised her eyebrows as she met his gaze. "My short life? You make it sound like I'm a kid and you're an old man. You're what? Maybe twenty-seven or so?"

"Or so," he muttered, mentally adding, *Give or take five hundred and thirty-three years.* "So what else have you done?"

Jo shrugged, her attention back on the lock as she stuck her tools in and fiddled with the inner workings. Her voice was absent when she said, "Loads of things. What about you?"

"Loads of things," Nicholas echoed wryly, and suspected he'd worked a hell of a lot more jobs than she had.

"Are you married?"

That question surprised Nicholas, and he glanced away as the usual shaft of pain shot through him at the thought of his late wife. Oddly enough, for the first time in fifty years, the pain wasn't crushing. The memories of his Annie and losing her hurt, but not with the brutality he was used to. His gaze shifted back to Jo. She was concentrating on the lock, but paused to raise a suspicious eyebrow his way.

"Are you?" she asked.

Nicholas shook his head, but then admitted, "Widowed."

Surprise flashed across her face, and then she turned her gaze back to the lock, murmuring, "My sympathies."

"It was a long time ago," he said quietly, and for the first time, it felt like that was true. It had been fifty years since Nicholas had lost his Annie, but for most of those fifty years the loss had felt as raw as if it were just yesterday. Yet now . . . His gaze slid to Jo and he frowned, feeling guilt writhe in his gut at the knowledge that he was finally letting go of his grief and moving on with life.

"You must have been babies when you married if she's been dead awhile," Jo murmured, squinting into the lock as she worked her tools.

He didn't comment to that, but instead asked, "Do you have a boyfriend or—"

"Nope," she interrupted. "No time. Full-time school and full-time work kind of leaves little time for guys. Besides, I see the worst of man at work."

Nicholas raised his eyebrows at the comment. He'd thought being a rogue hunter showed him the worst of mankind, but she sounded pretty certain. "How's that?"

Jo shrugged. "Given enough alcohol, even the nicest guy is an ass. You'd be amazed how many guys come in with their girlfriends, have a spat, and then when she marches out all upset, he leaves with another girl. Then he'd show up the next week with the original girlfriend again, who's probably completely ignorant that he was messing around the week before. Or—and this one just bugs my ass," she paused to add with a disgusted sneer before finishing, "there's no spat and they're all 'coochie coo I love you,' but the minute the girlfriend heads off to the bathroom, he's hitting on other girls."

"Hmm," Nicholas murmured, thinking stories like that were enough to make him glad he was an immortal and immortals tended to be monogamous.

"And the women are just as bad," Jo continued. "I always thought it was just the guys who screwed around, but I've learned different. The gals are just smarter about it. More cautious and discreet, not as loud or obvious so that you aren't really aware they're flirting, but then they disappear to the bathroom for a bit, and return rearranging their clothes and a smirking guy following doing up his pants."

"The same women whose men are hitting on other women while they're gone?" Nicholas asked curiously, thinking perhaps that explained the men's behavior. Maybe they had some sort of agreement, he thought, but Jo shook her head.

"That's the weird thing. As far as I can tell, cheaters rarely hook up with cheaters. It's like they recognize their own and avoid them, because Lord knows a cheater wouldn't want to be cheated on," she said wryly. "It seems like one is always faithful and the other does the cuckolding . . . Although it does occasionally happen where they're both stepping out on the other. I prefer seeing that. I figure they deserve each other."

"It sounds . . ." Nicholas hesitated. It sounded like her job at the bar had given her a very dim view of her fellow man and woman.

"Got it!" Jo exclaimed.

Nicholas had heard the click before her triumphant announcement and now watched with wonder as she withdrew her tools and stood to pull the door open. She did so with a little flourish, waving her hand and bowing as she gestured him out. It made him smile, but instead of stepping out and moving past her, he stood in front of her and waited for her to glance up before reaching for her, saying, "It seems now *I* owe *you* a thank-you."

Jo blinked in surprise. She'd expected Nicholas to rush out and flee as fast as his feet would carry him the moment she had the cell door open, but instead he caught her arms and drew her forward, his head descending toward hers. She didn't resist. Thank-yous were nice . . . at least with Nicholas. She already knew that and wasn't adverse to enjoying more passionate thank-yous with him, she thought, and then his mouth was covering hers and she was overwhelmed by the same amazing passion she'd experienced earlier.

Damn, he was a fine kisser, definitely worthy of the title *rogue*, Jo thought, letting the tools she held drop from her fingers so that she could slide her hands around his back. She hardly heard the varying clangs as the tools hit the hard concrete. Her mind was consumed by the waves of passion building and rolling through her, each one slamming against her brain with more strength as his mouth devoured hers. She wasn't aware of Nicholas moving, but suddenly felt the cold metal of bars against her back and briefly opened her eyes to see that he'd backed her up against the cell door opposite his, and then her eyes closed again on a moan as he pinned her there with his body, grinding his hips against her.

When his hands cupped her breasts through her top, Jo arched her back, pressing herself into the touch. Her hands moved to cover his, and she squeezed them encouragingly before reaching to run her own hands over his chest, wishing he wasn't wearing the shirt and she could touch his naked flesh. It was a rather startling thought for Jo. She wasn't a prude or a virgin, but she hardly knew this guy. In fact, other than his name, the fact that he was a widower and that he'd risked himself to help her, she didn't know a thing about him. But her body was acting like it knew him very well, or wanted to. *She* wanted to. She wanted to know every naked inch of him. She wanted—

Jo's thoughts died on a gasp as Nicholas suddenly tugged her T-shirt upward, baring her breasts. She wasn't big on bras. They all had ribs and wires and all sorts of nasty little things to dig into a body. Other than wearing them to work, she tended to avoid them and hadn't worn one tonight. Jo was very glad she hadn't when Nicholas covered one naked orb with his hand and then broke their kiss to bend his head and claim the other with his mouth.

"Oh God," Jo gasped, curling her fingers into the hair at the back of his head. This was . . . this was . . . She gave up trying to think what this was when his teeth and tongue came into action, his teeth catching the tender nipple and holding it as his tongue rasped over the sensitive nub.

Damn he was good, Jo thought, and she, who had never had a one-night stand in her life, decided they needed to move into one of the cells and put the cot to good use. Now, she thought as his leg suddenly slid between both of hers, rubbing against her and raising their passion to a whole new level. Growling with need, Jo tugged at his hair, demanding he stop what he was doing and kiss her before she absolutely exploded right there on the spot.

Nicholas let her nipple slip from his mouth and lifted his head at once to claim her lips, but his kiss was less than soothing. His tongue thrust into her mouth in imitation of what she was beginning to desperately hope would follow on that cot, and his hand replaced his mouth at her breast, his thumb and finger plucking gently and then rubbing soothingly.

"Nicholas," Jo gasped when he broke the kiss to run his mouth along her cheek to her ear. "I need . . . ohh," she moaned as he rubbed his leg against her more firmly. "Yes . . . I . . . what's that?"

He stilled at once and then turned his head toward the end of the hall, where muffled voices could be heard.

"Christ," Nicholas muttered, and they broke apart at once, both of them quickly straightening their clothes.

Jo started to slide into the empty cell beside them then, her only thought to hide. But Nicholas caught her hand and shook his head and tugged her behind him as he started up the hall, saying, "They're in the garage."

"What are you doing?" Jo hissed with alarm when she realized they were moving *toward* the voices.

Nicholas merely glanced back and placed a silencing finger to his lips and then continued forward, staying close to the wall.

Jo closed her eyes briefly, thinking the man must be mad, but followed silently. They were nearly to the end of the hall before they could see the men in the other part of the building. Two of the six garage doors were open, the nearest one and the one farthest away. Three men stood talking in the open far door behind one of the SUVs. Jo recognized Bricker and two of the men she'd been introduced to at the party tonight.

"What—?" she began, but Nicholas pressed a finger to her lips.

"Wait here," he whispered, and then was gone.

Jo glanced around with confusion that only grew when she saw him disappearing into the office, still in a crouch. The man moved *fast*. She had barely turned to peer worriedly back into the garage when he was suddenly beside her again, slipping something into his pocket.

"My receiver," he explained. "They took it when they locked me up."

"What's a receiver?" Jo asked with confusion and then shook her head. That didn't really matter at this point. She was more concerned about getting caught and hissed in a whisper, "Bricker could come in here. We need to hide."

Nicholas shook his head. "I need to leave."

"What? But—" Jo began with alarm, and then gasped in surprise as Nicholas dropped to his haunches, pulling her down beside him so that they were out of sight.

"This is the only way I'm going to get out of here," he said gently, raising a hand to brush his fingers lightly along her cheek.

Jo frowned. "But—"

This time he silenced her by kissing her quickly, and it *was* quick, just a swift brushing of his lips over hers. Nicholas then pulled back and whispered, "Thank you for freeing me."

Jo tried to speak, but he shifted his thumb to cover her lips and added, "They'll probably wipe your memory of me when they realize you still have it, but I want you to know I'll never forget you . . . and if you ever need me, I'll be there."

Nicholas then kissed her again, another gentle brushing of lips, and Jo let her eyes drift closed. When she opened them, he was already gone, slipping through the door to the garage in a crouch.

"Crap," Jo whispered with dismay, and waited for the inevitable shout as he was spotted. When no shout came, she hesitated and then moved swiftly to the door in a crouch. She took a deep breath and began to ease it open, freezing when it was still merely cracked and she spotted Nicholas on the floor beside the first SUV, slipping under the vehicle. She watched until he disappeared and then started to rise, thought better of it, and instead eased the door closed again and moved at a crouch into the office. Once in the safety of the shadows there, she raised herself up to peer through the windows into the garage.

Jo was just in time to see the men finish their conversation and break apart. Bricker immediately headed out of the garage and out of sight, but one of the two remaining men moved to the SUV they'd been standing behind while the other crossed the garage to the vehicle she'd seen Nicholas disappear under. Jo watched as first the far vehicle backed out and disappeared from view, but when the nearer vehicle did as well and the two doors began to drop closed, Jo quickly moved to peer out the window that overlooked the backyard.

By that time the first SUV had already turned itself around and headed up the drive, but she was in time to watch the second SUV do the same, and Jo bit her lip, scanning the bottom of the vehicle for any sign of Nicholas, but it was dark out and, if he was there, she couldn't see him.

That thought made her rush out of the office to the door leading into the garage. Jo pushed it open and peered at the empty spot where the first SUV had been, then ran along the vehicles just to be sure, but Nicholas wasn't there. Pausing at the end of the garage, she leaned weakly against the wall for a moment, hardly able to believe he was gone. But then she just as quickly straightened and started back along the garage, telling herself that she shouldn't be shocked that he'd left so abruptly, it was how he'd entered her life. Besides, what had she expected? Declarations of undying love because she'd set him free and kissed him a couple of times? A marriage proposal? A happily-ever-after?

Jeez, she needed to get a grip, Jo thought with self-disgust. The guy was a rogue. He probably kissed gals all the time . . . loads of them . . . and a lot of kisses each. The guy had certainly been good at it, and you didn't get that good without lots of practice, she was sure.

Sighing, she headed for the door, intending to leave, but then decided she'd best wait. If she was spotted coming out of the building, they'd probably check the cells and find Nicholas was gone, then stop the vehicles, and he'd be caught once more. If that happened, Jo definitely didn't think she'd be allowed anywhere near the garage again.

If she even remembered Nicholas, Jo thought with a frown as she recalled his saying that once they knew he was missing they'd realize she had her memories back and probably wipe them again. She didn't like that idea at all. Wiping her memory . . . How had they done that? Jo didn't doubt for a minute that they had, but how they'd done it was what bothered her.

It must be some sort of machine, she thought, and turned to peer first into the office and then toward the garage, wondering if she should search for a possible machine that might be used for that. It would help her kill some time while she waited to give Nicholas the chance to get away . . . and if she found it, Jo thought grimly, she'd destroy it and keep her damned memory, thank you very much.

Jo started in the office, feeling her way through the room like a blind woman on an Easter egg hunt. It was a great relief to finish in there and move into the lit areas of the building. She was heading for the garage when she recalled the tools she'd left outside the cell. Jo turned in that direction and hurried up the hall to collect them. She then carried them into the garage and quickly replaced them where she'd found them before starting a search of the garage.

Jo was quicker about this search. The light in the garage made it easier, but she was also hurrying more. She was sure Nicholas was probably off the property by now. The only thing that kept her there was the possibility of finding the machine they used to wipe memories, but the fact was Jo didn't really have a clue what she was looking for. She had no idea what it looked like or even how big it was. For all she knew it was a shot of some drug that was given to make the person more susceptible to suggestion and that the suggestion was then given to the person to forget all about certain things.

When she reached the end of the garage without finding anything, Jo decided she'd have to give it up and head inside. She moved to the nearest garage door and rose up on tiptoe to peer out. When she found the yard was again empty, Jo made her way quickly back into the entry hall and then to the door. She slid it open just enough to slip out, and then drew it closed and started quickly across the yard at a jog that was a flat-out run by the time she reached the house.

What Jo really wanted to do was to walk around

the house, get in her car, and get the heck out of there before it was discovered Nicholas was missing, but she couldn't. She'd ridden in with Alex. It was all right though, she reassured herself. Nicholas had told her that Mortimer would never hurt her or Sam. So she would stay as planned, wait for Nicholas's absence to be discovered, and face the music like a grown-up.

Although, Jo thought, she really would rather just get the hell out of there. While Mortimer might not hurt her, he was definitely not going to be pleased that she'd let Nicholas go and she wasn't looking forward to his anger when he figured out she'd been the one to help him.

Grimacing at this sudden streak of cowardice running through her, Jo shook her head and slid into the house. She could hear voices coming from somewhere at the front of the house. It sounded like Sam and Mortimer talking, and Jo found herself glancing at the kitchen clock as she moved through the room. Her eyes widened slightly when she saw that it was nearly three A.M. Her surprise wasn't because it was that late, but because it was that early. While it had been after midnight when she'd stepped outside for a walk, so much had happened since then that Jo wouldn't have been surprised to find it was nearly dawn. It felt like she'd lived a lifetime in the past few hours.

She moved silently up the hall to the stairwell, her heart beating a rapid tattoo, and was relieved when she made it up the stairs without encountering anyone. Jo was just thinking she'd get to her room and be able to avoid all this business until morning when the front door suddenly opened behind her. Freezing on the top stair, Jo turned and glanced down toward the door, a sudden wave of wariness rolling over her as she saw the man entering. Tall, blond, and grim as death, he had already spotted her before he lifted his first foot over the threshold, and he was looking at her with the same intense stare she'd suffered all night as Sam had introduced her to the men at the party.

Jo shifted uncomfortably under his piercing glare, her eyes sliding to the door of her guest room and the haven it offered, but before she could move, the blond said, "Come downstairs, Josephine. I need to decide what to do with you."

Jo blinked at him in surprise, startled that the stranger knew her name, and then her gaze slid to the doorway to the living room as Mortimer suddenly appeared there.

"Lucian?" he said with surprise and then glanced to Jo at the top of the stairs. He frowned when he spotted her. "Jo? You should be asleep. What are you doing still up?"

"She just came from setting Nicholas free," the man Mortimer had called Lucian announced.

Jo's jaw dropped at the words, and then her eyes shifted to Mortimer as he cursed and started up the hall toward the back of the house.

"Don't bother," Lucian growled, bringing him to a halt. "He's long gone."

Mortimer turned back, and then moved quickly to the door of the living room as Sam appeared there, her worried gaze seeking out Jo.

"Josephine Lea Willan. What have you done?" Sam asked with alarm, and Jo grimaced at the use of her full name. She knew she was in trouble when Sam brought out the big guns, and using the full name had always been considered a big gun in their home while growing up.

"I set him free," Jo said defiantly. "And why shouldn't I? I don't know what the hell's going on here, but Mortimer had no right to lock up Nicholas like he's some criminal. He's not a cop or anything, and Nicholas didn't do anything wrong."

"Oh, Jo," Sam breathed, and then leaned into Mortimer when he slid an arm around her waist. Jo couldn't help but notice, though, that her sister's worried gaze was on this Lucian, person, as if her main concern was what he might do.

Mortimer was also looking at the man, appearing to await something from him, Jo noted, and reluctantly turned her own gaze his way. It appeared this Lucian was the one in charge. A pity, she decided. He looked like a big meanie and his glare was making it hard for her to hold on to her defiance and not fidget nervously like a teenager caught returning after curfew.

"She is Nicholas's life mate," Lucian said suddenly.

Mortimer cursed and Sam muttered, "Oh crap," but Jo scowled at the man and asked, "What is a life mate?" She'd heard the term before from Mortimer and Bricker, but that had been in reference to Sam. She had just assumed it was the same thing as a girlfriend and she definitely didn't feel she could call herself Nicholas's girlfriend. A couple of kisses did not a girlfriend make.

Much to her annoyance the man remained silent,

his gaze solemn and intent, and Jo found herself grinding her teeth with frustration. Really, Mortimer had seemed all right up north in cottage country, but she was beginning to rethink her opinion of him. If a person was judged by his friends, he must be a weirdo because his friends were certainly strange.

A sudden snort of laughter slid from Lucian and he stopped staring at her to turn to Sam. "I like her. She's feisty like my Leigh. Tell her she may go to bed."

Sam's eyes widened and she glanced uncertainly from Lucian to Mortimer. When Mortimer nodded encouragingly, she cleared her throat and glanced to Jo. "Umm . . . Jo?"

"Yeah, yeah, go to bed," Jo muttered, and spun away to head up the hall. She slowed, however, once she was out of sight of the railing and paused to listen. Much as she was relieved to get away from the penetrating stare of the man below, she wanted to hear what he would say next.

"Is she really Nicholas's life mate?" Jo heard Sam ask quietly, and frowned at the worry in her voice.

"Yes," Lucian said. "Which works in our favor."

"How?" Mortimer asked quietly.

"He won't be able to stay away from her."

Jo's eyes widened at that proclamation. She felt a moment's excitement at the prospect of possibly seeing Nicholas again, but it was quickly washed away and replaced with alarm when Lucian added, "Put two men on her when she leaves here tomorrow, Mortimer. He'll show up eventually."

"You want to use my sister as bait?" Sam asked in a voice that was suddenly steel with anger. Jo was actually glad to hear it. Sam had seemed a bit alarmed and uncertain during the last few minutes, which was unusual for her. She was normally the "most efficient and iron-willed lawyer chick." The uncertain and anxious Sam had been rather worrying to Jo, and she would have given her sister a high five if she could have when Sam said, "I won't have it."

"You'd rather we wipe her memory and refuse to allow you to see her?" Lucian asked, annoying Jo all over again. Who the hell did this guy think he was? No one was going to keep her from seeing her sister.

Jo heard Sam curse and then Lucian said, "Let's move this conversation into the library. Jo's heard more than enough of it already."

Her eyebrows flew up at those words, and she couldn't resist easing up to the rail to peer down into the hall. Three pairs of eyes stared back.

"Go to bed," Lucian said firmly. "You are very tired."

And suddenly Jo *was* tired, and bed seemed the most desirable place in the world. Turning dutifully away, she moved up the hall to the door to her guest bedroom and went inside. She was undressed and in bed before it occurred to her to wonder how she could have gone from wired and tense one moment to relaxed and exhausted the next. Jo fell asleep before she could worry about it too much.

Chapter Five

The sun was shining bright and cheerful when Jo woke up. It made her groan and cover her eyes with the hope of easing the ache in her head. Damn, she had the mother of all hangovers. Too bad she hadn't had the good time to earn it. She hadn't had that much to drink last night, which meant the headache was probably thanks to the head banging she'd taken . . . or possibly the result of getting her memory back, she supposed, recalling the agony that had shot through her skull as the memories had come rushing into her mind.

Sighing, Jo removed her hand and forced her eyes open, grimacing and breathing deeply until the first stab of pain eased.

She'd say one thing for her sister, Jo thought as she shifted to a sitting position and then got out of bed. Sam certainly threw memorable parties. Not necessarily memorable in a good way though. Jo suspected this headache was going to stay with her for the rest of the day. Here was hoping her memories stayed with her as well.

Jo grimaced at the thought and then moved to the bathroom. She needed to shower, dress, and get out of this house. She didn't trust that Lucian guy not to try to "wipe" her memories. The idea of anyone messing with her head was rather alarming. She counted on her brain as everyone did, and the idea of pieces of it somehow being "veiled," as Nicholas had put it, was just scary to consider.

Jo turned on the water and took a quick shower, grimacing with pain the whole while. She'd hoped a shower would ease her headache, but instead the sound of the rushing water seemed to make it worse. She was glad to finish and step out, but less glad when she had to dry herself with a bath towel rather than the much larger beach towel she liked to use at home.

The thought of home made her sigh. Jo wished she was in her little apartment right now. She'd close the blinds, put a cold cloth on her head, and sleep until her head felt better. Eager to be able to do that, Jo left the bathroom as quickly as she'd entered. She dressed in record time, stuffed the overlarge T-shirt she'd slept in and the clothes she'd worn the night before into her backpack, and then slung it over her shoulder and immediately headed out of the room.

The hall was empty, and she hurried to the stairs. Jo jogged down them, pausing as the sound of voices reached her from the kitchen. She hesitated, eyes moving longingly to the door, but knew there was nothing for it. Alex had driven her here and she needed Alex to take her home.

Muttering under her breath, she set the backpack on the floor by the front door and then headed up the hall. The closer she got to the kitchen, the clearer the voices became.

"I still don't understand why we can't just explain everything to them," Sam was saying. "Others know about you. Cripes, Bricker says there's a whole town two hours south of here that knows about you guys."

"Knows what about you guys?" Jo asked as she stepped into the room.

Dead silence was her response as Sam and Mortimer turned to peer at her from where they sat at the kitchen table. Sam looked alarmed, she noticed, but Mortimer just looked irritated.

"Here you are."

Jo turned to find Bricker entering the kitchen behind her. His gaze sought out Mortimer as he said, "Sorry, I only stepped away to go to the bathroom and she was gone when I got back to her room."

"I have a guard now?" Jo asked with disbelief. She scowled at Bricker and asked, "And how did you know I'd left my room? Did you go in there?"

"No. I just cracked the door when I couldn't hear you snoring anymore."

"I don't snore," Jo snapped.

Bricker grinned and shrugged. "Okay, I cracked the door when I couldn't hear your *very* loud snorting, snuffling breathing as you slept."

"Ha ha," Jo muttered.

"Do you want a coffee?" Sam asked, getting up to retrieve a cup for her from the cupboard.

"Yes, please, but I'll get it," Jo muttered, moving to meet her at the coffeepot. She murmured a "Thanks" as she took the cup from Sam. "Where's Alex? Not up yet?"

"Oh yes. She was up and out of here early," Sam said, returning to the table.

"What?" Jo whirled to gape at her with horror. "She was supposed to drive me home."

"I know, but I told her I would," Sam said soothingly.

Jo frowned and leaned against the counter, her eyes moving warily from Bricker to Mortimer as she lifted the cup to take a sip. She stiffened when Bricker suddenly moved toward her, but he merely opened the cupboard door beside her and retrieved a small bottle that rattled as he plucked it from the shelf.

"What's that?" Jo asked when he offered it to her.

"Pills Sam had me pick up for her the last time she had a headache," Bricker said, opening his palm for her to read the label.

Jo accepted the pills slowly, her narrowed eyes searching his face. "How did you know—?"

"You have that same squinty-eyed look Sam gets when she has a headache," he said with amusement.

"God, you're a charmer this morning, aren't you?" Jo said dryly, making an effort to remove the "squinty-eyed look" from her face. "I don't remember you being this insulting when we first met."

Bricker grinned. "Yeah, but you're practically

family now. At least you're Sam's family, and she's like family now."

"Great," Jo muttered, setting down her coffee to open the pills. When she struggled with the chore, Bricker plucked the bottle away and opened it for her, forcing her to mutter another "Thanks" as he shook out a couple of pills and handed them over. She picked up her coffee and swigged down some with the pills as Bricker resealed the bottle and put it away. She then glanced to the table to see Sam and Mortimer still watching her. Sam was biting her lip as if there was something she wanted to say, but Mortimer was looking a bit wary.

"Do you want some breakfast?" Sam asked finally.

Jo shook her head, and then winced at the pain the action sent shooting through her skull. She must have bruised her brain or something last night when she hit the wall, Jo thought with disgust, and wondered if you *could* bruise your brain. It certainly felt tender this morning.

"No . . . thanks," she said. "I'd really rather just head home."

"I'll get my keys," Sam said, getting up at once.

"Why bother?" Jo asked. "Why not just let the guys that are supposed to watch me take me home. They can watch me up close then."

A moment of silence passed as Sam glanced to Mortimer. He stared at Jo with narrowed eyes for a minute, but then shrugged and said to Sam, "It will save you a trip, and that way I'll not have to worry about you." Before Sam could comment, he glanced to Bricker and said, "Anders is in the garage fee—having a drink."

"I'll get him and one of the SUVs and pick you up out front," Bricker told Jo, and moved toward the door leading into the backyard.

"I'll get my bag," Jo said, and set down her cup with relief. She'd be out of there soon . . . and with her memory still intact as far as she could tell.

"Jo?" Sam said, standing to follow as she headed out of the kitchen.

Jo slowed, but didn't stop as she started up the hall toward the backpack she'd left by the front door. "Yeah?"

Sam scooted to catch up with her, taking her hand as she reached the front entry and drawing her to a halt.

Jo turned, her gaze sliding up the hall to see with relief that Mortimer hadn't followed. Shifting her gaze back to her sister, she raised her eyebrow.

Sam hesitated and then asked, "Are we all right?"

Jo raised her other eyebrow now. "Why wouldn't we be?"

Sam wrinkled her nose and sighed. "I know this is probably all weird and incomprehensible to you, and—to be frank—I'm amazed you aren't asking a ton of questions about what happened last night, and—"

"Would they be answered?" Jo interrupted quietly, and when Sam peered at her blankly, explained, "If I asked questions about last night, would they be answered?"

Sam bit her lip, but then dropped the uncertainty

that was so odd coming from her and admitted bluntly, "No."

"That's what I thought," she said dryly. Besides, Jo suspected asking questions might lead to losing the memories she'd managed to regain. She wasn't sure why she thought that was so, but had decided to go with her instincts, keep her questions to herself, and get out of there.

"You always were practical," Sam said with a wry smile curving her lips.

Jo forced a smile in response and then said solemnly. "I am going to ask you one question though."

Wariness immediately crept over Sam's face. "What's that?"

"Are you happy?" Jo asked, and then raised her hand to stop her when Sam opened her mouth to answer at once. "Think about it. I mean it. Are you happy? It's all happened so fast. You've quit your position at the firm, moved in here with Mortimer, and started a whole new—and from what I can tell—very strange life. Are you sure it's what you want? Are you sure you won't regret any of this later? Is there any reason *at all* that I should be worried about you?"

Sam appeared to be seriously doing as Jo had requested and thinking about it. Then she let go of the breath she'd apparently been holding.

"I am very happy," Sam assured her solemnly. "It *has* all been very fast, but I am positive I won't regret any of the choices I've made. I love Mortimer and he really does love me, Jo. I know you don't understand a lot of what's happening, but—" Her words died abruptly as Jo hugged her. Her eyes were wide and questioning when Jo stepped back.

"That's all I wanted to hear," Jo assured her quietly. "It's enough. I won't ask questions you can't answer . . . for now," she added quietly.

Sam smiled crookedly and agreed, "For now."

"That's settled then," Jo said with feigned good cheer as she turned away to collect her backpack. She peered out the window at the driveway. Spotting the SUV pulling up, Jo gave Sam a smile as she opened the door. "Now I'm going home to bed. My head is killing me."

"Make Bricker stop and pick up some breakfast for you on the way home," Sam said firmly, following her out the door.

"I heard that," Bricker announced, slipping out of the front passenger seat to open the back door for Jo. He took her backpack, saying, "Get her breakfast. Will do."

"She'll be a good mother, don't you think?" Jo said dryly as she slid into the backseat.

"That she will." Bricker's voice was solemn as he set the backpack on the floor by her feet.

As he closed the door, Jo glanced to Sam, a frown claiming her lips as she saw the stricken look on her sister's face. Apparently Smart Sam hadn't connected being in love and having regular sex with possible future babies. Jo sincerely hoped Smart Sam hadn't forgotten about birth control. If she had . . . well, a baby would be an interesting development, she supposed. She didn't mind the idea of becoming an aunt.

"And we're off."

Jo turned her gaze forward to see that Bricker had hopped back in the front seat and was pulling the door closed. The moment it slammed shut, the man behind the wheel, a dark-skinned, grim-faced fellow, set the vehicle in motion.

Jo shifted forward on the backseat and peered at the driver more closely. She hadn't met him at the party, but she might as well have. Like all the others, he was a perfect version of himself, with glossy, short black hair, perfect pores, and shiny white teeth.

"You must be Anders," Jo commented, recalling Mortimer mentioning the fellow.

"Seat belt," was his growled response.

Jo raised one eyebrow and glanced to Bricker.

"Anders is a man of few words," he said almost apologetically.

"So I see," she commented dryly.

"Seat belt on or vehicle stops," Anders said firmly.

Jo snorted. "*Very* few words if he can't even bother with little words like *the*, *goes*, or *please*."

"The seat belt goes on, please, or the vehicle stops," Bricker said, using those little words Anders hadn't.

Jo chuckled at his imitation of the other man's deep growl, but sat back to do up her seat belt. She didn't miss the little sigh Anders released at Bricker's teasing, though, and it made her grin. She peered from Bricker's good-natured face to the back of Anders's head and said, "So how come you weren't at the party last night?"

Anders was silent for a minute and then glanced to Bricker. "Is she speaking to me?"

A snort of amusement slid from Bricker, but he nodded. "Yes, Anders, I'd guess she is."

He turned back to the road, and Jo was just deciding he wasn't going to answer her question when he said, "I was working."

"Really?" she asked with interest, leaning as far forward as her seat belt would allow. "Working on a Saturday night? What do you do?"

There was a pause and then he said simply, "Hunt."

Jo raised her eyebrows and drawled dubiously, "Right."

Silence fell in the vehicle as they reached the gates at the end of the drive. Two men were stationed at the guardhouse today, she noted. One rushed to open the inner gate for them while the second stood at the booth and watched them pass. She wondered briefly if the added security was because of Bad-Breath Boy's visit last night, and then they were out and heading up the road.

"So . . . Anders," Jo murmured, sitting back in the seat. "What's that trace of accent you have?"

His eyes met hers in the rearview mirror. They were narrowed at the moment and a beautiful black with gold flecks, she noted, and then his eyes shifted back to the road. "I don't have an accent. You do."

"Beg pardon," she said dryly. "This is Canada and I have a Canadian accent, which means I have no accent here. But *you* do, just a trace, but it sounds . . ." Jo paused, considering the few words he'd said so far and then guessed, "Russian?"

His eyes met hers in the mirror again. This time

there was a flicker that might have been something like appreciation in his eyes as he nodded.

"So is Anders your first name or last?"

"Last."

Jo pursed her lips. "Anders doesn't sound very Russian."

"It was originally Andronnikov," he admitted. "I got tired of North Americans mangling the name."

"Hmm," Jo said. "Russian. We should get along great then."

"Why?" he asked, and she couldn't help but notice that his tone was dubious as he met her gaze in the mirror again. There was also true confusion on his face. She suspected he doubted they would get along at all.

Jo met his gaze, smiled sweetly, and said, "Well, it just figures, doesn't it? I'm a bartender, you're a Black Russian. It's a perfect match."

Bricker burst out laughing, but Anders, she noticed, looked less than impressed, and Jo wondered if that crack would be considered racist. She hadn't thought so. Actually, she hadn't thought at all before saying it. Damn, she really needed to learn to think before she spoke.

"It wasn't racist," Anders said dryly. "It was a very bad play on the name of an alcoholic beverage, but not racist."

Jo peered at him sharply. "How did you know I was worrying about that?"

He hesitated, but then shifted his eyes back to the road and said, "You have that guilty look white people get when they're worried they've misspoken." Anders glanced back to the mirror and raised an eyebrow as he asked, "Or is it racist to call you white? Perhaps I should say Caucasian."

Jo snorted and then found herself babbling, "Hell if I know. You can call me white if you want. Although I don't really get the whole white business myself, I mean we aren't *really* white. Well, I suppose we can be when upset and we pale, but mostly we're kind of tan in the summer and pink like pigs in the winter."

"Shall I call you pig then?" he asked sweetly.

Jo's eyes sharpened on his face in the rearview mirror, but she caught the twitching of his lips and asked, "Was that an attempt at a joke?"

"It was better than yours," he said, and actually cracked a smile.

"Hmm," Jo muttered.

"Right," Bricker commented with amusement, "So now that you two have broken the ice and moved straight to the slinging of insults, where are we going for breakfast?"

"Do not look at me," Anders said dryly. "I do not eat . . . breakfast," he added when Bricker glanced at him sharply.

"You should," Jo said with feigned solemnity. "It's the most important meal of the day, you know."

"Is it?" Anders asked. "And what do you usually have for breakfast?"

"Dried-up day-old pizza or anything else I can scrounge up," she admitted wryly.

"Why am I not surprised?" Anders said in dry tones.

Jo frowned at his knowing expression. "It's my

pores, isn't it? They give away my bad student-type habits."

His eyes sharpened on hers in the mirror, bewilderment in their beautiful depths. "Your pores?"

"Yeah. I have big pores that give away my vices while you guys all have baby's ass pores."

"Baby's ass pores?" Bricker asked incredulously.

"Smooth and poreless like on a baby's butt," she explained dryly.

"Jesus," Anders muttered, his hand rising to rub his own cheek and his eyes examining his skin in the rearview mirror.

"Eyes on the road, big guy," Jo ordered. "You can look at your pretty self later."

Anders stared at her in the mirror briefly and then glanced to Bricker and muttered, "It's a shame I can read her. She's an interesting female."

"I know. I've been bemoaning it all summer," Bricker said on a sigh, and then added, "She's hot too."

Jo wasn't sure what the hell they were talking about with the reading business, but was relatively certain she'd just been given a compliment. It cheered her up and made her smile. Jo smiled a little wider when she realized that her headache was easing. Something to eat and some juice and coffee might help eradicate it completely, she thought. "There's a little place not far from my apartment that serves all-day breakfast."

"Address?" Anders asked, apparently reverting to his man-of-few-words persona.

Jo gave it to him and then leaned her head back and closed her eyes, hoping that relaxing a little on the drive would help ease the headache some more.

* * *

When Ernie's van pulled into the gas station, Nicholas scanned the street, spotted an open parking spot, and managed to maneuver into the tight space. He then glanced toward the gas station. Ernie obviously hadn't stopped there in search of gas. He'd parked on the edge of the lot and was now staring at the restaurant parking lot across the street.

While it was Ernie he had set himself the task of watching, Nicholas couldn't resist looking toward the restaurant himself. He was rewarded with a perfect view of Jo, Bricker, and Anders getting out of the SUV they had driven there in and heading into the restaurant. They disappeared through the front door, only to reappear a moment later in the large front window as they claimed an empty booth there.

When Nicholas then glanced back to Ernie, it was to find that the other rogue had shut off his van and looked like he was settling in for a wait. It seemed he could no longer deny the obvious; while he was following Ernie, Ernie for some unknown reason had set himself the task of following Jo, Bricker, and Anders. Mouth tightening, Nicholas shut off his own engine and sat back to wait as well, but it wasn't long before he was shifting uncomfortably in his seat and wishing he had the little foam cushion he liked to place at his back. Unfortunately, that was still in his old van, which he suspected was now in enforcer hands. At least the damned thing had been gone by the time Jo had broken him out of his cell, and he'd ridden out on the undercarriage of the SUV. He'd dropped to the pavement as it had raced past the spot where he'd left the van, taking a damned good road burn in the process, only to find his van missing.

It didn't take a rocket scientist to figure out that Mortimer had sent men out to find his vehicle after he'd been captured. He had no idea where they'd taken it to. They hadn't brought it back to the enforcer garage before he'd left, so he supposed they'd taken it somewhere to search it. Perhaps Argeneau Enterprises where Bastien Argeneau's science geeks could go over it with a fine-tooth comb.

It had been a great disappointment to Nicholas to find his vehicle gone. Aside from the fact that it held all of his meager belongings, it had meant a rather long walk for him. Had a car with some slightly drunken teenagers returning from a party not come by, he would have been forced to run all the way back to the city. Fortunately, he'd barely started out for town when they'd roared up the road in his direction. Nicholas had immediately taken control of the driver and brought the vehicle to a halt, then had gotten in to hitch a ride into town.

Nicholas holed up in a motel until morning and then headed out to purchase some supplies: clothes from a secondhand store, tools, and weapons, as well as this new van. Well, new to him, he supposed. It was used, but then he'd had to pay cash and didn't exactly have access to his previous wealth. Used or not, it had four wheels and ran. It would do for a while, he thought, watching as Jo laughed at something Bricker had said.

The sight was rather disturbing to him. Nicholas didn't like that Bricker was making her laugh, but it took him a moment to recognize what he was experiencing as jealousy. He wanted to be the one sitting there with her, making her laugh . . . and it was all his own fault that he couldn't.

Sighing, Nicholas shifted unhappily in the driver's seat. He couldn't claim Jo as his life mate. There was no way he would force her to live a life on the run, but fate wasn't helping him to stay away from her. After buying the van, his first instinct had been to go find where Jo lived and wait there for her, but he'd subdued that less-than-sensible idea and instead had headed after Ernie, following the tracker he'd placed under the man's van several days ago.

Nicholas had been rather shocked when trying to do the right thing, rather than what he'd wanted, had led him straight back to the enforcer house. Or at least to the neighboring house. He'd spotted Ernie's vehicle parked in the trees and glimpsed someone in the driver's seat.

Secure in the knowledge that his own windows were tinted and that Ernie wouldn't be able to tell it was he in the van, Nicholas had pulled into the driveway of a house on the opposite side of the road. It had been nearly noon when he'd shut off the engine to wait and see what unfolded.

He hadn't had long to wait before the SUV Ernie was presently following had driven by him. Nicholas had spotted Jo in the backseat as the vehicle passed, and his heart had lurched just to see her. It had lurched again when Ernie's vehicle had suddenly pulled out to follow the SUV. Nicholas had immediately started the engine and followed as well, worrying all the way into town. The only thing he could think was that Ernie had decided that going after Dani and Stephanie was too risky and so was making do with Jo instead. Perhaps he hoped to punish Nicholas for interfering last night by taking her. Ernie had probably heard him murmur that he couldn't read her when he'd tried and failed last night.

It was a worrying thought and something Nicholas didn't intend to allow to happen. He sat thinking of ways to protect Jo as he watched the trio in the restaurant talk to the waitress, receive their orders, eat, and then get the check. When Bricker threw some money on the table and the trio stood to exit the restaurant, Nicholas sat up and started the van engine, preparing to follow. His priority had changed. If Ernie had set his sights on Jo, then Nicholas wasn't letting her out of his sight for a minute.

Chapter Six

"Thanks for the breakfast, guys. Have fun watching my building. I'm going to bed," Jo said cheerfully as Anders stopped the SUV in front of the large Victorian house that held her little one-bedroom apartment. The house had been split into five apartments years ago. Hers was small, and the building was run down, but it was also cheap and close to work and school, both of which were important considerations for a university student supporting herself.

"Yeah, sure, rub it in," Bricker said dryly, and she glanced up from undoing her seat belt to find he'd already slid out of the front seat and opened the back door for her. The man had lovely manners, she'd say that for him, but Jo had noticed that earlier in the summer. He, Decker, and Mortimer all had lovely manners. Even Anders, who was dry as dust and spoke little, had fine manners.

Jo accepted the hand Bricker offered and climbed out of the vehicle. As she stepped onto the sidewalk and straightened, she suggested, "You could always go back to the house and tell Mortimer you lost me."

"Oh yeah, like he'd believe that." Bricker laughed, slamming the back door closed.

Jo grinned and shrugged as she turned away. "Have fun then."

She half expected him to follow her to the house and open the front door for her, but when Jo got there he was still standing by the SUV, watching her. She opened the door and entered, smiling as the muffled sound of reggae music met her ears. J.J. was home. The guy was white as a lily but fancied himself a born-again Jamaican, sporting colorful Caribbean clothes and dreadlocks. He smoked pot too, the malodorous stench often seeping into the hallway, usually on a cloud of the air freshener he used to try to mask the smell. Jo often wondered what it was exactly he was studying at the university, but she hadn't yet gotten around to asking him. He was always so stoned it was hard to hold a conversation with the guy.

Shaking her head, Jo passed the door to his apartment and climbed the stairs to the second level where her apartment waited. While there were two two-bedroom apartments on the main floor, there were three one-bedroom apartments on the second, and hers was the middle apartment. She had to pass Gina's apartment to get there, and as usual the door was open, allowing a glimpse of bright yellow walls, lots of plants, and Gina herself in an overlarge T-shirt and little else, curled up on a chair in her living room, the inevitable book in hand. Gina was a psychology major and today's book was abnormal psych. It was a course Jo herself had taken as an elective and quite enjoyed.

The sound of her footsteps as she reached the door brought Gina's head up. The blond smiled at the sight of her and called, "Yo!"

"Yo," Jo responded, pausing in her doorway. "How was the date last night? Did Dan finally try to get you into bed?"

"No." Gina closed her book with disgust, and uncurled to stand up and walk toward the door. "We had a lovely dinner, watched a great movie, and there were lots of kisses, what seemed like passionate kisses even, but that was it." She stopped to pick up Jo's spare keys from the hook. "We've been dating a year and a half for God's sake, what's his problem? I thought it was sweet and charming that he wasn't pressuring me at first, but now I'm starting to think there's something wrong with him . . . or me."

"Can't be you," Jo said with certainty, her gaze sliding over Gina's curvaceous figure. The woman was tall with legs that went on forever. She was also pretty. "You're gorgeous, Gina. It isn't you. Besides, most men would bang a Jabberwocky . . . or a hole in the wall if a Jabberwocky wasn't available."

"Then what's going on?" Gina cried with frustration. "He says he loves me, so why doesn't he want to *make* love to me? It's a natural expression of love, and vital to a healthy relationship."

Jo peered at her sympathetically and patted her arm as she suggested, "Maybe he's gay and in denial."

"Oh God," Gina breathed with horror. "Do you think so?"

Jo bit her lip. "Well, it could be erectile dysfunction or something else. But if that's the case, he should tell you rather than let you think there's something wrong with you."

"I don't know. He does like to shop and stuff, and guys usually hate that. Maybe he *is* gay," Gina said with mounting horror. "What do I do?"

"Hmm." Jo shifted uncomfortably, and then sighed, "Gina, honey, I'm the last person in the world you should be asking for advice from on relationships. I don't have them. Not lately anyway. Between work and study I just don't have time for men."

"Yeah, I suppose." Gina sighed, and then handed over her spare keys. "I fed Charlie last night and this morning and took him for a walk. He's been real good; no barking or tearing up the house while you were gone. He was sleeping at the foot of your bed when I checked on him earlier."

"Thanks," Jo said, taking the keys. "I owe you one."

"Nah." Gina grinned. "I love that dog. He's a sweetie."

"Yeah, he is," Jo agreed with a grin and started to turn away, but paused when Gina caught her arm.

"I forgot to ask, how was your sister's party?"

"Oh." Jo wrinkled her nose. "It was me, Sam, Alex, and a dozen good-looking guys, *and* it was boring as sin if you can imagine."

"No way," Gina said with amazement.

"Yes way," Jo said dryly. "I think they were all gay too . . . or most of them," she added, thinking Nicholas definitely hadn't been gay.

"They are not gay," Bricker suddenly exclaimed,

drawing her attention to the fact that he was walking up the stairs toward them. "God, woman, what scandalous rumors are you spreading here?"

Jo grinned at his horrified expression. "It's not rumor if it's true. What are you— Oh," she murmured when he held up her backpack.

"You left it in the SUV," he said.

"Thanks." Jo took it from him, and when his gaze slid to Gina, said, "This is my neighbor, Gina. Gina, this is Justin Bricker. A friend of my sister's boyfriend. He and another friend brought me home."

"Hello." Gina smiled brightly and held out her hand. Her eyes were positively eating Bricker alive, Jo noted, and thought that if Dan didn't get his butt in gear and make some moves on the girl, he was definitely going to lose her to a more interested party. Fortunately for Dan, while Bricker eyed Gina appreciatively in her skimpy attire, his smile was polite and he—thankfully—didn't give Gina the same penis-eye look that he'd first given her up north and that all the men at the party had been trying on last night.

"So," he said, turning away from Gina to raise his eyebrows at Jo. "You're going in your apartment and I'm going back out to the SUV and you're going to signal us if Nicholas shows up, right?"

"Dream on, buddy," Jo said with a laugh as she slung the backpack over her shoulder. Glancing to Gina then she said, "Later, G."

"Later, Jo," Gina responded absently, her eyes still examining Bricker minutely.

"Oh, come on," Bricker said, following when Jo

continued up the hall. "We're buddies. Practically family, and you hardly know Nicholas."

"True," Jo agreed with amusement as she paused to unlock her door. "But I didn't cut him loose last night just to turn around and help you catch him again. Besides . . ." she added, and then paused as she started to open the door.

"Besides, what?" Bricker prompted.

"Besides, you've never kissed me like he did last night," Jo admitted with a smile as she opened the door just enough to slide in. She turned to face him through the narrow opening then and added, "In fact, you've never kissed me at all. Tell the truth, all you boys that hang with Mortimer really are gay, right?"

Bricker's jaw dropped and Jo grinned and closed the door, calling, "Bye Bricker. Happy watching."

"Just a minute. Open the door. Hey, I'm not gay!" he shouted, knocking at the door. "Open the door and I'll kiss you to prove it. Come on, Jo."

"Sorry, not interested," she said on a laugh and started away from the door, only to jerk to a halt with a startled gasp when a dark shape came hurtling at her, nearly knocking her on her ass.

"Jo!" Bricker called, sounding worried now. He rattled the door. "Are you all right?"

"I'm fine," she said on a laugh as she managed to steady herself and began to pet the German shepherd who had greeted her so exuberantly. "It was just my dog, Charlie. Now go away, Bricker."

Charlie barked as if to sound his agreement. His

tail was wagging frantically, his tongue trying to swipe at her face as he did.

Laughing, Jo petted Charlie with one hand and tried to push his head away to keep him from licking her with the other. "Did you miss your mama?" she asked in a coo. "Hmm? Were you lonely here by yourself?"

Charlie barked, his tail wagging becoming even more frantic, and Jo laughed and urged the dog down, "Come on, I'll get you a treat for being so good while I was gone."

Charlie dropped down to all fours at once at the word *treat* and rushed ahead into the kitchen. Smiling, Jo shrugged the backpack off her shoulder and dropped it by the door. She then peered out the peephole to see that the hall was empty. Bricker had listened and left. Good.

Turning away, she went into the kitchen and got the promised treat for Charlie. Leaving him munching on a cheese-stuffed dog bone, Jo then wandered into the living room and dropped on the couch. An old beat-up television sat on its table looking lonely and dusty. Jo rarely had time to watch television, but now that she'd eaten she was wide awake, and the nap she'd looked forward to no longer seemed appealing. However, she didn't want to risk bringing on her headache again by reading or studying either, so she grabbed the remote and turned on the TV.

Jo flicked through the channels until she recognized the opening scenes of the original *Alien* movie. She then dropped the remote, curled her legs up on the couch, grabbed a pillow to cuddle, and relaxed to watch it. Charlie joined her several moments later, seating himself on the floor at her feet and eyeing her with hopeful eyes. Smiling wryly, Jo shifted her legs off the couch and patted the cushion beside her.

"All right, come on up this time, but you know this isn't going to be a regular thing. You still have to stay off the furniture most times," she warned as the dog leaped up onto the couch and settled beside her, his head resting on her lap. Smiling faintly, Jo petted the dog, her attention returning to the television screen.

The movie was nearly over when Charlie suddenly stiffened beside her and raised his head. Jo tore her eyes away from watching Sigourney Weaver shivering and climbing slowly and cautiously into a space suit hanging from the wall of the shuttle where she'd just discovered the Alien was on board. Jo glanced to Charlie curiously, and then toward the door where his attention appeared to be.

"What is it?" she asked, running her hand lightly over the dog. Realizing she'd whispered the question, Jo grimaced, but then stilled as Charlie began to growl deep in his throat, an almost silent sound of warning. Frowning, she urged Charlie's head off her lap and stood. Between the movie and Charlie's strange reaction, she was a bit freaked out, Jo acknowledged, her concern growing when Charlie leaped off the couch to stand in front of her. He was now blocking her way, eyes on the door and still growling that low, quiet warning.

"Jo?"

Her eyes shifted from the dog to the door at that call from Gina. It had sounded strangely wooden and stiff from the usually exuberant girl. Frowning, she moved around Charlie, headed for the door, but paused when the dog growled louder and nipped at the pant leg of her jeans as if to stop her.

"What is it?" Jo asked the dog with bewilderment and then nearly jumped out of her skin at a sudden shriek from the Alien on television. She had to stop watching these horrors, Jo thought with embarrassment over her own reaction.

"Jo?" Gina said again a little louder.

Feeling foolish, Jo shook her head and brushed Charlie away, making him release her jeans. "Come on, it's just Gina."

She started forward again, but Charlie was immediately in front of her, trying to trip her up and stop her.

"What is the matter with you?" she asked with irritation. "You know Gina. What—"

"Open the door, Jo."

That made her pause. It wasn't the words so much as the fact that they definitely sounded wooden and unlike Gina. Combined with Charlie's odd behavior, it was enough to make the hairs rise on the back of her neck. Jo swallowed and stared at the door, unsure what to do now. Charlie released another growl, this time a loud, angry sound followed by a worried whine that started Jo's heart pumping. Something was very definitely wrong.

Her eyes slid from the dog to the door to her windows, and Jo had the brief mad urge to rush over, jerk the window up, and climb out . . . But something was wrong and Gina was out there, possibly in trouble, and she couldn't just leave her.

"Crap," Jo muttered under her breath, and then patted Charlie reassuringly and moved to the door on her tiptoes.

Apparently satisfied that she now understood something was wrong, Charlie didn't try to stop her this time, but stuck close to her side as she rose up to peer out the peephole.

What Jo saw wasn't really all that alarming. Gina stood in the hall still in her T-shirt, a man at her side. In fact, if it weren't for the fact that her face was completely blank as if no one was home inside her head, and that Jo recognized the man, she would have simply opened the door. But Jo did recognize him—it was Mr. Bad-Breath Boy from last night.

Jo straightened from the door and stared at it, her mind working frantically. She had no idea what Bad-Breath Boy wanted, but it couldn't be good, and it definitely wasn't good that he had Gina.

"Jo, open the door or he'll hurt me." The words were spoken in the same dead voice, no emotion at all, and that was scarier than if Gina had been shrieking with fear.

Swallowing, Jo reached for the lock, and then hesitated, her head swiveling to the windows again. She could climb out and get Bricker and Anders and—

"Open the damned door, bitch, or I'll rip her throat open right now," Bad-Breath Boy snapped, his patience apparently at an end.

Cursing, Jo glanced to Charlie, and then quickly unlocked and threw open the door. Charlie was out of the apartment before she'd even opened the door all the way. Teeth snapping, he lunged at the man beside Gina, catching him by surprise and knocking him down, his teeth buried in his throat. Jo was hard on his heels, catching Gina, whose face was no longer blank, but now confused as she took in the chaos around her.

"What's going on?" Gina asked with bewilderment as Jo grabbed her arm.

"Run!" Jo shouted, urging her past the battling man and dog and up the hall. "Run outside and scream for all you're worth, Bricker will come."

"But—" Gina began uncertainly, craning her neck to peer back at Charlie and Bad-Breath Boy.

"Run!" Jo shrieked. She pushed Gina toward the stairs, and then turned away to hurry back up the hall to help Charlie. But Bad-Breath Boy had recovered from his surprise and was already hurling the dog off. Jo cried out as she saw Charlie fly through the air, and back through the apartment door. The dog's yelp of pain could be heard over the loud crash that followed, and the combination was nearly enough to stop her heart. In a panic now, Jo rushed past Bad-Breath Boy. The man was shifting to a sitting position, one hand pressed to a gushing wound on his neck. Charlie had gone for the throat.

Good dog, she thought grimly. Jo had only had Charlie for a year and a half. Despite his size, he was really still a puppy, but he'd already burrowed his way into her heart. Leaving him to run to safety herself wasn't even an option in her mind.

"Charlie?" She rushed into her apartment to find his still body lying on the remains of what used to be a small hall table just inside the door. Jo dropped to her knees beside the dog, relief roaring through her when Charlie opened his eyes at her voice. He looked stunned, but he was alive, she saw, and then stiffened when his eyes slid past her and he growled.

Jo glanced toward the hall, mouth flattening with anger when she saw that Bad-Breath Boy had let go of his neck and was getting to his feet. The dog had gone after him with a vengeance. It was rather surprising considering the man hadn't really been doing anything threatening. It was as if Charlie had some doggie sense that had told him the man was up to no good and so had done his damnedest to rip out his throat. As bad as the wound looked, though, it wasn't bad enough. Bad-Breath Boy wasn't only on his feet, he was coming toward them, ready to continue the battle.

Jo lunged forward to slam the apartment door closed. She managed to lock it just nanoseconds before he crashed against the other side with a roar of fury. The way the door shuddered under his weight was rather alarming, and Jo didn't think it would hold long.

She turned back to Charlie, swallowing hard when she saw the German shepherd trying to get to his feet, only to collapse back to the floor, landing half on the rag mat in the hall. Jo set her teeth and moved to kneel beside him again.

"It's all right, fella. I've got you. You just rest for now," she murmured, catching the edge of the mat and dragging it down the hall as Bad-Breath Boy hit the door again. She had gotten Charlie into the living room and was dragging him toward the door leading to the balcony over the garage when the third crash came. This time it was accompanied by a cracking sound that put her heart in her throat. They were running out of time. Where the hell was Bricker? Gina half naked and shrieking should have brought help at once.

Jo had nearly reached the door to the balcony when it suddenly opened behind her. She released the mat and whirled around, her eyes widening incredulously when she saw Nicholas standing there. Before she could say anything, Bad-Breath Boy hit the door again, and this time it gave way, crashing open with a thud. For one second everyone froze and simply stared at one another. It was a shout from the hallway that Jo recognized as Bricker's voice that started them all moving again. Bad-Breath Boy growled and started into the apartment. Nicholas grabbed her hand to drag her toward the door, and Jo grabbed for the mat Charlie lay on and pulled him along.

"Nicholas, wait, Charlie's hurt," she cried as he pulled her over the threshold. He stopped at once, his eyes shooting to Bad-Breath Boy and then the German shepherd. Before she could even blink he was past her, scooping up Charlie and turning back.

"Move!" he roared, and Jo moved, rushing out onto the balcony that serviced all three upper apartments. She heard the door slam behind them and glanced back to see that Nicholas had shifted Charlie under one arm like a football and was using the now-free hand to jam one of the wooden deck chairs under the door to slow the man chasing them. Once done, he whirled and pointed toward the backyard. "That way. The van!"

Jo turned in that direction, spotting the van parked on the grass in the backyard directly behind the garage. She led the way across the garage's flat roof at a run. The tarmac was tacky from the late summer sun heating it, which was why she and her neighbors rarely used it during daytime. The van's position was a lifesaver. There were no stairs off the balcony, but they could climb over the rail, drop to the van and then the ground, minimizing the chances of twisting an ankle, being slowed and caught.

Jo decided that was a very good thing when the door to the balcony suddenly burst open behind them as she reached the rail. The deck chair made a terrible scraping sound as it shot across the balcony under the impact.

"Go," Nicholas urged when she stopped at the rail. "I'm right behind you."

Jo didn't hesitate but practically threw herself over the rickety rail surrounding the balcony. She landed on the van with a thump and a gasp as her feet slid out from beneath her. She crashed hard onto her bottom facing the building. Nicholas immediately leaped the rail like an Olympic jumper and thumped onto the van roof beside her with Charlie cradled in his arms.

"Down," he barked, shifting Charlie again under his arm so he could push Jo toward the front edge of the van with his other hand. Unprepared, she slid down the front window on her bottom, and right off the front hood. Nicholas was there beside her, steadying her with his free hand so that she landed on her feet. Before she had even quite found her balance, he was hustling her around the van to the passenger door, half carrying her weight as well as her dog.

"The door."

Jo opened the door and climbed in without having to be told. The moment her butt hit the seat, she had a lapful of furry dog and the door was slamming shut. She instinctively reached for the seat belt, but her head shot around when the driver's door was opened before Nicholas could possibly have gotten around the van to it. Her jaw dropped in surprise when she saw that it was indeed he launching himself into the driver's seat.

"Seat belt," he barked, starting the engine.

Jo tugged the belt out, but that was as far as she got before the van shuddered as something heavy hit it. Nicholas shifted into reverse and hit the gas, sending the van racing backward. Jo clutched desperately at Charlie with one hand, the other had a death grip on the undone seat belt and was the only thing that kept them both from flying to the floor.

A thump from above brought her head up in time to see Bad-Breath Boy roll down the windshield and off the hood to crash to the ground as Nicholas backed away from him. They'd nearly reached the back of the yard, and Jo saw Bricker and Anders racing across the garage roof and Bad-Breath Boy getting to his feet. Then Nicholas suddenly spun the wheel, backing them around across the grass. He barely brought the van to a halt before shifting to drive and hitting the gas again as he spun the wheel in the opposite direction, steering them toward the alley.

Slamming back against the seat, Jo saw first Bricker and then Anders leap the balcony railing as Nicholas had done, with no more effort than she would have exerted to leap a curb. As they landed behind Bad-Breath Boy, she also saw him charging forward, pulling a gun from his waistband. Apparently Nicholas saw it too.

"Down," he shouted. Nicholas grabbed her shoulder and forced her forward off her seat so that her bottom landed on the van floor with a bruising bump as the back window of the van shattered under a bullet's impact.

Jo merely gritted her teeth and did her best to keep from crushing Charlie as they were bounced and bumped around and gunshots continued to ring out. She was pretty sure it wasn't just Bad-Breath Boy shooting. The gunshots were coming too close together and then they suddenly stopped. Another minute passed, however, before Nicholas said, "You can get up now."

Jo hesitated, her gaze dropping to Charlie. The poor dog lay still in her arms, eyes open, but otherwise unmoving, and that was rather worrisome. He hated being on his back, probably an instinctive reaction from a dog. Their bellies were vulnerable to predators when they were on their backs and so they avoided being there.

"It's okay, baby," Jo whispered, but rather than try to get both herself and Charlie up into the seat, she lifted the dog and set him on it so she could take a look at him. Jo quickly ran her hands over the animal, but couldn't find any injuries. He didn't whimper or indicate her touch caused pain in any way except when she gently felt his head, and then he whined and tried to avoid her touch. Frowning, she peered into his eyes, noting that the pupils were slightly dilated.

"Nicholas," Jo said worriedly. "I think we need a vet."

Chapter Seven

Nicholas tore his gaze away from the road to glance to the German shepherd lying silent and still on the passenger seat. The dog's eyes were open, but he looked rather dazed. "What happened to him?"

"Bad-Breath Boy threw him a good ten or fifteen feet into a wall. At least I think he hit the wall, I'm not sure. All I know is he landed on a table with enough impact to smash it." Jo frowned and reached out to pat the dog reassuringly. "Charlie seemed unconscious when I first got to him, but then he opened his eyes. He couldn't stand up when he tried though."

"By Bad-Breath Boy I presume you mean Ernie?" Nicholas asked. "The blond who was shooting at us and whom Bricker and Anders were shooting at?"

"Is that his name?" she asked with disgust. "He has the name of a geek but is an utter jerk. I guess Shakespeare was right, a jerk by any name is still a jerk."

Nicholas smiled faintly at her mangling of Shakespeare, but then said, "Charlie could have a concussion."

Jo appeared surprised. "You think? I didn't know dogs could get concussions too?"

Nicholas shrugged. "They have brains, don't they?"

"Right," she muttered, and Nicholas glanced over again to see her peering worriedly at the dog. The German shepherd's eyes were closed and he appeared to be sleeping now. He wasn't surprised when she asked, "Should I let him sleep? It seems to me I remember hearing somewhere you aren't supposed to sleep with a head wound."

Nicholas hesitated, his eyes on the road ahead. He wasn't sure if that was true or not. Jo began to shift out of the cubbyhole in front of the seat, and Nicholas glanced over to see her scooping the dog into her arms and resettling herself in the passenger seat with him on her lap. He suspected she'd done it as an excuse to rouse the dog rather than for her own comfort. She was peering down at the beast like he was a baby who was deathly ill. She obviously loved the mutt.

Sighing, Nicholas cleared his throat and asked, "Where can we find a vet?"

Jo took a moment to glance at their surroundings. They weren't really far from her apartment, and relief filled her face as she took in that fact and said, "Charlie's vet is two blocks up and one block right."

Nicholas merely nodded. He'd take her and the dog to the vet, but this was a perfect example of why he couldn't claim her. Stops like this were dangerous, especially so close to the apartment. Ernie and the others would be looking for them now, cruising the neighborhood and watching for the van. He hoped there was somewhere to park that would make it less noticeable.

"Thank you," Jo murmured the minute he took the turn onto the street the clinic was on.

"For what?" he asked with surprise.

"Everything," she said dryly. "You got us out of there and now you're taking us to the vet's. Thank you."

Nicholas didn't say anything, but suspected Jo wouldn't have needed saving if it weren't for him. He should never have kissed her with a rogue lying nearby. He should have at least made sure the man was down for the count first . . . and admitting that he couldn't read her had been a stupid slip that Ernie had no doubt heard. It was probably the only reason the rogue was now after Jo.

Aside from that, Nicholas had been foolish enough to count on Bricker and Anders to keep her safe when he'd first seen Ernie leave his vehicle and creep up on the house. It wasn't until the rogue had climbed through the building's ground floor window and disappeared while the two enforcers had stayed in their SUV talking that he'd realized they hadn't noticed the man.

Nicholas had wanted to race his van right up to the front door and charge in after the rogue, but had feared it might bring the two enforcers running . . . after him. He'd worried that by the time he'd convinced them that Jo was in peril, it would be too late. So he'd wasted time driving around to the back of the building and climbing up onto the flat garage roof that doubled as a balcony to get inside. Then he'd had to be sure they saw him in case he wasn't enough to keep Jo out of Ernie's clutches and had run to the front of the garage balcony to be sure he was spotted. That was how he'd ended up going to the right apartment, he'd heard the banging coming from inside her apartment as he'd run across the garage roof.

"You shouldn't have come," Jo said suddenly, drawing his startled gaze.

"Why?"

"Because Bricker and Anders were sitting outside," she said quietly. "Lucian said you wouldn't be able to stay away and they were sent to watch for you."

"I figured," he admitted on a sigh. "But I was following Ernie and he followed you guys from the house."

"So much for you not being able to stay away from me," Jo muttered, and then added, "I don't know what took them so long. I expected them to come running the minute Gina ran outside screaming."

Nicholas glanced at her uncertainly. "Gina?"

Her eyebrows rose at his confusion, and she prompted, "Blond . . . half naked . . . no doubt screaming her head off?"

Nicholas shook his head. "There was nothing like that. I knew Ernie was in there because I saw him go in, and the only reason Bricker and Anders came running was because I made sure they saw me climb up onto the garage roof to get to your door."

Jo frowned. "I wonder where the hell Gina went then."

"If she was half naked, she probably went to one of the other apartments rather than outside," he suggested quietly. "Her first instinct would be to get somewhere safe and probably call the police."

"Probably," Jo agreed with a sigh. "It should have been my first suggestion to her too."

Nicholas merely grunted. The mortal police wouldn't have been of much use against Ernie. He would have been long gone, taking Jo with him before they could even get there. Still, he asked curiously, "Why didn't you call the police?"

Jo was silent for a minute and then rather than answer, said, "It was pretty impressive the way you jumped over the balcony rail to the truck like you did."

"I used to be a high-jump champ in high school," Nicholas lied blandly.

"And I suppose Ernie, Bricker, and Anders were as well?"

Nicholas grimaced but merely said, "I wouldn't know."

"Right," she drawled dryly. "And Ernie managed to get through both of my apartment doors with little enough effort. No one I know could have done that."

"It's an old building," Nicholas said with a shrug.

"Yes it is," she agreed, but then added, "However, those weren't old or flimsy doors. I made sure they were solid oak doors and had the locks put on myself when I moved in. Ernie shouldn't have been able to break through as he did, and he certainly shouldn't have been able to send the deck chair flying either. It was heavy as hell and you jammed it in good, yet it hardly slowed him down."

Nicholas's mouth tightened, but he didn't comment. He'd pulled into the veterinary clinic parking lot and now sandwiched the van in a spot marked "reserved" between two clinic vans, hoping it would be enough to hide their vehicle. Turning off the engine, he opened his door, saying, "Sit tight. I'll come around and get Charlie."

He caught the startled way Jo glanced around and the suspicion that immediately lit her face when she saw where they were.

"How did you know where the clinic was?" she asked the moment he opened her door, and he noted the way her grip tightened on her dog when he reached for Charlie.

Nicholas raised one eyebrow and pointed out, "You said it was on this road."

"Yes, but—"

"And the big sign on the front lawn that says Hillsdale Veterinary Clinic was a help," he interrupted dryly. "I presume this is the right one and there isn't another clinic further up the road?"

"No," she admitted on a sigh and relaxed.

Nicholas leaned in to scoop up the dog and this time she let him. He then waited just long enough for her to slip out of the van and close the door before heading toward the clinic entrance. He walked at a good clip, just enough to keep her jogging to keep up with him so that she didn't have the time or breath to ask further questions. When he reached the door, he shifted the dog to open it himself and stepped inside, only to pause at the sight of the packed waiting room.

The cacophony of barking dogs, mewling cats, squawking birds, and yipping people that rolled over them as they entered seemed to put some life back in Charlie. He barked with excitement, body twisting and legs kicking in a demand to be set down, but Nicholas ignored him, ground his teeth, and walked straight up to the counter, his eyes zeroing in on the older of the two women behind it. By the time Jo caught up with him, the woman's face was blank and she was moving around the counter to meet them.

"What did you tell her?" Jo asked in an amazed whisper as they followed the woman to an examination room.

Nicholas caught the guilty look she was casting to those waiting with their pets, but wasn't sorry he'd taken control of the woman to speed the process along. They had a rogue and two enforcers after them, and the longer they were here, the more chance there was they'd be trailed and caught. He'd done what he had to do. Rather than answer her question, he set Charlie on the examination table, and then said, "I need to make a phone call," before slipping out of the room.

From the concern she'd shown over her pet, Nicholas had expected Jo would stay with the mutt. It would have been convenient. He had hoped to call the enforcer house and tell them to have Bricker and Anders pick her up here, and then watch the building from a safe distance to be sure Ernie didn't get to her first. Unfortunately, Jo was a smart cookie. She chased after him, catching him by the elbow at the exit.

"You're dumping us here," Jo said accusingly.

Nicholas avoided her gaze and lied, "No. Of course not. I told you, I need to make a phone call."

Her eyes narrowed, but she held out her hand. "Then give me the van keys."

"What?" he asked with amazement.

"If you're just making a call, you don't need the keys," Jo said with inarguable logic. "So give me the keys and go make your call or I start yelling rape and tell everyone here that you are the one who hurt Charlie, and while you're trying to fight off this animal-loving mob, I run out and slash your tires and neither of us goes anywhere."

"Jesus, woman," Nicholas muttered with amazement.

"I'll do it," she warned.

Nicholas opened his mouth, closed it, and then sighed and said, "Jo, I'm just calling Bricker and Anders to have them come get you. I wouldn't take off until I knew you were safe. You're better off with them. At the house Mortimer and the others can keep you safe."

"Oh yeah, because they've done such a bang-up job already, at the house last night and then just now at my apartment," she said dryly.

"That was . . ." Nicholas paused when she arched one eyebrow. Actually they hadn't done such a hot job of keeping her safe so far, he acknowledged. Still . . .

"I want answers, Argeneau," she said grimly. "I'm

worried sick about what my sister has got herself into. My dog has been hurt, and some crazy guy is after me, and I want to know what the hell is going on."

"Mortimer—" he began.

"Mortimer and those guys won't give me answers," Jo snapped impatiently. "From everything you've said they're more likely to wipe my memories instead, and then—what? Keep me an unwilling 'guest' at the house until this—whatever this is—all blows over?"

Nicholas grimaced guiltily; that was exactly what they would do. Sighing, he ran one hand through his hair agitatedly, and then asked, "What makes you think you'd get any answers from me?"

"Because I'm going to pester the hell out of you until I get them," she said bluntly. "Now, do I get the keys or should I start screaming my head off?"

Nicholas stared at her silently, a reluctant smile curving his lips. It was inconvenient as hell that he couldn't read or control her . . . but it certainly made life interesting, he decided. Pulling his keys from his pocket, he handed them over. "There. Now get back to Charlie."

Her eyes narrowed suspiciously. "What are you going to do?"

"I told you, I have a phone call to make," he said solemnly. "If you're done before I come back in, I'll be in the parking lot."

Jo hesitated, obviously suspecting a trick, but then she apparently decided to trust him and turned to walk back into the examination room.

Nicholas watched her go with admiration. He didn't doubt for a minute that she would have started screaming if he'd tried to leave, but that wasn't why he'd given her his keys. He had done so because Josephine Willan was one interesting woman: plucky, caring, strong, determined, and sexy as hell. He didn't want to leave her there and couldn't resist the temptation of keeping her with him for at least a little longer.

It might just have been the stupidest decision he'd ever made in his life, of course. But then Nicholas had made a lot of those in his five hundred and sixty years, and if he'd learned anything in that time it was that regret was a waste of time . . . and he'd wasted fifty years on that emotion already.

The examination door closed, cutting off his view of Jo. Nicholas sighed and started to exit the building, but paused when one of the other examination room doors opened. An older gentleman appeared, his face not dissimilar to that of the bulldog he was leading on a leash. As the man led the dog to the counter, Nicholas quickly slid into the fellow's thoughts. After finding out the man had a cell phone and where he was headed on leaving there, Nicholas went outside to wait for him. He'd use the fellow's phone to call the enforcer house and find out if Ernie was caught without risking the call being traced or the phone being tracked to him.

Jo stepped out of the clinic and paused to quickly scan the parking lot. The van was still there of course, she had the keys. But she'd still worried that Nicholas would either hot-wire the van, had another set of keys, or would leave on foot. That wasn't the case, however, the van was there, and so was Nicholas;

just visible inside the van. The moment she spotted him, however, he was opening the door and slipping out to hurry toward them.

"If you tell me which vehicle it is, miss, I'll take Charlie to it."

"Oh, sorry." Jo turned to offer the vet's assistant an apologetic smile. He was struggling to hold Charlie. She hadn't wanted to walk the German shepherd through the waiting room without a leash. Fortunately, the vet hadn't liked the idea either and had sent for one of his assistants to carry him out for her. The German shepherd was heavy, though, and also wasn't happy being carried anymore. The moment the vet had shown up, Charlie had suddenly regained his spirit. All through the examination, he'd wagged his tail happily, barked, and tried to lick the doctor in hello, basically acting like there wasn't a thing wrong with him.

Jo hadn't been at all surprised when the vet finally announced that it was no doubt a mild concussion as she'd feared, but that Charlie should recover quickly and be fine. He said to keep an eye out, and if Charlie started to vomit or demonstrate any other unusual behavior, she was to bring him directly back in, but he could go home for now.

"You can put him down now, thanks," Jo said. "Charlie won't run. I just didn't want him to be loose in the waiting room with the other animals."

"Oh, that's all right, Miss Willan," the assistant said, smiling despite the squirming dog. "I'm happy to help. I'll carry him to your car for you. We wouldn't want one of the other owners coming out with an animal and—"

He broke off with surprise as Nicholas reached them and plucked Charlie from his arms.

Jo's eyebrows rose, not at the peremptory way he took her dog from the young man, but at the scowl he sent the assistant as he growled, "She doesn't need your help. She has me."

The assistant swallowed. "Right. Well . . . I'll just . . ."

"Thank you," Jo called as the young man turned and hurried back into the building. The moment the door closed behind him, she turned a glare on Nicholas. "That was rude. He was just trying to help."

"You wouldn't think *I* was the rude one if you'd heard *his* lascivious thoughts," Nicholas said, striding toward the van.

"Lascivious?" Jo hurried after Nicholas. "What do you mean, if I'd heard his lascivious thoughts? You can't hear his thoughts . . . can you?"

"Open the door," Nicholas ordered rather than answer.

Jo frowned, but opened the back door he'd stopped beside.

"There's a blanket in that box there, on top. Spread it out for him."

Jo peered at the half a dozen boxes in the back of the van, spotting a plaid blanket on top of the nearest one. She grabbed it, surprised to find that it was incredibly soft rather than the prickly wool she'd expected. It felt nice, and she leaned into the van to lay it out for Charlie. The moment she finished and stepped aside, Nicholas leaned in and set Charlie on it. Jo then offered him the doggie bone the nurse had given her. He accepted it and began to chew on it at once.

"He's got an appetite, that's a good sign," Nicholas murmured, straightening. "What did the vet say?"

"Mild concussion. Bring him back if he starts vomiting or anything," Jo admitted on a sigh. "Of course, Charlie was all perky and happy to see the vet the minute he entered the room. Dr. Hillsdale probably thought I was a panicky idiot."

"Or a caring pet owner," Nicholas said, sliding the door closed. He then opened the front passenger door for her before moving around to the driver's side.

Jo climbed in and pulled the door closed. She was doing her seat belt up when Nicholas climbed in on the other side and held out his hand. "Keys?"

She automatically reached for the keys, but then paused and peered at him. "I want to know—"

"When we get somewhere safe," Nicholas interrupted firmly. "We can't stay here. It's too close to your apartment. They'll be cruising the streets looking for us. We have to get out of this area altogether."

Jo sighed and gave up the keys. She then sat back in her seat and closed her eyes, a small cyclone of thoughts rolling through her head. Memories of last night and today were flowing together making the oddities of what had happened obvious . . . All of it was odd, of course. Her life had been relatively normal until that party at Sam and Mortimer's last night, and now her life appeared to have exploded. She'd been attacked twice, her dog had been injured, and she was surrounded by men who seemed just a little different from the average male.

Jo didn't think anyone else she knew could have leaped that balcony rail with the ease Nicholas, Bricker, Anders, and even Ernie had. And certainly Mortimer was the only person she knew who had a trio of prison cells in his garage, not to mention a refrigerator full of bagged blood.

And then there was the passion of Nicholas's kisses. Perhaps it was the long dry spell she'd had. Jo hadn't dated in a couple of months, but the man had curled her toes and set her hair on fire with his kisses. She didn't doubt for a minute that, if they hadn't been interrupted, she would have had sex with the man right there in the garage and would now have bar imprints on her back.

The sudden silence of the engine caught Jo's attention and she let her thoughts slip away to peer around. They were in a parking garage.

"Where are we?" she asked, glancing to Nicholas.

"A hotel," he said quietly, opening his door to get out. "We can talk here and I need some sleep."

Jo glanced to Charlie. The German shepherd had remained quiet and still during the ride, but now he stood up, tail wagging and eyes bright. Happy to see him looking so much better, Jo smiled and patted his head, glancing around when the back door opened. Nicholas was leaning in to get a duffel bag. She watched briefly, but then reached for her door handle and got out. Charlie immediately followed and Jo murmured, "Good dog" as she closed the door, but then frowned as she recalled Nicholas saying they were at a hotel.

"Do they take dogs here?" she asked, walking to the back of the van.

"They'll take Charlie," he assured her, straightening and slamming the back door closed. "Come on."

Nicholas took her arm to lead her across the garage toward the hotel entrance.

Jo patted her leg, a silent order for Charlie to follow, though she needn't have bothered. He never left her side when they were out of the apartment. He rarely left it in the apartment. Charlie was definitely a one-woman dog.

It was mid-afternoon and the hotel lobby was busy as they entered, but most of the people were coming and going. There was only one person ahead of them at the check-in desk, a man in a business suit who finished his business and moved off as they approached.

"I'm Mr. Smith and we need a room," Nicholas announced, releasing her arm. "I'm paying cash."

"We need a credit card to secure a room, sir, and we don't allow dog— Very good, sir," the man interrupted himself to say suddenly, and Jo's eyes sharpened on the clerk. His voice had gone from polite disinterest to an empty wooden tone in a heartbeat, and his face was just as empty as he passed over a packet of card keys.

"Thank you." Nicholas took the cards, dropped several bills on the counter, and then urged Jo away.

"What did you do to him?" she asked with a frown.

"Nothing," he said at once. "You were there."

"Yes, I was, and he was politely refusing us a room

when he suddenly changed his tune and, I suspect, not all on his own. Somehow you made him—"

"Sir, I'm afraid dogs aren't allowed in this hotel."

Nicholas slowed, and Jo glanced around to see a man in the hotel's golden jacket approaching.

"The check-in clerk should have told you that, I'm sorry," the man continued, and then suddenly paused just a foot from them, smiled woodenly, and offered, "Enjoy your stay, sir."

Nicholas grunted and urged Jo forward again, hurrying her to the elevators with Charlie padding along at her side. The dog's head was turning this way and that as he examined this new environment, but he stayed close enough to her that his shoulder kept bumping her leg. They reached the bank of elevators just as one arrived, and followed another couple on board.

They all smiled politely at one another, but the woman's smile was a bit nervous as she glanced at Charlie.

"He doesn't bite," Jo assured her quietly, and the woman's smile widened a little, but she still eyed Charlie like he might leap up and muddy her skirt or chomp his teeth into her arm at any moment. It was a relief when the elevator stopped and the other couple got off. The elevator continued up then, and Jo watched the numbers light up. They rode nearly all the way to the top floor.

Nicholas led the way off the elevator and paused briefly before turning right. He led her up the long corridor, past a maid's cart. Jo glanced in the room as they passed, catching a glimpse of a maid making the bed, and immediately picked up speed to get Charlie past the door before the woman turned and noted his presence.

Nicholas led her all the way to the second to last door before he paused and inserted one of the card keys. When the light on the door blinked green, he pushed the wooden panel open, and then held it wide for Jo and Charlie to precede him.

Jo stepped past him, glancing appreciatively at the comfortable room as they went . . . and doing her best to ignore the fact that there was only one king-sized bed.

"Sorry," Nicholas muttered, glancing around as he entered behind her. "I should have asked for two beds. I can go down and—"

"It's all right," Jo interrupted. "The bed is huge. You could practically swim in it."

Nodding, he tossed his duffel bag on the bed and turned back to the door. "I need to go get something to eat. Make yourself comfortable, I won't be long."

Jo turned in surprise to find the door already closing behind him. Cursing, she crossed the room at a quick clip and tugged the door open, but when she stepped into the hall he was gone. The only thing out there was the maid's cart they'd passed earlier, otherwise the hall was empty. Jo stared up toward the elevators in amazement. It was as if he'd just disappeared.

Feeling a nudge at her leg, she glanced down to see Charlie peering up at her worriedly. The dog always got that look when she was upset. He seemed to pick up on the emotion and it stressed him out. Jo forced herself to relax and bent to pet him even as she urged him away from the open door. "Come on, buddy. I suspect we'll be evicted if you're seen without Nicholas around; back in the room."

Charlie turned in the doorway and moved back into the room, and Jo followed, letting the door close behind her. She then peered around the room again. A small single-cup coffeepot sat on a table beside a large armoire that she suspected held a television. Jo opened the front double doors to find she was right. She grabbed the remote and hit the button to turn on the television as she dropped onto the bed. It was that or pace, Jo thought, glancing to Charlie, who was sitting on the floor beside the bed, eyeing her hopefully. She patted the mattress beside her. "Come on, you can keep me company. You've had a rough day."

Charlie was on the bed in a heartbeat, settling beside her. Jo petted him absently as she flipped through the channels and discovered there was very little on at four-thirty. When the Sunday afternoon Disney movie flashed on the screen, she stopped. It would do. Jo set the remote on the bedside table, rearranged her pillows, and settled in to watch the show, realizing just how tense she'd been when her muscles all slowly began to relax.

Charlie wasn't the only one who'd had a rough day, Jo acknowledged, stifling a yawn.

Chapter Eight

Nicholas eased his teeth from the neck of the chambermaid and released her. He then turned her to face the bathroom of the suite he'd found her working in and stepped back as he withdrew from her mind. Once free of his control, the woman stood still for a moment, and then moved forward to continue the work he'd interrupted, with no memory of his arrival or her ever having stopped her work.

Nicholas slid away then, exiting as silently as he'd entered and continuing on to the elevators. As he waited for it to arrive, he considered what to do about food for Jo. Having to buy a new van and incidentals had really eaten into his funds, and the hotel on top of it all had nearly wiped him out. He had less than fifty bucks in his pocket. Surely that was enough to buy her something nice for dinner? And then tomorrow morning, he'd have to head straight to the bank to get money from his security box to feed her breakfast.

The elevator arrived and Nicholas stepped on board, absently rubbing his stomach as he went. The maid was the first feeding he'd had since the morning before. In his usual cautious manner, he'd taken only a little bit of blood, and while it had helped, it hadn't helped much. The cramps that had been attacking him since that morning had gone from almost unbearable to just really painful.

Another bite was in order before he returned to Jo. Otherwise, he risked snacking on her without meaning to. Nicholas had no idea where he'd get the next meal, but had no doubt an opportunity would come up before he got back to the room. He was very good at feeding off the hoof. He knew most immortals in North America now fed on bagged blood, but for a rogue, ordering a delivery of blood from the Argeneau Blood Bank was out of the question.

Nicholas left the hotel on foot, eyes scanning the street ahead. Every other storefront seemed to be a restaurant or fast-food joint of some sort, and he hadn't a clue which were good and which were bad. They hadn't had this variety when he'd last eaten. A lot appeared to have changed on the cuisine front since then. Nicholas had been vaguely aware of it on the periphery of his consciousness, but hadn't eaten a bite of food since Annie's death and hadn't paid close attention to the changing face of the food industry. Being confronted by it now was rather frustrating. He should have asked Jo what she wanted before leaving, but he'd worried she'd insist on coming with him and he wouldn't be able to feed.

That thought made Nicholas decide to feed now

and worry about what to get Jo after. Perhaps he'd be able to think more clearly if he wasn't so distracted by his cramping body. His gaze shifted from the business fronts to the people on the sidewalks. Most people were in groups of two or three, but he spotted one lone woman hurrying along. Middle-aged, with pink cheeks and some meat on her bones, she was rushing up the street, hands full of bags.

Nicholas focused on her briefly, slipping into her mind to ensure she wasn't ill or coming down with anything. It did little good to ingest blood from someone ailing; bad blood would just have to be removed from his system, using up what little blood he presently had to do so. She was fine, however, healthy and robust.

Nicholas kept his distance at first to prevent catching her attention and alarming her. He'd followed her for a block when she turned down a side street. Shortly after that, she started up the sidewalk to an apartment building. He then began to close the distance between them and was almost on her heels when she entered the lobby.

The front door wasn't locked but there was a doorman. Nicholas slipped into the man's thoughts, making sure he didn't see or stop him as Nicholas trailed the female to the elevator. It arrived disbursing a mixed group of people in their twenties. Nicholas followed the woman on board once it was clear and offered her a polite smile as he waited for the doors to close. The moment they did, he slipped into her mind and had her turn toward him. He stepped forward, intending to take her in his arms and feed on her, but paused as a fragrant odor enveloped him. Nicholas had been vaguely aware of the scent as he'd trailed her, but it had been faint then. Now that they were enclosed in the small elevator, it was impossible to ignore, and he glanced around curiously for the source. It reminded him of something from when he used to eat. Something . . .

Nicholas traced the smell to a bag she carried and took it from her to peer inside. All he saw was a box. He reached in to open it and was immediately hit with a strong wave of the scent. Fried chicken, Nicholas realized, smiling. Annie used to make it on Sundays. It had been his favorite.

That's what he'd get Jo, Nicholas decided, closing the box and peering at the bag. KFC. He recalled passing a restaurant with that logo.

"What are you doing with my chicken?"

Nicholas glanced to the woman with surprise. He'd gotten so distracted by his find that he'd released his control over her and she was now peering at him with confusion. Setting the bag on the floor, he slipped into her thoughts and took control again. Nicholas then quickly took her in his arms and sank his teeth into her neck, using more speed than finesse. His distraction had cut into the time he had for this endeavor. Fortunately, he still had time to do what he had to do. He'd finished feeding and just released the woman when the elevator dinged, announcing their arrival at her floor. Nicholas picked up the bag of chicken and gave it to her, and then sent her off the elevator before releasing her mind.

He felt much better now, the cramps had eased considerably. One more bite and he should be good to get the chicken and head back to the hotel, Nicholas thought as he hit the button to return to the ground floor.

The elevator had traveled down only two floors before it stopped to allow a young man on. The fellow was all alone, and a quick check of his thoughts proved he was healthy as a horse, a real health nut, in fact, into natural foods and something called green tea. Nicholas smiled to himself as the doors closed. It seemed fate was on his side for a change. He'd be back at the hotel in no time . . . then he just had to figure out some explanation to give Jo for everything that had been going on.

That or tell her the truth, Nicholas thought as he slid into the young man's thoughts and leaned in to bite his neck. His preference was to tell Jo the truth, but he doubted she'd be allowed to keep her memories of that truth once they had her back at the enforcer house . . . and he would eventually have to take her there. On the other hand, they hadn't taken away her memories after the first time. True, she didn't really know much, but still . . .

The elevator dinged. Nicholas finished feeding and stepped back from the young donor, rearranging his thoughts and making him move to the doors as they opened. He kept control of him until they were out of the building, and then released his thoughts and turned to make his way back to the busy street where he'd first spotted the chicken lady.

Twenty minutes later Nicholas let himself back into the hotel room, his arms weighted down with a large bag marked KFC. He let the door close behind him and strode into the room, mouth opening to speak, but closed it again when he spotted Jo sound asleep on the bed. He peered at her blankly and then to Charlie. The dog lay beside her, but his head was up, eyes open and alert.

Sighing, Nicholas set the bag on the small table by the window. The moment he did, Charlie was off the bed and at his side, tail wagging frantically.

"Hi, buddy," he whispered, giving him a pat.

Charlie promptly lifted up, resting his feet on Nicholas's leg so that he could reach more of him, and then turned to nose the bag of chicken curiously.

"Hungry, huh?" Nicholas asked quietly. "Luckily for you I thought you might be and got a bucket. But you'll have to wait until I strip the meat for you. I'm not sure you can handle chicken bones."

Charlie dropped back to sit on his haunches patiently, and Nicholas smiled wryly as he opened the bag to retrieve the food containers and paper plates inside. He then settled in one of the two chairs at the table and set to work, selecting three meaty pieces of breaded chicken and then using one of the plastic forks provided to strip the meat onto the plate. He'd barely started on the first piece of meat when he couldn't resist and popped a bite of the delicacy into his mouth. The flavor exploded on his tongue, making him moan softly. Charlie whined in complaint.

"Sorry," Nicholas muttered, making himself resist trying any more until he had the meat from the three pieces he'd selected stripped and cut into small chunks on the plate. He then set the plate on the carpet for Charlie, watched him begin scarfing up the treat, and then turned and pulled out a piece for himself. Nicholas hadn't felt like eating since Annie's death fifty years ago, but now had to wonder why. The chicken was incredible and he was reaching for a second piece before he'd even finished the first.

He'd just have one more and then he'd lie down and try to sleep before Jo woke up and started demanding her answers, Nicholas told himself as he finished the second piece. He hadn't slept since the day before and could really use a couple of hours of shut-eye before trying to explain things that she would no doubt find impossible and upsetting by turn. The bed was big enough she wouldn't even know he was there.

Jo was dreaming. She knew it was a dream because she was back at the party at Sam and Mortimer's place, but the dream was a little different than the reality had been. The buzz of the guests' conversation was incredibly loud yet at the same time muffled, so that she couldn't understand what was being said . . . and the light was a little off, wavering and almost watery. Jo was alone, walking through the group of men, each of whom turned and gave her the strange silent stare they'd all greeted her and Alex with last night. Their eyes focused briefly on her forehead as if she had a penis growing there and then they turned away indifferently.

Though she knew it was silly, each time one of them turned away it felt like a rejection, and Jo was relieved when her dream took her outside. But here too things were a bit off. The sounds of night creatures and the wind in the leaves was magnified and overloud, and the caress of the cool breeze on her skin was like hands brushing over her skin making it tingle and raising goose bumps over her body. Ignoring that, Jo continued around the corner of the house, completely unsurprised when Bad-Breath Boy, Ernie, came lunging out of the darkness at her. This time there was no fear in her at the sudden attack, and no pain as she hit the wall. In the dream, her eyes were open and she saw Nicholas suddenly appear and drag the man away from her.

Jo leaned against the wall, watching as the men struggled in a strange, slow, violent dance and then bent and picked up the same boulder she had last night and moved forward to slam it over the blond man's head. Ernie's head swiveled around at once, eyes glowing golden and teeth bared, showing long, pointy fangs. Jo stared with confusion because it suddenly felt more like memory than a dream. The magnified sound and watery feeling were suddenly absent, leaving everything sharp and clear. But then the sound came roaring back and everything began to waver again as the two men continued to struggle.

Jo simply stood there in the dream, watching until Ernie fell to the ground and Nicholas stepped over him to get to her.

"I can't read you," he said clearly, grabbing her upper arms, and then his head descended, his mouth closing over hers as his body pressed against hers and his tongue slid out to taste and invade her. Jo forgot about that moment of clarity and fell into the sensations rolling over her. The feel and taste of him forced everything out and brought the desire she'd experienced last night roaring back to life like a fire that had been banked, and then he tore his mouth away and tugged her T-shirt up and Jo gasped as his lips closed over one nipple.

As suddenly as that, the dream changed. They were in the garage now, the stark fluorescent lights overhead burning into her eyes, and the bars of a cell pressing against her back as he ran his hands over her body and his lips drew at the dusty rose nub he'd claimed. She closed her eyes again, running one hand over his arm and shoulder, the other knotting in the hair on his head as his teeth and tongue scraped over the excited nipple.

"Yes," Jo breathed, and then gasped again when one of his roaming hands slid between her legs, pressing against the core of her through her jeans. It was enough to make her wish she wasn't wearing them, that she could feel his touch without their inhibiting presence, and suddenly the jeans were gone, as was her T-shirt. The bars of the cell were cold against her back, a stark contrast to his warm mouth and fingers as he caressed her more intimately.

Jo moaned as his fingers slid over her slick flesh, but when one finger slid inside her, she couldn't bear the assault anymore and tugged at his hair violently, forcing him to release the nipple he'd been teasing and raise his head. The moment his lips were in reach, Jo kissed him, sucking frantically at the tongue Nicholas thrust into her mouth, and then sending her own tongue out to wrangle with his as she reached blindly to find the front of his jeans. Jo found the bulge of his excitement and squeezed it briefly through the heavy cloth, and then started to wrestle with his belt before recalling how nicely her own clothes had disappeared when she wished it. She immediately paused to wish his were gone as well, and suddenly she was touching naked skin. Jo released a relieved sigh and immediately clasped him in hand.

Nicholas broke their kiss on a deep chuckle.

"Impatient," he whispered by her ear as he paused to nibble at it briefly. "So eager."

"Yes," she breathed, "I need you."

The words made him chuckle again, but it died on a gasp as she tightened her fingers around him and let them slide his length. A growl followed, and then he caught her hand and pulled it away, pressing it against the bars by her head as he kissed her again. When she tried to reach for him with her other hand, he caught and lifted that too, then ground himself against her as he kissed her almost punishingly. Jo gave as good as she got, her own kiss becoming demanding, and—thinking it had worked so nicely with the clothes—silently wished he'd thrust himself inside her, but the dream Nicholas wasn't nearly as accommodating as their dream clothes. Instead of lifting her by the hips and thrusting himself into her, he broke the kiss to growl, "Not yet," and began to trail his mouth down her throat to her collarbone.

Frustrated, Jo twisted her hips, rubbing herself against him, and then gasped as his mouth dropped to one breast to briefly toy with her nipple again. He still held her hands, but was drawing them down with him as he lowered himself to kneel before her, his mouth trailing kisses across her stomach. Jo dug her nails into his palms with excitement as his lips then trailed lower to nibble at one hip.

"Nicholas," she moaned desperately, and then gasped and reached up to grab at a bar by her head to steady herself when he suddenly released one of her hands to catch her leg and lift it over his shoulder. The position opened her to him, and Nicholas took full advantage, leaning to press his mouth to the flesh his fingers had so excited.

Jo cried out and grabbed for the bars with her other hand as he released that too, needing the hold to keep herself upright. Her legs had suddenly lost all strength, and she didn't think she could have kept herself upright if he hadn't raised his hands to clasp her by the bottom and hold her in place as he drove her wild with his teeth and tongue.

"Please," Jo gasped desperately, releasing the hold she had on the bars to grab at his hair and tug demandingly. The pressure had built to a breaking point, and she wanted him inside her when that happened. She wanted to feel him filling her, their bodies joined, their breaths commingled.

Much to her relief, Nicholas left off his torment and suddenly looked up. His eyes were glowing a fierce silver with no trace of the blue they were in reality and then he surged upward, his mouth reclaiming hers. Jo wrapped her legs around his hips as he shifted and lifted her, slamming her back against the bars almost roughly, and then she opened her eyes as a muffled clang woke her up.

Blinking in confusion, Jo peered at the ceiling overhead in the darkening room, and then glanced toward the window as another clang and the murmur of voices reached her ears. Her eyes widened slightly when she saw window washers moving upward past the window on their mechanized scaffolding. She was just in time to see their knees and feet move out of sight, and she supposed they were calling it a day.

Jo let her breath out on a small sigh and then glanced to the side to find, not Charlie in bed beside her as he had been when she'd fallen asleep, but Nicholas. He was on the other side of the bed, a good couple of feet away, but his eyes were open and seemed to be glowing silver in the dimming room as he stared at her . . . as they had in the dream, she noted, and then he suddenly rolled off the bed and started toward the bathroom.

"Nicholas." She got up quickly, but he was in the bathroom and closing the door before she caught up. When Jo instinctively stuck her foot in the door to prevent it shutting, he paused abruptly.

His voice was a low growl when he said, "Unless you want to find yourself naked on the bed doing exactly what we were about to do in the dream, I suggest you remove your foot."

Jo's eyes widened incredulously at the words. "How do you know what I was dream—"

"Jo," Nicholas growled in warning. "You have one second to release the door. Otherwise I won't be responsible for what happens."

She closed her mouth and stared at him. One part of her mind really wanted to know how he could possibly know what she'd been dreaming. Another, much larger part of her mind—not to mention her body—was interested in the image he'd put in her head of the two of them naked on the bed finishing what had started in the dream. Her body was still humming with excitement over the interrupted interlude, her nipples were still hard and aching and the liquid heat that had pooled low in her belly had not dissipated.

Jo wanted him desperately. If Nicholas had meant to scare her off with the threat, he'd used the wrong tactic. To her, it had sounded like a challenge, and there was nothing she liked better than a challenge. Realizing that several seconds must have passed and he hadn't carried out his threat, Jo leaned up on her tiptoes and pressed her mouth to his.

As responses went, his was most gratifying. Her lips had barely brushed his when the door was suddenly wide open and Nicholas was pulling her into his arms. Turning her against the open door, he pressed his body against hers until every inch of them was touching as he thrust his tongue into her mouth. He seemed to be trying to punish her with the kiss, his tongue lashing her like a whip, but if it was punishment, it was one she enjoyed. As she had in her dream, Jo gave as good as she got, her tongue wrestling with his and fingers scraping along his scalp urging him on.

She was vaguely aware of the sound of tearing cloth, and then his hands were between their bodies and on her bare breasts. Nicholas growled deep in his throat, the sound vibrating its way into her mouth, adding to the excitement. She wanted to reach between them and find his erection as she had in the dream, but her arms were above his, blocked by his shoulders and arms, so Jo had to be content with arching her hips to rub eagerly against him.

Nicholas responded by immediately releasing her breasts and pulling far enough away to reach for the button of her jeans. It freed Jo to reach for his, and she managed to get his belt and the top button undone, but had worked the zipper only halfway down when Nicholas suddenly knelt to tug her jeans down her body.

Jo stepped out of the pants when he got them to her ankles, and then he tossed them aside and turned to run his hands up the legs he'd bared. Nicholas leaned his mouth to press a kiss just above her knee and then to her inner thigh, and then he suddenly lifted her leg as he had in the dream and pressed his mouth to the center of her. Jo's whole body shuddered as his tongue suddenly rasped over the swollen, excited flesh, and she grabbed for the door handle to stay upright, relieved when he didn't continue the torment, but suddenly rose up to reclaim her lips again.

Nicholas gave her one hungry kiss, his hands working at freeing himself from his jeans, and then muttered apologetically, "I can't wait."

"Neither can I," she breathed, and then gasped as he suddenly scooped her up in his arms and carried her out to the bed. Jo gasped again when he dropped her on the mattress. She bounced once and then sat up and glanced down at herself. In his impatience, Nicholas had ripped her T-shirt up the front. She shrugged it off quickly, finishing in time to see Nicholas pull his own T-shirt off over his head, muscles rippling on his chest as he did. He tossed that aside, sending it across the room where it landed on the desk lamp, and then immediately stepped out of his shoes and pushed his jeans off his hips. His actions were quick and efficient and Jo didn't get much of a chance to enjoy the view. The moment he'd bared himself, Nicholas lunged on top of her.

Jo fell back with a grunt of surprise and then slid her arms around him as he claimed her lips once more. He didn't thrust into her right away as she'd expected, but instead reached between them to begin caressing her again. Jo hesitated briefly, unsure if his own passion had waned as he'd stripped, or if he thought hers might have, but when she felt the hard length of him against her hip, she decided he must think she needed more fire stoking. She didn't. The dream had been almost more foreplay than her body could stand, and all she wanted now was to feel his hard length inside her.

Without breaking the kiss, Jo pushed at his chest. She managed to catch him by surprise and sent him tumbling onto his back on the bed. Jo rolled with him, her mouth still plastered to his, and hips straddling him. She raised herself up and then dropped back down, taking him inside her in one swift action. She froze then, groaning along with him as he filled her. Nicholas fit her like a glove, snug and perfect, and she broke the kiss to peer down into his face.

He opened his eyes, and she saw that they were pure molten silver now. They were beautiful, and like nothing she'd ever seen. Jo simply sat there, impaled on him and staring until he raised a hand to caress her cheek and then ran it around to the back of her head to pull the scrunchie from her hair. Nicholas then buried his fingers in the long strands and pulled her down to claim her lips once more. As his mouth covered hers, he sat up, his chest brushing against her breasts, and then he slid his hands beneath her bottom and urged her up and then back down.

Jo moaned at the sensation that shot through her, and then took over moving herself. Wave after wave of increasing pleasure lapped at her brain and urged her on, and then Nicholas released her hips to cover her breasts instead, squeezing the round orbs and toying with her nipples.

Jo broke their kiss on a gasp as he tweaked them, her head dropping back, hair trailing down and tickling her back as Nicholas nibbled his way down her throat. She felt a nip of pain as his teeth scraped the exposed flesh, but it was followed by unbearable pleasure that joined the sensations already assaulting her and made her scream as the tsunami of all orgasms exploded inside her.

Jo was vaguely aware of Nicholas pulling his head away and shouting out a heartbeat later, but then darkness descended and she slumped against him.

The first thing Jo saw when she opened her eyes was the glow of the digital alarm clock in the dark room. It was seven thirty-two. She was lying on the bed, Nicholas's warm body at her back, the heavy weight of his arm curled around her and tucked under her side.

Jo lay still for a moment, not wishing to wake

Nicholas, but her bladder was complaining and she finally had to move. Going slowly and carefully, she tried to ease out from under Nicholas's arm without waking him, but had barely started when his arm suddenly tightened around her, drawing her back against his chest.

"Where are you going?" he asked, his voice rough with sleep.

Before Jo could answer, his hand found one breast and covered it to squeeze lightly and he began to nuzzle her neck. She sucked in a breath, and wiggled her bottom back against him as desire stirred within her.

"Mmm," Nicholas murmured, urging his own hips closer against her so that she felt his erection even as it grew between them. He then released her breast and reached for her face, catching her by the jaw to turn her head so that he could lean over her and claim her lips.

Jo turned as he kissed her, rolling onto her back and sliding her free arm around him. With the one caught between their bodies, she ran her fingers over what she could reach of his chest as she kissed him back.

"You taste good," Nicholas murmured against her mouth, his hand releasing her face to drift down over her body.

"I—oh," Jo moaned as his hand stopped to palm and squeeze her breast. It then slid away to smooth over her stomach before gliding down to her hip, and she moaned again as it tickled over her hip bone. But then it shifted again, sliding around to her bottom to turn her further onto her side and press her hips to his.

"I need you again," he growled, his hand dipping under her bottom and between her legs to find the center of her excitement in a roundabout route.

"I need . . . oh." Jo paused to gasp as he left off the caressing to slip one finger inside her. When she caught her breath again, she finished, "To pee."

Nicholas stilled and then pulled back to peer at her.

"Sorry," she muttered wryly, and then pushed herself away from him to sit up. "Nature calls."

Nicholas fell back on the bed with a groan and then sat up to watch her scamper naked across the room to the bathroom door and growled, "Hurry back."

Her answer was a chuckle as she disappeared into the bathroom and closed the door.

Sighing, Nicholas flopped back on the bed again, a smile curving his lips. Jo was . . . well, she was a slice of heaven was what she was; beautiful in his eyes and smart and sassy . . . The perfect woman for him.

It was just too damned bad he couldn't keep her, Nicholas thought bitterly, and closed his eyes as the soft, warm feelings left by their lovemaking slid away to allow reality to intrude.

He never should have touched her. It was the dream's fault, of course. There were several signs that one had met a life mate; not being able to read or control them was just one of them. Another sign of a life mate was shared dreams, usually erotic ones, and Nicholas knew he hadn't been alone in the dream he'd had of their interlude in the cells at the enforcer house. He'd woken from that with a raging need and had tried to save them both the coming heartache by fleeing for the bathroom and a cold shower, but Jo hadn't let him. Nicholas didn't blame her. She had no idea what was going on here and had no doubt been as aroused by the dream as he, but his giving in to it had been a major mistake. It was just going to make it harder to give her up when the time came, and it was coming soon. He couldn't keep her with him. In fact, his plan to make love to her again seemed incredibly stupid now that he was thinking. It would just make things even harder.

Rolling off the bed, Nicholas stood up, eyes landing on the German shepherd asleep in the cushioned chair by the desk. He'd forgotten all about the dog and suspected he wasn't supposed to be sleeping on the furniture, but then remembered that Charlie had been sleeping on the bed with Jo when he'd entered and didn't disturb him. Instead, he moved around the room collecting his clothes and then laid them on the bed and sat down to wait when he heard the shower come on in the bathroom.

He would slip into the bathroom the moment she came out, subject himself to a cold shower to cool the raging passions just the thought of Jo caused in him, and then sit her down and explain the situation before things went too far. Nicholas had no doubt the moment Jo heard what he had to tell her, she'd be more than happy to let him take her back to the enforcer house and get him out of her life.

Chapter Nine

Jo was quick about her shower. It had been a spur-of-the-moment thing. She'd been about to rush back out of the bathroom after finishing her business, but when she spotted the tangled mess that was her hair in the bathroom mirror, she whirled to turn on the shower instead. Jo washed her hair, quickly lathered and rinsed her body, shut off the taps, and nearly killed herself in her rush to get out of the tub, tripping over the lip and only saving herself by grabbing for the towel rack.

Grimacing to herself, Jo straightened, taking a towel as she did. She ran it quickly over her body in the most perfunctory of drying jobs, and then wrapped the towel around herself toga style and headed back out into the bedroom with every intention of jumping on Nicholas and having her way with him again. Instead, she was barely out of the room before he was slipping past her, jeans in hand, saying, "My turn."

Jo whirled toward the bathroom door just in time

to watch it close. A smile curled her lips and she took a step toward it, thinking it would be fun to join him, only to come to a halt when she heard the lock being engaged. Her eyebrows rose slightly at the sound, but then she glanced around at a rustle from the corner of the room. She turned to see Charlie yawning as he sat up on the desk chair he'd apparently been sleeping on. The sight immediately made her scowl.

"You know better," Jo murmured, but couldn't be too angry. She'd been letting him up on the furniture all day. Besides, she wouldn't have wanted to sleep on the carpet either. Still, the mild reprimand was enough, Charlie jumped off the chair and came to sit on his haunches before Jo, eyes appearing almost apologetic as he looked up at her.

Jo smiled wryly and bent to pet him, wondering what he'd been doing while she and Nicholas had been "busy." She'd quite forgotten the poor guy, and silly as it sounded, she was hoping he was sleeping. It just felt creepy to think of him sitting there watching them during those passionate moments.

Shrugging the thought away, Jo straightened. She spotted her jeans lying outside the bathroom door, but left them and moved to the bed intending to lie down, only to pause when Charlie whined and moved to the hotel room door, came back, and then moved to the door again. Recognizing the signal that he needed a walk, Jo sighed and then went to fetch her jeans after all. She had pulled her panties and jeans on before going in search of her T-shirt. She found it on the other side of the bed, but the moment she picked it up, Jo recalled that Nicholas had shredded it.

Wrinkling her nose, she tossed it over a chair and was debating what to do when she spotted Nicholas's T-shirt on the bed. As she recalled, it had been tossed on the desk lamp earlier. He must have collected it to take in the bathroom and left it behind in his rush to get in there.

Jo shrugged and picked it up. His loss was her gain. She couldn't walk Charlie topless. Jo tugged it on over her head, smiling as she was immediately enveloped in his scent. She paused to inhale deeply before pulling it all the way on and tucking the over-large T-shirt into her jeans. She then glanced to the bathroom door, considering whether to tell Nicholas where she was going. Jo suspected that if she did he'd protest her taking Charlie out by herself It was probably better just to do it and get it done while he was in the shower, she decided. If she was lucky she might even get back before he finished showering, and he never need know about it.

Jo moved to the table to collect the KFC bag lying there. Her gaze dipped into the bucket as she went, noting with a small, amused smile that it was empty. Nicholas had apparently been hungry when he got back and she'd slept through the meal. She noted the licked-clean paper plate on the carpet, and supposed Charlie hadn't. Jo shook her head, grabbed the bag, a plastic fork, napkins, and one of the key cards from the packet on the table and walked to the door where Charlie waited, whining almost nonstop now. It seemed he really had to go, and Jo supposed she should just be glad he hadn't had an accident in the room while they were sleeping.

Afraid of running into problems on the elevator, Jo led Charlie to the stairwell door. He followed eagerly when she opened the door and then bounded ahead, padding quickly down the stairs at a speed that forced her to jog to keep up. All Jo could think was that she'd better let him run while they were out, because there was no way she was jogging all the way back up.

They managed to slip out of the building without encountering anyone, but it took a bit of time for Jo to find a park. Once she did, she waited patiently as Charlie, who had been whining with need the entire way, spent a good few minutes sniffing every tree before lifting his leg. He then had to find another spot worthy of his performing the more messy business. Jo cleaned up after him using the KFC bag, and then dumped his offerings in the garbage before leading him back the way they'd come. They were passing a pizza joint halfway back when the door opened and a waft of cooking pepperoni and tomato sauce struck her nose and started her stomach growling. Pausing, Jo peered in the window, her mouth salivating as she watched a worker inside slide a freshly baked pizza out of the oven. She was just debating slipping inside to buy one to take back to the hotel when Charlie suddenly emitted the same strange growl he had in the apartment when Bad-Breath Boy had been outside the door.

Glancing down, she saw that he was stiff and still, ears back and teeth bared as he growled at something to their right. Jo peered in that direction, but couldn't see what had him on edge. Still, it was enough to remind her that Bad-Breath Boy, or Ernie, as Nicholas had called him, was still out there somewhere, possibly looking for them, and Bricker and Anders as well. Now was no time to be wandering the streets unnecessarily. She needed to find out why this Ernie guy was after her . . . and why Bricker and Anders were after Nicholas. She'd thought it all some grand game when she'd let him out of the cell, but the incident at her apartment had convinced her it was serious.

Charlie released another growl, and Jo cast another glance around, but still didn't see anything. Suddenly nervous, she turned away from the pizza joint, eager to get back to the hotel.

She'd order a pizza when she got back to the room, Jo assured herself as she continued on her way, slapping her leg out of habit in a gesture for Charlie to come. As usual, the German shepherd hadn't left her side since leaving the room.

They were just approaching the hotel when Jo passed a cute little blond who reminded her of Gina. The girl brought her worries for her neighbor to the forefront of her mind. While she suspected Gina had run down to J.J.'s place or something rather than outside as she'd instructed, she would feel better if she knew for sure.

Frowning over that, Jo led Charlie around to the same fire exit door they'd used earlier. She nudged aside the stone she'd jarred there to keep the door from closing and led Charlie inside. The German shepherd immediately charged up the stairs, but Jo followed more slowly, grimacing at the climb ahead of her.

She was well out of breath by the time they reached their floor. Charlie, however, was still pretty perky, tail wagging and waiting impatiently for her to open the door. The moment she did, he rushed to their hotel room door with an unerring sense of direction that always amazed her. Jo opened that door as well, waited for him to enter, and then followed.

The shower was still running in the bathroom, but she didn't think they'd been gone more than ten minutes, possibly fifteen. She was passing the door when the water suddenly went silent, only to start up again in the next heartbeat. Eyebrows rising, Jo paused by the door and called out, "Nicholas? Are you all right in there?"

"Fine," came the muffled answer. "Just switching to hot water."

"Right," Jo drew the word out as she tried to sort out what he meant by *switching* to hot water. Had he been showering in cold before this, she wondered with a little confusion. Shaking the concern away, she crossed the room to the phone to make the calls to the pizza place and Gina. She called Gina first, relieved when her friend answered sounding perfectly fine.

"Gina? Are you all right?" Jo asked anyway.

"Jo?" Gina asked, and then said, "Yeah, sure I am. Why wouldn't I be? How was the party?"

Jo blinked at the question and then asked uncertainly, "The party?"

"Yeah, the party at your sister's place," she explained, and then added, "I fed Charlie this morning and took him for a walk, but he'll be wanting more food soon. I can go feed him again now if you aren't going to be home for a while, but surely the party's over?"

"Gina," Jo said slowly, trying to understand what she was hearing. Gina seemed to have no memory of her returning home earlier. Clearing her throat, she said, "Charlie's here with me. Don't you remember me coming home earlier?"

"What did you do, sneak past my door while I was in the bathroom?" Gina asked with a laugh. "You should have stopped in and let me know you were back."

Jo frowned. "You don't remember seeing me earlier?"

"What are you talking about?" Gina asked, and there was a frown in her tone now. "I haven't seen you since you left for Sam's yesterday."

Jo sank to sit on the desk chair by the phone, her head pounding. Gina didn't recall any of what had happened at their building that afternoon . . . just hours ago, in fact.

"Oh, hang on, someone's at the door," Gina said suddenly, and Jo heard a loud rustling over the phone as if she had pressed it to her chest. Gina's cheerful voice came muffled to her, and then a prolonged silence before the rustle came again and Gina said, "Anyway, where are you?"

"Who was at the door?" Jo asked suspiciously.

"The guy downstairs," Gina answered. "Now where are you? Your friend Justin came around earlier looking for you."

"Justin?" Jo echoed blankly.

"Good-looking, dark hair, and hot-looking in leather." Gina paused briefly and then added, "Had a tall, really hot black guy with him."

"Bricker," Jo breathed. Everybody called him Bricker and she'd actually forgotten his first name.

"Yeah, Justin Bricker, that's him," Gina said. "What a cutie. He wants me to call if you come home, so come home soon, 'kay? 'Cause he's hot and I want the excuse to call him."

"Yeah," Jo muttered. "I'm glad you're okay, Gina. I have to go now."

She hung up before Gina could ask anything else, and then simply sat there. Gina didn't seem to remember anything about the incident that afternoon. Jo recalled the blank look that had been on the other woman's face when she'd opened the door and first seen her in the hall with Bad-Breath Boy holding her arm. The memory made her frown. It was the same look that had been on the desk clerk's face earlier when they'd checked in. Like there was no one home and they were being controlled, she thought.

That was crazy thinking, Jo told herself silently. Nicholas had probably slipped the man some money without her seeing to make him more amenable, and Gina had probably been drugged to make her more quiescent. The drug had probably affected her memory, Jo assured herself, and then glanced to Charlie as he suddenly laid his head in her lap.

Jo smiled and petted him, her gaze sliding to the empty chicken bucket on the table. The sight made her remember that she was hungry and had planned to order a pizza.

Sighing, she pulled out the phone book and quickly looked up area pizza places. Jo ordered a large two-for-one special just in case Nicholas and Charlie were hungry by the time it arrived. She then pulled her wallet out of her back pocket. A quick check showed that a run to an ATM was in order. The shower was still going and she wouldn't be long, so Jo grabbed the room card again, patted Charlie reassuringly, and headed out of the room. This time she took the elevator, and was happy to be able to do so. Her legs still ached a little from the walk back up.

There was a little convenience store on the main floor of the hotel. Spotting the ATM sign in the window, Jo nipped in, made a withdrawal, and then purchased a couple of pops before heading back upstairs.

The shower had finally shut off in the bathroom when she reentered. Jo passed the door, set down the pops, and had grabbed up the ice bucket when the bathroom door opened and Nicholas came out.

"Finally, I was starting to think you'd drowned yourself in the tub," she teased as she took the clear plastic bag out of the bucket and opened it to set it back in. She then headed for the door. "I'll be right back."

Nicholas caught her arm as she made to pass him, concern on his face. "Where are you going?"

"To get ice," she said, raising the bucket slightly.

"I'll get it." He took both the bucket and card key from her, but when he turned to the door it was her turn to catch his arm.

"You might want to cover that magnificent chest of yours before you go, stud. You wouldn't want the maids fainting from the excitement of seeing you like that."

Nicholas glanced down at himself, smiling wryly when he saw he'd been about to head out in only his jeans. He glanced to her, his eyebrows rising when he took in the fact that she was wearing his shirt.

"You tore mine off," Jo reminded him with a shrug and then reached for the hem as if about to tug it up and off and asked, "Do you want this one back?"

"No!" Nicholas caught at her hands, stopping her, and then patted her arm and moved past her into the room, muttering, "I have another."

Jo leaned in the bathroom doorway, smiling with amusement as she watched him move to the duffel bag he'd brought up from the van. Nicholas looked a bit agitated as he quickly opened it to retrieve a clean T-shirt. He was definitely avoiding looking at her, and she suspected she'd definitely embarrassed him with her teasing.

"Sorry about your shirt," he muttered, tugging the fresh T-shirt on. "You can keep that one, of course."

"Thank you," Jo murmured, her eyes eating him up as he turned and headed back toward the door.

Nicholas paused as he came abreast of her, and for a minute Jo thought he was going to kiss her. But after hesitating a moment, his gaze on her lips, he turned his face away and continued on to the door, saying, "There's a brush in my bag if you want it."

Jo's eyebrows flew up at the comment as he slipped out of the room and then she turned into the bathroom and squawked as she caught a glimpse of her foggy outline. The mirror was covered with a film of mist from Nicholas's prolonged shower, but she could see herself well enough to note that her hair was a curly mess around her head. It was only then she recalled towel drying her hair and hurrying out of the room to jump Nicholas, only he'd gone running into the bathroom and she hadn't had a mirror to check herself before rushing Charlie outside so he could take care of his business.

Dear God, she'd taken Charlie for a walk in the park looking like this, Jo thought with dismay as she grabbed a towel and quickly began to wipe the mirror. It probably hadn't been as bad as this right after her shower, though, she reassured herself. Unfortunately, Jo had inherited her mother's naturally curly, flyaway hair. It tended to imitate Ronald McDonald's wild mass if it wasn't styled. That was why she normally scraped it back into a ponytail.

Jo finished wiping the mirror and sighed as she got a better look at herself. Wow, she was some femme fatale. It was no wonder Nicholas hadn't kissed her before leaving; she'd be lucky if he ever tried to kiss her again after seeing her like this.

Muttering under her breath, Jo moved out of the bathroom and to his duffel bag to find the mentioned brush. She then searched the bed until she found the scrunchie he'd tugged from her hair earlier and returned to the bathroom to fix her hair. It was a bit of a struggle. Her hair knotted like no other. In truth, it was one of the few things Jo hated about herself. She considered herself smart enough, she had an okay figure, and her face was pretty enough though her mouth was a little wide and her nose a little too tipped up. But her hair was a misery to her.

Jo had just finished getting the knots out and was

giving her hair one final brush to be sure she hadn't missed any when she heard the main door open.

"One bucket of ice," Nicholas announced as he entered the room.

Jo glanced to the reflection of the doorway behind her as Nicholas strode past with a heaping bucket of ice in hand.

"Thank you," she called, starting to scrape her hair back, gathering it for her customary ponytail. "There's pop on the desk if you want one."

"Shall I pour you one?" Nicholas offered, and then—a frown entering his voice—asked, "Where did the soda come from?"

Jo hardly heard either question, her arms were raised, hands holding the hair back from her face, and eyes locked on her now-revealed neck. Frowning, she peered at the marks there for a moment, and then finished putting the scrunchie in even as she leaned forward, arching her neck to get a closer look at the two small punctures. That's what they were—puncture marks. Weird, Jo thought. She had no idea where those had come from. She should have felt something like that. Sam had had two blackfly bites up north that had looked somewhat similar, but there were no blackflies in downtown Toronto.

"Jo? Where did you get the pop?" Nicholas suddenly appeared behind her, a can of pop in hand. "You didn't leave the room, did—?"

The question died as he saw what she was doing. His gaze slid over the puncture wounds, and then he turned and walked out of sight. Jo stared at the spot where he'd been for a moment, and then looked one more time at the puncture marks, glanced back to the empty doorway, and then turned and followed him out of the room.

Nicholas was standing by the table pouring pop over ice in two glasses. "Come sit down," he said without turning around. "I suppose it's time we got to those explanations you wanted."

Jo hesitated. Something about the way he said it made her suspect she was about to learn something she wouldn't like, but when he slid one glass in front of the seat across from where he stood and then settled into the opposite chair, Jo gave up her position and moved across the room to settle in the chair. She glanced at him warily, then picked up her drink and said, "I'm listening. What the hell is going on?"

"Right . . . well . . . I'm sorry. I bit you. I'm a vampire," Nicholas started, and then jumped up to rush to her side and thump her back as her drink went down the wrong way and she began to choke.

"All right?" he asked worriedly, his thumping coming to an end when her coughing and gasping slowed.

Jo nodded, wiping her face and breathing deeply as she waited for the stinging in her nose and lungs to stop. Drowning in pop, she decided, would be a terribly painful experience. Shaking her head at the completely inane thought, Jo picked up her drink again, took a sip to clear her throat, and then set the glass carefully back down and turned to glare at him where he still hovered beside her. "What kind of stupid idiot do you take me for? *I'm a vampire?* If that's your idea of a pickup line, it's about the most asinine, trivial bit of bullshit I've heard in a long time. I've had better lines from the computer geeks at the university. I— Crap," Jo cut herself off when Nicholas suddenly opened his mouth and his canine teeth extended into two very sharp, wicked-looking fangs. Jo was close enough she could see it was no trick. Those were his real teeth growing and shifting, she realized, and suddenly had a flash of her dream—Bad-Breath Boy Ernie, eyes glowing and fangs bared, growling at her like a rabid dog. Only it hadn't had the same feel as the rest of the dream and didn't now either. At that moment it felt like a memory that had somehow managed to stay veiled earlier when the rest had come back to her.

"Crap!" Jo repeated more loudly, and leaped out of her chair and away from Nicholas.

"Jo, wait a minute," he said quickly, grabbing for her arm as she tried to rush for the door.

"Don't touch me," she gasped, jerking away from his hold and facing him as she backed toward the door now.

"Okay," Nicholas said soothingly, hands rising, palms open in the traditional calming manner. "It's okay. I won't touch you. Just calm down. You're safe. I'm a good vampire," he added, and then grimaced as if he couldn't believe he'd spoken the words. Sighing, Nicholas tried a different tactic, saying, "I saved you, remember? From Ernie? Twice?"

Jo had backed into the small entry hall, but Charlie was still lying on the carpet under the table. The German shepherd was peering uncertainly from her to Nicholas as if unsure what they were up to. He didn't look especially worried, however, just kind of curious, like he was wondering what her problem was. Jo slowed to a halt as she realized she couldn't leave the dog behind, and then slowly considered Nicholas's words. He *had* saved her twice, she acknowledged, eyeing him warily, and if he'd wanted to hurt her . . .

Her eyes narrowed and her hand rose to her neck, running lightly over the puncture wounds there. They didn't hurt, and while she had a vague recollection of feeling a slight nip while they were . . . well, earlier on the bed, it hadn't really hurt then either. Still . . . "You bit me?"

Nicholas grimaced. "I'm sorry. I didn't mean to. I just got a little too excited and . . ." He shrugged unhappily. "I *am* sorry, Jo."

She relaxed a little, and then shook her head and said with disbelief. "A *good* vampire?"

"That wasn't maybe the best way to start off," he acknowledged on a sigh.

"You think?" she asked sarcastically.

"Yeah," Nicholas said wryly, and then added, "And I'm not really a vampire anyway, it's just what others like to call us."

Jo propped her hands on her hips. "Right. Sure. Tell me you're a vampire, flash some fang to prove it, and then tell me you're not a vamp? I saw the fangs and the bite, Nicholas. I mean— Oh, hang on," she interrupted herself suddenly. "You were running around under the sun today when you got me out of the apartment. Vampires can't go out in sunlight." Jo scowled. "What's the deal here? Are those fake teeth? Did you bite me with some kind of weird, trick Goth dentures?"

"No," Nicholas assured her solemnly. He then hesitated and suggested, "Why don't you come sit down again and I'll explain everything?"

Jo glanced to the table, and then to Charlie. The German shepherd had apparently gotten bored with their drama. He'd laid his head back down, his eyes closed. Her gaze slid back to Nicholas.

"You're perfectly safe with me," Nicholas promised, and then pointed out, "I was going to leave you at the clinic and have Bricker and Anders collect you to keep you safe. I'd hardly harm you now."

Jo felt herself relax a little. She kept forgetting that the first time she'd met the man was when he'd saved her from Bad-Breath Boy Ernie. She'd met him again today the same way. Why would Nicholas save her, just to turn around and hurt her?

"Fine," Jo said at last, and gestured to the table. "Sit down and I'll come join you."

Nicholas glanced from her to the door, and then to the table, no doubt worrying that she would flee the room when he turned his back to claim his chair. However, he nodded solemnly and did so.

Chapter Ten

Jo waited until Nicholas had scooted his chair in and glanced her way before giving up her position by the door and slowly crossing the room to reclaim her seat. She peered at him silently, and then merely raised her eyebrows in question. "So? Are you a vampire, or not?"

Nicholas hesitated. "Not in the traditional sense."

"Uh huh, and how does that work?" Jo asked dryly. "You see, to me that's kind of like an expectant mother saying she isn't pregnant in the traditional sense. Either she's preggers or she isn't, and either you're a vampire or you're not. Which is it?"

Nicholas frowned and picked up his glass to take a drink. His expression thoughtful, he swallowed, set down the glass, and said, "See now, I started this wrong. I started at the back end of the horse rather than the front."

Jo simply raised an eyebrow.

"Our vampirism is scientifically based."

Jo raised her other eyebrow.

"One of my ancestors was a scientist," he began, "and he was messing around with nanos and bioengineering, trying to find a way to repair injuries and cure disease from inside the body without the need for surgery. These nanos would be injected into the person and do the work . . . Kind of like— Have you seen that movie where they shrink this group of people and inject them into a sick guy in a shrunken ship?"

"I know what movie you're talking about," Jo acknowledged slowly, her curiosity piqued. "I can't remember the name, but I know the movie."

"Right, well that's kind of what he was trying to create, but only, as I say, with nanos instead of shrunken people."

"And he succeeded?" Jo asked with interest.

"Nah, he died," Nicholas said with a grimace. "I mean he did, but old age got him before he perfected it. Others took up where he left off, though, and eventually they did succeed . . . sort of. It wasn't quite as successful as they'd hoped." He paused to take another drink before adding, "Or perhaps it was more successful than he'd expected."

Jo raised her eyebrows again. "Which is it? Was it successful or not?"

"Both," he decided. "The end result worked, but . . . These bio-nanos did destroy illnesses in the body and repair injuries as intended, but once done they were supposed to disintegrate and be flushed from the bodies . . . only they didn't."

"They didn't disintegrate? Or they didn't leave the body?" she asked.

"Either," Nicholas said grimly, and then explained, "See, their program was general rather than specific. It wasn't like they created a bunch of different nanos with ones for cancer, ones to repair bones or skin, etc. They had one kind of nano with a very wide ranging and general programming, to repair the body and return it to peak condition and then basically self-destruct, but the body is in constant need of repair. Every breath we take sucks in pollution, the sun constantly attacks the skin. Just the simple passage of time sees a wear on cells and bones and tissue. The body is in constant need of repair, so—"

"So the nanos didn't disintegrate, but stuck around and continued repairing," Jo guessed, and he nodded, a smile curving his lips at her figuring that out.

"Exactly."

Jo considered that and then shook her head. "I don't see that as a problem. I'd think it would be a good thing to have something like that in your system, fighting off illness and repairing wounds."

"It is," Nicholas said solemnly. "But it comes with a price."

"Which is?" she asked with a frown.

"The nanos don't just see cancer or colds or a terrible burn as something that needs repair. They're programmed to repair *all* damage and keep their host at their *peak* condition . . . and they see the effects of even aging as something that needs to be repaired. They repair and fix it all."

Jo's eyes narrowed as she asked, "Are you saying people with these nanos don't age?"

Nicholas nodded. "And anyone over the age of twenty-five or thirty will actually reverse in age if given them."

Her eyes widened. "So it's kind of like a sip from the fountain of youth? You never get ill or age and the old become young again?" When he nodded, she smiled wryly and said, "Forgive me, maybe I'm just dense, but I'm not seeing a downside here. What's this price you mentioned?"

Nicholas grimaced. "The nanos use blood to perform these functions as well as to power and regenerate themselves."

"That's interesting," Jo said, eyes widening. "Smart too since our bodies make blood."

"But not enough to power the nanos," he said quietly. "They use more blood than a body can create on its own."

"I see," Jo breathed, sitting back as she understood the problem, and what he'd meant by not being a vampire in the traditional sense. "So I'm guessing the nanos gave you fangs so you can feed on others for that blood, but you aren't dead, and can go out in the sun, and I presume—since the source of your vampirism is scientific in nature—religious icons and items don't affect you?"

"No they don't," Nicholas agreed.

She was silent for a minute, her gaze returning to her glass as she now began to turn it on the table, her mind suddenly whirling with questions. She started with, "And you have these nanos in you?"

"Yes."

Jo nodded. It was nothing more than she'd expected. He'd flashed fang and apparently bit her earlier. She asked, "How long have they had this technology? I'm guessing not long," she added thoughtfully. "I'm sure it would be all over the news if—"

"Actually, it's been longer than you'd think," he muttered.

Jo narrowed her eyes on him as another question popped into her head. "How old are you? I mean you look like twenty-seven or so, but if the nanos make you look young again . . ." She paused. He was suddenly avoiding her eyes and looking uncomfortable and even reluctant. Jo got the distinct impression that this question was not something he wanted to answer, and she began to suspect he was much older than he looked. Probably her father's age or something, she decided. No doubt he was given the nanos because of heart disease or another infirmity related to old age. The thought made her sigh unhappily. She had never been into older men. At least not way older men. Her parents had died in a car accident when she was younger, but while her father might be dead, she wasn't looking for a replacement daddy. Five years was usually her limit for age difference with men. On the other hand, the guy looked her age. And he didn't act like a geriatric.

"So?" she prompted. "How old are you?"

Nicholas peered at her solemnly and then admitted, "I was born in 1449."

Jo released her glass and gaped at him. "What? I think I heard that wrong. What did you just say? What year were you born?"

"1449," he repeated solemnly.

"How—You can't—That isn't possible," she said finally. "They didn't have that kind of technology back then. Heck, they—"

"My ancestors did," Nicholas assured her quietly.

"Your *ancestors*," Jo echoed blankly. "Well, where the heck are *your* ancestors from? Venus? Saturn? Mars maybe?"

Nicholas smiled faintly, but shook his head. "No, they were mortals from a place called Atlantis that fell before the coming of Christ."

"Atlantis?" Jo echoed, eyes wide. She'd heard of the place, of course. She doubted anyone hadn't heard of Atlantis. There were all sorts of myths about the place. Even its very existence was something of a myth since most people weren't sure it ever existed. Apparently it had . . . and jeez, he wasn't kidding about advanced technology if they were playing with nanos there way back when.

Atlantis, she thought on a sigh. Wasn't it just like her that in a country full of Canadians she falls for the oddball guy from Atlantis? That thought reminded her of an old show that she used to watch in reruns as a kid, *The Man from Atlantis*. The memory of it made her glance at his perfectly formed hands and then lean to the side to peer at his shod feet under the table. Straightening, she asked, "Do you have webbed feet, like the guy on the *Man from Atlantis*?"

"No," Nicholas snapped with disgust. "Good God, woman, you saw me naked."

"It wasn't your feet I was looking at," Jo said

dryly, and then her eyes widened as the man actually blushed.

Releasing a pent-up sigh, he said, "That show was a load of nonsense. We're vampires, not fish."

"But not traditional vampires, Atlantean vampires," Jo suggested with gentle teasing.

Nicholas smiled reluctantly. "The fact is, we prefer to be called immortals rather than vampires, but the vampire thing is more expedient when explaining things."

"I suppose it would be," Jo agreed. She peered at him silently for a moment, but then asked, "So Mortimer and the guys run around hunting down Atlantean vampires? I presume that's why he has those cells and the blood in the office and such. He and Bricker and the others know about your existence and hunt you down?"

Nicholas hesitated, and then sighed and said, "Mortimer, Bricker, Decker, Anders, and all the other men you met at the party are also Atlantean vampires . . . I mean immortals," he corrected himself with a grimace.

Jo's eyes widened. "Mortimer? *My sister's boyfriend*, Mortimer, is a vampire too?"

He nodded.

Jo sat back in her seat with a frown. "So the blood in the garage . . ."

"Their supply," Nicholas said quietly. "We drink bagged blood now. It's against our laws to drink any other way."

When Jo arched her eyebrows at that and raised her fingers to the puncture wounds on her throat, he grimaced and added, "There are exceptions to the rule. It's allowed in cases of an emergency where bagged blood isn't readily available . . . or between lovers."

Jo almost smiled at the term. *Lovers*. She hardly knew the man. At least, she'd met him for only the first time last night, but *lovers* was a much nicer term than some she'd heard. She peered at him silently for a moment and then asked, "So Mortimer is one too and sneaks out to the garage for blood." She wrinkled her nose and shook her head. "God, I have to tell Sam. She'll be—"

"She'll know," Nicholas assured her solemnly. "She's his life mate. He would have told her and then eventually he will turn her."

"Turn her?" Jo asked sharply. "You mean make her one too? You can do that?"

"We're each allowed to turn one," he admitted.

"Wow," Jo breathed, unsure how she felt about that. She supposed it was good news in a way. She wouldn't have to worry about Sam getting ill or dying, but . . . a vampire . . . jeez.

"In fact, he should have already, but the scuttlebutt on the street is that she's refused for now because it would mean leaving you and your other sister behind in ten years."

"Really?" Jo asked, unsure how to feel about that. "Why would she have to leave us in ten years?"

"Not just you, everyone she knows in this life. It's to prevent anyone noticing that she isn't aging," he explained. "We have survived as long as we have only because our existence is kept secret from the general population."

Jo nodded. "Otherwise you guys would probably be hunted down and experimented on and probably drained dry so the fat rich could become like you."

"That is an issue now," Nicholas acknowledged. "Though until the last few centuries it was more a concern of being hunted down and killed."

Jo grimaced, but said, "You mentioned Sam is his life mate. Bricker has said that a time or two as well. I just thought it was some weird Californian term for girlfriend, but—"

"A life mate is much more than a girlfriend or even a wife," Nicholas interrupted her quietly. "She, or he, is rare and precious. They are the one person in all the world that an immortal can relax around and be him or herself with."

"Why?" Jo asked at once. "What makes them so special?"

"Ah . . . well . . ." Nicholas frowned and glanced away. It was a moment before he glanced back and said, "To explain that I have to explain some other things."

"Go ahead."

He nodded, and then took a breath and began, "The nanos gave us more than fangs."

"Speaking of which, I understand *why* the nanos gave you fangs, but *how* did they do it? Surely the nanos weren't programmed to alter you physically in that way?"

"No. They were programmed to keep us healthy and at our peak. In Atlantis, the fangs weren't necessary. Those who had been injected with the nanos were given transfusions to make up for the problem of not producing enough blood on their own to sustain the nanos. But then Atlantis fell and there were no more transfusions. Atlantis had been very isolated by the ocean and a ring of mountains. When it fell, it sank into the ocean and the survivors—mostly immortals—had no choice but to cross the mountains and rejoin the rest of society, but the rest of the world wasn't nearly in the same league technologically as Atlantis had been. The people were ages behind, still primitive. There were no more transfusions."

"I'm guessing that was a problem," Jo said dryly.

"Most definitely," Nicholas agreed. "So the nanos altered their hosts, giving them what they needed to survive in the new terrain. They gave them fangs, made them faster, stronger, and gave them better night vision, making them nocturnal predators."

"Why the night vision?" she asked. "You said you could go out in daylight."

"We can, but it's something we try to avoid," he said and explained, "The sun causes damage, and more damage means more blood is needed to repair it, and more blood needed means biting more people since we were forced to feed off the hoof back then."

"Off the hoof . . . cute," she muttered.

Nicholas shrugged apologetically.

Jo sighed and said, "So you avoided going out in sunlight to avoid the damage and reduce the amount of blood needed."

He nodded.

"Sensible," she murmured, and then cleared her

throat and said, "So you used to actually run around biting people, but now just get blood from the blood bank?"

Nicholas was silent for a moment and then cleared his throat and said, "It is against our laws to bite mortals now."

Jo's eyes narrowed. She hadn't missed the fact that he was avoiding her eyes as he said that . . . and that he hadn't really answered her question and said whether he'd bitten people in the past, but now fed on bagged blood. She let it go for now, however, and said, "What else can you do?"

Nicholas looked wary. "What do you mean?"

"The guy at the check-in desk downstairs and the other one who was telling us dogs aren't allowed in the hotel, but then suddenly did an about-face," she reminded him dryly, and Nicholas grimaced.

"Oh yes." He sighed. "Well, the nanos also make us able to read and control people. It makes it easier to hunt them, and that way we can make it so they don't feel the pain of the bite. We can send them our pleasure instead. We can also read if they're healthy and so on."

"Nifty," Jo said dryly, now wondering what thoughts of hers she'd been unknowingly sharing since meeting Mortimer, Bricker, and Decker up north . . . or more worrisome, when she'd been controlled and what she'd been made to do.

"The ability isn't just with mortals though," Nicholas continued quickly, probably noting her upset. "We can read other immortals too if they aren't guarding their thoughts and they can do the same with us. It makes it rather trying at times. Around other immortals we are constantly on our guard, constantly having to remember to keep up a mental wall to keep our thoughts and feelings our own . . . except with a life mate," he added solemnly. "They are that very rare person we can neither read nor control. Being with them is like finding an oasis in a desert. You can be yourself without having to guard your thoughts all the time. They are your mate for life, a very long life that gets terribly lonely if you don't have one."

Jo was silent for a minute and then said, "So not being able to read or control someone makes them a life mate?"

He nodded. "It's how we recognize them. That, and old appetites awaken."

"I don't understand, what do you mean by old appetites?"

Nicholas smiled wryly. "After a couple of centuries, most things become boring. Places, jobs, and so on. We have to move every ten years or so to prevent anyone noticing we aren't aging, which helps somewhat, and most immortals change careers every fifty to a hundred years or so, some even more often. But there are some things that we just drop and don't bother with after the first couple of centuries."

"Like what?" Jo asked curiously.

"Food."

"Food?" she echoed with surprise.

Nicholas nodded. "Food becomes little more than a troublesome bother and we tend to lose our taste for it around one hundred and fifty or so."

Jo raised her eyebrows, but supposed she could understand that. There were nights when she was trying to figure out what to make for dinner for herself and it just seemed a big bother. She suspected after a hundred years, which would be around thirty-six thousand, five hundred dinners and as many lunches and breakfasts, she too would think, *Why bother?* But . . . Her gaze slid to the empty chicken bucket between them. If Nicholas was truly born in 1449 he was well over the hundred and fifty marker, yet was eating. Jo didn't think for a minute that Charlie had eaten all that chicken on his own while she'd slept.

"And sex," Nicholas said suddenly, drawing her attention again.

Jo's eyes were incredulous as she asked, "Sex? You can get tired of that?"

He shrugged and said almost apologetically, "With non–life mates, it starts to become a lot like masturbation after a while."

"Oh right, you can control them and make them do what you want," she realized, and frowned, wondering if he'd done that with her. Had her passion been real? It had certainly felt real. She'd ached for him with every part of her body. Or thought she had. "So, was what we did—"

"It was real," Nicholas interrupted firmly. "I ca— didn't control you or put thoughts or feeling in your mind. I never have with any woman, at least not intentionally," he qualified with a frown.

She relaxed under the knowledge that he hadn't controlled her, and she did believe him when he said that. It might be foolish, she hardly knew the man, but when it came right down to it, Jo trusted Nicholas and had from the start. Just as Charlie did.

"So, sex can become boring," Jo commented, finding it hard to fathom.

"I'm afraid so," Nicholas said solemnly. "The best way to explain it is that it becomes just a function; repetitive and boring. There's no real feeling for the other person when you know you can read and control them, and once you've sown your wild oats, so to speak, it's just not that interesting anymore." He frowned and then glanced down and muttered, "Until you encounter your life mate."

"And what's it like with a life mate?" she asked quietly.

Nicholas sighed and looked unhappy as he admitted, "Then it's all brand-new again; incredible, passionate, all-consuming, and addictive. You can't get enough at first. Being in the same room with them makes your body hum and ache. Their scent is like an aphrodisiac, their smile makes you want to rip their clothes off, their touch makes you want to bury yourself deep inside them and stay there forever."

Jo swallowed. The man had lifted his gaze to her halfway through his words and his eyes were flaming that silver she'd noted earlier. She supposed it must have something to do with the nanos and the night vision thing, but didn't ask. The hungry look in his eyes was making her squirm in her seat and goose bumps rise on her skin. Jo was pretty sure her nipples were suddenly erect too; like a dog salivating at the sight of food, her body was responding to just his look.

"You can't read me," she said abruptly.

Nicholas stilled, his eyes losing some of their silver sheen and going wary. "What makes you think that?"

"Oh, I don't know," Jo drawled. "Maybe the fact that you said, 'I can't read you' last night in this kind of wondering tone after trying to send me back to the house."

"I was hoping you hadn't caught that," he muttered, flopping back unhappily in his chair.

Jo blinked. "Let me get this straight. You can't read me, and your appetite for food and, *I'd* say," she added dryly, "sex has returned?"

"Yes, but—"

"And according to you these are signs of a life mate. Yes?"

"Yes, but—"

"Also according to you," she continued over him, "life mates are rare and as wonderful as an oasis in the desert?"

"Yes, but—"

"But you don't want me," Jo finished for him bitterly, and then asked, "What? You're gay? 'Cause I have to say, if you're gay, you did a very good imitation of a straight guy here this afternoon."

"I'm not gay," Nicholas assured her on a sigh.

"And yet you don't want me . . . me, your life mate," she said with feigned good cheer. "Weird, huh?"

"It's not that I don't want you, Jo," he said, and then cursed with frustration and admitted, "Jesus, all I can think about is you. I nearly gave myself hypothermia taking a cold shower this afternoon, then nearly scalded myself with a hot one to warm up after, and I still can't think of anything but you. You naked, you half naked, or even you not naked but in a short little skirt that I pull up so I can bury myself in you."

Jo blinked as that image rose up in her mind. She didn't normally wear skirts, but she had one or two for special occasions and did have one little black leather number that would be perfect for what he suggested. If she'd been wearing it last night, Jo suspected Nicholas would have tugged it up and they'd have gotten a lot further than kisses and caresses before they'd been interrupted by the sounds from the men in the garage.

Damn, Jo realized with dismay, just a couple of words had gotten her hot all over again. Sighing, she said, "So what's the problem? You want me, I want you . . ." Jo paused and frowned, and then said, "Of course, I'm not talking marriage or anything here. We need to get to know each other better and I *am* very busy. But I wouldn't be averse to the occasional dinner or movie followed by really hot sex."

"Jo," Nicholas said quietly, and reached across the table, holding his hand out.

She placed her hand in his and felt a quiver of excitement shiver its way up her arm and then spread through her body when his fingers closed over hers. Jeez, she had it bad, Jo acknowledged, and then noted the way Nicholas stiffened, swallowed, and closed his eyes and suspected he was having a similar reaction. They both had it bad, and really she'd had enough talking, they should move this discussion to the bed and talk with their bodies, she thought faintly, running her thumb softly over the back of his hand. Nicholas released her at once and sat up.

"I want you," he admitted grimly, and his eyes were glowing silver again.

Jo suspected that was a tell with him. Like an inbuilt mood ring; when his eyes were sky blue, he was serene. Molten silver meant hot and horny. Which was fine with her, she was feeling rather hot and bothered herself.

"But I can't claim you," Nicholas added firmly.

"Claim me?" she echoed blankly, and then gave a laugh. "You make me sound like lost luggage, Nicholas. No one can *claim* me. I have free will."

When Nicholas looked all mournful and sad and merely shook his head, Jo rolled her eyes. She supposed it was some tortured vampire thing she didn't understand, but she wasn't in the mood for it, her body was still tingling from just holding hands with him, not to mention the memories of what they'd done earlier.

Standing, Jo moved around the table and dropped into his lap. She slid her arms around his shoulders and said, "Fortunately for you, I'm free and willing."

"Jo," he said sadly, but she didn't want to hear it and covered his mouth with her own. Nicholas kept his mouth closed and reached for her arms, presumably to push her away, but the moment she let her tongue slide out to run over his lips, he froze.

Jo smiled, and then slid her lips to his ear and nibbled briefly before whispering, "I ache for you."

Nicholas sucked in a harsh breath, and then it was like something snapped. Suddenly his head jerked around so his lips could claim hers, and he launched himself to his feet with her in his arms. In one quick step he was tumbling her to the bed, and then the phone rang.

"Ignore it," Nicholas growled, leaning to tug her borrowed T-shirt out of her jeans and push it up to reveal her breasts.

Jo gasped as he bent his head to suck the nipple of one into his mouth, and then scowled with irritation as the phone rang again. She never had been able to ignore a ringing phone. It might be something important. Cursing under her breath, Jo reached out to grab the phone and pulled it to her ear, gasping, "Hello?" as Nicholas drew on her nipple, sending excitement rocketing through her.

"Mrs. Smith? This is the front desk. There's a pizza delivery here for you."

"Oh . . . um . . . yes," Jo moaned as Nicholas pressed a hand between her legs. Shaking her head, she reached down to push his hand away, and cleared her throat before muttering, "That's fine. Send him . . ." She paused on a gasp as Nicholas nipped lightly at her nipple. Fortunately, the officious-sounding woman on the other end understood.

"I'm sorry, ma'am. We don't allow anyone without room keys past the lobby at night."

"What?" Jo asked blankly, grabbing at Nicholas's hand as he began to undo her jeans. He stopped at once and levered himself off the bed to begin stripping off his T-shirt.

Jo watched him, eyes eating up the wide expanse of chest revealed as the receptionist explained, "It's a security thing, ma'am. We've had some trouble with people breaking into the rooms and robbing the guests while they were absent, so we no longer allow anyone who isn't staying here past the lobby unless the guest comes to get them."

"Right," she breathed on a sigh as the T-shirt went flying and Nicholas started on his belt.

"The delivery man will be here at the desk waiting for you though."

"Right," Jo repeated and hung up blindly, feeling around for the phone hook rather than looking. She was too busy watching as Nicholas finished undoing his jeans and pushed them down. She sat up as he stepped out of them and scampered off the bed, barely missing being pinned by his body as he did a belly dive onto the bed.

Rolling over, he growled, "Your turn. Strip for me."

Jo felt liquid pool in her belly at the heated look in his eyes, but shook her head. "As soon as I get back."

"What?" Nicholas sat up in surprise as she headed for the door. He was on his feet and catching her arm before she could get the door wholly open. "Where are you going? Who was on the phone?"

Jo's eyes wandered naughtily down his body. The man was magnificent naked and smelled good enough to eat. She briefly considered dropping to her knees and doing just that, or at least licking and nibbling a bit, but then her stomach rumbled, reminding her that food waited below and that she was hungry.

"That was the front desk," she explained. "The pizza I ordered is here."

"You ordered pizza?" Nicholas asked with horror.

"Well you ate all the chicken you so kindly bought, presumably for both of us," Jo pointed out dryly.

"Oh, right," Nicholas muttered with chagrin and glanced guiltily back toward the empty bucket on the table, but then he frowned and turned back. "Why isn't the delivery guy bringing it up here?"

"Security. They don't let anyone without room keys past the lobby. She said they've had rooms broken into and robbed while guests were out, but I suspect it's to discourage guests from having prostitutes in. I have a friend who works in one of these hotels downtown, and she said they have a terrible problem with prostitutes propositioning guests in the hotel. I'm guessing security here is hoping a guy's less likely to have a prostitute in if the front desk makes them go down to collect them."

Nicholas grunted at this, but then asked, "What name did you give?"

"Smith," she said patiently. "It is the name you checked us in under . . . and I'm paying cash."

He relaxed, but frowned. "I don't know if I have enough money on me at the moment to—"

"I do." Jo pulled her wallet from her back pocket and waved it between them. "I don't carry a purse. My wallet is always in my back pocket. Comes in handy on those occasions when I'm on the run and hungry, huh?" Jo grinned and then leaned up and kissed him on the cheek, one hand sliding the wallet back in her pocket, the other reaching down to briefly squeeze the more than firm erection he sported. "Mmm, still hot and hard. Good thing pizza is good cold. We'll pick up where we left off when I get back."

Nicholas growled and tried to draw her into his arms, but she quickly slid away and ducked out the door, promising, "When I get back."

Jo heard him sigh a moment before the door closed and smiled to herself as she scurried up the hall to the elevator.

Chapter Eleven

Jo spotted the pizza guy the moment she entered the lobby. He stood by the concierge's desk and was hard to miss in his red jacket and red hat with the pizza place logo on the front. She paid him quickly, tipping him handsomely for having to wait, and then headed for the elevators, only to decide they might need more pop. She'd purchased only the two cans earlier; those were now open and no doubt going flat and watery as the ice melted in them and would probably be completely unpalatable by the time they got around to the pizza.

The thought of what would come before the pizza made her smile as Jo detoured toward the small convenience store. She walked in, automatically tossing a smile of greeting toward the cashier, but the man had his back to the till as he stocked cigarettes in the cupboard behind the counter. Shrugging, she continued on her way to the refrigerators at the back.

Once there, Jo shifted the pizza to rest on one hand

like a tray and used her other hand to open the glass door. She had just jarred it open with one knee so that she could reach in and grab a couple of cans when someone said, "This is where Jo made the cash withdrawal."

Jo stiffened, recognizing Bricker's voice. She also recognized Mortimer's when he said, "That was almost an hour ago. She won't be here now."

"No." This time it was Anders's voice. "But they're probably staying in this hotel."

"And the cashier might remember her," Decker suggested. "He might be able to tell us if she said anything that might indicate if they're staying here or what."

"Hmm."

Jo turned her head cautiously to peer toward the front of the store where the voices were coming from, but the rows of shelves were in the way and she couldn't see the front of the store. That meant they couldn't see her either, Jo decided as she took her hand off the cans in the refrigerator and gently eased the door closed.

"We're looking for a woman who was in here about an hour ago. She used the ATM and may have purchased something. She's about five foot four inches tall, cute, with dark brown hair she wears in a ponytail."

Jo closed her eyes, sure the man was about to admit she'd been in there, but instead she heard, "Sorry, no one like that today and it's been slow. I'd have remembered."

Jo's eyes blinked open and for one moment she thought the guy was covering for her, and then she recalled the wild mass her hair had been when she'd seen herself in the mirror after returning with the pop. She definitely hadn't looked cute then. She'd probably also seemed a couple of inches taller because of the hair.

"Maybe she's dyed her hair," Bricker suggested quietly. "Or Nicholas could have used the card."

Mortimer cursed. "We'll have to search the hotel. I'm going to watch the lobby and the elevators while I call in all the local enforcers. Decker and Anders, I want each of you at the stairwell exits. Bricker, you watch the door to the parking garage. Once we get some more people here we'll start going floor by floor. Nicholas is not getting away this time and he's definitely not taking Jo with him."

The words had grown more distant as Mortimer had spoken and then silence followed, suggesting that they'd left the store, but Jo waited where she was for a minute, not wanting to risk running into them. She had shifted the pizza to hold it with both hands and was standing there debating what she should do when the cashier said, "Miss? Is there something I can help you with?"

Jo glanced forward, but all she saw was the row of potato chips stacked on the first shelf next to the pop. She then glanced up and around, spotting the man in a rounded security mirror in the corner of the store. It was a damned good thing Mortimer and the guys hadn't checked out the mirror while in here, Jo thought as she met the cashier's gaze. One glance told her that they were gone, however, and she started for the front of the store.

"Hey, there were some guys in here a minute ago and you fit the description of the gal they're looking for," the cashier said as she stepped out from between the aisles.

"Yeah, thanks, I'll go find them," Jo lied cheerfully and hurried out of the store, only to pause just outside the door, unsure which way to go. She couldn't go back out into the lobby to catch the elevator, Mortimer was going to make his calls from there and would be watching them. She couldn't take the stairs either because he'd sent Decker and Anders to watch them. Jo was just debating finding a phone and calling the room to tell Nicholas to get out when someone grabbed her arm.

"Jo? Hey girl, how's it going?"

"Beth?" she asked with surprise, glancing to the brunette who had approached her. "Hey." She held the pizza box with one hand and hugged the girl with the other. "I knew you worked in one of the hotels downtown, but didn't realize it was this one."

"Yeah." Beth grimaced. "And I pulled a late shift tonight. You aren't delivering pizza now, are you? What happened to your job at the bar?"

"Oh . . ." Jo glanced down to the pizza box she held. "No. I still work at the bar. This is for me and a friend. We have a room upstairs."

"Oh?" Beth grinned and then nudged her. "A man in your life, huh? You never tell me anything."

Jo smiled nervously, and glanced warily toward the

front of the hotel. Part of the lobby was visible, but she couldn't see Mortimer.

"It's nice to hear though," Beth added solemnly. "All you ever seem to do is work. A social life is a good thing."

"Yeah, right, like you're any better. You work at least as hard as me," Jo murmured, turning back to her. She then asked, "Beth, is there a service elevator in this place?"

Beth's eyebrows rose at the question. "Yeah. Why?"

Jo hesitated and then decided a lie was really the only way to go. She could hardly start babbling to her about vampires and such and expect Beth to think her anything but nuts, so she said, "There's someone I want to avoid in the lobby. He's a customer who's been going all stalker boy on me and hanging out at the bar all the time."

"You mentioned him a couple weeks ago," Beth said with a frown, and Jo forced a smile, glad that she had. The customer had laid off lately, but was a good cover.

"Yeah, well, he's here and—"

"Say no more," Beth interrupted, patting her arm. "Come on, follow me."

Jo glanced toward the lobby again, but then followed Beth deeper to a narrow hall leading off to the left. At the end there were several doors and an elevator.

"Which floor are you on?" Beth asked, leading her inside and inserting a key in the elevator panel.

"Top floor," Jo murmured as the doors closed. During the ride up Beth chattered easily about the bio class they had together at university. Jo tried to keep up with the conversation, but was a bit distracted with her worries about how she and Nicholas were going to get out of there. She would have asked Beth to stick around and quickly grabbed Nicholas so they could ride down in the service elevator, but Mortimer, Bricker, and Anders were covering all the exits. Basically they were screwed, she thought unhappily, but forced a smile as she said, "Thanks for this, Beth. I owe you one."

"No you don't," she assured her. "You're always giving me free drinks at the bar. However, I *am* going to want to hear all about this new guy in class tomorrow night."

Jo smiled faintly, but her mind was racing, trying to figure a way to get out of the hotel without using the lobby or side exits. Maybe they could take the window washer's scaffold down, she thought as she recalled it passing the window earlier and waking her.

"Jo?"

She blinked and glanced to Beth who was peering at her with a small frown. "I'm sorry. Did you say something?"

Beth smiled wryly. "I just asked if you guys were only staying the one night or—"

"Not even the one night, I'm afraid," Jo said with a grimace. "We'll probably leave right away now that . . . er . . . my stalker is here."

"But you have pizza," Beth protested. "And you paid for the room."

"Yeah, well, we'll have to take the pizza elsewhere. I'm just not comfortable here anymore." Jo shrugged and grimaced, annoyed that she was unable to explain anything to Beth. She wasn't used to having to prevaricate with her friends. Sighing, she shook her head and then said, "The room's already paid for. We'll just slip out and . . ." She waved her hand vaguely.

"You really need to call the cops about this guy if he's getting this troublesome," Beth said with concern. "It was bad enough when he was just being creepy and hanging around the bar all the time, but now he's actually stalking you, Jo. This isn't good."

"I know," Jo muttered. "But for right now we'll just try to slip out without his seeing and following."

"I can help with that," Beth offered. "If you're quick about fetching your friend from the room, I can take you back down in the service elevator and then slip you out through the kitchens. There's a door into the parking garage for deliveries; that way you can avoid the lobby altogether and he can't follow you to the next place."

"Oh, Beth, that would be amazing. You're a lifesaver." Jo shifted the pizza to one hand and hugged Beth with the other. "Thank you."

"No problem." Beth hugged her back and then glanced to the number panel above the door as the elevator dinged. "Here we are. Give me the pizza. I'll wait here and hold the elevator while you run and get your friend."

"Thanks," Jo said, handing it over. "I'll be quick."

"Okay. I'll be waiting."

Nodding, Jo rushed off the elevator as the doors opened and hurried up the hall at a jog, pulling the card key out of her back pocket as she went. She had it up and ready to slip into the slot as she slid to a halt in front of the door, but never got the chance to put it in. Before she could, the door was pulled open and Nicholas was there, grabbing her hand and dragging her into the room.

"Finally," he growled, pushing the door closed and whirling to pull her into his arms. "I was worried sick."

"I—" Jo began, but got no further before his mouth was suddenly on hers. Jo groaned, but reached up to push at his shoulders, only to clutch at them instead as he suddenly walked her quickly backward. One hand at the back of her head, holding her in place, the other on her behind, he urged her hips against his so that she felt his erection as they moved in a strange, rather erotic dance across the room until the backs of her legs bumped up against the bed.

"I need you," Nicholas growled against her lips as he tugged her T-shirt upward, his hands palming and squeezing her breasts.

"Oh God," Jo gasped, reaching to clasp his hands. She'd meant to pull them away and explain that they had to move, but he was squeezing and kneading, and when she opened her mouth to speak, his tongue slid inside and Jo found herself clutching at his hands, squeezing them even as he squeezed her. In the next moment, Nicholas pushed her away, sending her toppling onto the bed while he remained standing.

Jo blinked her eyes open as she hit the bed, and then gasped as he caught her by the backs of the legs and drew her forward until her butt was on the edge, the jean-covered core of her pressed snugly against him and her thighs on either side of his hips. His eyes were molten silver, his erection standing at attention as he bent to work at the button and zipper of her jeans.

Jo sucked in a breath, shook her head, and then covered his hands and blurted, "Mortimer's here."

Nicholas froze and stiffened briefly and then his head jerked up, his eyes stabbed at her, suddenly more blue than silver. "What?"

Jo sighed and explained, "I went into the store to buy pop after I collected the pizza and Mortimer, Bricker, Anders, and Decker came in while I was there."

"Did they see you?" he asked with concern.

Jo shook her head. "I was at the back of the store. They couldn't see me, but I heard them talking. Mortimer's got the men watching each exit and is calling in more men so they can search floor to floor."

"Jesus," Nicholas muttered, running his free hand through his hair. "We have to get out of here. We'll use the stairs and—"

"They're downstairs watching the lobby and side exits until more men arrive. You have to dress quickly. I have a way out of here."

Nicholas was out from between her legs at once, and Jo flopped back on the bed with a sigh, aware that her body was throbbing and aching with need from just that brief but very hot almost-interlude.

Man, when Nicholas was like that, he was . . . *man*, Jo thought faintly, and then gave her head a shake and sat up. Nicholas already had his jeans on and was doing them up. She shifted off the bed and stood to move into the bathroom to check and see if there was anything in there. All she found that was theirs was his brush. Jo took it out and tossed it in his bag as he donned his shirt, and then glanced around that room as well, but she hadn't had anything with her but Charlie, and Nicholas's things were all in his bag.

He was tying up his shoes now, and Jo's gaze slid to the German shepherd as she quickly zipped up the duffel bag. He had been sleeping, but was awake, watching her with interest.

"Come, boy, we have to go," she said, and the dog was on his feet and at her side at once.

"I've got that," Nicholas said, taking the bag from her when she started to pick it up. "Lead the way."

Nodding, Jo turned and hurried out of the room and up the hall. When she bypassed the bank of elevators, Nicholas simply followed, apparently trusting her. His eyebrows rose, however, when they reached the service elevator and he spied Beth standing there with the pizza in hand.

"Beth, this is Nicholas," Jo introduced as she stepped onto the elevator, Charlie at her side. "Nicholas, this is Beth. We have a bio class together Monday nights."

"My, you are a hottie," Beth said with wide eyes as Nicholas stepped onto the elevator.

Jo grinned at Nicholas's discomfort and then said, "Beth's going to slip us out through the kitchens so we can avoid the lobby."

"About that," Beth said suddenly, tearing her eyes off Nicholas and down to Charlie. "I'm not sure I can take a dog through—" She paused abruptly, her face going blank as she said, "It will be fine," and turned to work the elevator.

Jo frowned and then glanced to Nicholas to see him concentrating on her face. It was the guy who had checked them in all over again, only this time she knew what was happening. Nicholas was controlling Beth.

"Stop that," she hissed.

"No," Nicholas said firmly. "We have to get out of here and she was about to back out of taking us through the kitchens because of Charlie."

Jo frowned, her gaze sliding to the dog and then to Beth. "Then we'll have to find another way out. I don't want to get her into trouble."

"She won't be in trouble," he said soothingly. "No one will see the dog."

"Right. How are you going to manage that?"

"The same way I'm managing Beth," Nicholas said calmly. "Now just relax. We're here."

Jo glanced around as the elevator dinged. They'd arrived at the main floor. She waited tensely for the doors to open, relieved when there was no one in the hall, and then quickly led Charlie off and into the small hall she'd passed through earlier.

"This way," Beth said lightly, sounding more like herself as she slid out to lead the way. She also didn't look quite so blank-faced, Jo noted, and glanced to Nicholas in question.

He merely shook his head and gestured for her to follow.

Sighing, Jo fell into step behind her friend, leaving

Charlie and Nicholas to follow. Beth headed straight for a door near the end of the hall. When she pushed it open, the sounds of clanging dishes, rushing water, and shouting voices rolled over them. Jo bit her lip and glanced nervously around, waiting for someone to notice Charlie, but no one even glanced their way.

Bewildered, she peered back at Nicholas to see his eyes moving quickly around the room, touching briefly on worker after worker before moving to the next as they walked. She had no idea what he was doing, but knew he was doing something to make sure they weren't noticed and stopped or interfered with.

The kitchens were brightly lit, hot and humid, and Jo was relieved when Beth pushed through a door, leading them into a cooler, darker area she recognized as the parking garage.

"Here we are," Beth said. "Are you guys parked in here or did you take the subway?"

"Nicholas parked here," Jo said, accepting the pizza Beth was holding out to her and hugging her quickly as she whispered, "Thank you, Beth."

"No problem," Beth said, hugging her back. "I'm sorry your night was ruined. Promise me you'll call the police and get a restraining order or something on that stalker guy of yours though. He's just getting beyond creepy."

"I will," Jo assured her as she stepped back. She glanced to the side with surprise when Nicholas then took Beth's hand.

"Thank you," he said solemnly, concentrating briefly on her face. He then released her and stepped back and glanced to Jo. He took the pizza from her and said, "We have to go. I'll take Charlie to the van."

Jo nodded and glanced back to Beth to see her staring after him wide-eyed. "He is *so* hot."

She smiled wryly. "Yeah."

"Enjoy the rest of your night," Beth said with a grin and turned back to the door. "I have to get back to work."

"Okay, thanks Beth. See you in class," Jo added as she turned to hurry after Nicholas. She caught up to him quickly, and asked with a sigh. "What did you do to her?"

"I just removed Charlie's presence from her memory so it wouldn't be a problem," he said quietly.

"And the workers in the kitchen?" she asked.

"I just gave them a psychic suggestion that they not notice our presence," he muttered. "Beth won't be in trouble and we got out without being spotted. It's all good."

Jo blinked at the words. It just sounded odd to hear such a contemporary comment like "It's all good" from him. It made her realize that he normally sounded a bit formal and even a little old-fashioned. His age, she supposed, and then glanced around sharply as he suddenly caught her arm and drew her to a halt.

"What is it?" she asked worriedly. They weren't far from the van. It was perhaps four vehicles away, but they had to pass the hotel's guest entrance from the garage to get to it, Jo realized, and immediately recognized the problem. The guest entrance was a double set of glass doors with wide glass windows on either side of it, and she could see Bricker inside. His back was to them at the moment as he peered into the hotel, but if he turned a little to the right . . .

"What are we going to do?" Jo asked with worry.

Nicholas didn't answer at first, his eyes were slipping around the parking garage, and then he suddenly ushered her between the two vehicles next to them. When he dropped to his haunches, she did as well and peered at him in question, automatically petting Charlie when he slid his furry body between her and the car on her right.

"Wait here," Nicholas ordered. "I'll get the van and pick you up."

"How will you—" Jo began, but he was already gone. It happened so fast she was left blinking in amazement, and Jo rose up a little to look around for him. She barely caught a glimpse of him disappearing around his van, and Jo shook her head at his speed as she glanced toward the door where Bricker stood. She never could have moved that quickly, but he appeared to have managed to make it past the guest entrance without being noticed.

A deep-throated growl from Charlie made Jo drop back down to her haunches and peer around with worry.

"What is it, boy?" Jo asked as she saw that he'd left her side to move to the front of the car on their left and was growling in the direction they'd come from. She heard the van start up and moved toward Charlie in a crouch. Pausing beside him, still between the cars, Jo leaned her head out a little, but all there was to see was the dim garage interior and the rows of vehicles.

Jo ran her hand along Charlie's stiff back, frowning when he gave that strange growl again. It was the same one he'd given when Bad-Breath Boy had been outside the apartment door, and Jo swallowed as she felt the hairs on the back of her neck stand up. This wasn't good.

Much to her relief the van pulled in front of them then, stopping just past the vehicle on their left. Jo immediately launched herself to her feet and hurried forward. She started out intending to run around the van to the passenger door, but a shout drew her attention to the fact that Bricker had spotted them and was now pushing through the hotel door, heading for her. Knowing how quickly immortals could move, Jo stopped abruptly at the back of the van, pulled the door open, and turned to see Charlie still standing at the front of the car they'd been hiding beside. The fur on his back was standing on end and his ears were down as he growled in earnest.

"Charlie come," she shouted, glancing nervously back toward Bricker. He was moving faster than she would have thought humanly possible.

"Get in," Nicholas roared, and Jo threw herself in the back of the van, grabbing at the still-closed door to stay inside when Nicholas immediately hit the gas sending the van jerking forward.

"Charlie come!" Jo shrieked, holding the other door open for him as the van moved forward and he came into view. The German shepherd was still standing, growling, but turned at her call and launched himself toward the van. Charlie ran up behind the vehicle and was about to launch himself through the open door when Bricker was suddenly there, catching him in mid-jump.

"Get out of there, Jo!" Bricker shouted, holding on to her dog. "Get out of there!"

Jo stared at him silently, watching Charlie struggle to get out of his arms. Bricker wasn't hurting the German shepherd, but he wasn't letting him go either. Grinding her teeth together, she pulled the door closed as Bricker yelled, "Dammit, Jo, he's a rogue. Get the hell out of there!"

The door slammed shut, and Jo leaned her head briefly against it, her eyes closing. She knew Charlie would be safe with Bricker. He'd probably take him back to the house and Sam would look after him, but she felt like she was abandoning a child. She was also suddenly questioning her decision to stay with Nicholas. She'd been following her instincts, but Bricker's words were ringing in her ears making her wonder if she should have. *Jo, he's a rogue. Get the hell out of there!* The worry and upset on Bricker's face as he'd yelled that had given the words more weight than she liked and she was suddenly having doubts where previously there had been none.

"Hold on to something, Jo," Nicholas ordered, and she glanced around briefly and then simply threw herself to the floor as the van suddenly shot around a corner. Jo slid with the boxes in the back of the van, slamming up against a tire well. She tried to grab it and hold on, but it was smooth with nothing to grasp, and in the next moment she was rolling away and sliding down to hit the back doors as the van straightened out and careened up the street.

"Are you all right?" Nicholas called with concern.

Jo grimaced, but glanced up to see him peering back worriedly.

"Watch the road," she muttered, and crawled to her hands and knees to make her way to the front of the van. Doubts or not, she was there now. Besides, despite everything, she for some reason trusted the man.

"Charlie will be all right. They'll take care of him," Nicholas said quietly as she climbed past the pizza box and into the passenger seat.

"I know," Jo said wearily, pulling out the seat belt and buckling herself in. She closed her eyes briefly and sank back into her seat. "Bricker said you were a rogue."

"Yes."

She opened her eyes and peered at him, but his face was as expressionless as his voice had been. "What does that mean exactly?"

Nicholas hesitated and then sighed. "Maybe I should take you to the enforcer house. You'll be with Charlie and they can explain everything."

"Do you honestly think they'll tell me anything? From all I've learned, they're more likely to wipe my memory, right?"

Nicholas was silent for a minute and then sighed and said, "Maybe that's for the best."

"What?" she asked with amazement, and then growing angry asked, "Is this the immortal version of wham-bam-thank-you-ma'am? Show me the best sex ever and then dump me off with your buddies so that they can erase it all from my memory?"

"They aren't my buddies . . . anymore," he added wearily. "And I never should have—" Nicholas cut himself off, swallowed, and said, "I have nothing to offer you but a life on the run, Jo. I can't even rent a cheap motel room tonight. I used up the last of the cash I had on hand for the hotel and chicken. I have nowhere to take you and I can't—"

"I have somewhere we can go," Jo interrupted quietly. "Sam's place."

When he glanced at her sharply, she shrugged and said, "It's her old apartment. Sam moved in with Mortimer, but couldn't break her lease. It's fully furnished and I keep telling Sam she should sublet, but she hasn't got around to it yet . . . which works nicely for us. I have a key. It's free and we have pizza," Jo pointed out. "We can stay there tonight and talk. You can explain what a rogue is and why you're one and then I'll decide whether to let you dump me at the enforcer house or not."

Nicholas was silent for a moment, considering the suggestion, and then asked, "What's the address?"

Chapter Twelve

"I thought you said you had a key?" Nicholas asked grimly, his wary gaze sliding over the closed apartment doors in the hall outside Sam's apartment.

"I do." Jo didn't even glance up from the lock she knelt before. "At home. The only thing I had in my pocket when we left so precipitously was my wallet. Don't worry, though, I've got this."

Nicholas shook his head and continued to watch the other doors, thinking he should have left her at the hotel for Bricker to catch, or, failing that, he should have taken her straight to the enforcer house.

"It's a good thing you had all those tools in the van though. What do you use them for?" Jo asked as she fiddled with the lock.

"Stuff," he muttered, and she paused to glance at him, one eyebrow arched. Nicholas merely shrugged. He could have told her he hadn't used them for anything yet. They were all new, purchased that morning to replace the tools he'd lost with his old van, but why bother?

"Stuff, huh?" Jo asked dryly, and then turned back to what she was doing, saying, "It must be pretty technical stuff for you to have these tiny screwdrivers and—Got it," she interrupted herself happily as a click sounded. Retrieving the borrowed tools, she straightened and opened the door.

Nicholas followed her inside with relief, glancing around as she flipped a switch on the wall and a light burst to life overhead. His eyes widened as he saw that the apartment was still fully furnished. Sam hadn't yet taken out anything; even knickknacks and pictures still decorated the place. The decor was modern, the colors muted and calming.

"The pizza's probably cold by now," Jo said, turning into a room off the hall. "Sam has a microwave though."

Nicholas grunted and followed her into what turned out to be a kitchen. His gaze slid over clean white cupboards and stainless steel appliances and back to Jo as she crossed the room away from him.

"Look, we even have wine," she said happily, and he followed her gesture to a wine rack on the counter holding half a dozen bottles as Jo added, "Pop is better with pizza, but beggars can't be choosers, right?"

Nicholas glanced back to Jo as she opened a cupboard door and retrieved a couple of plates. She sounded anxious; the good cheer she was trying for seeming forced. He crossed the room, set the pizza on the counter, and then slid his arms around her from behind. Jo stiffened at once, and he pressed a kiss to her cheek and started to withdraw his arms, saying sadly, "You're afraid of me now."

"No." Jo released the plates she'd started to grab and caught at his hands to keep them where they were. She hesitated then, but finally sighed and assured him solemnly, "I'm not afraid of *you*, Nicholas. I'm more afraid of what you have to tell me."

He remained still for a moment, regret sliding through him. She had every right to fear what he had to tell her. Once Jo knew what he'd done, she wouldn't only be afraid of him, she'd no doubt loathe the very sight of him. The thought was painful to even consider and Nicholas tightened his hold on her briefly, holding her while he still could. He was about to turn her in his arms and kiss her when a scent reached his nose that made him frown and sniff delicately.

"What is it?" Jo asked, and tilted her head back to peer at him.

Nicholas lifted his head, pausing when he noted the glossy sheen on her hair. Withdrawing one arm from around her waist, he brushed a hand over the tightly bound strands, his fingers coming away greasy. Raising his hand, he sniffed at the oily liquid, and then glanced to her face, his eyebrows rising when he saw some on her cheek as well.

"What is it?" Jo asked again, frowning at the liquid he'd removed from her hair.

"Motor oil," Nicholas said wryly. "You must have got it on you when you were rolling around in the back of the van. It's old so I bought a bottle of oil in case . . ." His words died off as Jo stepped away from him to raise her hands to feel her hair. His gaze then dropped over the rest of her and he grimaced. She had it all over her. The bottle must have opened. The back of the van was probably covered with it now too. It looked like she'd rolled in it.

"Ew," Jo muttered, glancing down and catching sight of what he had. Sighing, she let her hands drop from her hair and moved past him. "I'm going to shower and find something less 'car mechanic' to wear. I'll be quick. You heat yourself some pizza and open the wine, I'll be right back."

Nicholas turned to watch her go, telling himself he'd best get used to it. He suspected soon she'd be walking away and not returning. When Jo disappeared from view, Nicholas turned to collect two plates and a couple of wineglasses. He set them on the counter and then moved to the wine rack to consider the selection as he heard a door close somewhere in the bowels of the apartment. It was followed by the muffled sound of running water that sounded far away, and Nicholas wondered where the bathroom was, and then frowned as he realized he hadn't seen anything of the apartment other than the kitchen.

Deciding it was in his best interests to check out the rest of the place and all the exits in case of problems, Nicholas turned from the wine rack to do a quick exploration. He passed back out into the hall, and then walked through the living room, noting the black leather and chrome furniture, and state-of-the-art entertainment system before continuing on into a hallway that had three doors off it. One door was closed, the sound of rushing water coming from beyond it.

The bathroom, obviously, Nicholas thought, and forced away the sudden image in his mind of Jo stripping her clothes and stepping under a steaming spray. It wasn't an easy task, mostly because he was enjoying the vision. Of course, he'd prefer the reality, but that was definitely out of the question. Jo would take her shower, he would let her eat and then tell her what he'd done to make himself a rogue, and quickly return her to the enforcer house when she requested it. Nicholas had no doubt she would.

Pushing that thought away as firmly as he had the image of Jo showering, Nicholas glanced into the first open door, and then flipped the light switch on. The room had been set up as an office with a desk, an expensive leather chair, and shelf after shelf of books, most of them legal in nature. He flipped off the light and moved on to the next room. This light was already on and the closet doors open to reveal the first signs that Sam had actually moved out. The closet held only a few items of clothing, what he suspected were rejects left behind when she'd taken the rest of her clothes. Hopefully Jo would be able to find something among them to replace her own oil-stained clothes.

His gaze slid to the bed next, taking in the voluptuous red satin comforter and arrangement of pillows on it. For one moment Nicholas envisioned Jo lying on that bed, her naked body pale against all that deep, rich red, and then he forced himself to look away and moved back out of the room to retrace his steps back to the kitchen.

Nicholas had reached the wine rack when the sound of the shower died. He glanced toward the door, but then forced his eyes back to the wine to consider the selection, eyebrows rising as he noted the bottles with little blue penguins on them. For some reason it made him smile. His gaze slid over the other bottles, but then returned to the penguins, and he picked one of those. It had been fifty years since he'd had wine and he had no idea what was considered good, but three out of the six bottles bore the penguins and suggested it was a house favorite.

Taking the bottle, he crossed back to the counter, found an opener and quickly uncorked it and set it aside to breathe as he opened the pizza box.

Nicholas had two slices on a plate ready to go in the microwave—whatever that was—and was pouring wine into the glasses when Jo padded back into the kitchen. Setting down the bottle, he glanced over his shoulder and then turned and simply watched as Jo crossed the room toward him. Her feet were bare, her hair damp, and her face completely lacking makeup. She would have looked about twelve were she not wearing a sleek, red silk robe that clung in spots where she'd still been damp when she'd donned it, emphasizing that her figure was a woman's.

"It's the only thing Sam left behind that will fit," Jo said wryly as she reached the counter. "She's as skinny as a rail. So I threw my clothes in the wash and this will have to do until they're dry."

"It's lovely," Nicholas said, frowning when he heard how husky his voice was. Clearing his throat, he picked up one of the glasses of wine and held it out to her.

"Mmm, Little Penguin," she said, glancing at the bottle on the counter as she accepted the glass. "It's my favorite among the not ridiculously expensive wines. Sam's too."

"That explains the three bottles then," Nicholas said with amusement.

Jo smiled and took a sip as she moved around him to the microwave. She opened the door, grabbed the plate of pizza, and placed it inside.

Nicholas watched as she started hitting buttons, but knew he'd never be able to replicate the action himself. It seemed if he was going to be eating again, he had some things to learn. Though it was possible his desire to eat would disappear once Jo was out of his life as it had when his first life mate, Annie, had died.

Swallowing at the painful thought, Nicholas turned and picked up the other wineglass to take a drink. Losing Annie had been hard, but he knew losing Jo would be harder. She wouldn't be dead, but simply beyond his reach. He would forever be the poor and hungry young lad peering at the fine cake in the shop window, able to see the sweet that lay beyond, but never to touch or taste it.

"A couple minutes and we can eat," Jo announced, turning toward him as the microwave began to hum. "Do you want to eat at the table or in the living room?"

Nicholas stared down at her silently, watching her drink from her glass. When she lowered it, her lips were wet and a drop of the red liquid remained on her lower lip, just one drop of the smooth wine, trembling there, but it fascinated him. Nicholas couldn't seem to tear his eyes away, and then it began to roll off and her tongue slid out to catch it and he growled, "The table."

"Okay," Jo murmured. "Well—"

Whatever she'd been about to say died and her eyes widened in surprise as he suddenly took her wineglass and turned to set it on the counter with his own. Nicholas then turned back, scooped her up, and carried her to the table. Her eyes were wide and questioning when he sat her there.

"What are we doing?" Jo asked uncertainly, but he knew she had a good idea of what he was up to. He could smell the excitement coming off her and could see her nipples beginning to grow and harden to press against the silk of her robe.

Nicholas raised a hand to lightly brush one finger over the pebbling nipple through the silk and growled, "I'm hungry."

"Oh," she breathed.

Nicholas smiled and raised the finger to run it over her lips, feeling how soft and giving they were. He then let it trail to her throat, and finally down to follow the collar of her robe. Jo shivered as his finger slid along the neckline, cresting the curve of her breast, and then he suddenly changed direction, moving to the side and pushing the cloth before it until he exposed her breast.

Jo's breathing had become low and fast, but stopped altogether when he paused to run his finger lightly around the nipple he'd exposed. He knew she was excited, her response was hitting him too, and he felt it shoot upward in strength as his finger followed the circle around the pale rose areola, lightly brushing the outside of the darker nipple as it went.

"Nicholas," she half breathed and half moaned.

Smiling, he bent his head to rasp his tongue over the erect tip. The shiver that caused in her rolled down his own back as well and made him close his lips over the nipple and draw on it lightly, and then more urgently as their mutual excitement grew and reverberated between them. This was another sign of a life mate—shared pleasure, his feeling hers and her feeling his. The first time he'd taken her in the hotel, Nicholas hadn't gotten the chance to enjoy this. Wound up as they'd been from the shared dream, their first time had been a blur of need and urgency driving them on, but this time he intended to enjoy this aspect of their relationship, he decided, and released her breast to straighten abruptly.

Jo blinked her eyes open and gasped as he suddenly tugged her robe completely open, revealing all of her to him. Nicholas met her gaze, watching her as he clasped her knees and drew them apart so he could step between them. He then slid his hands around her back and lifted her, forcing her to arch upward so he could merely bend his head and lave first one nipple and then turned his head to do the same to the other. Jo clutched at his shoulders, her head dropping back on a moan as he licked, nipped, and suckled her, sending wave after wave of need and excitement coursing through them both.

"Nicholas, please," she moaned, wrapping her legs around his and pulling him tight against her, but he knew this might be his last chance to be with her and he wanted it to last. He wanted it to be something he could remember on all those long, lonely nights ahead.

Reaching up, Nicholas caught her hands in his and pulled them away from his shoulders as he pressed her back on the table with his own body. Holding her down, he then released the nipple from his mouth and ran his mouth down over her stomach, pausing to dip his tongue into her belly button. She smelled of oranges. Obviously it was a result of the soap she'd used in the shower, but Nicholas couldn't resist licking and nibbling her sensitive skin, making it jump and tremble as he moved lower to trail his mouth along her hip bone.

Jo was gasping and panting now, her body trembling and her nails biting painfully into his hands as she held on to the hands holding hers. But Nicholas hardly felt the nip of her nails, his own body was awash with the same mounting excitement she was experiencing . . . but it wasn't enough. Hooking the nearest chair with his foot, he drew it behind him, and dropped to sit on it. Nicholas then released her hands, spread her legs wider, and drew her forward to make a meal of her.

Jo screamed, her hips bucking on the table as Nicholas buried his face between her legs as if she were a slice of melon. She felt his tongue rasp over her sensitive core, and then closed her eyes and gasped for breath as he proceeded to drive her crazy. Her body was suddenly as taut as a bow string, her muscles straining toward the satisfaction he promised, and her brain was hit with wave after rebounding wave of pleasure that seemed magnified with each rush and soon became almost unbearable.

Either she would find that satisfaction or she would explode into a million pieces, Jo thought dazedly, grabbing at the table edges and squeezing until it hurt. Just when she thought it would be the second option and that her mind would shatter under the pressure, Nicholas suddenly rose up between her legs. She blinked her eyes open to see that while he was still fully dressed, his jeans were open. She closed her eyes again on a moan when he caught her by the hips, drew her forward, and finally thrust himself into her.

Nicholas froze then, and Jo forced her eyes open to see that his own eyes had closed. His face was a portrait of what appeared to be pleasure-pain. Jo waited a heartbeat and then clasped her legs around his and sat up on the table to touch his cheek.

When his eyes blinked open in surprise, Jo whispered, "I'm hungry too," and then kissed him, her hips shifting against him in demand. A sigh slid from his mouth to hers and then Nicholas began to kiss her, his arms enveloping her and his hips beginning to move, withdrawing and then thrusting into her again and again until the world shattered around them and they fell into the gentle darkness waiting for them.

* * *

Jo woke up to find herself splayed on the table like some sort of human sacrifice. Her body was sated but a bit chill, her legs were hanging off the table, dangling in the air, and Nicholas was nowhere in sight. Frowning, she sat up, drawing the robe around her as she did, and started to slip off the table, nearly stepping on Nicholas. Pausing abruptly, she teetered on the edge of the table and gaped at the man lying slumped on the floor at her feet.

"Nicholas?" she said with alarm, and managed to drop to the cool tile surface without stepping on him. Jo then knelt at his side and reached for his face. The moment her palm touched his cheek, Nicholas rolled over, his eyes opening.

"Oh, hello," he mumbled sleepily, reaching for her head and drawing her down as if to kiss her, but Jo resisted.

Pressing against his chest, she took in his eyes and coloring, trying to see what had happened to put him on the floor. "What happened? Are you all right?"

Nicholas chuckled at her concern and sat up. He pressed a quick kiss to her lips before shifting to get to his feet and drew her up with him.

"Maybe you shouldn't get up," Jo said fretfully as they straightened. "You seemed to have passed out or something and—"

"I'm fine," he interrupted her soothingly. "I just fainted."

"Fainted?" she asked with dismay, clutching at his hands. "Are you short of blood or something? Do you need to feed? We can—"

"Jo, it's all right. It's perfectly normal. I'm fine," Nicholas repeated.

"Normal?" she echoed with disbelief. "It's not normal to faint, Nicholas. It's—"

"It is for life mates when they make love," he said patiently, and Jo stilled. She stared at him blankly for a minute, then glanced to the table where she'd woken up and realized that she'd rather blacked out after . . .

"Oh," she said weakly, but glanced back to him with uncertainty. "Why?"

Nicholas hesitated, and then said, "I'll explain while we eat."

Jo opened her mouth to insist he explain now, but the rumbling of her stomach changed her mind. Nodding, she moved to the microwave and checked the pizza inside. Enough time had passed that the slices she'd heated were room temperature again. Clucking her tongue, she put them on for another minute and then picked up the wineglasses and glanced to the table. Just looking at the damned thing brought back memories of what they'd done there, and she felt her body responding to those memories.

"Maybe we'll eat in the living room," she muttered.

"This time," Nicholas murmured, eyes flashing silver as he took the wineglasses from her.

Jo flushed at the naughty glint in his eye, her body tingling with remembered pleasure, and when he bent to press a kiss to her lips, she opened for him at once and started to raise her arms to slide them around his neck.

"Food first," he growled, withdrawing quickly from her reach. "Food, and then talk."

Jo watched him walk out of the kitchen, a little sigh slipping from her lips. At that moment she didn't care if she ever ate again. She just wanted to feel Nicholas's body against and in hers again. She wanted . . .

The microwave beeped, announcing that it was done, and Jo gave her head a shake and turned to it thinking that Nicholas was like a drug. She couldn't seem to get enough of him. Sighing, she retrieved the pizza slices from the microwave, divided them between the two plates, and carried them out to the living room.

Nicholas had set the wineglasses on the coffee table and settled on the couch before it. Jo dropped to sit beside him, and then handed him one of the plates and settled in to eat. While she would have been happy to bypass eating moments ago in the kitchen, now that the smell of pizza was wafting under her nose, she was more eager to feed herself . . . first. It had been quite a while since she'd had that breakfast with Bricker and Anders, and she was really quite hungry.

Jo might have been hungry, but Nicholas was absolutely ravenous. He seemed to almost inhale the slice of pizza and had finished it before she had finished even half of hers. With a little direction, he managed to warm up the next two pieces and brought them out to the living room just as she finished her first piece. Jo had three slices before stopping. Nicholas was on his sixth piece when she set her plate down and turned to him expectantly.

"So? Explain how fainting is normal," she prompted as soon as he chewed and swallowed his last bite.

Nicholas peered at his now-empty plate, glanced toward the kitchen as if considering fetching another, but then set the plate down and explained, "The combined pleasure is too much for the mind to take at first and in response, the brain sort of overloads and winks out as the orgasm overwhelms it. It's perfectly normal for the first year or so that life mates are together."

"What's this combined pleasure business?" she asked at once.

"I feel your pleasure and you feel mine," he said simply.

"So when you were . . ." Jo paused and bit her lip, trying to think of a way to describe what he'd been doing without having to use a crude term that would demean the beauty of it.

"Every time I kiss, caress, or touch you, I experience your pleasure as if it was my own," Nicholas said solemnly, solving the problem for her. "I experienced your pleasure, and it mingled with mine and then bounced back to you, mingling with yours again and bouncing back even stronger, and so on until neither of us could take it anymore."

That explained the overwhelming pleasure she'd experienced, Jo supposed, and then asked, "So this combined pleasure business only happens between life mates?"

Nicholas nodded solemnly, and then asked, "Why are you smiling?"

"Because you're over five hundred years old and

have probably bedded a load of women and I'm glad as gonads that you didn't experience this with them."

"Glad as gonads?" Nicholas asked, wincing at the term. Shaking his head, he smiled reluctantly, but then admitted quietly, "I have experienced it once before, Jo."

"Your wife," Jo remembered.

He nodded solemnly.

Jo considered his almost guilty expression and then shrugged mildly. "I guess I can deal with that. I'm still the only one alive you can enjoy it with, so . . ." She climbed onto his lap and slid her arms around his neck, commenting, "I imagine that makes infidelity less likely."

"We are a monogamous people for a reason," Nicholas murmured, clasping his own arms around her. "Once you find a life mate, no other woman can compare. It's like trying to kill pain with aspirin after years of morphine."

"That seems an apt description," Jo assured him quietly. "Because I find you're like a drug I can't get enough of. I want you again already."

She raised her eyes to his to find that the blue was fading, replaced with silver again.

"So," Jo whispered, moving her face forward so that their lips were almost touching. "If I were to kiss and caress and touch you, I'd get to experience your pleasure too, right?"

Nicholas gave a very slight nod.

"That's a pretty cool deal," she murmured, reaching down to clasp him through the cloth of his jeans. He was hard and grew harder at her touch, and she shuddered at the excitement it sent shooting through her.

Damn, Jo thought faintly, he was right. She had been so consumed by the rush of passions that had overwhelmed her earlier as he'd ministered to her, Jo hadn't understood what was happening, but now . . . She squeezed him gently and closed her eyes as another rush of pleasure slid through her. In the next moment, she'd slid off his lap and between his legs to rest on the floor as she reached for the button of his jeans.

"Jo, wait, we have to talk," Nicholas said, trying to stop her.

"Later," she said quietly. "It's my turn now."

Nicholas met her gaze briefly, a conflict taking place on his face, and then he stood up, pulling on her hand to urge her up with him.

"What—?" Jo began uncertainly.

"The bedroom," Nicholas growled, tugging her around the table and toward the hall. "I fancy waking up in a bed this time rather than sprawled on the couch or the living room carpet."

Jo grinned and teased, "Where's your sense of adventure?"

Nicholas paused abruptly in the hall and whirled to take her in his arms. His mouth was demanding, his hands stripping away her robe before her chest even came to rest against his, and then he pinned her to the wall, grinding himself against her and thrusting his tongue into her mouth as he kicked off his shoes.

Moaning at the pleasure coursing through her, Jo clasped his bottom. She squeezed briefly, and then managed to work her hands between their bodies to undo the button and zipper of his jeans. They both groaned with pleasure when she slid her hand inside and found him, and then Nicholas broke their kiss to step back and remove his clothes. His T-shirt was dragged up and off in one step, and then his jeans followed and he was back, clasping her by the upper thighs and pulling her legs around his hips so that his erection rubbed against, but didn't enter her.

Jo grabbed for his shoulders, kissing him frantically as he pressed her back against the wall and drove them both wild, and then she tore her mouth away with a cry as he suddenly thrust into her.

Nicholas paused then. Breathing heavily, he briefly rested his forehead against her neck, and then raised his head enough to lick her throat, kiss it, and then nibble a trail up to her ear.

Jo moaned as he withdrew and slid into her again, pressing her back into the wall.

"Is this enough adventure for you?" he growled, and then chuckled breathlessly when she nodded. "Good," Nicholas murmured, then caught her lips in a gentle kiss before thrusting almost violently into her again. Breaking their kiss again then, he added, "The real adventure is seeing whether we can make it to a soft surface before passing out."

Jo blinked her eyes open and peered at him. "How—?"

Her question died on a gasp as he suddenly stepped back from the wall, taking her with him, and turned toward the end of the hall. Jo's legs tightened instinctively around him, but she needn't have bothered, his hands were clasping her bottom, holding her in place as he started up the hall.

"Let's see how many steps it takes to blow our minds," Nicholas said through gritted teeth as he walked, their bodies rubbing together with each step.

"Oh God," Jo breathed, burying her face in his neck and closing her eyes as wave after wave of mounting pleasure rushed through her. She suspected they wouldn't make it to the bed and just hoped the padding under Sam's carpet was a soft one.

Chapter Thirteen

"That's a serious expression."

Nicholas glanced down at Jo. She lay half on his chest, her face questioning and raised to his. They were in the bed, finally. On the first attempt they'd made it only halfway up the hall before their passion had overwhelmed them both. He'd done his best to protect Jo as he'd lost consciousness, and supposed it had worked. She'd seemed fine when he woke up. Not that he'd gotten the chance to ask her. She'd awakened before him and immediately decided to finish what she'd tried to start in the living room. Nicholas had woken to find himself fully erect, her mouth working over him, and both of them halfway to exploding all over again.

Jo had woken up before him the next time as well, but they'd made it to the bedroom door that time. It had taken two more tries to get to the bed. The last time, they'd woken up at almost the same time and had made it to the bed before their mutual need had overwhelmed them. This time, Nicholas was the first to wake, which was a shame because it had given him a chance to think.

"What's the matter?" she asked, worry clouding her face.

Nicholas hesitated, but then said, "Nothing. I was just thinking."

Jo was silent for a minute, and then asked, "Nicholas?"

"Hmm?"

"Tell me about your wife," she said quietly.

Nicholas stilled briefly, his mind suddenly blank. He had no idea what he should say.

"You said you were married and she was a life mate too?" Jo prompted.

Nicholas let out the breath he hadn't realized he was holding and nodded. "Yes."

"How long ago was it that you and she—?"

"We met, married, and she died all in 1959. It was the best and worst year of my life . . . until now," Nicholas added solemnly, and knew it was absolutely true. He had been fortunate enough to find another life mate, a very rare occurrence, and he was going to have to give her up. Definitely best and worst.

"Did you not turn her?" Jo asked, frowning.

Nicholas shook his head. "She was born immortal."

"But . . ." Confusion reigned on her face for a moment and then she shook her head. "But then how did she die? If she was immortal, she should have—"

"*Immortal* isn't truly the proper word for us,"

Nicholas said on a sigh. "We can die, it's just harder to kill us than a mortal. Illness won't do it, and being shot will only incapacitate us until the bullets are forced out, but decapitation or having our heart removed can kill us."

"And Annie had one of those things happen to her?" Jo asked with a frown.

"Annie, and our child along with her, died in a car accident," Nicholas said quietly.

"But how? If bullets won't kill you, surely an accident . . ." Jo paused, her eyes widening, then asked, "She wasn't decap—"

"Yes," Nicholas interrupted gruffly, then sighed wearily and said, "They told me it was a freak thing, but probably for the best since the car burst into flames, and had she not died quickly, she would have suffered horribly."

"Oh," Jo murmured. "I'm sorry."

Nicholas remained silent, but bent and kissed the top of her head.

"Was it her you were thinking of when I woke up?" she asked quietly.

"No," he assured her, and then sighed and admitted, "I was just wondering how they found us at the hotel."

Jo closed her eyes briefly and sighed. She then shifted off him and moved to pull the sheets and blankets over them both before sitting up to lean against the pillows at the top of the bed. "That's my fault. Apparently they were able to track my bank activities and found out I'd made a withdrawal from the hotel store's ATM."

"You withdrew money from—" Nicholas began with horror, sitting up beside her, but she interrupted.

"I'm sorry. I had no idea they could track things like that," she said apologetically. "I mean, jeez, who would have thought that Mortimer and those guys could do something like that?"

He would have, Nicholas thought, but didn't say as much. She hadn't known and he hadn't told her so he could hardly blame her for the mistake. The good news was it meant they hadn't put some sort of tracker on her or anything and weren't going to burst in on them here.

"I am sorry, Nicholas. I won't use my debit card again. I just never thought—I mean, it never occurred to me they would or even *could* do something like that. Checking bank activity is like a cop trick or something."

Nicholas was silent for a minute, but then decided it was time they got the big talk out of the way. "Jo . . . Mortimer and those guys *are* cops. They're enforcers, rogue hunters, the equivalent of vampire cops. They have access to any technology the cops do, any technology out there if they want it. They hunt rogue immortals."

Jo was silent for a minute and then said, "Bricker said you were rogue."

"Yes," he said solemnly.

She remained still for a moment, not looking at him as she digested that and then asked carefully, "What is a rogue immortal, exactly?"

Jo hadn't moved, but Nicholas could feel her withdrawing from him, putting some emotional distance between them. He could feel the emotional tearing as she began to draw a protective wall around herself, and his heart ached. Forcing himself to breathe deeply, he waited for the pain of it to pass and then said, "A rogue is an immortal who has broken our laws."

"You have laws?" she asked with surprise.

Nicholas smiled faintly. "Of course. No society exists without laws."

"Of course," Jo murmured, and then sighed and asked. "Tell me your laws."

Nicholas hesitated and then said, "We can turn only one in a life time."

She nodded.

"Couples are allowed to have only one child every hundred years."

"One?" Jo asked with surprise. "How do you manage that? I mean what do you do if one of your females finds herself pregnant sooner than a hundred years?"

Nicholas shrugged. "It's easily managed. Actually, getting pregnant and carrying to term have usually been the problem in the past."

"The nanos?" she asked.

Nicholas nodded and reminded her, "They are to keep the host healthy and at their peak. They see a baby as a parasite, using up the blood and nutrients the host needs. For one of our women to get pregnant, she has to double up on blood to keep the nanos busy and continue to double up on it until the baby is born. Otherwise the host's nanos will abort the fetus."

"I see," she murmured, frowning. "Is that what happened to Lucian's wife?"

"Lucian?" Nicholas asked with surprise.

"I heard Mortimer say that Lucian and Leigh had been traveling a lot since she lost her baby," Jo explained, and then added, "I assume they're both immortals too?"

"Yes," Nicholas said quietly. He hadn't realized that his uncle's life mate was with child. The man must have been over the moon about it, and had probably fallen just as far when she'd lost the child.

"So did she lose the baby because she didn't feed enough?" Jo asked.

Nicholas shook his head with certainty. "No. I'm sure that's not what happened. Lucian would have made sure she'd fed enough."

"Then how could she have lost the baby?" Jo asked with confusion. "The nanos should have—"

"The nanos repair illness and injuries, but they don't fix genetic problems, so I'd imagine there was a genetic flaw and she had a natural miscarriage," he said, and then thought that probably explained why the triple wedding with Lucian, Leigh, and two other couples had been delayed yet again. On the run and rogue though he might be, Nicholas had still managed to keep up with things in his family's life. While he'd had to avoid other immortals, there were mortals who worked for his cousin's company, Argeneau Enterprises, and he'd occasionally looked one or another up and read their minds and then blanked their memories of his presence.

It was in this way Nicholas had found out about the triple wedding. It had started out as a single wedding for his cousin Bastien and his life mate, Terri. But then Lucian had found Leigh and the two couples had decided to have a double ceremony. And then his uncle Victor and Elvi had been added to the roster and it was to be a triple wedding. However, the original date had been changed and the wedding delayed when his aunt Marguerite had gone missing, and then he'd recently learned it was to be delayed again, but the secretary he'd read hadn't known why. Nicholas suspected Leigh's losing the baby had been the cause of the last delay and wondered if the triple wedding would ever take place at this rate.

"So," Jo said, drawing him from his thoughts. "You can turn only one, can have only one child every hundred years . . ." She raised her eyebrows. "What else?"

"We aren't allowed to bite or kill mortals," Nicholas said.

"And?" she asked.

Nicholas shrugged. "That's about it, other than we just aren't supposed to do anything that would make our presence known to mortals."

Jo nodded, was silent for a moment, and then asked, "So did you bite or kill a mortal? Or did you do something that would make the presence of immortals known to mortals?"

Nicholas looked away, but reluctantly forced himself to say, "I guess I bit and killed a mortal."

There was a long silence this time, and Nicholas

wanted to look at her and see her expression, but didn't have the courage to do so. When Jo spoke, he wasn't surprised to hear anger in her voice.

"You *guess* you did?" she asked, finally. "What do you mean you *guess*? Did you or didn't you?"

"Apparently I did," he admitted on a sigh and finally turned to look at her to see her blinking and shaking her head.

"Nicholas, this is one of those yes or no questions again. You seem to have a problem with those. Did you or did you not kill a mortal?"

Nicholas frowned and shook his head with irritation. "Yes, I guess I killed a mortal."

Jo blew her breath out with exasperation and flopped back against the bed frame. "No, you didn't."

"Yes, I apparently did," he said at once.

"Oh?" She snorted. "You can't even say it without a qualifier. I *guess* I did, *apparently* I did . . ." Jo shook her head. "You couldn't have done it. You can't even *say* it."

Nicholas scowled with irritation. He'd been loathing making this confession, afraid to see the fear and hatred cross Jo's face as she realized what he'd done. However, he'd never once imagined her reaction would be disbelief. Mouth compressing, he said firmly, "Jo, I killed a woman, a pregnant woman. I ripped her throat out and fed on her."

"Right," Jo said with disbelief, and then suggested, "So tell me about it."

"What?" he asked with amazement.

"Tell me what happened," she insisted.

"I'm not going to—"

"Because you didn't kill anyone," Jo interrupted with a certainty that was almost defiant.

Nicholas stared at her with amazement. Truly, she was something else; beautiful, funny, sweet, sexy, surprising . . . and frustrating as hell. Sighing, he said, "Jo, I wish it weren't true too, but—"

"It's simple, Nicholas. If you did it, tell me about it," she insisted. "Who was the woman?"

"I don't know," he admitted uncomfortably. Nicholas had fled the Toronto area, and Canada itself, that fateful day fifty years ago and not returned . . . At least, not until the start of this summer when he'd trailed a particularly nasty nest of rogues from the northern states and all the way up into Canada and Ontario's cottage country. That being the case, Nicholas had never had the chance to find out who the woman was. He suspected that was a good thing. Her face already haunted his nightmares. Knowing her name would only make it worse.

"You don't know?" Jo asked dryly. "Well, okay, so how did you meet this woman you didn't know but for some reason killed?"

Nicholas grimaced at her sarcasm, and then leaned his head back against the bed's headboard and closed his eyes. "It was after Annie died. I was . . . I didn't take it well. I shut out family and friends and basically wallowed in my grief," he admitted with self-disgust.

"I think that's probably natural," Jo said softly.

"Yes, well . . ." He licked his lips and opened his eyes to stare up at the ceiling overhead as the events played out in his mind. "That day I found a birthday gift Annie had got for a friend of hers at work. She'd bought and wrapped it ahead of time and it had been sitting on her craft table."

"Craft table," Jo murmured in a disbelieving voice, and when he glanced at her, she flushed and shrugged and muttered, "It just seems odd to think of a vampiress doing crafts. That's so . . . mundane," she finished finally.

"We're just people, Jo," he said quietly.

"Yeah, I suppose. People with fangs, who drink blood, live a long time, and apparently do crafts." She shook her head.

Nicholas smiled faintly, but tilted his head back again and continued. "I probably wouldn't have taken the gift to Carol if—"

"Carol?" Jo interrupted in question.

"Annie's friend at the hospital," he explained. "They worked the night shift together."

"What did Annie do at the hospital?" Jo asked curiously.

"She was a nurse in the critical care unit," he said, smiling faintly at the memory. "Annie was . . . She was special. She liked to help people and—" Nicholas paused abruptly as he realized it was probably bad form to go on about the wonders of a past life mate to a present life mate . . . even if he couldn't claim her.

"Anyway," he muttered, "as I was saying, I probably wouldn't have taken the gift to Carol, but I wanted to ask her if she knew what Annie . . ." Nicholas paused as he realized he'd left something out. "I should tell you that the night before Annie died, she called me in Detroit and said—"

"What were you doing in Detroit?" Jo interrupted.

"I was hunting a rogue," he explained. "It was going to be my last case. Annie was nearly due and I didn't like being away from her when she was so close to delivery."

"You were hunting a *rogue*?" Jo asked slowly, and then, "You were a rogue hunter too?"

"We're actually called enforcers. I mean they are," Nicholas corrected himself with a frown.

"But you *were* one?" she insisted.

"Yes," he admitted.

"Better and better," Jo muttered. "Go on. Annie called you in Detroit and said . . . ?"

"She said she had something to tell me when I got back. She was excited and I was curious, but she wouldn't tell me what it was over the phone. She said she wanted to see my face when she told me."

"But she died," Jo prompted.

"Yes. She died and I forgot all about it for a while."

"But then you saw the gift and you thought you'd deliver it as an excuse to ask this Carol if she knew what it was Annie was going to tell you when you got home."

Nicholas nodded, releasing his breath on a slow sigh. Jo was making this as easy as she could for him. She was also very quick at putting things together.

"Did this friend Carol know?" Jo asked curiously.

Nicholas shook his head. "I never found out. I put the gift in the car and drove to the hospital, but as I was crossing the parking lot to go inside a woman came out. She was petite and blond like my Annie. She even looked like her a little . . . and she was very pregnant."

"Like your Annie," Jo suggested.

"Yes," he said wearily, closing his eyes. "I remember being really angry, furious even that this mortal woman lived while my Annie, an immortal who should have lived for centuries, was . . ."

"That's normal too, Nicholas," Jo said softly, slipping her hand into his and squeezing gently. When he glanced at her with obvious disbelief, she nodded solemnly. "Shortly after my parents died, I met my friends at this restaurant for lunch where there was this older couple seated at a table across from us. They were ancient. White hair, wrinkled, they had to be in their eighties or nineties . . ." She paused and shook her head. "I don't know what it was about them. Perhaps it was how they smiled at each other, or the way she shared her food with him, but for some reason it made me think of my parents, and for one moment I was absolutely furious that these two old codgers were alive and happy while my parents, so much younger, were dead." Jo sighed unhappily at the memory and then shrugged. "I think it's probably a natural part of grieving."

"Did you take the old couple home and slaughter them?" Nicholas asked grimly.

Jo's eyes shifted to meet his, sharp and hard. "Is that what you did?"

Nicholas looked away and shrugged. "Apparently."

"There's that word again," she said dryly. "I don't want to hear *apparently*. Tell me what happened. You saw her and were angry and . . ."

Nicholas frowned as he sifted through his memories trying to find the ones that covered what happened next. Finally, he just said, "I ripped her throat out and fed on her."

"Right there in the parking lot?" Jo asked with shock.

"I—No . . ." He reached up to rub his forehead unhappily. "At my home. In my basement."

Jo was silent for a long time again, and when he finally glanced to her, she was peering at him as if sorting out a puzzle. Finally she shook her head and said, "How did you get her there? Did she say something to really piss you off? What happened?"

"I don't know," he snapped with frustration. "I just remember looking at her, and being really angry. The next thing I knew Decker was shouting my name and I opened my eyes to see that I was sitting on the floor of my basement with the pregnant woman, dead in my arms. There was blood everywhere, including in my mouth. I killed her, Jo."

Much to his amazement, Jo suddenly smiled and leaned back against the headboard. Her voice was satisfied as she said, "You didn't kill her."

For some reason her calm certainty infuriated him. "Goddammit, Jo, I did."

"Then why don't you remember it?" she asked calmly.

"I must have been in a blinding rage," he said at once. It was the only explanation he'd been able to come up with after all these years. Not that he'd thought about it often. He'd been so horrified by what he'd done that Nicholas had done his best not to think about it at all until the night he'd met Jo. Since then it was constantly in the back of his mind.

What he'd done, why he'd done it, how he'd ruined his chances to be with her.

"Nope, you weren't in a blinding rage," Jo said with certainty, snapping his attention back to her with disbelief of his own.

"Well I sure as shit wouldn't have killed her if I hadn't been in a blinding rage," he snarled.

"Nicholas," she said patiently, shifting to kneel beside him on the bed. "Think about what you're saying. You saw her and were angry because she looked like your Annie, was pregnant like your Annie, but was alive when your Annie wasn't. Your anger was natural, and if you'd told me you'd struck out at her right there in the parking lot, one angry shot that had killed the woman, I might have believed you'd killed her in a blinding rage. But that's not what happened. Supposedly, in this blinding rage, you transported her to your car, got inside, drove her to your place, and took her down into your basement and killed her . . . without ever coming out of your blinding rage. Without remembering a thing about it until you *opened your eyes and peered down to find her dead in your lap*?" She shook her head. "Nope. Didn't happen that way."

Nicholas merely stared at Jo blankly as she suddenly sat back and looked thoughtful, and then she asked, "You say Decker was shouting your name? That's what woke you up?"

"I—Yes," he said on a sigh.

"He did it then," she decided calmly, and as Nicholas began to shake his head, she said, "Yes, he did. He took control of you and took you both back to your place and killed the woman, set her in your lap, and then released his control."

Nicholas closed his eyes wearily. "Decker didn't do it, Jo. Decker wouldn't kill a mortal. He's a rogue hunter, he protects mortals and immortals alike. He wouldn't kill anyone but rogues."

"Yet *you* would," she asked dryly, and pointed out, "You were an enforcer too."

"Yes, but I was grieving, my head wasn't on straight. I was—"

"Controlled," Jo said firmly.

Nicholas wished he could agree with her and say that was what had happened, but shook his head. "Immortals can't be controlled."

"You said you can read each other's thoughts just like you can mortals," Jo said at once. "Perhaps an older immortal can also control a younger one. Decker probably—"

"Decker is younger than me," he interrupted. "And yes immortals can read each other, but only a very new turn can be controlled. I was centuries old."

"You're sure about that?" she asked, eyes narrowing.

Nicholas ran a hand through his hair and nodded solemnly. "Yes. It would take a three-on-one to wipe my memories and control me—three older immortals working together to do it. The minute you try to erase or bury an immortal's memories, the nanos will be trying to bring them back to the surface. They have to be buried and reburied over and over again. It takes days, and it was still the same night when Decker got there. I wasn't controlled, and

I didn't have my memory erased," he assured her regretfully.

"Then you were drugged," she decided promptly.

"Jo," he said wearily.

"Stop fighting me and help here," she snapped. "You're wallowing in your supposed guilt. Stop that and use your noggin. It just doesn't make sense, Nicholas. You apparently risked getting captured and killed earlier in the summer to help Dani and Stephanie, and then just the other night you did it again to save me. I was a complete stranger and I presume Dani and Stephanie probably were too, but you risked losing your own life to save us. That doesn't sound like a man who would kill a woman just because she looked like your life mate." She paused to suck in a breath and then said, "Honestly, you'd be more likely to control the woman and keep her to play house with and pretend your Annie was still alive."

Nicholas frowned at her words. "But she was in my lap."

"But you don't remember how she got there," Jo said at once. "Does that seem right to you? How did you get her there? What happened to the gift for Carol? Did she say anything to you to set you off? Did she cry and beg for her life? Did you take control of her and keep that control as you drove to your place? And why the basement?"

Nicholas peered at her blankly as her questions rained over him. When she put it that way, it didn't really seem right. Surely she was correct and if he'd lost it, he'd have killed the woman there in the parking lot or at least remember something about getting her home, but . . . "Drugs don't work on us."

Jo paused and tilted her head. "No drugs? Not at all?"

"Well . . ." He hesitated and then admitted, "Weaker drugs will be removed by the nanos before they can do anything, and stronger ones wouldn't have as strong an effect or work for more than twenty minutes to half an hour."

"How long a drive was it from the hospital to your house?" she asked at once.

"Ten minutes," he said quietly. "I didn't want Annie to have to drive far to get to work."

Jo raised an eyebrow. "So you could have been drugged, taken home, the woman killed and set in your lap before you woke."

"Her blood was in my mouth," he reminded her.

She rolled her eyes and suddenly bounded from the bed and hurried from the room. Nicholas stared after her with surprise, and then threw the sheets and blankets aside to follow. He found her in the living room, bent over, picking up something from the table. His eyes slid over her bare derriere with interest totally inappropriate to the conversation they'd been having and he grimaced to himself, and said, "What—?"

That was as far as he got. At the sound of his voice, Jo suddenly straightened, turned, and threw a glass of wine in his face.

Nicholas gasped in shock, eyes instinctively shutting as the liquid splashed over him, hitting his face and upper chest.

"Oh look, you have wine in your mouth. Did you drink it?" she asked sarcastically.

Nicholas opened his eyes slowly to stare at her.

"Wake up, Nicholas," Jo snapped, setting down the glass. "This is your future. Stop just accepting that you killed the woman and start considering other possibilities, because the story you told me makes no sense at all, but everyone believes it and that can get you killed."

Turning abruptly, she walked into the kitchen. Nicholas simply stood there, watching her ass as she walked away. Once she disappeared, he glanced down at himself, noting that the wine was running down his body and dripping onto the carpet. He was about to go find a towel or something to clean up when Jo reappeared from the kitchen with a dish towel in one hand and a slice of cold pizza in the other. She tossed the dish towel to him and then dropped onto the couch and took a bite of pizza, glaring at him the whole while.

Nicholas grimaced and began to dry himself off under her glare, but then his lips began to twitch. The woman had thrown a glass of wine at him and was now glaring at him as if *he* was the one who'd done something wrong. Annie would have never done that. Annie had been like a soothing balm, a gentle angel. Jo was the opposite, a firecracker. Yet they'd both been his life mate and he could have lived happily with either, but he suspected life wouldn't be anywhere near restful with Jo. Or it wouldn't have been if he could have claimed her . . . and if what she was suggesting was true, he might be able to claim her someday.

"Right," he said suddenly. Finishing with the towel, Nicholas tossed it on the coffee table and dropped onto the couch beside her. "Let's do this."

Jo's glare immediately disappeared. Placing the nasty cold pizza on one of their used plates on the table, she turned to face him on the couch and said, "You saw the pregnant woman who looked like Annie in the parking lot . . . and then what?"

Nicholas sought his memories, but there just weren't any, which really was rather odd. Finally he said, "And then we were in my basement and she was dead."

"How did you get her there?" Jo shot the question at him like a bullet.

"I must have driven," he said uncertainly.

"In a blinding rage?" she asked dryly, and then snapped, "What happened to the gift for Carol?"

"I . . . don't know," Nicholas admitted with a frown.

"Okay, go back to what you do remember. You got out of the car and started across the parking lot. You saw the woman, she reminded you of Annie . . . Did she say or do anything? Hello, or good evening?"

"I don't recall her saying anything," he muttered, searching his memory. "I think she smiled and . . ." Nicholas frowned.

"What?" Jo asked eagerly. "You're remembering something. What is it?"

"It's not much," he said wearily. "I just . . . She was walking toward me, she glanced up, met my gaze and smiled, and then her eyes traveled past me to something else."

"Probably to whoever it was who drugged you," Jo said with certainty and in that moment, Nicholas knew he loved her. She was so certain of his innocence, believing in it even when he didn't. Decker, his cousin and best friend, hadn't doubted his guilt when he'd seen him there in the basement. All of his family had accepted his guilt without hesitation. Even he himself hadn't doubted it these fifty years, but Jo, who had known him for only a matter of a couple of days, hadn't believed he was guilty for even a heartbeat . . . and he loved her for it . . . for that, and her spirit of adventure, courage, and intelligence and perky nature. *He loved this woman.*

"Do you remember feeling any kind of jab or anything?" Jo asked, completely oblivious of his thoughts. "Maybe a sudden sharp pain in the neck or arm that might have been a needle? Or— Oh!" she interrupted herself suddenly, eyes widening. "It could have been a tranq gun. I bet an elephant tranquilizer would have taken you out for half an hour."

"It could have been," Nicholas agreed quietly.

Standing suddenly, Jo moved around the coffee table and began to pace the carpet, arms crossed under her breasts and pushing them up. The woman was completely and utterly nude and apparently totally unselfconscious about it as she murmured, "How it was done doesn't really matter. I mean we can supposition on that all we want. You were probably drugged, the woman was probably controlled. You were taken home, she was killed, placed in your lap, blood splashed on you and in your mouth, and all just in time for Decker to show up and witness it. But none of that really helps. We can't prove it now. We need to figure out *why* it was done."

Nicholas nodded, his eyes drifting from her breasts to her behind as she turned to pace back again. Damn, she had a killer figure. He doubted the nanos would have much work to do body wise when he turned her. The thought drew him up short, and Nicholas swallowed the sudden lump in his throat. For the first time in fifty years, he had hopes for a future. But it was a false hope if they couldn't work this out.

"Did you have any enemies?" Jo asked suddenly, spinning to peer at him.

Nicholas shook his head. "No, not that I know of."

She clucked at that with disgust. "You were a rogue hunter, Nicholas. You probably had loads of rogues who weren't happy with your capturing them."

He winced, but then sighed and explained, "Most rogues don't live to be unhappy about it. Mostly they're staked and baked shortly after we bring them in."

"Staked and baked?" she asked.

"Staked out to bake in the sun all day," he explained. "After centuries of avoiding the sun we're pretty sensitive to it. It does a lot of damage. The nanos repair as much as they can but run out of blood to work with and start attacking the organs in search of more. It's pretty painful," Nicholas admitted with an almost embarrassed grimace.

"It's pretty Draconian," Jo said dryly.

"Yes," he acknowledged. "It's supposed to be a deterrent to others to convince them they don't want to go rogue and risk having that happen." Nicholas cleared his throat and added, "I think they may have stopped that practice the last couple of years, though, I'm not sure."

"Hmm," Jo murmured. "But they did that when you were still an enforcer?"

Nicholas nodded uncomfortably. "But not by me. Enforcers just bring them in. We aren't supposed to kill them. They get a trial just like a mortal would, and then the Council has them staked and baked and beheaded."

"Nice," she said on a sigh. "So no one you brought in could be behind this."

Nicholas was nodding in agreement when she added, "But family members could be, someone who had a rogue relative and blames you for bringing them in."

He shook his head again and peered down at his hands as he said, "Relatives tend to shun rogues. They're upset and embarrassed by them and often even deny their existence or relationship to them."

"Is that what happened to you?" Jo asked quietly.

Nicholas simply shrugged, but it *was* what had happened. From his checks on his family through mortal employees he knew that his brother and sister never spoke of him anymore and that Jeanne Louise, his little sister, who had adored him and made a pest of herself visiting all the time, often catching him and Annie in inopportune moments, even denied his existence now. As far as she was concerned, he had never been born.

"I'm sorry," Jo said quietly, and he glanced up to see she'd moved around the coffee table and now stood before him in all her nude glory. Just the sight of her perky breasts peering him in the face was enough to cheer him somewhat, but when Nicholas reached for her, she skipped out from between his legs and the coffee table to move back to the open area of carpet, out of his reach. "Right, so it probably isn't about being an enforcer. We have to think about this."

Nicholas sank back against the sofa with a sigh as she continued her pacing.

"So . . ." she murmured. "Annie called you and said she had something to tell you, but died before she could tell you what it was . . . in a fiery car accident where she was decapitated." Jo grimaced and paused in her pacing to turn and ask, "How did the accident happen? I mean decapitation in a car accident is pretty rare, I would think. Did she crash under a semi or something?"

"No," he said quietly. "She drove off the road on her way home from work. She must have been tired or maybe she was avoiding an animal in the lane. She went off the road, and slammed into a tree. Seat belts weren't mandatory at that time and she went through the windshield."

Jo stared at him with confusion. "How did that decapitate her?"

"The windshield did it," Nicholas said on a sigh. "The steering wheel caught her body and kept her in the car, but her head slammed out the window. It didn't shatter like it should have. The bottom stayed intact and her head went out and down and—" He shrugged unhappily. "It was a freak accident. One in a million they said."

Jo started to pace again, murmuring, "A freak accident, one in a million."

Nicholas nodded, recalling his horror as they'd broken the news to him, and then Jo said, "That must be it."

He raised his head to peer at her. "What?"

"Don't you see?" she asked, turning to look at him, eyes sparkling. "Annie was going to tell you something when you got back, but died in a totally freak car accident that decapitated her . . . one of the *very few* ways to kill an immortal. And then you were heading to see her friend Carol to give her a gift Annie had bought for her before her death *and* ask her about what Annie had been going to tell you, but you wind up in your basement with a dead woman in your arms and on the run for fifty some years, completely forgetting all about the question you'd wanted to ask."

Jo paused to peer at him. "What would have happened had you not run?"

"I probably would have been executed right away," he said slowly.

"No trial?" she asked.

"Well, maybe a ghost of a trial. I doubt they would have put much effort into it. Decker saw me, I thought I'd done it . . ." He shrugged.

"It doesn't matter," Jo assured him. "Either way you wouldn't have been around to ask about what Annie wanted to tell you."

Nicholas's eyes widened incredulously at her words. She was simply stating what had happened, things he'd already known, but they had an entirely different connotation when she said it like that. He'd never really connected the two events, never even considered they might be connected. But then he'd just assumed, as everyone else had, that he'd killed the woman found dead in his arms. Everyone had . . . but Jo.

"I think we need to find this friend Carol and see if she knows what Annie wanted to tell you," Jo said solemnly.

Chapter Fourteen

"Nicholas?" Jo asked quietly, moving around the coffee table to peer down at him. He'd gone quiet all of a sudden and bowed his head. Pausing in front of him, she bent to brush her fingers over his cheek. "What is it?"

He lifted his head, and she felt worry slide through her at the stark look in his eyes, but then he cleared his throat and asked, "Why do you believe in me?"

Jo straightened in surprise at the question. "What do you mean?"

Nicholas reached out to take her hand and said solemnly, "Jo, you hardly know me. We only met yesterday morning and yet when I told you I killed a woman, you didn't believe it for a minute. My entire family, most of whom have known me for centuries, had no doubts, but you did. Jeanne Louise and Thomas, my own sister and brother, didn't doubt it and now won't even acknowledge my existence." He paused and looked away, but not before she saw the pain streaking across his face. It was gone when Nicholas turned back, and his face was expressionless as he asked, "Why do you believe I'm innocent when I wasn't even sure about it myself?"

Jo stared at him, unsure she knew the answer herself. Perhaps she simply didn't want to believe it, but from the moment Nicholas had said he'd bitten and killed a woman, her heart had rejected it. Perhaps it was blind faith at first and a desire not to think it possible that someone she was coming to care for could do something like that. Perhaps had he told her minute by minute how and why he'd done it, she would have believed it, but the moment her brain had gotten over the shock of the declaration and Jo had heard the *I guess*es, and the *apparently*s, and then the complete lack of memory behind the claim . . . Jo had known, to the very core of her being, that this man hadn't killed some innocent, pregnant woman all those years ago.

Oh, she had no doubt he could kill in the right circumstances, but she was pretty sure that for Nicholas it would have to be to save another or stop a rogue. Jo didn't even think he could kill in a blinding rage, not on purpose, and she was positive no blinding rage would last through the time needed to bundle a woman into his car, drive the ten minutes home, drag her into the basement, and rip her throat out. It just wasn't logical, and Jo fancied herself a logical person.

Of course, the feelings she had for Nicholas weren't really all that logical. While she was grateful he'd saved her twice, the feelings she was experiencing for this man were far and away from simple gratitude. Jo liked Nicholas. More than that, she trusted him, and she lusted after him. Even now, she hungered for him and wanted nothing more than to climb into his lap and reexperience the mind-blowing sex only he could give her. The only thing keeping her from doing just that was the possibility that if they didn't find out what had happened that day so long ago and prove he was innocent, she would lose him forever. The very thought scared her silly. Jo wasn't ready to acknowledge that she might want a future with this man, but Jo was damned certain she would do everything she could to make sure she had the opportunity if she did want it.

"I don't know," Jo said finally, and smiled wryly as she added, "Maybe your nanos are talking to me."

Nicholas smiled faintly. "I don't think they're capable of doing that. I wish they could," he added wryly. "They could probably tell us what happened that day, but then so could the walls of my house, the floor, the . . ." He sighed wearily. "But they can't."

"But Carol might be able to help us figure it out," she said encouragingly. "Let's find out where she is now and talk to her. What's her last name? We'll call information and get her phone number. We can call her right now and maybe solve this whole thing."

Nicholas was silent, his eyes shifting away from her suddenly excited face, and then he shook his head. "It's nearly dawn, too late to be doing anything."

Jo followed his gaze to the window where the first streaks of sunlight were just visible through Sam's sheers.

"Well that's good then," she said. "Carol will definitely be home sleeping. You immortals normally sleep during the day, right?"

"Right," Nicholas murmured, and then turned to her adding, "But we also don't have phones in our sleeping rooms as a rule. Too many sales calls," he added dryly, catching her hand and tugging her forward.

Jo gasped as she landed in his lap, exactly where she wanted to be, but had been fighting going herself. She still fought it now, pushing at his chest when his mouth started to lower to hers. "But we could try."

"Later. When night falls," he said solemnly, his mouth lowering toward hers.

"But—" Jo turned her head away. "Nicholas, this is important. We really have to—"

"*You're* important," Nicholas interrupted quietly, catching her face and turning her to peer at him. "You're the most important thing in the world to me, Jo. I love you. Let me have this moment."

She stared into his face, stunned into silence by his declaration and unsure what she should say in response. Jo wasn't ready to say the feelings that had grown so quickly in her were love for this man. Fortunately, he didn't seem to expect her to. He didn't seem to expect her to say anything at all. His mouth lowered to cover hers and his arms tightened around her, drawing her closer as he kissed her.

Jo sat unresponsive in his lap for perhaps a heartbeat, but just his mouth on hers and his tongue slipping out to glide between her parted lips was enough to overcome her protests. Sighing, she gave in and slid her arms around his neck, her mouth opening further for him as he suddenly stood, scooping her up in his arms.

A couple of hours wouldn't hurt, Jo told herself as he began to carry her to the hall and the bedroom that waited beyond. They would call Annie's friend Carol when darkness fell again.

Nicholas finished dressing and moved to peer down at Jo where she lay on her stomach in the bed. She was sleeping soundly as her body worked at replacing the blood he'd taken from her this last time they'd made love. This time it hadn't been an accident of his getting overexcited. He'd deliberately bitten her, and had deliberately taken more blood than he normally would have just before they'd both found their ecstasy and passed out. It had been his hope that doing so would ensure she slept longer and he would have the chance to get away. Apparently, his plan had worked like a charm. Jo was dead to the world, and Nicholas found it odd that the realization saddened him rather than satisfied him. But then he supposed that while he knew this was the best thing he could do for her, it didn't mean he had to be happy about having to do it.

Sighing, Nicholas bent to brush the hair away from her cheek. She was smiling in her sleep, but he wasn't surprised. He'd allowed her to think all would be well and that when they woke up, they would head out, find Carol, and ask her about what Annie had been going to tell him. Jo was positive that would lead to solving the whole matter of what had happened all those years ago and, hopefully, point to another culprit . . . But that was only because he hadn't told her everything.

Because Annie and Carol were friends, Jo had assumed Carol was an immortal. She wasn't. She had been a mortal coworker, and while she and Annie had been friends, Nicholas doubted his deceased wife would have told the woman anything to do with immortal business. Which meant Carol probably wouldn't know anything, because if he *had* been drugged and someone else had murdered the pregnant woman all those years ago, it had to have been an immortal who did it.

Still, if it had been preying on her mind, he supposed Annie might have let something slip about whatever she'd wanted to tell him. Only it was fifty years later, and Carol would be in her nineties now if she even lived.

Nicholas didn't hold out much hope. He suspected he'd have to try alternate ways to find out what Annie had wanted to tell him back then . . . and Nicholas had no intention of dragging Jo around while he did it. She had family, friends, school, her job, and a life to live, and he had nothing to offer her but running and hiding and the dangers that entailed. Playing investigator was going to be a lot more risky than just life on the run. He'd spent the last fifty-plus years always moving, never staying in one place for long. But to try to find out what Annie had been thinking of would mean staying in Toronto, and he wouldn't be able to prevent leaving a trail for Mortimer and the men to follow. His biggest fear was of Jo getting herself hurt or killed trying to save him should the enforcers catch up to them.

He wouldn't risk that.

Nicholas straightened with a sigh and turned away from the bed. It was better this way, he told himself as he slipped out of the room. He paused in the living room to check the phone there, but it was dead. While Sam hadn't sublet the apartment, she apparently had canceled the phone and cable. The water and electricity were obviously included in the rent, because they were both still on.

He set the phone back in its rest and left the apartment to take the stairs down to the main floor lobby. It was empty when Nicholas first entered, but he only had to wait a moment before a young woman entered and moved toward the buzzers in the entry. Nicholas slipped into the woman's thoughts, bringing her to a halt. He took a moment to search her thoughts and be sure she had a cell phone and then turned her toward the door as he moved forward to open it for her.

Nicholas let her in, urged her to a pair of seats in the lobby, had her take her phone out and then sit while he quickly punched in the number for the enforcer house. He placed the phone to his ear, grimacing when a woman's voice answered.

"Sam?" he asked reluctantly. It was the same woman who had answered the phone when he'd called from outside the veterinary clinic, and he knew Jo's sister lived at the house with Mortimer. When she answered yes in a surprised voice, he cleared his throat and said, "I need to speak to Mortimer."

There was a pause and then she asked politely, "Who shall I say is calling, please?"

"Just put Mortimer on, Sam," he said quietly.

"Nicholas?" she asked sharply. "I recognize your voice from the last time you called. Mortimer told me it was you after he hung up."

Great, Nicholas thought dryly.

"Where's my sister?" she asked, her voice grim.

"If you give Mortimer the phone I'll tell him where she is so he can come get her," he said patiently.

"Is she okay?" Her voice was worried now, and Nicholas rolled his eyes, wishing someone else had answered the phone.

"She's fine, Sam. She's sleeping right now. Please get Mortimer on the phone."

"Mortimer said she's your life mate." It wasn't phrased like a question, but he knew it was one.

"Yes, Sam. Jo is my life mate," Nicholas said apologetically and wasn't at all surprised when she cursed. Sighing, he said, "I know it's not quite what you were hoping for when you set out to find your sister a life mate."

"You're damned right it isn't," Sam snapped. "You're rogue."

"Yeah, well, no one's perfect," he muttered under his breath.

"Ha ha," she said coldly. "Put her on the phone."

"Sam," he said, growing a little impatient now. "I'm trying to get her back to you where she'll be safe. If you'd get Mortimer I'll tell him where she is and he can send Bricker and Anders to come get her. So put him on the goddamned phone and—"

"Nicholas?"

He paused abruptly at the male voice. "Mortimer?"

"Yeah. Who's M. Johansen?"

"What?" he asked with bewilderment.

"The name on call display," Mortimer explained. "M. Johansen."

"Oh." Nicholas grimaced, his gaze dropping to Ms. Johansen, who sat blank-faced on the chair before him. "Just a kindly visitor of an ex-neighbor of Sam's who loaned me her phone. Jo's at Sam's old apartment. Come and get her. And this time, keep her safe."

Jo was up before she woke up. In fact, that was what woke her, her body sitting up and climbing out of bed. Startled awake by the activity, she blinked her eyes open and glanced wildly around, confused even as to where she was at first. It took only a moment to recognize that she was in the bedroom of Sam's apartment. It took another moment to spot and recognize the man standing by the bedroom door, and apparently controlling her, Jo realized as her body straightened beside the bed.

Bad-Breath Boy, Ernie.

"It's not my fault," he snarled, managing to sound both angry and petulant at the same time. "It's because of the blood. We have to have it but it gives us bad breath."

He was in her thoughts and had heard her nickname for him, Jo realized. Apparently, it had pricked his ego. She knew she was still half asleep when her only thought was that his excuse didn't carry much weight since Nicholas didn't have bad breath and that perhaps Ernie should consider brushing his teeth. As first thoughts went in this situation, it was rather inane, she acknowledged.

"Yes, it is," Bad-Breath Boy Ernie growled unpleasantly, and then added, "And why should I brush my teeth? The nanos keep me from getting cavities."

Well, that pretty much said it all, Jo supposed, and was amazed when she was able to ask, "Where is Nicholas?"

She wasn't completely under his control, she realized as she waited for his answer and began to try to move. Jo was able to wrinkle her nose, lift and lower her eyebrows, and move her mouth. But that was it. Everything from her neck down appeared to be under his control. It was not a pleasant sensation. In fact, it made her feel terribly vulnerable.

"You *are* vulnerable," Ernie said suddenly, making her realize he was still in her head. "At least you know it. Most mortals walk around completely oblivious to the fact that superior beings walk the earth who can make them do anything they want at any time."

Jo felt the sneer that claimed her lips at those words. "Superior? That's what you think it is to make me stand here naked? It seems more perverted than superior to me."

He gave a harsh laugh at that. "Don't flatter yourself. I'm old enough that sex holds no interest. You're nothing but a walking blood bag to me."

A quiver of fear ran up Jo's back at those words. While Nicholas had bitten her twice now, she suspected his bite and this man's would be two entirely different things, and she was pretty sure she wouldn't enjoy Bad-Breath Boy's bite.

"You didn't answer my question," Jo said, trying to change the direction of his thoughts. "Where is Nicholas? What have you done with him?"

Ernie stared at her resentfully for a moment and then moved out of her line of vision as he said, "I haven't done anything to him. He left."

"Left?" she squawked with disbelief, trying to see what he was doing. Jo could hear rustling and walking, but couldn't turn her head to see what he was up to.

"Yes, left," Ernie said with irritation. "Believe me, I'm not pleased either. I was intending to surprise you while you were sleeping and capture you both. Nicholas blew that plan all to hell. As I was about to slip out of the stairwell, he came sauntering out of the apartment. Fortunately, he took the stairs at the opposite end of the hall. I followed." Ernie came back around the bed into her line of vision, his eyes scanning the room. "I thought he'd be heading to the van, but he went to the lobby, borrowed a phone from a woman there, and called Mortimer to come and get you. Then he went to the parking garage and drove out of here."

"You're lying," Jo snapped, but was afraid he wasn't. It was just the dumb, stupid, caring kind of thing the big idiot would do. Have Mortimer come and get her thinking she'd be safer at the enforcer house. Men were such boobs sometimes, she thought with disgust, and then noted the odd way Ernie was looking at her and supposed he was still reading her thoughts and had heard all that. She couldn't tell what he made of it.

Rather than comment, Ernie simply said, "I decided it was too risky to jump him and came up to get you instead. It's not as good as both of you, but I think Father will still be pleased."

"Your father," Jo said frowning. "What would your father want with me?"

"You're Nicholas's life mate," Ernie said, and actually sounded resentful. "And Nicholas is the reason five of my brothers were killed. My father will consider you a worthy gift. And then he'll realize that I am as good as my brothers," Ernie said grimly and moved back out of her line of vision as he gloated, "None of them were able to locate the new enforcer house. None of them have even tried since Basha convinced him to lay low for a while. I'm the only one who knows where it is and when I bring him its whereabouts and Nicholas Argeneau's life mate, he'll realize that just because I'm immortal instead of no-fanger doesn't mean I'm inferior."

Jo stared at Ernie as he came around in front of her and she could see him again. He wasn't bad-looking, or wouldn't be if he showered and maybe fixed himself up a bit, but the man looked like he did everything he could to make himself look as bad as possible. He also made absolutely no sense to her. She had no idea who this Basha was, or what he meant when he said he was immortal instead of no-fanger. What the hell was a no-fanger? All she'd gotten out of that little speech was that Ernie seemed to be jealous of his brothers and felt his father appreciated them more than him and planned to deliver her to him in the hopes of earning his approval. Great, she thought unhappily.

"Where are your clothes?" Ernie asked suddenly, sounding irritated. "We have to get out of here before Mortimer shows up but I can't find your damned clothes to make you dress."

"They're in the wash," Jo answered at once. She was not averse to the idea of not having to stand around naked any longer.

"In the wash?" he asked, and actually looked amazed. As she'd suspected, laundering his clothes obviously wasn't something he bothered with often. He probably wore his clothes until they fell off. His top was covered with stains, no doubt from being a messy eater. She'd had a friend like that once who always seemed to wear the day's meals on her clothes like a walking menu. There appeared to be only one dish on Bad-Breath Boy's menu, blood. She was sure that's what all the stains were.

"If they're in the wash they'll be wet," Ernie said with irritation.

"Yes, well, that's my problem, isn't it," Jo said dryly.

Ernie sighed with exasperation and gestured a hand toward the door. "Well, lead the way then. I can't take you to my father like this. I may not be interested in sex, but not all my brothers are past that stage yet, and taking you like that would be seen as an invitation. They'd tear you to pieces before I could tell Father who you are."

Jo managed not to wince at his words, but merely

said, "You have to release me if you want me to—" Her voice died when her knees suddenly went weak and she nearly collapsed on the bedroom carpet. She had been released. Catching herself, she sighed and headed for the door to the hall.

Jo considered making a run for it the minute she reached the door, but had barely had the thought when Ernie was suddenly in front of her, barring the door.

"Don't waste my time with escape attempts. I'm inside your mind, reading your thoughts as soon as you have them. Any little plan you come up with, I'll know the moment it's hatched and I can take control of you again in a heartbeat. So do what you're told like a good little cow and don't strain my patience."

Jo stared at him wide-eyed, knowing that everything he'd said was true. There simply was no escape for her. He was privy to every thought she had, and even if an opportunity for escape did suddenly arise, he could take control of her before she'd got one step away from him. She was a goner.

"Good. Now that you have a grasp of the situation, get your clothes and get dressed, or I will take you as you are and let my brothers do what they will."

When Jo swallowed and nodded, he stepped out of the way. She immediately moved into the hall to the end closet. She opened it to reveal the stacked washer and dryer inside and started to reach for the washer door before noting that the dryer was humming. It was on, she realized, staring blankly at the empty washer, and then slammed that door and reached for the dryer door instead.

The moment Jo opened the dryer door, her borrowed T-shirt fell out. It was dry, she noted, and realized that Nicholas must have thrown the clothes in the dryer for her when he'd gotten up, probably before he'd even dressed to leave. She was amazed he'd even thought of it, and the consideration it showed made her swallow as she quickly tugged the T-shirt on. Jo then reached in to grab the jeans and panties still inside. Like the T-shirt, the panties were dry, however, the jeans were still a bit damp. But then, Jo supposed at this point catching a chill from wearing damp jeans was the least of her worries and she pulled them on without hesitation.

"Good," Ernie said as she quickly did them up. "Now let's go. I don't want to be here when Mortimer arrives."

Jo turned with resignation and started up the hall, trying very hard not to think at all. Not just about possible ways to escape, but about anything at all. It was terribly uncomfortable knowing someone could hear your every thought, and she had no desire to share any thoughts with this man.

They went down the stairs rather than the elevator, Jo leading the way. On the main floor, he had her take the side exit and then walked her to a car in the visitor parking area. Jo glanced around as they crossed the short distance, hoping to see Nicholas or Mortimer or just *anyone*, but it was early enough that there was no one.

"How did you find us here?" she asked, once they were both in the car.

"I was in the parking garage at the hotel when you

came out. Your dog sensed me," Ernie added grimly as he started the engine. "Fortunately, I'd stopped to feed on a guest and was in their car when the two of you came out. I simply followed you. Nicholas was looking for SUVs on his tail. He didn't notice the car."

"How did you know we were at the hotel?" Jo asked quietly as he steered them out of the parking lot. She was pretty sure he couldn't have been tracking her bank card as Mortimer and the others had.

"Gina," Ernie answered, sending a chill down her back. "I was the one who came to the door while she was talking to you. I read her mind, saw she was on the phone with you, and instructed her to ask where you were."

"But I didn't tell her," Jo said at once.

"No, I know. So I had to punch in the code for last call return when you hung up. The reception desk at the hotel answered."

"And Gina?" she asked quietly.

"Safe and oblivious in her apartment." Ernie glanced to her briefly, his lips twisted as he added, "I was hungry, but I wanted to get to the hotel so I simply wiped her mind and left. That's why I was feeding in the parking garage."

Jo sighed to herself and sank back in her seat. It appeared that when it came to being on the run, she was a dud. She'd led the enforcers to them by using her bank card, and led Ernie to them by calling Gina. The position she was presently in was all her own fault. She was just glad Nicholas had left and Ernie hadn't caught them while passed out after one of their lovemaking sessions, or she'd be sitting there suffering all kinds of guilt rather than just terror.

Her thoughts drifted to Nicholas, and Jo hoped he wouldn't take her death too badly, but worried he'd blame himself for leaving her there alone. It didn't really seem fair. He'd spent fifty years feeling guilt over a murder she was pretty sure he hadn't committed, and she suspected would now flagellate himself over her death as well when that wasn't his fault either. She wished she could talk to him and tell him that.

Jo wished she could tell Nicholas what he meant to her too. He'd told her he loved her and she'd simply stared at him like a dummy. She wished she had that moment back again for a do-over. This time she'd tell him she loved him too, because Jo was pretty sure she did. It was funny how knowing your death was looming could clarify things like that. She loved her sisters and had many good friends, but if given a chance to spend ten minutes or even one minute with anyone in the world before she died, Jo knew she would choose Nicholas. Just to be near him and inhale his scent and feel his arms around her one more time would make accepting death easier. Jo supposed she should be grateful that she'd gotten to meet and enjoy knowing him before she died, but she wanted more. She—

"Dear God, if you're going to go getting all weepy and maudlin on me, I'm going to put you to sleep. I'm not listening to this crap the entire way."

"Then put me to sleep," Jo said through her teeth, and the last word had barely left her lips when she felt darkness dropping over her.

Chapter Fifteen

Jo was moving before she was awake again. It was a horrible way to wake up, disorienting and scary, she decided as she opened her eyes to find herself crossing what appeared to be a motel parking lot. Her gaze slid quickly around, noting the neat walkway, the pretty plants hanging from the awning that ran along the motel, and the number six on the door she was approaching. When a hand reached past her to open the door, Jo's eyes followed it up an arm, shoulder, and neck to Ernie's face.

It seemed they'd arrived. Jo sucked in a deep breath as the door opened, trying to prepare herself for what was to come, and then her body moved forward. Her mouth was dry, and her heart was pounding with fear as she peered a bit frantically around the room she was entering. She was looking for Ernie's father, the man who would no doubt kill her as payment for Nicholas's assistance in capturing his sons. There was no man, however, just a young woman asleep on one of the two queen-sized beds in the room.

Jo heard the door close as her body came to a halt in front of the occupied bed, but couldn't see it, so looked at what she could see, the woman. The female appeared to be in her early twenties like Jo, but that was where any resemblance ended. She had short, spiky black hair, was heroin-addict thin, had a small tattoo of a bat under the outside of her left eye, and had multiple piercings in her ears, one through one eyebrow, and a ring through her nose. She wore skin-tight, black leather pants and a black fishnet top over a lacy black bra. She looked . . . interesting.

"Where's your father?" Jo asked quietly as Ernie moved into view, approaching the bed.

"Several days' drive south of here," he said shortly and then added, "We'll head out after I've caught some sleep. I've been up for two days watching the apartment. I'm too tired to start a long drive right now."

"Two days?" Jo asked with amazement. She'd thought it had been only one night, but then recalled how many times she and Nicholas had made love and that they'd passed out and slept between each and realized it could have been two days. No wonder she was starved. They'd taken breaks a couple times to eat up the rest of the pizza, and Jo had found some canned soups left behind that she'd warmed up for them at one point . . .

Yes, it definitely could have been two days, she thought now and then wondered about the defensive tone of Ernie's voice as he'd spoken. It was as if he thought he had to make an excuse for not heading out right away and she might think less of him for having to sleep. She had no idea why he'd care what she thought.

"I *don't* care," he snapped and then kicked the bed, making it shake violently. Jo presumed it was an effort to wake the girl in the bed, but if so, it failed. The girl moaned, but didn't wake up.

"Goddammit, Dee, wake up," Ernie snarled, bending over the bed to slap her violently across the face. The crack of sound in the room was loud enough that Jo winced in sympathy, but it worked. The girl woke up. She seemed sluggish and a bit out of it, however, and Jo wondered if her lack of body weight really was a result of heroin addiction. The woman Ernie had called Dee moaned in protest as she opened her eyes, a moan that died when she spotted the man bent over her.

"Ernie?" Dee sat up slowly, relief covering her face. "You were gone so long, three days, I thought you'd left me."

"I told you I'd be back," he growled with disgust. As reassurances went, Jo thought it was rather poor indeed, but then if what Ernie had said about not having any interest in sex was true, she wasn't his lover. It left Jo wondering just what this Dee was to him.

"She's dinner . . . and my servant," Ernie announced, obviously reading the question in her mind. He glanced to Dee. "Aren't you?"

"Yes, Ernie," she answered almost absently, her eyes full of resentment as they traveled over Jo. Her voice was bitter when she asked, "Who is she? My replacement?"

"She's for my father," Ernie said shortly. "Now get up and make yourself useful. Have you eaten since I left?"

"Yes. Three meals a day as you ordered," she said quickly, slipping her feet off the bed to get up. "And I've been taking the IV blood too. A bag a day even though you weren't here."

"Good, order something else now, I'll be hungry when I wake up and you're no good to me if you're too weak to drive after I feed."

Dee nodded and moved to the phone beside him to begin punching in numbers . . . which told Jo they'd been staying here long enough for the girl to memorize the number of the local delivery places, but she had other things on her mind. Turning on him with disbelief, she asked, "You have her take transfusions and then feed off of her? Why don't you just drink the bagged blood and leave her alone?"

"I don't like cold food," he said, glaring at her. "Be glad I'm not feeding on you."

"Why aren't you?" she asked at once.

"Would you give a dinged-up gift to your father?" he asked dryly.

Jo grimaced. She supposed she should be grateful, but it was hard to be grateful that he wasn't going to hurt her before he handed her over to his father to do what he would.

Ernie glanced to Dee as she placed her order. He frowned as she ordered a calzone with a side salad and then said, "Make sure it's enough for two." When the girl glanced at him in question, his eyes narrowed. "Don't question me, order it. She's eating too."

Jo glanced to him with surprise at the comment. She hadn't expected him to bother.

"Even a condemned prisoner gets a last meal," he muttered. "I'm not an ogre."

"Forgive me," Jo murmured dryly as Dee hung up the phone. "But you're hoping to buy your father's affections like a john buys a prostitute's favors by giving me to him . . . knowing he'll kill me. I just assumed you were a bastard."

Ernie's eyes narrowed, a growl issuing from his throat, and then he suddenly turned and grabbed Dee by the hair at the nape of her neck, yanked her head back, and sank his teeth into her throat with a violence that made Dee cry out in pain.

Jo tried to turn guiltily away, knowing the woman's unnecessary suffering was her fault for angering Ernie, but he'd taken control of her body again and she couldn't move. Her eyes wouldn't close either when she tried. He wanted her to watch what she'd brought about and she gave in with resignation, knowing it was little more than she deserved for angering him and causing it in the first place. It seemed since he didn't want to take a "dinged-up gift" to his father, Dee was going to pay for any temper she stirred in him.

Ernie removed his teeth and whirled to glare at Jo. "This time," he snarled, blood coating his teeth and rimming his mouth. "She paid for you this time. But bear in mind that my father doesn't know about his gift, and I can always drain you dry and go after

Nicholas or one of the other girls to give to Father should you push me too far."

Jo's gaze slid to Dee. Ernie was still holding her head back by the hair at what appeared to be a painful angle. It left her wound exposed, and Jo swallowed as she peered at the ragged, angry-looking bite mark. In his anger, he hadn't just punctured her neck, he'd torn it somewhat, and the two wounds were seeping blood.

Ernie glanced back to Dee and released her abruptly, snapping, "Take care of your neck."

Dee stumbled a couple of steps and then caught herself and moved into the bathroom. The moment the door closed behind her, Ernie turned back to Jo, and she found herself walking to the small two-person table and chairs beside the bed. She heard a drawer open and close behind her, and when her body sat down in the chair in the corner without her input, Ernie was walking toward her, rope in hand.

"Just so you don't get any ideas about trying to escape while I sleep," he commented, moving behind her chair, and jerking her arms back painfully to tie her wrists together. "I'm afraid if you did try to escape, Dee would probably club you over the head and kill you. She doesn't like you," he confided, seeming amused.

Jo didn't have to ask how he knew that. She supposed he'd read it in Dee's thoughts, and said through gritted teeth, "She doesn't know me."

"She's jealous," he said with amusement as he jerked on the rope, tightening it painfully around her wrists. "She wants me to turn her and she's afraid you might be a threat to that."

"So tell her I'm not a threat," Jo suggested as he finished with her wrists and moved to work on her ankles, binding them together now as well.

"Why?" Ernie asked, and seemed truly surprised at the suggestion. "I'm her master. I do what I want and she has to accept that whether she likes it or not. As will you." He finished with her ankles and stood to survey her with displeasure. "Nicholas should have made you aware of your status. You are inferior. We feed on you, milking you like the cows you are. We can control you, make you do anything we want. We are faster, smarter, stronger . . . we *are* superior."

"If you're so superior, why do you run around with greasy hair and in filthy clothes?" she asked dryly.

"Because I can," he said coldly. "I do what I want."

Jo stared at him, the thought running through her mind that she was in the hands of a very dangerous, snot-nosed, spoiled, petulant, little pissant. She supposed she shouldn't have been surprised at the fury that suddenly covered his face. But after a lifetime where her thoughts had always been her own and private, it was hard to remember that this was no longer true and he could read her mind. When his hands balled into fists and one raised, Jo steeled herself for the blow about to come, wondering if she would make it to Ernie's father or die here in this room. A moment passed, but no blow fell, and Jo opened her eyes warily to find the hand back at his side and relaxed. The man was even smiling.

"I'm not going to kill you," he said calmly. "I'll leave that to my father."

Jo forced the tension from her muscles and merely peered at him, thinking it really made no difference. Here now, or later at his father's hands. It was all the same. Dead was dead.

"Oh no, it's not the same," Ernie assured her solemnly, picking up on her thoughts. "My killing you would be a mercy. My father will cut you to pieces as slowly and painfully as he can. He's a no-fanger."

"You say that like I should know what it is," she said with false indifference.

"Don't you?" he asked with surprise.

Jo shook her head.

Ernie frowned, and then apparently deciding she wouldn't be sufficiently scared if she didn't know what she was in for, he explained, "No-fangers are immortals without fangs, a result of the first trials with nanos. One in three don't survive the turn and those who do . . . well." He smiled cruelly. "Half of them come up mad and mean and completely unfeeling. They keep mortals like the cattle they are and slice and dice them whenever they want a meal."

"And your father is one?" Jo asked slowly.

"Oh yes. He's the oldest no-fanger known to be alive." Ernie said with what sounded like pride and not a little glee, and then added, "And the older they are, the more powerful and cruel they are."

Jo considered that and then tilted her head and asked, "But you're not a no-fanger?"

"No," he muttered, some of his glee waning.

"Why not?" she asked. "If your father is no-fanger, surely you—"

"My mother was immortal."

"So if the mother is immortal and the father is no-fanger, the baby can come out immortal or no-fanger?" she asked curiously.

"The baby will *always* come out whatever the mother is," he said with disgust. "The father only ever passes the sperm. The blood makes the baby. If the mother's immortal, the baby's immortal, if the mother is no-fanger, the baby is no-fanger. My mother was immortal, so I was too," he muttered.

"You don't sound too happy about that," she pointed out quietly.

Ernie shrugged, but then scowled and said, "Why should I be? Most immortals are weak and soft-hearted like Lucian and his gang. They protect mortals rather than farm them as we should. They give us all a bad name," he added with disgust.

The bathroom door opened then and Dee came back out. Jo tried to twist in her seat to see her, but Ernie hardly glanced her way, merely turning on his heel and moving to the bed.

"Feed her when the food comes," he ordered, dropping to lie on the bed. "And make sure she doesn't get away. Wake me when night falls."

Ernie closed his eyes and completely relaxed, seeming to drop off to sleep at once, and then Dee moved into view beside Jo. The girl was looking toward Ernie, watching as his breathing became slow and steady, but Jo was looking at the girl's throat. All there was to see was a large, neat bandage covering the wound on her neck, and then the girl turned to look at her. If Ernie hadn't already told her Dee didn't like her, the look she gave Jo then would have told her so. Dee's eyes were lasers of hatred, slicing her to ribbons.

"He's mine," Dee hissed, glaring at her.

"You're welcome to him," Jo said solemnly, keeping her voice low. "In fact, if you want to untie me, I'll happily get out of here."

Dee hesitated, and Jo felt a moment's hope, and then Dee glanced to Ernie. Jo did as well, her heart sinking when she saw that his eyes were open and focused on them.

"If she escapes, you die, Dee," he said calmly, and then closed his eyes again.

Dee's breath hissed out and she scowled at Jo and then moved to the dresser, opened the top drawer, and retrieved something. It wasn't until she turned and headed back to the table that Jo saw it was a gun. She watched the other woman drop into the seat across from her and set the gun on the table. Jo stared at what to her appeared to be a very large gun barrel pointing in her direction, and then glanced to Dee and asked, "Yours?"

"Mine now," Dee said defiantly, and picked it back up to examine it briefly as she said, "We got it off a cop on the way out of Texas. He stopped us for speeding."

"You don't sound like you're from Texas," Jo said quietly.

"I'm not. I'm from here." She set the gun down again. "We were just passing through Texas on the way back to Canada."

"And the policeman you took the gun from?" Jo asked.

"He won't need it anymore," Dee said with a shrug, and then added defiantly, "He was an arrogant prick anyway. He shouldn't have insulted Ernie."

"Right," Jo said on a sigh, trying not to imagine some poor police officer stopping a car on a lonely road at night, never knowing it would be the last car he'd stop. Forcing the image away, she asked, "So how did you end up traveling through Texas with Ernie if you're from here?"

"His father took me south," she muttered.

Jo felt herself tense. Ernie's father was who she was being taken to, and it did seem smart to learn all she could about him. "Why did he take you south? What's he like?"

"He's crazy mean," Dee said quietly, beginning to rotate the gun slowly on the table. "He and a couple of his sons showed up at our farm earlier in the summer."

Jo blinked in surprise, not at the news that Ernie's father and his brothers had shown up at Dee's farm, but that she actually came from a farm. With her piercings and dress, Jo would have guessed she was a city girl.

"They came in the middle of the night, killed my father, kept cutting and feeding on my mother, sisters, and me for a couple days, and then they killed my mother and two of my sisters and took my younger sister and me and headed south. They fed on just the two of us on the journey, occasionally dragging in another person to feed on. Usually a girl. They seem to prefer girls, but then probably because they didn't always just use us to feed on. Ernie's father mostly left us alone except to bleed us, but his brothers . . ." She swallowed and shuddered. "They liked to do other things too."

Jo didn't need her to spell out what those other things were. Ernie had said some of his brothers weren't past the sex stage. She could figure it out. "I'm sorry," she said quietly. "It must have been awful."

"It was," she said in a vulnerable voice that made her seem much younger than Jo had at first thought she was, and then she suddenly straightened and sounded much stronger as she said, "But then we got to Ernie's place."

"Where was that?" Jo asked, but Dee shrugged.

"I was pretty weak the last leg of the trip. I slept a lot when they weren't bothering me. All I know is I'm pretty sure it wasn't America anymore when we stopped. It was hot, the people all spoke gobbledygook, and the signs were all in Mexican or something."

"South America then, probably," Jo murmured. If that's where Ernie's father was it meant a long drive to get there. Days even. She might get an opportunity to escape, she thought, and then glanced up as Dee continued.

"Ernie was nice to me." When Jo's eyebrows rose in surprise at the suggestion, Dee scowled and said, "He was. He'd bite us, but he didn't do those other things."

Afraid the girl would get angry and shut up, Jo smoothed out her expression and nodded quickly.

Dee relaxed a little and continued, her voice grim. "When he said he was heading out on a trip, his father gave me to him 'for the road.' I think he thought Ernie would only get another meal out of me and be dumping me on the side of the road somewhere, but Ernie didn't feed on me. *He* fed *me* and got me healthy again. He took care of me and fed on others like that cop, and only once I was strong again did he start feeding on me again. I'm his now and he looks after me."

"And your sister?" Jo asked quietly.

"She died before we left," Dee said dully.

"I'm sorry," Jo repeated on a sigh. She was silent for a moment, considering what she'd learned, and then asked, "So was Ernie the only brother there who had fangs?"

Dee nodded. "The rest of them had to cut us . . . except Basha."

Something in Dee's voice made Jo peer at her more closely as she asked, "Basha?"

"She's like Ernie, she has fangs," Dee said, her voice sounding admiring. "She's not crazy like the rest of them. Basha's beautiful with this long, gorgeous, icy blond hair and these cold eyes . . . and she's powerful, icy cold and so strong . . . None of the boys mess with her. The second day we were there, one of them said something to anger her, and she threw him through a wall."

Jo frowned as she recognized the hero worship in the other woman's voice. "What did he say?"

"I'm not sure. They were in the next room and he suddenly came crashing through the wall and fell at my feet, and then she stepped through the hole his body left and glared down at him and said, 'Remember to watch your tongue around me or you'll be tongueless as well as fangless.' And then she stormed off." Dee sighed with very definite admiration, and then added, "Even Ernie's father listens to her. She's the one who convinced him to lie low for a while and stay out of Canada until things blew over. Ernie's father really is a cruel bastard," Dee told her, and almost managed to look pityingly on Jo. "He's going to hurt you bad when Ernie gives you to him."

Jo stared at her silently and then sat forward in her seat, ignoring the pain it sent shooting through her arms as she said a little desperately, "You could help me escape. We could both go. I know people who could keep us safe."

"Like they kept Ernie from taking you?" she asked dryly, and shook her head. "Oh no. I'm his. I'm not betraying him and giving him a reason to kill me. I want to be strong and powerful like Basha. I want to be turned, and if I'm loyal he'll turn me," she said with certainty.

Jo sat back wearily and shook her head. "He's not going to turn you, Dee. He sees us both as little more than cattle. He'll use you up for as long as it pleases him and then he will dump you at the side of the road like his father expected."

"No," she said at once, almost desperately. "He took care of me when we left his father. He cares about me."

"Yeah, that bandage on your throat and the way he's treated you since I got here show a whole lot of caring," Jo said grimly.

"He was angry. It was your fault," Dee said at once.

Jo stared at her silently, wondering why Ernie would have bothered nursing the girl back to health. She didn't think for a minute he cared for the girl, but . . . "Who did the driving on the way up here?"

"He did at first, but after the first couple of days when I was feeling better, he slept during the day and I drove, and then I slept at night and he drove," she said proudly. "He trusted me."

"He *needed* you," Jo corrected firmly. "Feeding you a couple of meals and not raping you was enough to get you to feel so grateful you took over the day driving. It cut the journey in half for him."

Dee merely glared at her.

"Why didn't he fly?" Jo asked abruptly.

"What?" Dee asked with confusion.

"Why did he drive all the way here rather than fly? He could have saved himself a lot of time," she pointed out.

"He doesn't like flying," Dee said coldly, and then added almost reluctantly, "His father and brothers teased him about that, said it was another sign of his inferiority, that a no-fanger wouldn't be afraid of flying. But they're the ones who are inferior. They don't have fangs and have to cut to feed, and Basha has fangs and she's the smartest and strongest of all of them."

Jo was silent for a minute. The girl definitely had a hang-up about this Basha woman. Sighing, she leaned forward and tried again to reason with her, "You're fooling yourself if you think he's going to turn you, Dee. You aren't going to be like Basha.

You're just as dead as I am when we get back there. Once we're there, he won't need you to drive anymore and he'll hand you off to his brothers to finish what they started on the first journey down south."

"Shut up," Dee snarled, her hand tightening on the gun and raising it just as a knock sounded at the door.

"The food's here," Jo murmured, eyeing Dee warily. The girl was obviously unstable after all she'd been through, which was to be expected. Unfortunately, Jo didn't think she was going to be able to help her see that there was no future for her with Ernie. At least not before it was too late. Dee seemed to be so grateful that he'd let her live and wasn't raping her that she saw his cold, heartless treatment of her as some sort of caring . . . and that was going to get her killed. The question was whether Jo would be there with her when it happened . . . or die here in this room, she thought as Dee stared at her, the gun pointed at her chest and quavering slightly.

"The food," Jo said again, her stomach beginning to churn with tension as she considered her death might be imminent after all.

Dee cursed under her breath and stood up, slipping the gun into the waistband at the back of her leather pants as she moved to the door. She then pulled a wad of cash out of her back pocket with one hand as she opened the door with the other. The moment Dee started to open it, the door crashed open, slamming into her and knocking her backward.

Jo sucked in a quick breath as Dee tumbled back over the chair, relief like she'd never known slamming through her as Nicholas stepped into the room. He wore the clothes she'd last seen him in, but now had a long jacket over them. She understood the reason for the long coat when he pulled a crossbow from under it as he took in the scene. His gaze found her, flickered with relief, then slid to Dee sitting up on the floor next to the table, peering at him blankly, and finally to Ernie rearing up on the bed. He aimed at Ernie and pulled the trigger.

Jo never saw the arrow hit Ernie, her gaze was already swinging to Dee as she released a cry of animal pain and pulled out the gun she'd tucked in her jeans.

Jo didn't think in that moment, she merely reacted. Her ankles were bound, her wrists tied behind her back, so she did the only thing she could do. Screaming "No," she did her best imitation of a dolphin leaping out of the water and threw herself out of the chair at Dee. She soared through the air to land on the other woman—and the gun—as it went off.

The impact of the shot was like a punch, and Jo gasped for air that suddenly seemed absent. She was vaguely aware of Nicholas shouting her name and then he was there, lifting her away from Dee. He gathered her in his arms, his face panicked as he peered over her.

"Jo. Jesus, you're hit," he muttered, standing to carry her to the bed.

"Dee," she gasped anxiously, afraid the girl would shoot him in the back.

Nicholas paused to whirl back, just in time for both of them to see the girl flee the room. Nicholas growled deep in his throat as she disappeared through the still-open door, but didn't try to stop her. Instead, he turned back to continue on to the bed.

"The gun," Jo breathed as he set her down next to the prone Ernie. "She could come back."

"The gun's empty," Nicholas growled, and she supposed he'd read that information from Dee's mind.

Jo glanced down as he jerked up her shirt to get a look at her wound, and silently echoed the voluble curse that he issued. It was bad. She was no doctor, but it was real bad. The hole itself wasn't that big on this side, but blood was gushing out of it like a water hose at half pressure. That didn't seem good to her.

"Hungry?" she asked with a forced smile.

The look Nicholas turned on her should have singed her eyebrows off.

"Sorry," Jo muttered, and then closed her eyes as he turned and rushed into the bathroom. She supposed it *had* been a poor attempt at humor, but really, she wasn't feeling well. Actually, that was kind of an understatement. She felt horrible. It was getting harder to breathe, and she was growing weak.

"Stay with me, Jo."

She forced her eyes open at that growl to see that Nicholas had grabbed a towel from the bathroom and was pressing it down on her chest. Jo watched him, thinking that it should probably hurt, but it didn't. That probably wasn't good either, she thought a little hazily, and peered at his face. He looked frantic, but his eyes were flaming silver as they did when they made love and she mumbled, "Your mood eyes are reading horny again."

"What?" He peered at her face with confusion and then frowned at whatever he saw there. Taking one hand off her chest, he reached for her face, his eyes burning into hers as he touched her cheek and said harshly, "You have to stay with me, Jo."

"I'm here," Jo mumbled, and then opened her eyes and said, "I love you." She didn't know where that had come from. She hadn't planned on saying it, but knew it was true. She did love the big lug. He was handsome, and smart, and so built . . . and he had more honor in his pinky finger than most men had in their whole body. Nicholas had been born to help people, to save them, as he had saved her over and over. Jo was certain of that. She was also certain she wasn't going to be around to help him with it, which was a shame, because she really wished she could be.

Jo wished a lot of things, that she could help him solve the mystery of the past so he could stop running and settle down to enjoy life, preferably with her. She wished they could have a life together full of love and squabbles and making up. She wished she could have his babies and . . .

Jo closed her eyes wearily, but forced them open again to get one more look at him, because as the darkness crept up the sides of her vision, she knew she would have none of what she wished for.

"Jo?" Nicholas said anxiously when she closed her eyes again. He reached up to slap her face lightly and then shook her a bit in an effort to wake her up, but it wasn't working.

Cursing, he glanced around wildly and then back

to her chest wound. He had been trying to stanch the blood, but it still seeped out around his fingers, and he cursed with frustration, wishing she was immortal. The nanos would stop the bleeding at once if she had any, he thought, and then froze as his mind suddenly cleared.

He had to turn her. It was that simple. The moment the thought struck his brain, Nicholas raised his wrist to his mouth, bit in, tearing away a flap of skin, and then forced Jo's mouth open and placed his wrist over it. He watched silently as his blood gushed over her lips, instinctively lifting her head up with his other arm so that the blood would run down her throat. When the bleeding slowed and then stopped, he eased her back onto the bed and ripped open another patch of skin on the same arm. This one he let bleed into her wound until it too slowed and stopped.

Nicholas glanced to her face then, holding his breath as he waited for some sign that he hadn't been too late. He knew he should have turned her right away rather than trying to stop her bleeding, but he hadn't exactly been thinking clearly. In truth, he hadn't been thinking clearly from the moment he'd seen Ernie pass him in a car and realized it was Jo in the passenger seat beside him.

Nicholas's gaze slid to Ernie. The man was as still as death, the arrow protruding from his heart ensuring he wouldn't be getting up again. At least not until the arrow was removed. Of course, the female who had escaped was a problem that would have to be dealt with later . . . preferably by someone else. If he was left to deal with it, Nicholas would probably wring the little bitch's neck for shooting Jo, and he didn't care that she'd actually been aiming at him and Jo had thrown herself on the weapon.

Jo moaned, and Nicholas leaned eagerly closer, watching her face.

A second moan came from Jo as she turned her head weakly. He closed his eyes and whispered, "Thank you, God," as he realized she was turning. He hadn't been too late.

His eyes opened again on the third moan, however, and Nicholas frowned with a new worry. The turning was excruciating to both the body and mind. It was known to bring on nightmares and hallucinations so horrible that turnees could be driven mad by it. Nicholas wasn't willing to risk it. There were drugs and tricks to help her through it, and he was going to make damned sure she got them.

Standing abruptly, he glanced around the room and then back to Jo and finally to Ernie. He wanted to leave the rogue behind, but couldn't risk that the mortal girl who had shot Jo might not return, remove the arrow presently incapacitating Ernie, and help him escape. Turning, he headed out of the room, pulling the door not quite closed so that it wouldn't lock behind him. He then quickly crossed the parking lot to his van, jumped in, started it up, and moved it over to back it up to the motel room door.

Back inside the room, he took a moment to tug Jo's T-shirt back down, untie her, tie up Ernie with those ropes, and then make sure the arrow was still planted firmly in his chest. Nicholas then carted Ernie out to the van. He tossed him inside, satisfied by the thud of his body hitting the metal floor, and then hurried back inside to collect Jo as well. He started to pick her up, but paused as he noted the bloodstain on her shirt from the gunshot wound. He planned to set her in the front seat, and the bloodstain would draw more attention than he wanted to deal with at that moment.

Nicholas set her back, glanced around, and then moved to grab a leather jacket that lay over the back of one of the chairs at the table in the room. The female's, he supposed as he grabbed it up. It would do. Moving back to Jo, he laid it over her chest, and then scooped her up and carried her to the door.

Nicholas stepped out of the room just in time to catch Dee creeping into the back of the van. He didn't even slow, but took control of her, made her finish climbing inside and seat herself against the wall as he climbed in himself.

Kneeling in the back of the van, Nicholas shifted Jo to rest across his knees and quickly pulled the doors closed. He then scooped her up and moved to the front of the van in a crouch. Nicholas set Jo in the passenger seat, strapping her in with the seat belt, and then got behind the wheel and started the engine before reaching for his cell phone. He'd felt two pockets before recalling he didn't have one anymore.

Cursing, Nicholas closed his eyes briefly and then opened them with a start when someone knocked at the driver's side window. Turning his head, he peered out and saw a good-sized man in his early fifties standing there, a frown on his face. Nicholas unrolled the window.

"Everything all right there, friend? Your lady doesn't look so good. Does she need help?" the man asked in a bluff voice full of both concern and suspicion.

Nicholas glanced to Jo, noting her pale, unconscious face, but the jacket was still in place, held there by the seat belt and hiding the bloodstain on her chest. He turned to peer at the man, his gaze sliding past him to the anxious woman standing nervously on the other side of the car now parked beside the van. They must have pulled up while he was strapping Jo in, Nicholas thought, and then shifted his gaze back to the man at the window.

"Do you have a cell phone?" he asked.

The man blinked. "What?"

Too impatient to be polite, Nicholas slipped into his mind and took control. The man immediately reached into his pocket and handed over a phone.

"Thanks," Nicholas murmured, and quickly punched in the number to the enforcer house. Much to his relief, it was Mortimer who answered this time. Nicholas got right to the point. "I'm bringing Jo in. She—"

"You're *bringing* her in?" Mortimer interrupted with disbelief.

"Yes. She's starting the turn. You'll need whatever it is they've come up with to help her through it."

"You know we won't let you leave," Mortimer warned quietly.

"I know," he said grimly, his gaze sliding past the blank-faced man at his window to see that the wife was starting to look concerned. She couldn't see her husband's face, but apparently suspected something was wrong. He shifted his attention back to the phone and said, "I ask for only one favor. Two, actually."

"What?" Mortimer asked.

"I stay with her until she's through the turn."

"Okay," Mortimer agreed.

"And I get to talk to her once she's awake before I'm taken in for judgment," Nicholas said, and then frowned and changed it to, "I want a night with her before you call Lucian."

There was silence for a minute and then Mortimer said, "Okay. I agree. What—"

"We'll be there in twenty minutes," Nicholas interrupted. "Get on the phone and get what she needs there."

He then slapped the phone closed, handed it back to the man at his window, and took a moment to rearrange his thoughts before touching on the man's wife as well.

Nicholas rolled up the window as the couple turned and moved to the door of their own motel room, and then shifted into gear and steered the van out of the parking lot. Jo moaned for the fourth time as he pulled onto the street. This time she didn't stop.

Chapter Sixteen

Nicholas laid on the horn the moment he could see the woods at the edge of the enforcer property. He didn't take his hand off it until turning into the driveway at the gate.

As he'd hoped, the enforcers guarding the gate took his horn honking as an announcement of his arrival and had the outer gate open as he turned in. They'd kept the inner gate closed as a precaution, but one of the men was at it, and the moment he recognized Nicholas at the wheel, he grabbed the inner gate and began to run, pulling it open as well.

Nicholas roared through both gates and tore up the driveway, taking the turnoff to the roundabout in front of the house. He slammed to a stop before the front door as it opened, and caught a glimpse of Mortimer hurrying out, followed by Bricker and Anders, but then shifted the van into park and leaped out to hurry around the vehicle to the front passenger door.

Mortimer had reached the van and was grabbing

for the door handle as Nicholas got there, but he knocked his hand away with a growl to open it himself. Jo was his. No one else was touching her.

"Ernie and a mortal female named Dee are in the back of the van," Nicholas snapped as he pulled the door open.

"Is this Dee injured?" Mortimer asked with a frown in his voice as he tried to get a look at Jo around Nicholas's shoulder.

"No," he said coldly, undoing the seat belt he'd strapped around Jo. It had managed to keep her in her seat when she'd started to shift and flop about as the pain she was suffering had increased. As the seat belt snapped back into its holder, Nicholas scooped Jo up into his arms, adding bitterly, "She should be hurt, but I didn't have time. I wanted to get Jo here before the turn got too far."

He swung around with her in his arms to see Mortimer's raised eyebrows and bit out, "Her brain's broken, she's on Ernie's side and shot Jo."

"What?"

That high-pitched screech brought his gaze around to a thin, dark-haired woman on the steps. Jo's sister Sam, he guessed. There was a definite resemblance, though the woman was an emaciated version of Jo, all gangling arms and bony legs in the shorts she wore. With a little meat on her, she'd be almost as pretty as his Jo though, Nicholas decided, but then dismissed her from his thoughts and turned to warn Mortimer, "I controlled the mortal all the way here, but released her as I got out of the van. About now, she's probably pulling the arrow out of Ernie's heart."

Mortimer nodded grimly."Bricker, Anders, take them to the cells. We'll deal with them later."

"On it," Bricker said, already moving to open the van door beside them. Once it was open, he peered inside and shook his head. "Nicholas said you'd probably be doing that. Naughty, naughty," he muttered, and then climbed into the back of the van and pulled the door closed as Anders got in the front.

"Sam, honey," Mortimer said, pulling her away from Nicholas as she tried to get a look at Jo. "Let's get her inside and settled in her room, okay?"

"Yes, of course," Sam muttered, and pulled away to bustle back into the house, leading the way.

"After you," Mortimer said quietly, but Nicholas was already following the woman.

"Did you get what she needs?" he asked as he followed Sam up the stairs inside.

"They're on the way," Mortimer assured him, and then raised his voice to be heard over Jo as the jostling made the volume of her moaning increase. "They should have beat you here, but I suspect you were speeding just a little bit."

"Yes," he muttered, pressing Jo a little tighter and peering worriedly at her face. It was now a mask of pain and she was beginning to writhe in his arms. He'd broken a lot of road laws in his determination to get her here quickly, pushing the van to go as fast as it could, running red lights and stop signs and controlling a cop or two to get them off his tail when they'd come after him.

"They'll be here soon," Mortimer said reassuringly as Sam led them into a bedroom. "In the meantime,

I had Bricker bring up rope and we can get her tied down."

"Tied down?" Sam asked with horror, stopping abruptly.

Nicholas moved impatiently around her to get to the bed as Mortimer said soothingly, "It's for her own good, honey. So she doesn't hurt herself."

"Yes, but—"

"Where's the rope," Nicholas snapped as he started to strip Jo's jeans off her. His concern was all for Jo. Mortimer could soothe Sam after they took care of Jo.

Much to his relief, Mortimer was on the other side of the bed almost at once, holding out the rope. Nicholas tossed aside the jeans, but left her T-shirt and the jacket that covered her chest for now as he took the offered rope. They worked together, each taking a wrist, fastening one end of rope to it and then fastening the other end to the metal bed frame, before moving down to do the same with her ankles. The moment they were at the bottom of the bed and out of her way, Sam was beside Jo, pulling away the leather coat that had covered her chest. Nicholas wasn't surprised by her gasp of horror as she saw the hole in Jo's shirt and the blood staining it, but ignored her until he'd finished what he was doing.

"What happened?" she asked with dismay, pulling Jo's shirt up.

"I told you. She was shot," Nicholas growled, straightening and moving back up to the head of the bed. He didn't even glance at the woman on the opposite side of the mattress; his eyes were on the wound in Jo's chest. It was no longer bleeding and looked a little smaller to him, and he supposed the nanos had started repairing it before doing anything else. It meant they'd be using up what little blood she had left to do it though, and they'd be attacking the organs in search of more.

"She needs blood," Mortimer said, his thoughts moving along the same lines as Nicholas's. "I'll get it."

The immortal was out of the room before the last word had left his mouth, moving at speed. A loud thud a heartbeat later told Nicholas Mortimer had probably bypassed the stairs and jumped the hall rail to the main floor below to save time. He'd be back just as quickly, Nicholas knew, and glanced to Sam to see her gaping at the doorway Mortimer had just disappeared through. He raised an eyebrow when she glanced back to him.

"It always startles me to see him move that quickly," she muttered for explanation and then frowned as she peered down at Jo. "What happened to her?"

"I told you, she was shot," he said grimly for the third time. The woman was obviously in shock if she couldn't grasp the concept.

"Yes, but *how*?" she asked with frustration. "Why did the girl shoot her?"

Nicholas settled on the side of the bed, his eyes fixed on Jo's pale, contorted face as he tried to gather his thoughts.

"Here."

He glanced up with surprise to see Mortimer at his side, several bags of blood caught between his arm and his chest, and another in his hand that he was holding out to Nicholas.

"Start her with that, but only give her one. We'll give her the drugs and set up an IV as soon as the delivery gets here with them."

Nicholas nodded, and muttered, "Open her mouth."

He raised the bag of blood to bite off one corner as Sam immediately bent over Jo from the other side to do as he asked so that he could begin to pour the thick, red liquid in.

Nicholas sat back once he'd finished. Jo had calmed a little, the moaning dropping a bit in volume, but not stopping altogether. He supposed the nanos had left her organs alone and were collecting the blood she'd just ingested to do their thing. But he knew this calm wouldn't last long. They'd use the blood to generate more nanos, start spreading out in her body to cover the more important areas like her brain and heart, and then they'd set to work and she'd be in agony until it was done. At least, until the worst of it was done.

"What happened?" Mortimer asked, echoing the question Sam had asked earlier. "You called and said to come get her at Sam's place, but when the men got there she was gone."

Nicholas sighed unhappily and ran one hand through his hair as he balled up the empty blood bag in his other. That seemed like months ago to him, but had been only a matter of a couple hours, if that.

"I called you from the lobby after I left the apartment," he explained, his words and tone short and emotionless. "Then I went to move the van so your boys wouldn't find it. I was walking back, planning to watch the building until your men got there when

Ernie drove past with Jo in the passenger seat. I ran back to the van, jumped in, and followed them to a motel. I parked at the edge of the parking lot while he took her inside and then crept up to the window to listen to see what I was up against. If Leonius or anyone else was inside, I planned to call you, but it didn't take me long to figure out there was only Ernie and a mortal woman inside with Jo and I decided I could handle it on my own."

Nicholas's mouth tightened as he silently berated himself for that decision. He should have called Mortimer at once and gotten some backup. Jo might not have been shot had he done that.

"What happened?" Mortimer repeated.

Grimacing, Nicholas reached out to brush a finger over Jo's cheek. "I wanted to rush in there, but Ernie told the woman to order food for her and Jo, and then said he was going to sleep. I thought it would be better to wait. Ernie would be asleep and the woman would think it was the food delivery. I could take them all by surprise and save the day," he said bitterly, and then ground his teeth and continued, "I waited, I knocked, and as soon as the woman started to open the door, I slammed it into her, and stepped inside. The woman was on the floor, Jo was tied up in a chair, and Ernie just rising up from the bed. I shot Ernie in the heart with my crossbow, heard Jo scream, and turned in time to see . . ." Nicholas paused and took a breath, forcing down the lump that had risen in his throat as he recalled that moment.

"She was tied up," he said with what even he recognized as bewilderment. "Her wrists were tied behind her back, ankles bound together, but she was throwing herself at the mortal. The woman was lifting a gun to aim at me, and Jo—she was trying to save me, for Christ's sake, like a little bullet would hurt me."

Mortimer placed a hand on his shoulder, squeezing in what he supposed was sympathy, and Nicholas finished, "The gun went off as she landed on the mortal."

"So she took a bullet meant for you?" Sam asked, and then added, "Why would that woman even try to shoot you? Did she realize you were there to save them?"

"She didn't want saving," Nicholas said grimly. "She's broken. His pet."

"I'll say she's broken," Bricker said grimly, drawing their attention to the fact that he and Anders had arrived and were crossing the room. "She's a mess, Mortimer. She saw her whole family slaughtered by Leonius and his boys. The father was strung up by his heels from the rafters in the barn the night they stormed the farm. They slit his throat over a pail and then passed the pail around, drinking from it while his whole family watched."

"And that was the kindest thing they did to that family," Anders muttered.

"Christ," Mortimer said on a sigh, moving around to slip his arm around a horrified Sam and draw her against his chest.

"She had a mother and some sisters too," Bricker muttered. "Only she and a younger sister survived to leave the farm. They were raped and fed on by turn until the little sister died. Dee, that's her name," he added, pausing beside the bed to peer down at Jo. "She was pretty near death when Leonius gave her to Ernie to snack on, on the road. He feeds her, hasn't raped her, and bites her rather than cut her up so she's pretty much decided that makes him her hero."

Bricker glanced to Mortimer and added, "She'll need a three-on-one."

"The three-on-one is when three immortals wipe a mortal's mind at once, isn't it?" Sam asked quietly.

Mortimer nodded, but said to Bricker, "That could destroy her mind."

"There's very little of her mind not destroyed," Anders said dryly. "A three-on-one might be her only chance of anything approaching a normal life now. Wipe her as clean as a slate and let her start over if there's anything to start over with."

"I'll suggest it to Lucian," Mortimer murmured, and then glanced to Nicholas. "I presume you turned Jo after she got shot?"

He nodded.

"Did she consent?" Mortimer asked.

"No. She was unconscious . . . and dying. I made the choice for her."

Mortimer nodded, but glanced to Sam. Nicholas suspected the other immortal was wishing he'd been given the chance to do that himself with her. Sam would be immortal now as well which was a safer state for her considering the work Mortimer did. Ernie's getting onto the property and attacking Jo must have driven home how fragile his life mate was as long as she refused the turn.

It must be a sort of hell, for the man, Nicholas

thought. He couldn't imagine having to have suffered that worry for all the months Mortimer had. After only a couple of days of worrying himself sick over Jo, it was a huge relief to know she was now going to be an immortal . . . Even if he wouldn't be with her, at least Nicholas would die knowing she would be well . . . barring a freak accident or murder, he thought grimly, and then glanced to the phone by the bed as it began to ring.

Mortimer answered, listened, and then hung up. "The drugs and IV have arrived. They just passed through the gate."

Jo's first thought as she woke up and opened her eyes was that she felt like she'd been hit by a Mack truck. Her next was to wonder who'd been driving it.

"Jo."

Her name was a soft, relieved sigh, and she turned her head and managed a smile as she found herself peering at Nicholas. He'd been sitting in a chair beside the bed, but now stood to bend over her, and he looked like he hadn't slept in days. He was gray-faced with big bags under his eyes and looked a good ten years older than normal, which was kind of encouraging, Jo decided. It seemed these immortals weren't always pretty people. They too could look like hell.

"Hi stud," she whispered, and frowned when the words came out a dry croak that actually hurt her throat.

"Here." Nicholas picked up a glass off the bedside table and sat on the bed to slip an arm under her back. He lifted her up and pressed a glass to her lips. "Drink."

Jo obeyed the quiet order and drank the water he tipped into her mouth. He gave her only a sip, and then lowered the glass and asked, "More?"

When she swallowed and nodded, Nicholas tipped the glass up again.

"Better?" he asked, lowering the glass when she gestured that she'd had enough.

"Yes. Thank you," Jo murmured on a little sigh as he twisted slightly to set the glass on the bedside table again. When he turned back, she asked, "What happened?"

A concerned frown immediately claimed his lips, but he asked, "What do you remember?"

Jo dropped her gaze, peering down as she did a quick search of her memory. She grimaced as she found the pertinent memories.

"Dee shot me," she said with disgust, and then added, "Or maybe it would be more fair to say I got myself shot. She was aiming for you."

Jo smiled with wry amusement, but Nicholas wasn't smiling back. His expression was solemn as he nodded. His voice was equally solemn as he said, "I appreciate what you were trying to do, Jo, but it was a foolish risk. I could have taken a bullet or two with little problem, but you . . ." He shook his head and closed his eyes briefly as he finished, "You could have died and nearly did."

"That explains why I feel like crap," she murmured, and then turned her face into his chest to nuzzle him as she added, "But I didn't, and we're both safe and well, and you can't dump me with Mortimer and those guys while I'm healing, so it's all good."

When he didn't say anything, Jo raised her head and peered at him solemnly as she said, "I know you were trying to keep me safe by leaving me in the apartment, but bad things happen when you aren't around. Maybe it's a sign we're supposed to stay together."

"Ernie won't be a problem anymore," Nicholas said quietly.

"And Dee?"

"Mortimer is taking care of both of them," he assured her.

She considered that and then asked, "What will they do to Dee?"

"They'll probably wipe her memories and then have her be found somewhere public. The mortal authorities will think her lack of memories is due to the trauma she went through when she was taken by the people who killed her family. They'll help her start a new life. She'll be fine."

"Good," Jo decided. The girl had probably been a perfectly normal nineteen- or twenty-year-old before Ernie's family had happened on them and subjected her to countless horrors. Hopefully, without the memories of that time, Dee could have something resembling a happy life. Jo didn't bother to ask what Mortimer would do with Ernie. She already knew the punishment for rogues. He'd no doubt be executed, with or without a stake and bake, depending on whether they still did those or not. And while Jo didn't really want to think about that, the knowledge that he wouldn't be a problem again, crashing into her life and trying to take her to his rather horrible-sounding father, was a relief. Besides, it meant they only had one problem left to worry about, she thought, and said, "Then we can concentrate on finding out who really killed that woman all those years ago."

Nicholas hesitated, but then said, "Jo, you were hit pretty bad."

"Yes, I know," she murmured. Recalling watching her own blood gushing from the hole between her breasts, Jo glanced curiously down at her blanket-covered chest. "It doesn't hurt at all. I ache all over, but my chest doesn't hurt any more than the rest of me. Weird, huh?"

"No. Actually, it's to be expected," he murmured, and then scooped her into his arms. Once he had them settled more comfortably on the bed with her in his lap, Nicholas said, "Jo, honey, it was a mortal wound."

Jo tilted her head back to peer at him blankly, the hair on the back of her neck rising as she noted the way he was avoiding meeting her gaze, and pointed out, "But I'm alive."

Nicholas lowered his gaze to meet hers and nodded solemnly. "Because I turned you."

Her eyebrows flew up, and Jo stared at him for a moment and then asked, "Turned me? You mean you gave me nanos and now I'm like you?"

Nicholas nodded grimly, and then blurted, "I'm sorry, Jo. I know I should have asked you first, but you were unconscious, and dying, and I couldn't—"

He broke off as Jo suddenly began to struggle in his arms. Nicholas released his hold on her at once, muttering, "You hate me now. I knew you'd be upset at the choice being taken away, but I couldn't see you die."

The moment she was free, Jo rose up and tossed away the blankets he'd scooped up with her. She was completely naked and peered down at her chest, noting with some wonder that the gunshot wound was now a scar that looked a couple of years old. Jo glanced at Nicholas. His expression was apologetic, and he said, "I'm sorry."

"Are you kidding?" Jo snapped, and then crawled to straddle his hips. Once there, she leaned back, spreading her arms wide. "Look at me. No nasty, blood-gushing hole in my chest."

Expression uncertain now, Nicholas slid his gaze down her body, but then returned his eyes to hers and asked, "You aren't angry?"

"You must be joking," she said dryly. "I'm alive, Nicholas. And I'm immortal like you. This rocks!"

Laughing, she threw her arms around his head and hugged him to her breasts, then just as quickly released him and sat back on his legs. "Let's make love and see if it feels different now that I'm an immortal too."

"Jo, no," Nicholas said quietly, catching at her hands as she reached for his belt buckle. "Honey, we have to talk."

"Later," she said, grabbing his shirt and tugging it

up his chest instead. "Enough talk for now. I'm immortal and want to celebrate."

"But—

"No buts," she said firmly, pausing to peer into his face. "I thought I was a goner, Nicholas. I thought I was missing the chance to be with you and off to meet my Maker. But I'm alive. We still have a chance. Celebrate with me. Make love to me and make me feel alive. We can talk about all our worries and what we have to do later. But for now, make love to me . . . Please."

"God, Jo. You don't know how much I wish I could," he said sadly. Eyes closing, he bowed his head to rest his forehead against her chest. "You don't know how much I wish for that, but . . ."

"But?" she asked with a frown, and then stiffened at the sound of a door opening behind her. Twisting in his lap, she glanced over her shoulder, her eyes widening in shock when she saw Sam standing in the open doorway.

"You're awake," Sam said with relief.

Jo tore her gaze from her sister to finally take note of the room she was in. Her eyes widened with horror as she recognized the guest bedroom.

"We're at the house," she said weakly, turning back to Nicholas. "What are we doing here?"

Nicholas lifted his head and swallowed. "You were turning. It can be dangerous without the drugs to help you through it. Others have been known to go mad or die. And to make it worse, you'd suffered a gunshot wound. I didn't know if that would cause problems, weaken you enough that the turn might finish what the gunshot had started. I needed to get you help."

Jo stared at him blankly, and then asked, "But why are *you* here? Why didn't you just have Mortimer and those guys come and get me? You—"

"I didn't know how long I had to get you to the drugs before the turn could do you damage, Jo. Besides," he added with a sigh, "like you said, bad things happened every time I left you alone. I couldn't risk that Leonius hadn't followed Ernie north and might grab you, or some other damned thing might happen. I had to get you here and see you through it myself and be sure you were going to be all right."

"Leonius is laying low in South America," she said furiously. "And how the hell am I going to be all right now? They have you here. They'll judge you and execute you and I'll be all alone."

"Jo," Sam said gently, approaching the bed. "He did what he thought best."

Jo turned on her sharply. "Sam, you have to help me get him out of here. He didn't do it. He didn't kill that woman. We have to—"

"She can't help you get him out of here. There are guards on the door and the balcony outside the window."

Jo peered to the door where Mortimer stood, and then glanced down as Nicholas grabbed the sheet and pulled it up to cover her.

"I'm sorry, Jo," Mortimer continued, moving into the room. "But there is no getting him out of here. We'll be checking every vehicle that leaves the house, and the men have orders to call the house and have someone check to be sure Nicholas is present before any vehicle is allowed to leave. He isn't leaving here."

"Not alive," she said bitterly, and then climbed off Nicholas. Dragging the sheet with her, she stomped over to sway before Mortimer, glaring. "He didn't kill that woman. If you kill him, it will be murder."

"I just catch rogues," Mortimer said quietly. "The Council will judge him. If he's innocent, they'll find out."

"Forgive me if I don't put my faith in them," she snapped, and then asked. "How long?"

"How long?" Mortimer asked uncertainly.

"How long until he's judged and executed?" she asked impatiently.

"Oh." Mortimer grimaced. "I promised him he could see you through the turn and have one night with you before I call Lucian."

Jo glanced out the window to see bright sunlight shining in. They had until tomorrow morning. Less than twenty-four hours, she thought, and turned to peer at Sam. "Where are my clothes?"

"Jo?" Nicholas stood up and moved to take her arm. "Come back to bed. You need to rest."

"I don't have time to rest," she muttered, shaking off his hand and glancing around. "You saved my life, now I have to save yours. I'm going to find Carol and find out what Annie wanted to tell you and prove you didn't kill that woman."

Spotting her jeans lying in a heap beside the bed, she moved to collect them.

"Jo," he said wearily. "Carol was mortal. She was in her forties. She'll be dead by now. She can't help us."

Jo paused abruptly and turned to stare at him. "What?"

Sighing, he shook his head. "It's true. You were so hopeful that we could get to the bottom of things that I didn't want to tell you at the apartment, but Carol will be long dead. There's no way to find out what Annie was up to now."

Jo stared at him silently for a moment and then straightened her shoulders and turned to continue to collect her jeans. "Then I'll have to ask others in your lives at that time. She must have talked to someone else. I'll find out what it was."

"Dammit, Jo. Get in bed. You— What the hell!" Nicholas cursed and grabbed up the sheet she'd just dropped to don her jeans. He quickly held it up, blocking Mortimer's view of her as he snapped, "Put those down and get into bed. You're still going through the turning."

"I feel fine," she assured him, tugging the jeans on and doing them up before glancing around for her T-shirt. Spotting it on the floor on the other side of the room, Jo started to move around the bed, but paused when Nicholas shifted to block her. Frowning, she perched her hands on her hips and snapped, "Move."

"No. I love you, Jo."

Jo's face softened and she reached out to touch his cheek. "And I love you. That's why I have to do this," she added, turning and climbing onto the bed to walk over it.

Cursing, Nicholas hurried to follow, the sheet held out, trying to block her from Mortimer's view.

"Goddammit, Mortimer. Get out of here," he said with frustration as Jo leaped off the other side of the bed a step in front of the sheet he was trying so desperately to hide her with.

"You're kidding, right? I'm not missing this," Mortimer said with amusement, and then grunted.

Jo glanced over to see him doubled over, clutching his stomach and Sam glaring at him, rubbing her fist.

Grimacing as he straightened, Mortimer muttered, "I meant the argument. Not seeing Jo naked, babe. She's not you."

"Oh." Sam bit her lip and moved closer, her expression turning apologetic. "I'm sorry, honey. Are you all right?"

"Yeah, I'm okay. You got quite a punch there though, sweetie."

"You're just being kind," Sam murmured, leaning up to kiss him. "You probably didn't even feel that."

Shaking her head, Jo bent to pick up the T-shirt. She grimaced when she saw the blood on it, but it was all she had, so she tugged it on.

"Jo, please," Nicholas said quietly, tossing the sheet aside as she tucked the top into her jeans. Taking her arm, he turned her toward him and clasped her face in his hands. "Please just get back into bed . . . Don't take these precious hours away from me. I traded my life to be sure you'd be all right and for the promise of one last night with you."

Jo peered into his tortured face. He looked so sad and desperate she could have wept, and she almost weakened, but then she leaned up to kiss him gently. Before he could deepen the kiss, she pulled back.

"I'm all right," she assured him, and then stepped around him and headed for the door, adding, "and I'm trading that night for a lifetime."

Chapter Seventeen

"Jo, wait."

Jo glanced over her shoulder to see Sam chasing after her, but the hallway was empty other than the two men stationed outside the door. She was surprised Nicholas wasn't trying to stop her, but glad as well. It had been hard as hell to walk away from him once. Jo wasn't sure she could do it again.

"Where are you going?" Sam asked, reaching her side and matching her stride as Jo started down the stairs.

"I need to talk to anyone and everyone who knew Annie."

"Who's Annie?" Sam asked.

"Nicholas's first wife. I think this all has to do with her."

"What does?" Sam asked. "That woman he killed fifty years ago?"

"He didn't kill her," Jo snapped, pausing halfway down the stairs to turn on her furiously.

"Okay." Sam held up her hands soothingly. "Don't bite my head off. Just tell me what's happening and I'll do what I can to help you."

"I would never bite you," Jo assured her quietly, but found herself staring at Sam's throat and noting the way the vein was visible when she turned her head a certain way. Frowning, Jo said, "I think I can hear your blood rushing in your veins."

Sam's eyes widened and then grew wary, and she suggested, "Maybe you should have some blood while you explain things to me. Mortimer said you'd need a lot of it for a while."

Jo tore her gaze away from Sam's throat, forcing herself to look her in the eyes as she admitted, "I don't know how to—I mean I'm not sure I could drink—"

"It's okay." Sam patted her arm and then urged her to continue down the stairs. "We'll take this slowly."

"I don't have time to go slowly," Jo said unhappily. "If I don't find out what happened all those years ago they'll stake and bake Nicholas . . . But I'm sure he didn't kill that woman, Sam."

"Okay. We'll sort it out then," Sam assured her as they stepped off the stairs. "Blood first though."

Jo remained silent as Sam led her to the kitchen, but her eyes widened when Sam opened the refrigerator door to reveal it was filled half with food and half with bags of blood. "That wasn't here the night of the party."

"No. Mortimer moved it out to the garage the night you guys stayed over. We didn't want you and Alex opening the fridge in search of orange juice and freaking when you found this instead," Sam admitted wryly as she took out a bag. "We moved it back the next day."

"Hmm," Jo murmured as Sam closed the door and turned to her. When she offered her the bag, Jo hesitated and then said, "A glass maybe?"

"I don't know," Sam said with a grimace. "The men all just pop it to their fangs."

Jo immediately ran her tongue around her mouth, but grimaced. "No fangs yet. Maybe it takes a couple of days for them to show up. Nicholas said I was still turning."

"They aren't out all the time," Sam said with a faint smile.

Jo nodded. Nicholas didn't always have fangs. In fact, she'd seen his only once, when he'd shown them to her to convince her he was a vampire. Sighing, she asked, "Well, how do they bring them on then?"

"The smell of blood will do it if you're hungry enough," Bricker announced, bringing their attention to the fact that he had followed them and was now standing in the doorway. Straightening when they glanced to him, he lifted his finger to his mouth as he crossed the room. Jo thought he was biting a nail or something, but when he reached her, he withdrew his finger and she saw a flash of his fangs. She then glanced down to the finger he was holding out, her eyes widening as she saw the bead of blood on the tip.

Bricker had bitten his finger, Jo realized as he moved the digit closer. The faint scent of blood reached her nostrils, and she couldn't help but inhale it more deeply. Much to her surprise, there was an immediate shifting in her mouth. Reaching up, Jo felt her teeth with both fingers and tongue, her eyes going wide as she felt the pointy fangs now protruding from her upper jaw.

"There we go," Bricker said with satisfaction as he took the bag of blood from Sam. "Open up."

When Jo opened her mouth, he popped the bag to her teeth, grabbing the back of her head as he did to keep her from instinctively jerking away. Once she'd relaxed and reached to hold the bag, he released her and stepped away, saying, "There, now just relax and let your teeth do all the work."

Jo relaxed, surprised at how quickly the bag emptied, but the moment she pulled away the empty bag, Bricker was handing her another.

"Your body is still turning," he explained as she reluctantly took the bag. "You'll need a lot of blood for the next little while. Otherwise you won't recognize the symptoms of hunger and might end up biting the nearest mortal."

"That would be me," Sam muttered.

"Yes." Bricker grinned at her, but then turned back to Jo and said, "I'd recommend four bags now, and another three before dawn."

Jo sighed, but popped the bag to her still-extended teeth. She actually felt a little better after the first bag. She'd been feeling dried out and a little slow in the thinking area since waking, but the one bag had eased some of that. Jo needed all her faculties if she wanted to save Nicholas.

The phone rang as Jo waited for this second bag to empty.

Sam started to move to answer it, but paused when the ringing stopped before she could reach it.

"Mortimer must have grabbed it," she said with a shrug, turning back.

"Here you go."

Jo glanced around as Bricker held out a third bag and then glanced down with surprise to see that the second bag was empty. She tore it away and traded the empty bag for the fresh one and slapped that to her teeth as well. It seemed to go just as quickly as the first two, and Jo had just traded it for the fourth bag when they heard the front door open. Bricker moved to the kitchen door to look up the hall, and she saw the surprise cross his face.

"Thomas," he said, and disappeared from view as he started up the hall, but they heard him say, "What are you doing here?"

They also heard someone answer, "Bastien said Nicholas is back on the radar and I wanted to know how he is and how close you are to catching him. Bastien wouldn't answer any questions though and said I'd have to come out and ask Mortimer myself."

Thomas. Nicholas's brother, Jo realized and unthinkingly ripped the half-empty bag from her teeth, and then cursed when blood squirted everywhere. She tossed the bag in the sink, but didn't bother about the mess she'd made and hurried up the hall toward the two men in the entry.

Apparently Sam wasn't too concerned about the mess either, because she was hard on her heels.

"I thought you were in England with your life mate," Bricker was saying, a worried frown on his face.

"We travel back and forth a lot on the company jet. It's only seven hours," Thomas answered, glancing curiously to Jo and Sam as they stopped behind Bricker. Raising his eyebrows in question, he said, "Hello?"

"You're Nicholas's brother, Thomas?" Jo asked grimly, which made his eyebrows rise even further. They drew down in anger though when she added, "The brother who didn't doubt for a minute that he was guilty of murder and who won't even acknowledge he ever existed?"

Turning to Bricker, Thomas asked, "Who the hell is she?"

"Nobody," Bricker said at once, taking his arm and trying to urge him toward the door. "You really shouldn't be here, Thomas. Let us deal with—"

"I'm not going anywhere until I find out what the hell's going on with Nicholas," Thomas said grimly, shaking off his hand.

"Oh, like you care," Jo said with disgust. "You and everyone else who were supposed to love him turned your backs on Nicholas fifty years ago."

Thomas stared at her with amazement and then turned to Bricker again. "Who *is* she? And why the hell is she barking at me like an annoying Chihuahua?"

"More like a German shepherd I'd say, and her bite is worse than her bark," Nicholas said wearily. They all turned to see him standing at the top of the stairs, peering down at Jo affectionately. And then he frowned and said, "Speaking of which, where is Charlie?"

Jo's eyes widened incredulously as she realized she'd not thought to wonder that herself. She turned to Sam.

"He's at Anders's place," Sam whispered.

Jo's eyes widened even further at this news, but before she could ask why, Thomas had pushed past her to reach the bottom of the stairs, his voice shocked as he said, "Nicholas? They caught you?"

Jo scowled at the suggestion. "Of course they didn't. He's too smart for that. Nicholas turned himself in . . . to save me," she added bitterly, and when Thomas glanced to her in surprise, asked, "Does that sound like the actions of a man who'd kill a completely innocent pregnant woman he didn't even know?"

Thomas scowled at her. "No, but then I never thought he did it."

"Then why have you refused to acknowledge his existence all these years?" she snapped.

"I haven't," Thomas said at once, and then frowned. "Who *are* you?"

"My life mate, Jo Willan," Nicholas announced, moving down the stairs with Mortimer and Anders on his heels.

Thomas turned to Jo with amazement. "You're my brother's life mate."

Jo scowled at him and then glanced to Nicholas as he reached the bottom of the stairs. He slid his arm around her and kissed her on the nose. Smiling sadly, he turned to his brother and explained. "I was told you won't talk about me anymore. I thought it meant you too believed I was guilty."

"I won't talk about you because it upsets the women," Thomas said dryly. "It made Aunt Marguerite and Lissianna sad, and you know how close Jeanne Louise was to Annie. She burst into tears every time your name or Annie's was mentioned after what happened. It was just easier to not mention you in front of them, and then it was easier not to have to explain the whole mess to others. But I never believed you had killed that woman . . . at least not without good reason. I don't care how messed up you were after Annie's death, you just wouldn't do it. But you weren't around to ask and—"

"Wait a minute," Jo said, interrupting him. "Jeanne Louise was close to Annie?"

"Yes." Thomas glanced to her curiously. "She was always over there visiting with her."

"Always over there pestering us, you mean," Nicholas said with wry affection. "And usually at the worst possible times. I was always throwing her out."

Thomas smiled faintly. "Jeanne Louise was over there all the time when you were off hunting rogues too. She and Annie would shop together and stuff. She even slept over when you were gone for days so Annie wouldn't be alone. They were like Siamese twins when you weren't around."

"They were?" Nicholas asked with surprise.

"She might know what Annie wanted to tell you then," Jo said, turning to Nicholas with excitement. "We have to talk to her."

Nicholas hesitated, but then frowned and shook his head. "She would have told me if she knew anything."

"Not if she didn't know it was important," Jo pointed out, and then turned to Thomas. "Where can I find Jeanne Louise?"

"She's at Aunt Marguerite's with my wife, Inez," Thomas said slowly. "The ladies wanted a girly day with Inez, so I dropped her there and went to see Bastien, who," he added dryly, glancing back to Nicholas, "brought up the fact that Nicholas had made a reappearance. Then he wouldn't answer any of my questions except to say that if I wanted to know anything I should come to talk to Mortimer at the house."

"He was trying to keep his promise without keeping his promise," Mortimer said dryly, stepping off the stairs and moving to Sam's side.

"What promise is that?" Nicholas asked.

"I had to clue him in to what was going on when I called about his sending out the IV and drugs for Jo's turn, but I made him promise not to mention your presence here."

"Why?" Thomas asked with surprise.

"Because I made a promise to Nicholas that if he brought Jo in, he could see her through the turn and have one night with her before I called Lucian. I didn't want word getting out before that promise was fulfilled."

"Thank you, Mortimer," Jo murmured, grateful that he'd kept his word. Otherwise, she could have woken to the news that Nicholas had already been judged and executed and wouldn't now have the hope of saving him. Patting the man's arm, she smiled and then turned to Thomas. "You need to take me to your sister."

"He needs to take both of us to see Jeanne Louise," Nicholas corrected her grimly, and then pointed out, "You have no idea what was happening at that time. I can find out more from her."

"You're right," she agreed and glanced to Thomas. "You need to take us both to Jeanne Louise."

"Just a minute," Mortimer muttered, moving between them and placing a hand on Nicholas as if suspecting he might make a run for it at any moment. "Nicholas isn't going anywhere."

"You said he could have a night with me," Jo said accusingly.

"Well, yes, but *here*," he said at once. "Not gallivanting around the city."

Jo arched an eyebrow and glanced to Nicholas. "Was there any mention of where that night would be?"

"No. Just one night with you," Nicholas said with a grin.

Nodding, Jo turned to Mortimer. "Are you a man of your word or not? You promised him one night with me. I want to go to Aunt Marguerite's. Hence he has to go."

"Jeez," Bricker muttered. "She sounds like Sam when she pulls on her lawyer face."

Mortimer scowled, his voice hard when he said, "I agreed he could have one night with you. I also said that if he came here, we wouldn't let him leave. The agreement that the night in question would be here was implicit. Whether you choose to spend that night with him here or not isn't my problem, but I am not letting him leave. I'm already going to have to talk fast when Lucian finds out I let him see you through the turn and spend that night with you here, so don't push your luck."

"Why do you want to talk to Jeanne Louise?" Sam asked quietly, joining the small circle now. "What are you hoping she can tell you?"

Jo sighed and then explained. "It all goes back to Annie's death. The night before the accident she called Nicholas in Detroit—he was a rogue hunter then like Mortimer," she paused to add in case Sam didn't already know that. "Anyway, she told him she had something to tell him when he got back. But that night she died in this car accident that decapitated her, *one of the few ways an immortal can die*. And the beheading on the windshield was a *freak* accident," she said grimly. "A one-in-a-million type thing they told Nicholas when he got home." She arched her brow meaningfully, satisfied when Sam started to get her narrow-eyed look.

"Anyway, so then a couple weeks later Nicholas sees this gift Annie had bought for her friend at work, this mortal gal named Carol. So he takes the gift and heads over to see Carol, thinking he'll ask her if she knows what it was Annie had been all excited about. He remembers driving there, and then crossing the parking lot and seeing this pregnant woman who looked like his dead life mate. The next thing he remembers is Decker calling his name, him *opening his eyes* and finding the pregnant woman dead in his arms, her blood all over him.

"He never connected the two things, but I think it's pretty odd that she died before she could tell him something she was pretty excited about, and then he suddenly finds himself accused of murder and on the run before he can ask this Carol what it might have been about."

Jo paused, and silence reigned for a moment, and then she shifted impatiently. "Don't you get it? Nicholas has absolutely no memory of killing the woman. He remembers nothing between seeing her in that parking lot and finding her dead in his lap. Is that possible if he killed her? With your nanos, those memories should be there, shouldn't they? I think he was drugged and he and the woman taken back to his place, the woman killed and placed in his lap for Decker to find.

"I think it was all to keep him from finding out what his Annie had to tell him," she announced triumphantly.

"Why not just kill him then?" Bricker asked uncertainly. "Why kill the mortal?"

Jo frowned at the question. She hadn't considered that herself. She did now, but it was Thomas who said, "Because we don't die easy or often. Annie and Nicholas both dying so close together would have made us all suspicious. But his being executed for killing a mortal in the throes of grief would have been something we all wanted to forget and not think about."

Jo glanced to the man with surprise. "Nice one, thank you."

He smiled faintly, but nodded.

"I suspected Decker was behind it all," Jo announced now. "It was pretty convenient how he showed up when he did, but Nicholas is sure he wouldn't have done something like that."

"Mortimer?" Sam asked, glancing to him. "It's possible Jo could be right. Nothing Nicholas has done speaks of a murderer to me. He has repeatedly risked himself to save others, and even turned himself in to save Jo. What if she's right and Nicholas didn't kill the woman?"

When he remained silent, a frown on his face, Thomas said quietly, "The memories should be there, Mortimer. It's odd they aren't."

"Maybe they are and he's lying," Mortimer pointed out reluctantly. "We won't know until Lucian reads him."

"You don't have to wait for Lucian," Bricker pointed out quietly. "If he's anything like you and Decker, his mind should be an open book now that he's met his life mate. Read his thoughts."

When Mortimer glanced to Nicholas, he nodded. "Go ahead. I won't fight it. I want you to read them."

Jo watched Mortimer, noting the sudden concentration on his face, and then glanced around to see that Bricker, Anders, and Thomas all had the same expressions on their faces as well and suspected all four were reading him.

"It jumps from seeing the woman in the parking

lot to her dead in his lap," Thomas murmured suddenly.

"He's angry when he sees the woman though," Mortimer pointed out with a frown.

"But the memory skips from seeing her to opening his eyes and her being dead in his lap, like a record with a scratch. Jo could be right," Bricker pointed out and then muttered, "Jeez, Nicholas try to keep your thoughts on that night. I don't need flashes of a naked Jo in my head."

"Sorry," Nicholas muttered, and he actually blushed. "You're the one who mentioned Jo. My mind just reacted."

Jo rolled her eyes. It figured. Mention her name and does an image of her being clever or amusing come to his mind? No. He immediately thinks of her naked. *Men.*

"All right," Mortimer said with a sigh, his face relaxing. "I'll agree this needs more investigation. But I don't know about letting you leave here."

Jo was just winding up to snap at him when he added, "We'll call and have Jeanne Louise come here so we can question her."

"I'll call," Thomas offered as Jo relaxed.

"You'll have to find some way to get her here without mentioning Nicholas," Mortimer warned. "Or we'll have Lucian breathing down our necks."

Thomas nodded and glanced around. "A phone?"

"My office," Mortimer said at once, and moved to lead the way, saying, "You call Jeanne Louise and then I'll call the front gate to watch for her. Bricker, keep an eye on Nicholas."

Jo watched them go and then glanced to Nicholas, frowning when she noticed how pale he was. "Are you feeling all right?" she asked with concern.

"I'm fine. I just need to feed."

"Come on," Bricker said at once. "There's plenty of blood in the refrigerator. I could use some myself and Jo has another bag to go I think."

"And a mess to clean up," Jo said dryly and moved ahead as Anders and Bricker positioned themselves on either side of Nicholas. She grimaced as she entered the kitchen and saw that a good amount of blood had gotten out of the bag before she'd dumped it in the sink, and then sighed and headed for the roll of paper towels hanging under the counter.

"So, why is my dog at your place, Anders?" Jo asked as she tore off several sheets of paper towel and began to clean up the mess she'd made in the kitchen.

"He followed me home," Anders said dryly, moving to the refrigerator to retrieve several bags of blood.

"Yeah, right," she muttered, swiping at the blood on the floor.

"Actually he did," Sam said quietly as she and Nicholas collected paper towels and bent to help her clean up her mess. "He stuck pretty close to Anders after they got back from the hotel, and then followed him out to his vehicle and hopped in when he went to go home. We figured since Charlie liked him, and Anders didn't mind, he could keep Charlie at his place until you returned to us."

Jo frowned at this news. Charlie had always been

her baby, preferring her company over anyone else's. She wasn't sure she liked the idea that he'd attached himself to Anders in her absence. Still, she hadn't been around and the man had apparently looked after her beloved pet for her, so Jo muttered a reluctant "Thanks for looking after him."

"My pleasure," Anders said as he watched them clean up the last bits of blood. "Although I must say I find it hard to believe he was raised by you. Charlie does as he's told and is much quieter than you. I quite enjoyed *his* company."

Jo glanced sharply at Anders as Nicholas helped her to her feet, caught the spark of humor in his eyes, and gave a reluctant chuckle. "Yeah, well, they say to trust the instincts of dogs and children, so I guess you can't be as bad as you pretend."

Anders's response was to hand her a bag of blood with one hand and pop a bag to his own mouth with the other.

"You guys have a nice setup here," Nicholas commented as he took the used paper towels from Jo and Sam and tossed them in the garbage. "It's a lot more organized than it was when I was a hunter."

"You still *are* a hunter from what I can tell," Bricker said dryly. "A renegade hunter, maybe, but a hunter just the same."

Nicholas chuckled. "Yeah, that's me, the renegade."

Bricker smiled and said, "But you're right. It is a lot more organized now. We have to be. We've lost a couple hunters lately and are shorthanded. It makes things a little difficult."

"Lost them how?" Nicholas asked curiously.

"Well, Decker resigned. He doesn't want to leave Dani alone until we catch Leonius. Not that he'd have been any good anyway. You guys are pretty useless for the first little while after you meet your life mates."

"Where *are* Dani and Decker?" Jo asked curiously. "I thought they were staying here with you guys?"

"The whole Ernie thing spooked him. He took Dani and Stephanie for a trip until things calm down," Sam explained quietly.

Jo frowned at this news and was about to tell them it was safe enough here, that Ernie had been the only one to figure out where the house was and that Leonius was apparently lying low for a while somewhere in South America, but before she could, Bricker continued, "So he's out of the picture for now, and then we lost two more when Lucian made Victor and DJ stay in Port Henry."

Nicholas raised an eyebrow. "Port Henry?"

"It's a little town south of here," he explained. "The entire town knows they have vampires there."

"*What?*" Nicholas asked with amazement.

Bricker nodded. "They don't know about the nanos or anything, they just think they're traditional vampires. Still, that's more than they should know."

"That's going to be a problem," Nicholas said grimly.

"Yeah." Bricker sighed. "Lucian says the same thing. Apparently a lot of the people think it's all just a joke, but just as many don't. Lucian thinks that's going to explode eventually and he made Victor and DJ stay there to deal with it when it happens."

"Hmm," Nicholas murmured, accepting the bag of blood Bricker held out.

"Well, maybe Nicholas and I could take their place and help after we get this all sorted out," Jo suggested.

Nicholas had been about to pop the blood bag to his mouth, but paused abruptly and turned a horrified look her way. "What?"

"Well," she said reasonably, "you were already one, and I'd be a great hunter now that I'm an immortal too."

Anders snorted, and Bricker muttered, "Yeah, right. It would be like *I Love Lucy* meets *Dracula*."

"What's *I Love Lucy*?" Jo asked with confusion. She thought she might have heard of some old show called that, but had no idea what it was about.

"Never mind," Nicholas muttered, and then glanced to the doorway as Mortimer led Thomas in.

"Jeanne Louise is coming," Thomas announced as Mortimer moved to the refrigerator to retrieve himself a bag of blood. He held it up and offered it to Thomas, and when Nicholas's brother took it, fetched himself another.

"Good," Jo said with a smile of relief. "Then this could all be over soon."

"Jo," Sam said with concern.

"What?"

Sam hesitated, and then gestured for her to follow and headed out of the room.

Jo raised her eyebrows, but trailed Sam out of the kitchen and up the hall to the living room.

When her sister settled on the couch, Jo dropped to sit beside her and asked, "What is it?"

Sam bit her lip, but then sighed and said quietly, "I know you're hoping that Jeanne Louise knows something that will help here. But even if she does know what Annie wanted to tell Nicholas that night, it might not be enough to exonerate him."

"It has to," Jo said quietly. "Nicholas didn't kill that woman. I know it."

"I know you believe that, and I tend to agree with you. He certainly doesn't act like someone who could kill a woman, but . . ." She paused and shook her head. "I just don't want you to get your hopes up and then crash if things don't work out."

"Hope is the only thing I have right now, Sam. I don't know what I'll do if we can't prove Nicholas didn't kill that woman." Jo swallowed, and then said, "I love him, Sam. More than anything or anyone in the world. And I'm not going to see him die. I can't."

Sam closed her eyes and shook her head. "I'm so sorry."

"For what?" Jo asked quietly.

"For everything. This is all my fault. I didn't want to turn and leave you and Alex behind in ten years, so I had that party hoping you and Alex might be life mates for immortals."

"I am," Jo pointed out quietly. "And we'll find Alex someone too."

"But what if Nicholas is executed?" Sam asked worriedly.

Jo was silent, but then shook her head and stood

up. "I can't think about that. I *won't* think about it. Nicholas is innocent and I'm going to find a way to prove it . . . either that, or I'll find a way to get him out of here and live on the run with him. I'm not losing him now. I can't."

"Jo," Sam began worriedly, but she shook her head.

"Save it, Sam," Jo said quietly. "You aren't going to talk me into being reasonable. I'm not like you."

"What does that mean?" she asked with a frown.

Jo glanced away, but then turned back and said, "I just mean you're overly cautious. You think more with your head than your heart. Which is good in some ways, but it means you take the safer route *all* the time. No matter how you feel. You weigh and measure all the pros and cons and then base your decisions on what sounds least risky rather than what your heart tells you." She sighed and then added, "It's why you stayed with your ex so long after you should have left and why you haven't let Mortimer turn you yet."

"I haven't let Mortimer turn me yet because it would mean leaving you and Alex in ten years," Sam said at once.

"Bullshit," Jo responded.

"What?" Sam asked with surprise.

"I said, bullshit," Jo repeated grimly, "You haven't let him turn you because you're afraid that he'll turn out just like your ex and suddenly stop loving you and start finding flaws. That's what happened with that jerk Tom, so the data tells you that could happen with Mortimer. You're just using Alex and me as your excuse."

"No, I—"

"You could have turned and then tried to find life mates for Alex and me," Jo pointed out. "You would have had ten years to find them, but you didn't go that route . . . because turning would make it irrevocable." She paused and then said, "I'm turned now. What excuse will you use if you find Alex a life mate too?"

Sam bowed her head and admitted in a low voice. "I don't know how he can love me, Jo. He sees me through rose-colored glasses right now, but how long will that last? One day he's going to wake up and notice that I have no boobs, and I have knobby knees, and—"

"Sam, he already knows that," Jo said quietly, and then glanced toward the door as a phone rang in another room. It rang twice and then stopped, and she glanced back to her sister with a sigh. "Sam, Mortimer loves you as you are. And from what I understand, that doesn't change between life mates."

Sam glanced up, her expression torn as she pointed out, "But Tom said he loved me too."

Jo sat down next to her again and took her hands in her own. She waited for her sister to meet her gaze and then said quietly, "Sam, the problem isn't that *he'll* fall out of love with you, but that *you've* never learned to love yourself." She let that sink in and then forced a smile and said lightly, "Besides, the nanos put us at our peak, right? So maybe they'll put some meat on your bones." She squeezed Sam's hand and teased, "You might even get boobs and finally be able to shed training bras."

"Nice," Sam muttered dryly.

Jo chuckled and then glanced to the door at the sound of approaching footsteps. Her eyebrows rose in question when she saw Bricker appear in the doorway.

He glanced at them curiously and then said, "Mortimer sent me to tell you that Jeanne Louise is on the way up the drive."

Chapter Eighteen

"I guess I should make coffee then," Sam murmured standing up. When Jo glanced at her with surprise, she explained, "Jeanne Louise is young enough I gather she still eats and drinks."

"Oh," Jo murmured.

"There's no need for you to move, Sam," Bricker assured her. "Mortimer was putting the coffee on as I left, and the guys were helping him put together a tray of cookies too. In fact, I have to get back to help. You two just sit down and relax."

Jo and Sam watched him go, and then glanced at each other.

"Mortimer is domestic?" Jo asked with surprise.

"Mortimer does whatever needs doing," Sam said quietly. "He's good that way."

Jo nodded and wondered if Nicholas was like that too. He'd helped heat up pizza at Sam's apartment and had helped clean up her mess in the kitchen just a few moments ago, but she had no idea what he was like day to day. She supposed they still had a lot to learn about each other, and she just hoped she got the chance.

The sound of the front door opening made them both glance toward the entry.

Eager to meet and question Nicholas's sister, Jo hurried across the room, aware that Sam was following. She paused abruptly in the doorway when she saw the woman entering the foyer. Tall, shapely, and gorgeous, the brunette looked amazing in a bright red summer dress. She also had an air of command about her that didn't seem to suit a young immortal, at least not in Jo's mind.

"Jeanne Louise?" she said uncertainly as the woman turned and spotted her.

"No, dear. I'm her aunt Marguerite," the woman answered, eyeing her with lively interest.

"I'm Jeanne Louise," another woman announced as she stepped into the entry.

This woman was more what she'd expected, Jo thought as she took in her lover's sister. She was tall but slender, her hair midnight-black and pulled back into a bun. She was also dressed much more conservatively than her aunt, wearing dark slacks and a white blouse.

"And this is her other aunt and my sister-in-law Leigh," Marguerite announced as a shorter brunette entered on Jeanne Louise's heels. "And this is Jeanne Louise's sister-in-law Inez."

Jo glanced at the woman with curly dark hair, and a darker complexion, and then to the next woman to enter, a blond replica of Marguerite who carried a small child in her arms as Marguerite continued the introductions with "My daughter Lissianna and her darling baby girl Lucy."

Marguerite turned back and smiled as she admitted, "Thomas was very mysterious on the phone and we were all curious so we decided to come with Jeanne Louise."

"Hell," Sam sighed behind her, and Jo could only silently agree. Unless there were two Leighs in the family, then they presently had Lucian's wife in the house. Great. There was no way they were going to be able to keep Nicholas's presence a secret from Lucian now.

"Aunt Marguerite!"

Jo glanced up at that alarmed cry to see Thomas leading the men up the hall, each of them carrying a plate of cookies, cups, or a tray with cream and sugar on it. At least he had been leading them up the hall, but stopped abruptly now and whirled to start pushing them back toward the kitchen.

"Oh, don't bother, Thomas," Marguerite said with amused exasperation. "I've already read these two lovely young women and know who they are and that Nicholas is here."

"Nicholas?" Jeanne Louise gasped. Jo glanced to her to see that she'd gone pale as she stared at the crowd of men, her eyes searching them for the presently hidden Nicholas.

"Come," Marguerite said suddenly. "Let's move into the living room."

She began to herd the women toward Jo and Sam and then said, "Sam, would you be a dear and show Lissianna somewhere she might lay Lucy down for her nap? She fell asleep in the car on the way over and doesn't need to hear this anyway."

"Of course," Sam murmured, and slipped past Jo to lead Lissianna upstairs.

"Come Jo, let's get settled in the living room, shall we," Marguerite urged, turning her into the room with a hand on her arm. Glancing up the hall, she added, "And you boys bring the goodies . . . as well as Nicholas. There's no sense hiding him now."

Jo moved reluctantly into the living room, only to pause by the nearest chair and glance back toward the door for Nicholas.

"Thomas, you and Inez sit on the couch with Jeanne Louise," Marguerite ordered gently. "She's a little upset. Nicholas . . ." She turned to the door as he entered behind the other men. "Come give me a kiss."

Nicholas moved to his aunt and she immediately pulled him into an embrace, murmuring, "We've missed you."

"Thank you," he said quietly as she kissed and hugged him.

She smiled and patted his cheek and then ordered, "You take the end chair there with Jo. We'll get this all sorted out."

Nodding, Nicholas released her and moved to sit in the La-Z-Boy Jo stood beside, then caught her hand and tugged, urging her to sit in his lap, but she shook her head.

"I want a coffee. Would you like one?" she asked.

"Yes, please," he said softly.

She moved to the coffee table where the men had set the trays and plates and quickly poured both herself and Nicholas a cup. She then moved back to hand Nicholas his before seating herself carefully in his lap. Jo sipped at the bitter liquid as she watched the others milling around getting themselves coffees and some taking cookies, but then they all began to settle into seats.

"We can make room here on the couch, Aunt Marguerite," Thomas said as the chairs began to fill up.

"Good, then Lissianna or Leigh can sit there. I think I'll take the rocking chair since I'm now a grandma. Everyone else find a seat where you can."

"I'll bring some chairs from the dining room," Bricker murmured, heading out of the room with Anders on his heels, but Jo hardly noticed. Her surprised gaze was on Marguerite as the woman settled in her rocking chair. She didn't look anywhere near old enough to be a grandmother.

"I'm over seven hundred years old, dear. Old enough to be a great-great-great-great-great grandmother or more if fate had been more accommodating," Marguerite said with a little sigh as Lissianna and Sam returned with Bricker and Anders on their heels. Each of the men carried two chairs.

"Well, there we are then," Marguerite said once everyone was seated. She glanced around the group, her gaze pausing on Jo. "So you think our Nicholas is innocent of murdering that mortal and hope Jeanne Louise knows something that will help prove it."

Jo blinked in confusion, and then grimaced as she realized the woman must have read her. Jeez, she really needed to learn how to guard her thoughts, Jo decided, and leaned forward to set her mug on the coffee table.

"Nicholas isn't innocent," Jeanne Louise said in a low, angry voice. "He killed that woman."

Jo peered at her, anger rolling up inside her until she saw the sad, tormented look on the woman's face. She looked ready to cry and was obviously upset to think that her brother could have done such a thing. Forcing her anger back down, Jo asked quietly, "Do you really believe that?"

Jeanne Louise looked at Nicholas uncertainly, but then said, "Decker saw him do it."

"Decker saw him *with a body*," Jo corrected gently.

"He said there was blood all over him," she argued in a firm voice, and Jo sat back with exasperation.

"You people and your seeing-is-believing!"

"Jo," Nicholas said in warning tones as she leaned forward to pick up her coffee.

"I'm just going to drink it," she muttered, and proceeded to do so. As Jo lowered the cup, she glanced to his sister and asked, "But if I *had* thrown this on you, Jeanne Louise, and you were covered with coffee, would it mean you drank it? Or even that *you* spilled it?"

When Jeanne Louise just stared at her, eyes widening slightly, Jo said firmly, "Nicholas didn't kill that woman. He has no memory between when he first spotted the woman in the parking lot and when he opened his eyes in his basement to find her lying dead in his arms. Someone set him up. And if it wasn't Decker, then they got super lucky that he showed up when he did, or I bet they somehow arranged for him to show up."

"But how could they have managed it?" Jeanne Louise asked quietly. "How did they get Nicholas there with the dead woman in his arms?"

"Drugs would be my guess," Jo said, and when Jeanne Louise merely bit her lip and looked uncertain, she shifted impatiently. "Look, it doesn't matter if you believe in his innocence, I do. So just tell us if you know what Annie might have wanted to tell him."

Jeanne Louise sighed, but shook her head. "I don't know."

Jo sagged with defeat, sure the girl wasn't even trying because she didn't believe.

"Jeanne Louise," Marguerite said softly, suggesting she thought the same thing.

"I don't," Jeanne Louise insisted. "We talked about loads of things. Her work, my work, family, shopping, movies, men . . ." She shrugged helplessly. "Everything."

"Wasn't there *anything* she talked about more than others?" Jo asked pleadingly.

"I'm sorry, no. Not that I recall," Jeanne Louise said unhappily.

Jo sighed and glanced around the room. "Well then maybe she mentioned something to one of you?"

When her gaze settled hopefully on Marguerite, the woman's gaze turned apologetic and she shook her head. "I'm sorry, dear. I really want to help, but we only met three times. The first time was when she and Nicholas first got together, and she was quiet and shy then. The second time was at the wedding, and we didn't get a chance to talk much at all, and then the last time was a couple weeks before she died. She and Jeanne Louise came for a visit while Nicholas was away, and as I recall . . ." She paused and frowned. "I think she mostly asked me about Armand."

"Armand?" Jo asked.

"My father," Nicholas told her.

"She was naturally curious about him," Marguerite murmured.

"Why naturally?" Jo asked with a frown.

"Because she hadn't met him."

Jo glanced to Nicholas and back to Marguerite with confusion. "Surely he attended the wedding?"

"No," Marguerite said quietly. "He couldn't bring himself to attend."

"He hasn't left his farm since his last wife died," Thomas said quietly. "He's become a total recluse."

"His *last* wife?" Jo asked sharply. "How many has he had?"

"Three. Each has died within a handful of years after their marriage," Thomas said and then added, "My mother lasted four years or so. She was the longest."

"He's had three life mates?" Jo asked with amazement.

"No," Marguerite said at once. "Only one was a life mate. Nicholas's mother. Armand turned her. The second wife, Thomas's mother, was an immortal. She was a bit wild, became his lover and got pregnant. Obviously, she wanted to or she wouldn't have been drinking enough blood to even start the pregnancy, let alone keep it long enough to know she was pregnant," she added dryly, and then shrugged. "She told Armand, and he, of course, married her. It was the eighteenth century," she added. "And at that time, an unmarried girl simply didn't have a child on her own. No one in the immortal community would have been too distressed, but we were all trying to fit in as mortals. They married for propriety's sake, but agreed it would only be until one or the other met their life mate." Marguerite grimaced. "Instead, she died."

"The last wife, Jeanne Louise's mother, was also immortal," Nicholas announced. "Father was lonely, and I think she felt sorry for him. She also wanted a child of her own and so they made an agreement—a temporary marriage for companionship until one or the other met their life mate."

"But she died too," Jo murmured.

"Yes," Marguerite said with a sigh. "Armand has had absolutely no luck with wives."

Jo raised her eyebrows. "You're kidding, right?"

Marguerite raised her own eyebrows. "You think losing three wives is good luck?"

"I think an immortal losing three immortal wives one after the other is completely unlikely," she responded grimly. "Let me guess, they all died in weird accidents?"

"Well, yes," she admitted with surprise. "Nicholas's mother died in a fire, and—"

"You didn't tell me fire can kill you?" Jo said, turning on Nicholas accusingly.

"It usually can't," he said quietly. "We can take a lot of damage and still keep moving and get out of the fire and then repair. But my mother was trapped and . . ." He grimaced and shrugged.

Jo shook her head and glanced at those surrounding her. "You guys are immortals, hard to kill. What are the chances of one of you losing three wives in a row? Don't you think that's odd?"

"That's what Annie said," Jeanne Louise murmured almost thoughtfully.

"Did she?" Jo turned on her quickly.

Jeanne Louise nodded. "I'd forgotten about that. She was curious as to why Father hadn't attended the wedding, and when I told her about his misfortunes with wives, she thought it was weird too and started asking all these questions . . ."

"She was very interested in how they died and so on that day you both came for tea," Marguerite murmured.

"She asked me about Uncle Armand and his wives too," Lissianna said. "I didn't think anything of it at the time."

"She did talk about it a lot," Jeanne Louise said, turning wide eyes to Jo. "You don't think that has something to do with what she was going to tell Nicholas?"

"It could," she said thoughtfully. "I certainly would have thought it odd and been curious about it. And if she started looking into it and learned anything that suggested even one of the deaths wasn't accidental . . ."

"Then it would be a very good reason for someone to want her dead before she could tell Nicholas what she'd learned," Thomas said grimly.

"Yes," Jo murmured, not noticing the sudden silence in the room, until Bricker broke it by standing up.

"I need to feed," he announced, heading for the door. "Does anyone else want something?"

There were murmurs from several people, but Jo was distracted with considering what it was Annie might have learned . . . and how she'd learned what she had. The deaths had happened so long ago, it was hard to imagine she'd learned anything.

"I think I heard Lucy chattering as I crossed the hall."

Jo glanced up at Bricker's comment to see that he'd returned and was passing out bagged blood.

"I guess I'd better get her. She'll need feeding," Lissianna said, and stood to slip from the room.

"Oh, she forgot her bag," Leigh said, standing to follow her.

Jo watched them go and then glanced back to the group and said, "It seems to me we need to talk to Armand. He might be able to help clear things up. We should at least get some idea of where to look or what step to take next."

"I'm not sure," Marguerite murmured. "If Armand knew anything I think he would have said so at the time."

"It can't hurt to check. He might know something without realizing it," Nicholas murmured and then glanced to Thomas. "Is he still on the farm?"

Thomas shook his head. "He has a new one now.

Well, he's bought several since you left and rotates them; ten years at one, then ten at another while foremen run the others."

"He never leaves though," Jeanne Louise said quietly. "And he doesn't allow visitors at all anymore. Not that he ever allowed me out there," she added bitterly.

Thomas rubbed her back sympathetically as he pulled out his phone. "Bastien will know where he is now and the number. Father still gets blood delivery."

"You know, it occurs to me that we might learn something useful from Armand after all," Marguerite said suddenly, and when everyone turned to her, said, "I've always assumed he locked himself away and cut himself off from family and friends because he was bitter at the loss of his wives, but if Annie's death is connected that puts a different complexion on things."

"I get it," Jo said slowly. "Perhaps he suspected the deaths of his wives weren't all accidents either. Perhaps he was trying to keep everyone out of the line of fire."

"Do you think so?" Jeanne asked, her eyes widening with hope.

When Marguerite nodded, Nicholas grinned and slid his arm around Jo. "She's very clever, isn't she?"

"Very," Marguerite agreed solemnly. "The nanos were right on the money as usual. She's exactly what we needed." She glanced to Thomas. "Call Bastien. The sooner we talk to Armand, the sooner we may be able to clear all this up."

Nodding, he started to punch buttons on his cell,

but paused and glanced toward the doorway along with everyone else when they heard the outer door open and the sound of someone entering the house.

Mortimer stood up with a frown and started across the room, but froze when a tall blond man filled the doorway. There was a good-looking, dark-haired man on his heels, peering over his shoulder into the room. Jo had no idea who the dark man was, but recognized Lucian from the night of the party. It was pure instinct that had her standing and shifting to block Nicholas from his view. She knew it had been the right decision when Marguerite, Thomas, and Jeanne Louise suddenly stood and positioned themselves around her, helping to hide Nicholas.

"How lovely to see you, Lucian. What are you doing here?" Marguerite asked, sounding completely calm and even welcoming.

The woman was a master at hiding her emotions, Jo decided. The way she'd moved quickly to step beside her and help hide Nicholas proved she wasn't exactly happy to see him.

"When Greg and I got to the house to pick up our wives, we were told you had all come over here so we followed," the blond man said, his eyes narrowing.

"Pick them up?" Marguerite asked with surprise and glanced at her wristwatch, clucking her tongue as she said, "I hadn't realized it had grown so late."

"The men are supposed to call if anyone arrives," Mortimer said, drawing Lucian's concentrated gaze off Marguerite.

"Yes, so I read from Xavier when he stopped the car," Lucian said dryly.

"You read one of your *own* men?" Thomas asked with amazement.

"He seemed exceedingly nervous when he realized I was in the car with Greg," Lucian said grimly, and Jo supposed that was his idea of explaining himself. "I convinced him calling ahead was totally unnecessary and would merely piss me off."

Mortimer grimaced and the room fell silent as Lucian glanced from one person to another. Jo frowned as she recognized the concentration on his face. She'd seen it before. It was the penis-eye look. Damn. He was reading people, she realized with dismay and had her suspicions proven when Jeanne Louise whispered in a panic, "He's reading me."

"Think of a nursery rhyme and block him," Thomas hissed.

"I'm trying, but he's—"

"Is no one going to introduce me?" Jo said quickly in the hope of getting Lucian's attention off the panicked Jeanne Louise. It worked . . . too well, Lucian's sharp eyes slid off Jeanne Louise and onto her instead. Feeling an immediate ruffling in her mind she assumed must be his trying to read her thoughts, she began to babble a little hysterically, "I mean, we have sort of met before, the night of the party, but no one introduced us properly. Sam?"

Responding to her panicked cry, Sam hurried to her side, adding her own body to the human wall blocking Lucian's view of Nicholas. She took her hand and said, "Yes, of course. Jo, honey, this is Lucian Argeneau. He's . . . well, he's Mortimer's boss."

"And our uncle," Thomas announced. Jo suspected

he was trying to draw Lucian's attention from her. She suspected that was also what Marguerite was doing when she added, "And my brother-in-law . . . Although, legally, perhaps he isn't my brother-in-law anymore now that Jean Claude is dead and I have remarried."

Marguerite's efforts were more successful. Lucian immediately tore his attention from Jo. His flashing eyes shot to Nicholas's aunt and he growled, "I shall always be your brother-in-law, Marguerite. We have been family for seven hundred years and will remain family no matter who you are married to."

Jo was just releasing a sigh of relief that she was free of the man's efforts to read her thoughts when his eyes suddenly shot back to her and the ruffling started up all over again.

"Think of a nursery rhyme," Thomas whispered beside her. "Recite it out loud if you have to, but concentrate on the words as if they were the most important thing in the world."

Jo nodded and began to recite, "There once was a girl from Nantucket—"

"Oh, for God's sake," Nicholas snapped, and was suddenly pushing past her to stand at the front of the group who had been trying to hide him.

"Nicholas," Jo cried with a combination of alarm and fury. She quickly shifted around to stand in front of him, placing herself between him and his uncle.

"Jo, honey, the very fact that you all were trying not to let him read you simply would have made him more determined to find out what you were hiding," he pointed out grimly, and then shook his head and added, "And 'There once was a girl from Nantucket'? That's the only rhyme you could think of?"

"I work in a bar," she pointed out dryly. "Trust me, you wouldn't want to hear the version of Little Bo Peep I learned there."

"Yes, well, we shall have to . . . er . . ." Nicholas frowned. "Have you considered a career change? Perhaps a bar isn't the best—"

"Watch it, nephew," Lucian growled.

"Aunt Leigh owns and runs a bar," Thomas explained under his breath, moving a little closer.

Jo couldn't help but notice that he wasn't the only one. Marguerite, Sam, and Jeanne Louise had all squeezed protectively closer, and the others in the room were slowly gravitating toward them. While she hadn't actually seen any of them move, they were closer than they had been. Encouraged by this show of solidarity, she raised her eyebrows at Nicholas in question. "So, what do we do now?"

"There's very little we can do now," Nicholas said quietly.

Jo gawked at him with amazement. "*Excuse* me? Please tell me you are not thinking you will just hand yourself over to this asshole dictator to be sliced and diced or shaked and baked or whatever it is you guys call it."

"Asshole dictator?" Thomas echoed, amazed amusement on his face.

"Well he is," she muttered, casting a resentful glance to the man who stood across the room, stone-faced as he listened. "And you can't let him shake and bake Nicholas."

Thomas rolled his eyes. "It's *staked* and baked, Jo. We aren't pork chops."

"Whatever," she said with complete disinterest and then turned to Nicholas. "The point is, you should have stayed right where you were and let us handle this. Now we're going to have to tie up your uncle and put him in one of the cells or something until we sort out everything and can prove your innocence."

The dead silence that followed her words was an exclamation point to the shocked horror suddenly on the faces surrounding her. Even Nicholas was peering at her as if she were quite mad.

Scowling, Jo glanced from face to face and asked, "What? Surely you agree with me? I know none of you are now so sure Nicholas killed that girl. I think most of you even agree with me that he probably didn't. But even if you just have some doubts that Nicholas is guilty, you can't just let Bossy Boy over there execute him."

"Bossy Boy?" Thomas echoed with disbelief.

Nicholas glared at him, then took both of Jo's hands and said, "Honey, I'm afraid they don't have much choice. If Lucian decides—"

"Of course they have a choice," she interrupted with disgust. "He's just one vampire."

"He's one very old and powerful vampire," Nicholas said quietly.

"You're *all* old," she pointed out dryly. "You're five hundred and something. Marguerite is seven hundred and something. You're all just fricking *ancient*."

"You say that like it's a bad thing," Thomas said with amusement.

"Well, it is a bad thing if you're all so set in your ways and used to Sourpuss Pants over there running things that you'll just let him slaughter an innocent man," she snapped.

"Mr. Sourpuss Pants! God, I love her Nicholas," Thomas crowed. When he noticed that neither Nicholas nor Inez looked impressed by the words, he added quickly, "In a totally sister-in-law type fashion, of course."

Nicholas and Inez hrrumphed together and then Nicholas turned to Jo and said, "Honey, you don't understand. Lucian is *very* old. He's also on the Council. He has a lot of power. He—"

"I don't care how old and powerful he is," Jo interrupted impatiently. "I love you and I'm not letting him kill you without a fight."

Jo tugged her hands out of Nicholas's, and then turned a determined glare on the head of the Argeneau clan as she started across the room, saying, "Nicholas didn't kill that woman. He has no memory of killing her. We think someone drugged him and set him up to stop him from finding out something Annie had learned about the deaths of Armand's wives. We need to find out what that was."

She paused in front of Lucian Argeneau, swallowed, and added, "I love him. I don't know what I'll do without him. What good is living hundreds of years if you take him from me? Please don't?"

Lucian peered down his nose at her dispassionately. "You were doing very well in your arguments right up until you started into the lovey-dovey crap. And the begging at the end was just over the top."

Jo stared up into Lucian Argeneau's cold face and felt a fury rise up in her like none she'd ever experienced. The man held the life of the man she loved in his hands. Her whole future rested in his palms and he stood their smugly critiquing her attempt to save both? All her fear and frustration balled into one blast of rage, and before Jo quite knew what she was doing, she was slapping the coldhearted bastard across the face.

"Jo," Nicholas barked with alarm and quickly dragged her behind him, placing himself firmly between her and his uncle as he said, "She's upset."

"So I see," Lucian said grimly.

Jo scowled and poked Nicholas in the side. "Don't apologize for me, especially not to Captain Crabby here who plans on killing you."

"It's all right, dear," Marguerite murmured, moving to Jo's side to run her hand soothingly up and down her arm, "Captain Crabby won't kill Nicholas."

"Marguerite!" Lucian snapped.

"Well, you won't," she said firmly. "Surely you've read everyone in the room by now and know further inquiry is needed before any decisions can be made about Nicholas's future?"

Lucian scowled at the woman for a moment, but then sighed and admitted, "Yes."

Jo moved around in front of Nicholas again to ask uncertainly, "You're not going to execute him?"

"No," Lucian said dryly.

"Really?" she asked, almost afraid to believe him.

"Yes really, I have no intention of killing Nicholas."

"Oh!" With joy exploding through her, Jo impulsively threw herself at the man to hug him in gratitude, saying, "Maybe you aren't such a bad uncle after all, Lucian."

"Yet."

Jo froze as the word reached her ears, and then pulled back to scowl at him. "What do you mean by *yet*?"

For some reason that made his lips twitch with what she suspected was amusement. He then glanced to Nicholas and said, "She's rather tempestuous, isn't she? Impetuous as well. It is good you decided it wasn't safe to keep her with you on the run. She'd have been dead in a week . . . or would have got you killed." He paused and then added, "Although she may have done that anyway since you turned yourself in to save her. We shall have to see."

Jo's mouth turned down and her eyes narrowed on him unhappily. "I don't like you."

Lucian arched one eyebrow. "That's a shame. I quite like you."

"You could have fooled me," Jo muttered with disbelief.

"I often do," Lucian agreed. "Fool people, that is."

"He does," Leigh assured her, reentering the room with Lissianna following.

Jo glanced to the woman, wondering what on earth she saw in Lucian Argeneau, but then just shook her head and asked, "What do you mean you aren't going to execute him yet? Are you or aren't you?"

Lucian turned his gaze to Nicholas. "I'm not executing you now because I'm not certain of your guilt. I've read the situation in everyone's mind, including your own. There is no memory of your actually killing the woman. In fact, there's a rather suspicious blank space where that memory should be."

"I told you," Jo said triumphantly.

"So you did," Lucian agreed dryly with a nod in her direction. He then turned back to Nicholas to continue, "I intend to get to the bottom of this and find out what did happen that day. If you killed her and have somehow blocked it from your memory, you'll be executed. If not . . ." He shrugged and then said, "Jo probably will eventually get you killed with her impetuousness anyway."

Jo felt herself stiffen at the words, but then noticed a suspicious gleam in his eyes that made her think he was goading her and she merely muttered, "Ha ha."

"Ha ha, indeed," Lucian said dryly, and then turned to Mortimer. "Now, let's get Dee and Ernie ready for transport so that you can prepare Nicholas's cell."

"Cell?" Jo asked indignantly. "You're going to lock him up?"

"Yes," he said calmly. "And I'm going to have you locked up as well."

"What?" Now Nicholas looked furious. His eyes were frigid silver as he stepped up to his uncle, fists clenched and growled, "Locking me up is one thing, Uncle, but Jo hasn't done anything to deserve being treated like a criminal."

"She's already plotting ways to help you escape in case I can't get to the bottom of this," he said quietly.

Nicholas turned to Jo with surprise and she felt herself flush guiltily. She actually had started thinking about ways to get him out of there. It seemed she was still incredibly readable.

"Maybe she is," Nicholas acknowledged reluctantly as he turned back to his uncle. "But, still, she hasn't done anything wrong yet. You can't lock her up for something she *might* try to do. Besides, I'll talk to her. I'll—"

"Locking her up with you will keep her from getting herself or anyone else killed with her amateurish efforts to break you out," Lucian interrupted firmly.

"Amateurish?" Jo squawked. "I got him out, didn't I. I picked the damned lock and set him free."

"Very impressive," Lucian assured her and then turned to Mortimer to say, "Make sure they're only given plastic utensils and don't allow them anything small enough to use to pick the lock this time."

"Crap," Jo muttered irritably, wishing she'd stopped to think before speaking. Her eyes narrowed on Lucian as she thought she saw his mouth twitch, and then he turned to Nicholas and continued.

"I will have Ernie and Dee transported to the Council for judgment. Mortimer will remove the cot from one of the cells and have a double bed moved in to replace it." He turned to Jo and Nicholas and said, "We shall give you candlelight and wine and roses and put a curtain on the cell so that the two of you can entertain each other *safely* and in privacy while I look into the matter of Annie and the mortal."

"Wouldn't it be easier just to keep them locked in one of the rooms in the house?" Sam asked with a frown. "It would be much more comfortable and—"

"And only mean four men would have to stand guard at the hall and balcony doors," Lucian interrupted dryly, and then shook his head. "We are already shorthanded. They go in the cells."

Sam didn't look pleased, but did nod unhappily. However, she also asked, "Can they have books or a television or something out there so they don't get bored?"

Jo thought her sister's concern was very sweet but totally unnecessary. It was hard for her to imagine growing bored with Nicholas around. Judging by the arched eyebrow Lucian turned on Sam, he thought so too.

"They are new life mates, Samantha," he said dryly. "As you still are yourself. Do you really think a television is necessary or would even be turned on?"

"Oh, right," Sam muttered, flushing as Mortimer grinned and slid his arm around her waist.

"Indeed," Lucian said dryly. He then glanced over the group and raised his other eyebrow. "Well? What are we waiting for? Let's get to it so these lovebirds can enjoy Nicholas's reprieve."

"Right." Mortimer turned to the group. "Bricker and Anders, you're with Nicholas and Jo until we put them in the cell. I'll get some of the men outside to help me with Ernie and Dee. Sam, honey," he said, his voice softening notably when he glanced to her. "Maybe you could make a list of what you think Jo and Nicholas will need in the cell and start organizing it; clothes, sheets, which bed to take, and so on?"

"Of course," she murmured.

Nodding, Mortimer kissed her quickly and then turned to head out of the house, Lucian on his heels. The moment the door closed behind them, Nicholas's aunt Marguerite stood up. Jo eyed the woman, still amazed that she could be seven hundred years old, but her voice had the ring of authority as she said, "The girls and I can help you with the list and gathering the things on it, Sam. And perhaps Thomas and Greg could help with shifting the cot from the cell and moving a double bed out?"

"Of course," Thomas and Greg murmured together.

Much to Jo's amazement, the room cleared out quickly then, everyone moving off to perform his task. Everyone but she, Nicholas, Bricker, and Anders, that was.

They all stared at one another for a moment and then Nicholas said, "I'd like a moment alone with Jo."

When Bricker glanced to Anders in question, he considered the matter and then shrugged and said, "The men will still be on the balcony outside the guest bedroom and we can guard the hall. It should be all right."

Bricker nodded. "Okay."

Nicholas urged Jo to her feet and out of the room. The hum of voices was coming from the kitchen as they made their way to the stairs, and Jo supposed the women were in there making their list. They were stepping off the stairs into the upper hall when Thomas and Greg came out of the room Jo had woken up in, one carrying a mattress all on his own, the other the box spring. Nicholas urged Jo nearer to the wall to let them pass and then urged her to continue on to the room.

Anders stepped inside and crossed the room to check and be sure the men were still out on the balcony. He opened the door and leaned out to have a word with them and then closed the door, nodded to Nicholas and Jo, and then slid back out of the room, pulling that door closed as well.

"Well," Nicholas murmured, glancing to the bare bed frame and headboard still remaining in the room. He then urged her toward the two overstuffed chairs arranged by a small round table at the opposite side of the room. He settled himself in one and drew her into his lap.

"I'm sorry about all of this, Jo," he said finally, running his hands soothingly up and down her back and thigh.

"You need to stop apologizing to me, Nicholas," Jo said quietly, leaning into his shoulder. "None of this is your fault. You're a victim here too."

"Maybe, but you wouldn't be about to be locked up in a cell with me if it weren't for my baggage. Had I stuck around fifty years ago, maybe this all would have been solved ages ago."

"Or maybe you would have been executed, or murdered, or maybe you wouldn't have been skulking around after Ernie that night and he might have taken me and I'd be just another Dee or dead," she pointed out. "Besides, I can think of worse things than being locked up with the man I love for a while . . . in a cell with a double bed."

"And wine and roses," he reminded her wryly.

"Hmm," Jo murmured, but shook her head. "I suspect Lucian was teasing about that. Your uncle doesn't seem the romantic type."

"You're probably right, that was probably sarcasm," Nicholas agreed with a grin. "But I bet you ten thousand kisses that Aunt Marguerite will insist Sam put them on the list anyway."

"You can have the ten thousand kisses without the bet," Jo assured him with a smile and then placed her hand to his cheek and said solemnly, "I love you Nicholas, and whether it's in a cell or this room or a cheap motel, there isn't anywhere I'd rather be than with you."

"I hope you feel the same way if this drags on for ten or twenty years," he said on a sigh.

"I feel that way now, and will feel that way forever," she assured him solemnly, and then frowned. "Surely they can sort it out faster than ten or twenty years?"

"I hope so, but . . ."

"But?" she asked.

Nicholas grimaced, and then pointed out, "It's been fifty years and we don't have much to go on. And while I don't think the Council would execute me without being certain that I did it, they might be reluctant to set me free without the same certainty that I didn't."

"So . . . what?" Jo asked with alarm. "They'd just keep you locked up here forever?"

"No, not forever," he said slowly, considering it, and then said quietly, "But they might keep me locked up for the length of the life I was accused of taking."

"You mean fifty or sixty years?" Jo asked with dismay.

"More like eighty or ninety since there was a baby involved," Nicholas said quietly, and when she stared at him wide-eyed with horror, quickly said, "I could be wrong. I'm just guessing based on various different decisions they've made over the centuries."

"This has happened before?" Jo asked, and thought she might be hyperventilating now. Eighty or ninety years? Dear God, she thought, so much for school . . . and her job would definitely be toast if she didn't show up for that long. Although, she supposed marine biology wasn't a very practical career for a vampire, and managing the bar had just been a temporary gig anyway while she attended school.

Sighing, Jo forced herself to calm down. Everything would work out. It had to. And if it didn't and they ended up spending eighty or ninety years in a cell together . . . well, from what she understood they'd have centuries together afterward, and maybe the Council would give Nicholas time off for good behavior as well as already having had to live on the run for fifty years. And maybe they'd cut the time in half or something because she would be sharing it with him.

"Jo."

"Hmm?" she asked absently, her mind on whether she should ask Sam to represent them to approach the Council, or if someone who was actually immortal and knew all their laws and such might be a better bet.

"They might let you leave and not have to be locked up if you promised not to try to break me out and meant it," Nicholas said quietly, and when Jo turned on him sharply, added, "At least that way you'd have a life while you waited for me."

"Dream on, buddy," she said dryly. "You aren't getting rid of me that easily. I'm staying with you."

"But—"

Jo caught his face and kissed him to silence, and then lifted her head and said, "You turned me, you're stuck with me now."

"I am, huh?" he asked with amusement.

"Yes. You am. Now and forever, stud. So learn to like it."

Chuckling, Nicholas drew her against his chest and hugged her tightly. "God, woman, I love you."

"Good, that's a start," she said promptly.

"A start?" he asked with a laugh.

"Well, this is the forever kind of deal, Nicholas. You have to love *and* like me to stand me for as long as we're going to be together."

"We're good then, because I liked you from the start," he assured her.

Jo smiled, pleased, and then murmured, "I love and like you too."

"What should we do about that?" Nicholas asked quietly, the hands that had been soothing a moment ago shifting to slide over her body with a decidedly different intent now.

Jo released a little sigh and melted against his chest. "Oh, I don't know. I can think of a thing or two."

"So can I," he growled, claiming her lips.

Jo sighed again as he kissed her, and then moaned as his hand slid around to begin tugging up her top. She moaned again for an entirely different reason, however, when a knock sounded at the door.

"We need to get the bed frame and headboard," Thomas called out as they broke apart to glance toward the door.

"And Mortimer just came in and said we can move you down to the cells," Bricker added through the door as Nicholas opened his mouth, Jo suspected to tell Thomas to get lost.

Sighing, Nicholas leaned his forehead against hers. "It looks like forever starts now."

"Looks like," she agreed, and then forced a smile and slid off his lap. Grabbing his hand, she gave him a tug. "Come on. We can finish off the dream sex we had in the cells, but for real this time."

"You always find the silver lining," he said with a small smile.

"Well, how do you think I found you?" she asked as he stood up.

When he peered at her uncertainly, Jo explained, "Your eyes go silver when you're turned on."

"They must be silver all the time when you're around then," Nicholas said dryly as she led him to the door.

"Good, then I'll always be able to find the silver lining, won't I?" she asked lightly, determined to keep his spirits up until this was all over. Jo just hoped she could keep her own up as well.

Epilogue

"Knock, knock."

Jo blinked her eyes open and frowned as she shifted her head on Nicholas's chest to peer toward the curtained cell door.

"I think it's your sister," Nicholas mumbled sleepily, his hand rubbing over her back.

"Knock, knock," Sam said again from the other side of the cell door. "We're coming in, so make yourselves decent or suffer the consequences."

Jo grimaced and grabbed up the sheets and blankets, tugging them up to cover her and Nicholas as the curtain moved and Mortimer appeared to unlock the cell door and open it.

"Oh good, you're awake," Sam said brightly as she sailed into the room, a tray in her hands.

Jo rolled her eyes with amusement. "Well, we weren't but certainly are now."

"Ah well, it was about time you woke up. You

guys have been sleeping—or not sleeping," she added dryly, "for two weeks now."

"We have slept some," Nicholas assured her, pulling himself into a sitting position. He leaned back against the headboard and dragged Jo up to lean against his chest.

"Besides, it's not like there's anything else to do," Jo said quietly. "It's that or worry."

"I wasn't criticizing," Sam said gently. "Mortimer and I were much the same way when we first got together. Well, not quite as bad, maybe. We had to come up for air on occasion, but then we weren't living with the possibility that one of us could be executed."

Jo swallowed and cuddled close to Nicholas, rubbing her nose against his chest. She'd been doing her best not to think about that for these last two weeks. Both of them had. They'd drowned themselves in each other, doing little else but make love and sleep and make love again, with breaks to eat when food was brought out, feed when they needed it, or be escorted up to the house for a quick bath or shower.

In fact, except for the small detail that they couldn't leave the cell when they wanted, and couldn't bathe or shower together, the last two weeks had been rather grand, she thought, peering around the room they'd occupied for two weeks. It didn't look much like a cell anymore. Sam, Marguerite, and the other women had worked magic in the room in the very short time allotted, placing a screen around the toilet to allow privacy, installing a coffee machine, flowers, bedside tables, an area rug, and even books, though those hadn't even had their bindings cracked. Jo could have almost pretended they were on a lovely vacation in a hotel were it not for the fact that the knowledge that this might be her last days with Nicholas was always at the back of her mind . . . and Nicholas's too. She'd seen that knowledge in his eyes many times, and the sadness it had brought to his eyes had nearly crushed her.

"Anyway," Sam said, sounding incredibly cheerful. "I know I'm early with breakfast this morning, but I couldn't wait. So, here you are."

"Why couldn't you wait?" Jo asked curiously even as Nicholas said, "Thank you, Sam."

Sam ignored Jo's question in favor of smiling at Nicholas as she set down the tray.

"You're welcome," she said, and smiled as she straightened. She then turned to head to the door, saying, "Oh, by the way, Anders brought Charlie back."

"He did?" Jo asked with surprise, and then her gaze dropped as Mortimer opened the cell door again and Charlie suddenly came running in and straight to the bed. Jo promptly sat up, taking the sheet with her. She patted the mattress. It was all the invitation Charlie needed; he leaped onto it at once and dropped across her lap like he thought he was a lapdog rather than the large German shepherd he was.

"Hi Charlie. Hello baby, was Anders nice to you?" Jo asked, petting him affectionately. "I missed you, boy."

Sam waited until the dog had settled and then smiled and nodded. "Anders said Charlie was a good dog and he'd have to get one, but now that everything is resolved you'd probably want him back."

"What?" Jo stiffened and glanced to her again. "What's resolved?"

"Did she forget to tell you?" Mortimer asked, stepping into the cell now himself.

"Oh, I guess I must have," Sam said innocently, and then slid her arm around the man and said, "You go ahead. You took the message."

Mortimer glanced to Jo and Nicholas. "Lucian called. He'll be here in an hour."

"And?" Nicholas asked tensely.

Mortimer hesitated, and then glanced down to Sam. "Go on."

Grinning widely, she announced. "You're innocent, Nicholas. You didn't kill that woman. He didn't explain the details on the phone, he wanted to do that in person, but he said to tell you you're free."

"Thank God," Jo breathed as Nicholas crushed her to his chest.

"So you two have an hour to eat breakfast, shower, dress, and present yourselves at the house. The whole Argeneau family is on their way over to hear about it. Congratulations, you two," Sam said with a laugh, and then slapped her leg. "Come on, Charlie."

The German shepherd hesitated, but then climbed reluctantly off the bed and moved to the door.

"He'll be waiting for you at the house," Sam assured them. "We all will."

Jo watched them leave and then turned to Nicholas and raised a hand to caress his cheek. "You're free."

"And innocent," Nicholas said solemnly.

"I always knew that," she whispered.

"But I didn't," he admitted. "And it's been a stain on my heart for decades."

Jo smiled softly. "You're a good man, Nicholas Argeneau."

"And you're a good woman," he said, twisting his head to kiss her fingers. He turned back and smiled. "How would you like to be a good wife?"

Jo blinked in surprise at the words and then frowned and asked with disbelief, "Are you kidding me? After everything we've gone through, *that's* your idea of a proposal?"

Nicholas's eyes widened. "I—"

"Because if so—" Jo crawled into his lap, straddling him. She clasped his face in her hands, scowled at him briefly, and then dropped her fake scowl, smiled, and whispered, "Then the answer is yes."

"Damn, Jo," he breathed. "If I were a mortal, I'd be dead of a coronary by fifty."

"Good thing you're not mortal, then, huh?" she asked with a grin, pressing a kiss to the side of his mouth, and then the other side, and then his nose, and eyes . . . "I love you Nicholas Argeneau."

"And I love you, soon-to-be-Mrs. Argeneau. Now and forever."

"Now and forever," she agreed as he drew her against him.

Can't get enough of Lynsay Sands?
Then turn the page for a sneak peek
Of her newest historical

TAMING THE HIGHLAND BRIDE

Coming February 2010
From Avon Books

"There it is."

Merry raised her head and drew her mount to a halt behind the men as they suddenly cleared the woods and a castle loomed before them. D'Aumesbery was a large, imposing fortress, perched on a hill and overlooking the land surrounding it. It was much bigger than Stewart, which didn't bother her except to make her wonder how her father had managed to arrange such an advantageous marriage. He'd always claimed it had come about through friendship with the late Lord d'Aumesbery, claiming the two men had met at court while young and started a friendship that had lasted a decade. D'Aumesbery's son, Alexander, had been born five years before her, but the moment Merewen had been born, the two men had sealed their friendship with the marriage contract.

Merry suspected the friendship had not lasted long after that. At least she didn't ever recall visiting between the families. She suspected her father's drinking may have had something to do with it. Her mother had once said that while her father had been a hard drinker when younger, he had not grown really bad until his own father's death when Merry was two. It seemed his grief combined with the new responsibility as laird had pushed him that final step to prefer the happy, fuzzy state of drunkenness to the sober reality of his life.

"Here we are, Merry." Her father turned to beam a smile on her. One that was reflected on her brothers' faces as well, she noted as he added, "Ye'll meet yer betrothed now, and soon ye'll be a married lady with a passel of bairns to chase about."

Aye, rather than three grown drunks, Merry thought, but didn't speak the words aloud. Why bother? Very soon she would be free of that chore. She'd have a husband of her own, one who, hopefully, would be nothing like her father and brothers.

With that hope firmly in mind, Merry urged her mare past the men and up the hill. It was late enough in the morning that the drawbridge was down and the gate open. Still, they were hailed as they approached; Merry stopped and left it to her father to answer the hail and explain their presence. She then followed his mount into the bailey and straight to the steps of the keep, knowing the news of their arrival would reach it before they did.

Merry was dismounting when she heard the keep doors open. Once on the ground, she saw that a seasoned soldier was rushing down the stairs toward them. It was not her betrothed. He was only five years older than she, and this man looked to be fifteen or twenty years older at least. Wondering who he was, Merry moved to stand beside her father as the man reached them.

"Laird Stewart," the man greeted, holding out his hand as he stepped off the stairs. "'Tis a pleasure to meet you. I am Gerhard, Lord d'Aumesbery's . . . man."

Merry's eyebrows rose slightly at his hesitation. It appeared to her that he hadn't been sure what to call himself, or what his station was. Odd, she thought as she watched the two men shake hands. Then the Englishman was turning to her, beaming brightly.

"And you must be Lady Merewen. A pleasure, my lady. Welcome to d'Aumesbery."

"Thank you," she murmured, and then waited patiently as her father introduced her brothers. Gerhard greeted both men politely and then shifted his attention to the rest of their party, who had dismounted and now stood about uncertainly.

"I shall have your horses and wagon attended to directly. In the meantime, perhaps we should go in."

Her father nodded, and took Merry's arm to lead her to the stairs, asking, "Where's d'Aumesbery? He should ha'e been here to greet us. He isna away, is he?"

"Nay, nay," Gerhard assured them as he followed them up the stairs, Brodie and Gawain trailing behind. "In fact, you are most fortunate in that way. Had you arrived on the morrow, we would have already left for Donnachaidh."

"Donnachaidh?" Merry asked with surprise, halting to turn to the man with surprise. Donnachaidh was the Duncan stronghold, and less than a half-day's journey from Stewart.

"Aye. Alexander's sister, Evelinde, recently married

the Devil of Donnachaidh and he wishes to check on her," Gerhard said as her father urged her forward once more. "Actually, we were supposed to leave this morn, but Alex is . . . er . . . indisposed."

Merry felt trepidation slide through her at his choice of word. *Indisposed* was the term she used when referring to her father and brothers when they were nursing a sore head after a night—or several days—of drinking. And what did he mean they were supposed to leave that morn? The man had sent for her. Surely he hadn't then planned to leave ere she arrived?

"All's well that ends well, eh?" her father said with a bluff laugh before she could ask any of her questions. He tugged on her arm once more, drawing her up the last few steps to the keep doors.

"Aye, of course," Gerhard agreed quickly. "But I should explain—"

"No need, Lord d'Aumesbery can explain," her father, Eachann, interrupted, pulling the door open and urging Merry inside. He hustled her several steps forward, but then paused, and they both stood blinking in an effort to make their eyes adjust to the sudden dearth of light. As with most castles, the great hall was much darker than it was out in the sunlight and the sudden shift left them both briefly blinded. That being the case, Merry actually heard the occupants of the hall before she saw them. Raucous shouts and cheers assaulted her ears and drew her blinking gaze to a crowd of men gathered in a small tight bunch.

"Is he among that group?" Eachann Stewart asked, glancing about for the man who had greeted them.

Gerhard nodded as he hurried to catch them up. "Aye, but—"

It was all her father needed to hear. Waving the man to silence, he again hurried Merry forward, this time steering her toward the group by the trestle tables.

Gerhard rushed after them. "But I should tell you that he is suf— Bollocks!"

Merry glanced over her shoulder to see that the man had tripped over something in the rushes. He stopped to pick up whatever it was, and then her attention was drawn forward again when her father suddenly drew her to a halt. They'd reached the edge of the group, and her father was now tapping the nearest man on the shoulder. The fellow, as large as a small building, turned a glare on them for interrupting whatever was going on, but quickly killed the glare when her father announced in a bluff voice, "I am Laird Stewart and this is me daughter, Merry, soon to be yer lady. Where is her betrothed, Alexander d'Aumesbery?"

The fellow's eyes widened, slid to her, and crinkled slightly as he smiled, but he didn't answer her father's question. Instead, he turned to nudge the man next to him. Once he'd gained his attention, he whispered something in the fellow's ear, and that fellow peered around with surprise before nudging someone else. Within a moment every face in the crowd had turned to look at her. No one, however, was stepping forward and announcing that he was her betrothed.

Merry was just growing uncomfortable under their stares when Gerhard caught up.

"Really, Laird Stewart, I should explain . . ." he

tried again, but paused as a sudden roar of fury sounded from the center of the group of men before them. It was followed by shuffling and shifting as the men whirled back to whatever had held their attention earlier. Merry stood on her tiptoes, trying to see what was happening, but couldn't see a thing. Then Gerhard shifted past her and pushed his way through the crowd, Merry quickly following in his wake. When he paused, she stood up on tiptoes again to peer over his shoulder, and this time was able to see what was happening. Two men were rolling about on the floor, a slender, smaller man attempting to defend himself as a larger man appeared to be trying to throttle him to death. The sight had apparently startled Gerhard to a halt, but only briefly, he was already moving forward, barking at the others, "I told you to hold him down, dammit!"

The rebuke had several men moving forward to help as Gerhard struggled to drag the one man off the other. It took a bit of effort, but eventually they were able to separate the two. Merry suspected it was only because the larger man had grown weary of the struggle, or perhaps he'd got over whatever it was that had made him attack the smaller fellow in the first place. It appeared to her that the larger man simply stopped fighting and allowed the others to pull him upright and away. The smaller man immediately scrambled out of reach, and, shaking his head, Gerhard quickly stepped forward. He brushed down the larger man and straightened his clothes, saying, "Your betrothed is here."

Merry sucked in a breath as she realized that the man presently swaying in the grasp of the men still holding him upright was her betrothed. She was not the only one shocked. Alexander d'Aumesbery appeared absolutely appalled by them and gasped, "The Stewart Shrew? What the devil is she doing here?"

The men surrounding them all turned wide and even apologetic eyes her way, and Merry felt herself flush with embarrassment, but lifted her chin as Gerhard hissed, "She's right here, Alex, right in front of you."

He then urged his lord toward her, and Merry's eyes narrowed as she noted how unsteady her betrothed was on his feet. Gerhard was having to help him stay upright with the grasp he had on his upper arm.

"My lord, your betrothed Lady Merewen Stewart," Gerhard introduced, drawing the other man to a halt before her. Or at least he tried to; while Gerhard's hold on his lord's arm should have stopped him, Alexander d'Aumesbery's feet were slower to get the message, so that he nearly walked right into Merry before the hold on his arm made him swing in a clumsy half circle. Gerhard immediately caught the man by both arms and turned him to stand before her like a naughty little boy. He then repeated grimly, "Lady Merewen Stewart."

Seeming oblivious of Gerhard's pained expression, Alex peered blearily at Merry, and then blew whiskey fumes all over her, saying, "Damn me. You're pretty. You don't look like a shrew."

There was a collective gasp of dismay from those around them, and Eachann Stewart actually drew himself up as if to say something, but Merry placed a hand on his arm and merely said in dry tones, "Thank you."

Really, what else could she say? The man was obviously beyond drunk and wouldn't remember any reprimand anyway.

"You're welcome." He beamed at her and then in the next moment grimaced and turned to tell Gerhard, "I don't feel so good."

The last word had barely slipped from his lips before he suddenly fell forward and flat on his face on the floor.

For a moment, the room was silent and still as everyone stared down at the unconscious man. But Merry's thoughts were not silent. Her mind was wailing in loss and fury as every last dream she'd had on the way here died a sudden, horrible death. She had gone from the pot into the fire, leaving one home of drunks to live in another, but this was worse. This drunk had rights to her bed and body. And he'd been in a drunken rage, throttling another man just moments ago, so he appeared to be a mean drunk.

Merry closed her eyes, depression and misery settling over her. She would never get away from drunkards and fools. She allowed herself a moment of self-pity, then she straightened her shoulders and forced her eyes open again. Finding everyone now peering not at the man on the floor, but at her, Merry controlled her expression and raised her head.

"Well," she said grimly. "Diya no think ye'd best carry yer laird's worthless hide up to his bed?"

Glances were exchanged and then there was a

sudden rush as every single man present began to shuffle forward. There were too many for the task. In the end only four were needed, each taking an arm or leg to cart him toward the stairs. The others followed, however, even the man whom her betrothed had been throttling when she'd first arrived.

Merry watched them go and then started to glance toward her father, but her gaze caught on a woman she hadn't noted earlier. Standing on the other side of where the men had been, the brunette appeared a good fifteen years older than she. She was also taller, with a thick frame and small eyes presently narrowed thoughtfully as she looked after the men carrying Alexander away. Merry peered at her curiously, wondering who she was. Then the woman glanced toward her, offered an anxious smile, and rushed forward.

"Good morn, Merewen. I am Edda, Alexander's stepmother. Welcome to d'Aumesbery."

"Thank you," Merry murmured as her hands were clasped in the woman's larger, strong hands. "Pray, call me Merry."

"Thank you, dear." Edda smiled, but it was a crooked smile, tinged with worry, and she rushed on, "I am ever so sorry you saw that. Did Gerhard explain matters to you?"

"Aye," Merry said dryly. "He explained when he greeted us that my betrothed was indisposed."

"Oh, good." She looked relieved. "I feared you might get the entirely wrong impression. But truly, while Alexander has been away these three years, I am quite positive he has not become a drinker and normally does not down a full pitcher of whiskey first thing in the morn. These are somewhat unusual circumstances." She smiled wryly and then urged Merewen toward the table. "Come, sit yourselves down. Have you broken your fast yet this morn?"

"Nay," Merry's father answered as they settled themselves at the trestle table. "We reached yer woods late last night and camped out there until this morning, but Merry was up early and through with her ablutions by the time the rest o' us woke so we rode straight here."

Edda nodded and then glanced to a maid who was hovering several feet away. "Lia, fetch some mead for Lady Merewen and . . ." She paused and glanced to Eachann Stewart. "For you gentlemen?"

"Mead fer them too," Merry said firmly.

"Merry," Eachann protested, "We've been traveling for days without a drop o' whiskey, surely we—"

"—shall manage without it so long as ye're here," she said grimly and then leaned forward to hiss in a voice she hoped Edda could not hear, "I'll no ha'e the three o' ye embarrassing me while ye're here. There'll be no whiskey fer ye."

He scowled, but didn't protest further, and Merry turned to Edda and offered a relieved smile. "They are fine with mead too."

"Mead then for the men as well, Lia, and something for them to eat." The moment the girl rushed away, Edda turned back and offered a smile. "I hope your journey here was a pleasant one."

Merry grimaced. "Riding from dusk until well past dawn fer days on end is rarely pleasant, but we were fortunate and didna run into bandits or trouble o' that sort."

"From dusk until dawn?" Edda asked with surprise.

"Aye, well, meself and me sons are all here, are we no?" her father said defensively. "We left one o' the men in charge o' Stewart while we're away, but 'tis no the same as me being there."

Merry snorted at this, earning a glare from her father before he continued, "We wanted to get the gel here, see her wed, and then get back to Stewart."

"Oh, aye, of course," Edda murmured sympathetically. "I suppose you must get back as quickly as you can. 'Tis a reflection of your caring for Merry that you would all come to see her wed and leave someone else in charge."

Merry managed not to snort as her father and brothers all puffed up under the compliment. 'Twas not caring, but eagerness to be rid of her, she was sure, but didn't say so.

"Aye, just so," her father said staunchly and then added, "That being the case, mayhap ye can send fer yer priest and—"

"Father," Merry snapped.

"What?" he asked defensively. "Yer betrothed wishes to get to Donnachaidh and we need to return to Stewart. There is no reason to delay."

"Except fer the wee matter of the groom bein' unconscious," she pointed out dryly.

"Aye, that does put a bit of a wrinkle in things," Edda said with a twinkle in her eye. "But I am sure he shall be recovered by the sup, or by tomorrow morn at the latest. There is no reason the wedding cannot take place first thing on the morrow and then everyone may set out on their journeys."

Her father and brothers agreed quickly, but Merry remained silent. She was no longer eager to be married, but there was really no reason to delay. The contract was binding and she would have to marry him eventually. Realizing that Edda was peering at her in question, apparently looking for her agreement, Merry sighed and nodded.

"Good!" Edda said brightly. "Then after you have eaten, I shall hunt down Father Gibbon while you talk to Cook."

"Me?" Merry asked with surprise.

"Aye, well, you will be the lady here by the morrow and in charge of everyone. You may as well begin now. Besides, 'tis your wedding, dear, and while it may be a bit rushed, you should really be the one to chose the menu for the wedding feast and so on."

Merry smiled uncertainly, but again nodded. Put that way, there really seemed little reason for her not to be the one to talk to Cook. She just hoped Cook agreed and would take orders from her despite the fact that she hadn't yet married his lord and officially become his lady.